The Short Stories of

CHARLES DICKENS

The Short Stories of Charles Dickens

Selected and Introduced by Walter Allen

Illustrated by Edward Ardizzone

THE HERITAGE PRESS

NORWALK, CONNECTICUT

The Contents

The Color Plates

mirer of Poussin, he likes to design moving figures in a stage-like setting. Thus, as every actor on a stage contributes to the action in a well-directed play, every figure in an Ardizzone illustration contributes to the dramatic effect of the picture. Studying the Dickens stories, he noticed a progression in the author's style from caricature to characterization and he suited his own style to that development—moving, as he put it, from Cruikshank to Luke Fildes.

Examples of Ardizzone's paintings can be found in the Tate Gallery; he has written and illustrated a series of charming and popular children's books; but he is most proud of the work he did as an official War Artist in the Middle East, Italy and Sicily, Normandy, and Germany. Some three hundred of these paintings and sketches are now owned by the Imperial War Museum. *The Young Ardizzone*, "an autobiographical fragment," was published in 1970.

The Heritage Club Dickens series—which has been described by neutral observers as the most readable Dickens ever made—runs to many titles, and is so popular that we are unable to keep them in print. All are in formats based on a typographic plan that Joseph Blumenthal designed for our *David Copperfield*, back in 1937.

Blumenthal was honored in 1966 with an exhibition at the Pierpont Morgan Library in New York, a showing of the books and ephemera produced at his Spiral Press over the preceding four decades. It was an extraordinary accolade from an institution devoted almost exclusively to treasures of the past. The material has since been displayed in the national libraries at Brussels, The Hague, and Edinburgh. Blumenthal is also a recipient of the medal of The American Institute of Graphic Arts.

For *The Short Stories of Charles Dickens*, as in his earlier Dickens creations for The Heritage Club, he has utilized that unusual and effective arrangement in which each heading is set at the right of a thumbnail drawing. But in this instance he has provided each story with its own distinctive title page.

These display pages are set in the Bulmer types, which Blumenthal combines subtly with the Baskerville of the text. There is, of course, an affinity between the two faces in spite of the latter's horizontal stress as compared with the vertical stress of the former. Both are eighteenth-century types, transitional between old-style and modern designs. William Martin, who cut the Bulmer type about 1790 for the head of the Shakespeare Press and named it after him, had been a pupil of John Baskerville, hence the family resemblance.

THE HERITAGE CLUB

Sandglass

ISSUED TO THE MEMBERS OF
THE HERITAGE CLUB
NORWALK, CONNECTICUT

The Short Stories of Charles Dickens

H E WAS STAGE-STRUCK all his life. As a child he worshipped the clowns in the traveling circuses that visited his town. As a young law clerk he spent his salary on cheap seats at the Drury Lane, Covent Garden, and Haymarket theaters. A gifted amateur performer, he applied to a London stage manager for a job, describing himself as an actor with "a strong perception of character and oddity," and a "natural power" of mimicry. Before he could appear for his scheduled audition, however, he was offered a chance to become a reporter and he opted for a literary career. It was not, all things considered, a bad decision for Charles Dickens.

I

THE THEATER was an excellent writing school for him. From the great tragedians and comedians of the day he learned how to present characters directly, in their own words, and how to capture his reader's attention with boldly displayed oddities of speech and dress. He saw life as a vast drama and he was able to transfer to literary productions his excitement over scenes that he witnessed. This heightened, dramatic vision is shown in all the novels and, as is apparent in *The Short Stories of Charles Dickens*, it is also revealed in the shorter pieces that Dickens wrote for the periodicals.

When we asked Walter Allen, English novelist and teacher of the novel, to select and introduce Dickens's short stories for us, he wrote enthusiastically: "I do think ... that the idea of publishing a selection of Dickens stories is really excellent. So far as I can find out, no one has done anything like this before, and there is a great deal of material which is very important and, for the most part, known only to Dickens experts."

In this volume you will find the comic Dickens, the grotesque Dickens, Dickens the social critic, and Dickens the unabashed sentimentalist. He grows into his full power as a writer before our eyes, as the first lively but conventional *Sketches by Boz* give way to the hilarious and terrifying inventions of his later years.

More important, there are at least a

Introduction

"THE INIMITABLE": it was Dickens' own phrase for himself, and he used it throughout his life. He was the great original, and after all the influences on them have been tracked down, his novels are still utterly unlike any one else's.

So are his stories. They remain relatively unknown, for they have been overshadowed by the novels. "The genius of Dickens needed space to attain its full stature," someone has said, and it is obviously so: important and challenging as it is, *Hard Times,* the shortest of the novels, is not among the greatest. But we wouldn't be without it, and indeed we think much more highly of it today than any one did in the nineteenth century. Dickens' genius was inexhaustible. He never repeated himself; and we cannot have too much Dickens, so that not to know the stories is to miss part of the richness of Dickens.

But in what sense are Dickens' stories stories as we understand the word today? Certainly they tell stories: we read on, wanting to know what will happen next — and we read on not in a perfunctory way but drawn by the spell laid upon us by his endless fertility of invention. Nevertheless, Dickens' stories are not stories in the modern sense; they are not what is called the modern short story; they are nothing like the stories of Hawthorne or Poe or Chekhov or Sherwood Anderson or Lawrence or Hemingway. They are as far as possible removed from Frank O'Connor's definition of the short story, "the lonely voice." Often they lack the unity we take as axiomatic in the short story; often, in fact, they tell not one story but two or even three. But what is certain is that they belong to the Dickens world. Only Dickens could have written them.

Inevitably, today, we see Dickens as primarily a novelist. Rightly — to be as great a novelist as Dickens was is job enough for one man.

But it is doubtful whether Dickens saw himself as primarily a novelist. He was throughout his writing life a journalist and an editor. He did in fact found (although he himself edited only the first seventeen numbers) a daily newspaper which survived him by more than eighty years. It seems to me unlikely that he differentiated in any real sense between his novels and his journalism. From the beginning, the novels were written in the conditions in which journalism is usually undertaken. The early novels were published first in monthly parts, with the author writing as publication proceeded — and often writing two novels simultaneously. The later novels appeared first of all as continued stories in Dickens' own weekly magazines, *Household Words* and *All the Year Round,* magazines that contained serial novels by the editor and other writers as well as stories and articles some of which Dickens wrote himself or in collaboration with others.

So he was a journalist as well as a novelist, and his first book was a collection of journalistic pieces, *Sketches by Boz,* papers reprinted from a number of newspapers and magazines. It was published when he was twenty-four. He had not then quite discovered the nature and scope of his genius, but *Sketches by Boz* is brilliant work, brilliant as journalism and foreshadowing the greater, the real Dickens, who emerged so soon afterwards in *Pickwick Papers. Sketches* is subtitled "Illustrative of Every-day Life and Every-day People," and that defines it. It was a kind of journalism that is still with us, the feature or the documentary, the personal impression of existence around us. It was very much like what Stephen Crane and Theodore Dreiser began by writing. It is always close to fiction, by which one means nothing more than a greater play of the imagination on observed facts. One section of *Sketches* is called "Tales." According to Dickens, in his preface to the 1850 edition, these were often "extremely crude and ill-considered, bearing obvious marks of haste and inexperience." The Dickens who had just written *David Copperfield* had the right to say this. Nevertheless, the *Sketches* and the tales among them are still interesting in their own right, and I have chosen four of them for this selection. They seem to me to pass through the barrier between the reporting of fact and the imaginative transformation of fact into the richer experience of fiction. "The Boarding House" — and one remembers how often in his later work Dickens was to return to the boarding house — is farce; but it is farce most adroitly handled and more important — because unlike farce generally, "The

Boarding House" creates characters, representations of people who may be imagined as living outside and beyond the confines of the story, notably Mr. Tibbs, the landlady's henpecked husband, who "always went out at ten o'clock in the morning, and returned at five in the afternoon, with an exceedingly dirty face, and smelling mouldy. Nobody knew where he was, or where he went; but Mrs. Tibbs used to say with an air of great importance, that he was engaged in the City." There is, even in this early story, an air of spaciousness, of command over material.

These tales from *Sketches by Boz* are perhaps simple. They are journalistic assignments, written to a specified length. The situations are commonplace, the stock material of popular comedy for centuries. But it is impossible to read them without excitement, so uncannily do they fore-echo the later Dickens. "The Bloomsbury Christening" is apposite here. Old Dumps, the man who hates little children, is invited by his nephew to be godfather to his new-born son. The christening is pure Dickens:

> The ceremony (which occupied about five minutes) passed off without anything particular occurring. The clergyman had to dine some distance from town, and had two churchings, three christenings, and a funeral to perform in something less than an hour. The godfathers and godmother, therefore, promised to renounce the devil and all his works — "and all that sort of thing" — as little Kitterbell said — "in less than no time". . .

But even more characteristic is the earlier passage in which Dumps meets Kitterbell's request that he should be godfather of the child:

> "Not born yet!" echoed Dumps, with a gleam of hope lighting up his lugubrious visage. "Oh, well, it *may* be a girl, and then you won't want me; or if it is a boy, it *may* die before it is christened."
>
> "I hope not," said the father that expected to be, looking very grave.
>
> "I hope not," acquiesced Dumps, evidently pleased with the subject. He was beginning to get happy. "I *hope* not, but distressing cases frequently occur during the first two or three days of a child's life; fits, I am told, are exceedingly common, and alarming convulsions are almost matters of course."
>
> "Lord, uncle!" ejaculated little Kitterbell, gasping for breath.
>
> "Yes; my landlady was confined — let me see — last Tuesday: an uncommonly fine boy. On the Thursday night the nurse was sitting with him upon her knee before the fire, and he was as well as possible. Sud-

denly he became black in the face, and alarmingly spasmodic. The medical man was instantly sent for, and every remedy was tried, but —"

"How frightful!" interrupted the horror-stricken Kitterbell.

"The child died, of course. However, your child *may* not die; and, if it should be a boy, and should *live* to be christened, why I suppose I must be one of the sponsors." Dumps was evidently good-natured on the faith of his anticipations.

"Thank you, uncle," said his agitated nephew, grasping his hand as warmly as if he had done him some essential service. "Perhaps I had better not tell Mrs. K. what you have mentioned."

"Well, if she's low-spirited, perhaps you had better not mention the melancholy case to her," returned Dumps, who of course had invented the whole story; "though perhaps it would be but doing your duty as a husband to prepare her for the *worst.*"

This is surely wonderfully well controlled as well as wonderfully high-spirited comic writing; and, among other things, it shows perfectly Dickens' debt to the theatre. It also pinpoints the fascination of *Sketches by Boz* for us today, the constant glimpses we get of the mature Dickens, the Dickens of the novels.

Still, the Boz of the *Sketches*, though he was already the "Inimitable," was not the complete Dickens, and the bulk of his stories appeared in his two magazines. By the time he turned editor he had long been world-famous — indeed, for all his comparative youth, probably the most famous of living novelists; he had already written *Pickwick Papers, Oliver Twist, Nicholas Nickleby, The Old Curiosity Shop, Barnaby Rudge, The Christmas Carol, Martin Chuzzlewit, Dombey and Son,* and *David Copperfield.* The stories Dickens wrote for his own magazines show us the whole range of his genius, even if in miniature, and they contain characters and passages which deserve to be as famous as anything in the novels. Many of them were brought together in the volume published after his death called *Christmas Stories.* In a way, the title is a misnomer. The stories do not necessarily have anything to do with Christmas as a festival; they do not belong to Dickens' specifically Christmas writing like *A Christmas Carol* and *The Chimes.* The title comes from the fact that they all appeared in the Christmas numbers of the magazines. They are not mere by-products of his genius, but part of his mature work.

From *Christmas Stories* I have selected seven pieces on very different themes and of very different lengths. The first of these, and the shortest, *Nobody's Story*, appeared in the Christmas number of *Household Words* for 1853; in other words, it was written more or less as Dickens was writing *Hard Times*, and that is significant. "Nobody's Story" represents the sombre Dickens of *Hard Times* and *A Tale of Two Cities*, a novel generally underrated because it is not funny. "Nobody's Story" is not funny. It is a parable of what was called at the time the "Condition of England" question and seems to me an extremely powerful piece of writing. "Nobody" is, as it were, a generalized character. His name, Dickens tells us, is also Legion. "Nobody" is also everybody, everybody in the sense of what in our time has been called the Common Man. In mid-Victorian England that meant the poor, the poor in whose slums disease was bred (in Victorian terms, typhoid especially) and from where it spread throughout the nation. Against Nobody Dickens sets the Bigwig family, the masters, the quarreling ruling class of the political parties. The wife and child of Nobody's master are killed by slum-bred disease. Nobody says:

"Master, 'tis hard to bear — I know it — but be comforted. I would give you comfort, if I could."

The Master thanked him from his heart, but, said he, "O you labouring men! The calamity began among you. If you had but lived more healthily and decently, I should not be the widowed and bereft mourner that I am this day."

"Master," returned the other, shaking his head, "I have begun to understand a little that most calamities will come from us, as this one did, and that none will stop at our poor doors, until we are united with that great squabbling family the Bigwigs yonder, to do the things that are right. We cannot live healthily and decently, unless they who undertake to manage us provide the means. We cannot be instructed unless they will teach us; we cannot be rationally amused, unless they will amuse us; we cannot but have some false gods of our own, while they set up so many of theirs in all the public places. The evil consequences of imperfect instruction, the evil consequences of pernicious neglect, the evil consequences of unnatural restraint and the denial of humanising enjoyments, will all come from us, and none of them will stop with us. They will spread far and wide. They always do; they always have done — just like the pestilence. I understand so much, I think, at last."

But the Master said again, "O you labouring men! How seldom do we ever hear of you, except in connexion with some trouble!"

"Master," he replied, "I am Nobody, and little likely to be heard of (nor yet much wanted to be heard of, perhaps), except when there *is* some trouble. But it never begins with me, and it never can end with me. As sure as Death, it comes down to me, and it goes up from me."

The story carries a note of despair:

There was so much reason in what he said, that the Bigwig family, getting wind of it, and being horribly frightened by the last desolation, resolved to unite with him to do the things that were right — at all events, so far as the said things were associated with the direct prevention, humanly speaking, of another pestilence. But as their fear wore off, which it soon began to do, they resumed their falling out among themselves, and did nothing. Consequently the scourge appeared again — low down as before — and spread avengingly upward as before, and carried off vast numbers of the brawlers. But not a man among them ever admitted, if in the least degree he ever perceived, that he had anything to do with it.

"Nobody's Story" is a passionate plea for the acceptance of social responsibility on the part of the rich and privileged, the ruling class. It is, it seems to me, the most Radical statement Dickens ever made.

Like the novels with which it has affinities, "Nobody's Story" is a special case. With the other stories, we are in the characteristic Dickens world. "Going into Society" is the fantastic Dickens, though it also has its element of the parable, a picture of the world translated into terms of a fairground; for the man who sets out to go into society, does so, and opts out of it again, is the dwarf "Chops," Major Tpschoffski.

"Somebody's Luggage" is again different. It appeared in *All the Year Round* in 1862 and in form is typical of Dickens' later stories. It is, in other words, a gathering together of stories, which are linked either by a single narrator or by its situation in a single place. The unifying factor in "Somebody's Luggage" is the narrator, the head waiter Christopher, who is worried about a trunk which has been kept against the discharge of a debt by a guest who had disappeared years earlier. Christopher buys the trunk from the landlady, finds the two stories which are at the centre of the whole thing, and sends them to the "conductor" of *All the Year Round*, Dickens himself. He is examining the proofs just at the moment that — but let me not spoil the effect by anticipating it. The first of the two stories is Dickens at his most sentimental; the second is much more interesting, a fable on the nature of the artist, which links up with the nature of the luggage-owner himself. But what contains everything and makes it possible to see the work as a single story is the narrator, Christopher. This is Dickens at not far from his most brilliant. As "Somebody's Luggage" opens, Christopher is telling his own tale, explaining the mystery of being a waiter, which is something to which one can only be bred:

> You were conveyed — ere yet your dawning powers were otherwise developed than to harbour vacancy in your inside — you were conveyed, by surreptitious means, into a pantry adjoining the Admiral Nelson, Civic and General Dining Rooms, there to receive by stealth that healthful sustenance which is the pride and boast of the British female constitution.

He identifies himself totally with the craft and mystery of being a waiter — and one feels that long years of study on Dickens' part, of sitting in restaurants and hotel dining rooms, have gone to Christopher's making, so close do we find ourselves to the Platonic idea of the waiter. For Christopher identifies himself totally with his occupation and the hotel he is serving in:

> We are a bed business, and a coffee-room business. We are not a general dining business, nor do we wish it. In consequence, when diners drop in, we know what to give 'em as will keep 'em away another time. We are a Private Room or Family business also; but coffee-room principal. Me and the Directory and the Writing Materials and cetrer occupy a place to ourselves — a place fended off a step or two at the end of the coffee-room, in what I call the good old-fashioned style. The good old-fashioned style is, that whatever you want, down to a wafer, you must be olely and solely dependent on the Head Waiter for. You must put yourself a new-born Child into his hands. There is no other way in which a business untinged with Continental Vice can be conducted. (It were bootless to add, that if languages is required to be jabbered and English is not good enough, both families and gentlemen had better go somewhere else.)

It is the speaking voice of Christopher that binds into a whole the stories that make up the piece. It imposes unity on what at first sight seems diverse, and like the speaking voice of all Dickens' major characters, it is totally idiosyncratic, unique. Christopher could appear in any one of the great novels, and he would be famous.

And this is even more so of the Mrs. Lirriper of the two stories

"Mrs. Lirriper's Lodgings" and "Mrs. Lirriper's Legacy." In both, there is the loving observation, this time of a London boarding house, that one might well believe came from years of first-hand experience, so completely have the atmosphere and very details of everyday existence been registered. But it is the character of Mrs. Lirriper, the widow who takes to boarding-house keeping after her husband's death, that makes these stories so triumphant. Like Christopher, the Head Waiter, she speaks in her own voice, a unique voice. "Mrs. Lirriper's Lodgings" has been called by Professor J. Isaacs, of London University, "one of Dickens's most neglected masterpieces," and so it is, because of Mrs. Lirriper. "There," Professor Isaacs goes on, "you will find comic prattle of supreme accomplishment. There James Joyce found Mrs. Bloom." I doubt whether this can be proved, but in the interior monologue through which Mrs. Lirriper tells her stories we certainly have an astonishing anticipation of stream-of-consciousness as Joyce uses it in the last chapter of *Ulysses*. This is in itself a striking instance of something that becomes more and more apparent the further Dickens recedes into history: his extraordinary modernity. He may have been unlike the writers who were his contemporaries, with the exception of Dostoevsky, but his affinities with later writers become increasingly plain.

Throughout the two stories, Mrs. Lirriper is talking to herself, or perhaps to a single listener who never speaks, never interrupts. In her own inconsequent words Mrs. Lirriper unrolls the sequence of her life, for that by implication is what the stories reveal, and reveals too, all artlessly and unconsciously — for it is Dickens her creator who is the conscious artist — the simple beauty of her character. Dickens — it is one of the few failings of his genius — was not commonly successful in his portrayal of good women, mainly, I think, because, where women were concerned, the notion of goodness tended to inhibit his comic sense. There is not, for instance, so far as I can recall, a female equivalent of Joe Gargery. Mrs. Lirriper is a comic figure, comic very much as Mrs. Nickleby is; but she is also admirable in her simple goodness. And she has a splendid foil in the character of her principal boarder, Major Jemmy Jackman, who again seems to me a major creation who would be famous if he had figured in any of the novels.

Mrs. Lirriper encloses all the action, all the incidents, within herself, within her speaking voice. That is everything. It redeems what might seem the appalling sentimentality of the central situation, the story of a young wife abandoned by her husband and dying in child-birth, her son being brought up, the apple of their eyes, by Mrs. Lirriper and Major Jackman. Here is the speaking voice:

> I am an old woman now and my good looks are gone but that's me my dear over the plate-warmer and considered like in the times when you used to pay two guineas on ivory and took your chance pretty much how you came out, which made you very careful how you left it about afterwards because people were turned so red and uncomfortable by mostly guessing it was somebody else quite different, and there was once a certain person that had put his money in a hop business that came in one morning to pay his rent and his respects being the second floor that would have taken it down from its hook and put it in his breast-pocket — you understand my dear — for the L, he says of the original — only there was no mellowness in *his* voice and I wouldn't let him, but his opinion of it you may gather from his saying to it "Speak to me Emma!" which was far from a rational observation no doubt but still a tribute to its being a likeness, and I think myself it *was* like me when I was young and wore that sort of stays.

That is surely great writing, and it is kept up throughout the two Lirriper stories, which essentially are one. Together, they are among Dickens' masterpieces, the best, perhaps, of Dickens' fiction outside the novels and worthy to stand by their side.

These later stories of Dickens', for they date from the last decade of his life, have an additional interest in that they show us a Dickens experimenting with technique and form. "Somebody's Luggage" and the Lirriper stories are, one might say, feats of ventriloquism: in them one see Dickens rendering character in itself, *from* itself, every-thing depending on the nuance of the character's spoken word and tone of voice. To use Henry James's phrase, there is no "going be-hind" the characters: they are completely dramatized. Not to know these stories is not to know an aspect of Dickens that isn't immedi-ately apparent in the novels. To this group of stories belongs also "Doctor Marigold," which begins: "I am a Cheap Jack, and my own father's name was Willum Marigold. It was in his lifetime assumed by some that his name was William, but my own father always con-sistently said, No, it was Willum."

In "Mugby Junction" Dickens is experimenting in a rather differ-ent way, a way that points to a minor mode of the novel that was popular in the 1920s and 1930s, in which the unity of the work was imposed by the place in which the action was played out. One still remembers, partly because of the film that was made from it, Vicki Baum's *Grand Hotel*. For Dickens, who was born in the last great days of the stage-coach era, knew it at first hand as a newspaper reporter, and celebrated it so wonderfully in his early novels, the railroad was a very powerful symbol. As comes out clearly in *Dombey and Son,* it stood for rapid industrial change, ruthless technological progress. In "Mugby Junction," which is generally thought to signify Rugby, an important railroad center in the English Midlands, Dickens exploits the dramatic possibilities of a large station:

> A place replete with shadowy shapes, this Mugby Junction in the black hours of the four-and-twenty. Mysterious goods trains, covered with palls and gliding on like vast weird funerals, conveying themselves guiltily away from the presence of the few lighted lamps, as if their freight had come to a secret and unlawful end. Half-miles of coal pursuing in a Detective fashion, following when they lead, stopping when they stop, backing when they back. Red-hot embers showering out upon the ground, down this dark avenue, and down the other, as if torturing fires were being raked clear; concurrently, shrieks and groans and grinds invading the ear, as if the tortured were at the height of their suffering. Iron-barred cages full of cattle jangling by midway, the drooping beasts with horns entangled, eyes frozen with terror, and mouths too: at least they have long icicles (or what seem so) hanging from their lips. Unknown languages in the air, conspiring in red, green, and white characters. An earthquake, accompanied with thunder and lightning, going up express to London. Now, all quiet, all rusty, wind and rain in possession, lamps extinguished, Mugby Junction, dead and indistinct, with its robe drawn over its head, like Caesar.

That is Dickens at his most authentically sinister, the Dickens of the Doré-esque imagination; and the stories that begin and end "Mugby Junction" are no less mysterious and sinister. The surprise, however, comes in the middle, which begins: "I am the boy at Mugby. That's about what *I* am. You don't know what I mean? What a pity! But I think you do. I think you must. Look here. I am the boy at what is called The Refreshment Room at Mugby Junction, and what's proudest boast is, that it never yet refreshed a mortal being." Dickens is again at his work of impersonation and ventriloquism. It is as it were the layer of comedy in the sandwich that

"Mugby Junction" is. It is one of Dickens' most brilliant pieces of satirical writing, for as the boy tells his story we learn of Our Missis's report to her assembled staff on her tour of inspection of refreshment rooms in French railroad stations, a totally horrifying and unnerving experience:

> "Shall I be believed when I tell you, that no sooner had I landed," this word with a killing look at Sniff, "on that treacherous shore, than I was ushered into a Refreshment Room where there were — I do not exaggerate — actually eatable things to eat?"
>
> A groan burst from the ladies. I not only did myself the honour of joining, but also of lengthening it out.
>
> "Where there were," Our Missis added, "not only eatable things to eat, but also drinkable things to drink?"
>
> A murmur, swelling almost to a scream, ariz. Miss Piff, trembling with indignation, called out, "Name!"
>
> "I *will* name," said Our Missis. "There was roast fowls, hot and cold; there was smoking roast veal surrounded with browned potatoes; there was hot soup with (again I ask shall I be credited?) nothing bitter in it, and no flour to choke off the consumer; there was a variety of cold dishes set off with jelly; there was salad; there was — mark me! *fresh* pastry, and that of a light construction; there was a luscious show of fruit; there were bottles and decanters of sound small wine, of every size, and adapted to every pocket; the same odious statement will apply to brandy; and these were set out upon the counter so that all could help themselves."
>
> Our Missis's lips so quivered, that Mrs. Sniff, though scarcely less convulsed than she were, got up and held the tumbler to them.
>
> "This," proceeds Our Missis, "was my first unconstitutional experience. Well would it have been if it had been my last and worst. But no. As I proceeded further into that enslaved and ignorant land, its aspect became more hideous. I need not explain to this assembly the ingredients and formation of the British Refreshment sangwich?"
>
> Universal laughter — except from Sniff, who, as sangwich-cutter, shook his head in a state of the utmost dejection as he stood with it agin the wall.

There follows Our Missis's outraged description of the French Refreshment Room sandwich, with Our Missis's indignation rising all the time.

The remaining stories I have chosen for this selection come from *Reprinted Pieces*, published in the "Library Edition" of Dickens' works in 1858. The volume was made up from contributions to *Household Words*. However, in The New Oxford Illustrated Dickens, which I have been following, some of the items, "Nobody's Story" among them, are transferred to "Christmas Stories," where they seem more properly to belong, and pieces hitherto uncollected have been added. Among these are "Hunted Down" and "George Silverman's Explanation." The former was specially written for *The New York Ledger,* where it first appeared; the other story appeared first in *The Atlantic Monthly,* which paid the author what was then the record price of £1000. "Hunted Down" may best be described as a detective story; it seems to have been based on one of the most notorious of nineteenth-century criminal cases, that of the poisoner and forger Thomas Griffiths Wainewright, of whom Oscar Wilde was also later to write in *Intentions.*

"George Silverman's Explanation," it has been said, "is possibly the least characteristic of Dickens' shorter writing," and it has mystified most critics. The study of a poor clergyman, from a slum childhood, it is certainly a very ambiguous work and, as Dickens' modern biographer Edgar Johnson has written, "one feels as if it were haunted by Dickens's troubled consciousness of ambiguities within himself." This seems borne out by Dickens' own comment on the story in a letter to a friend: "I feel as if I had read something (by somebody else) which I should never get out of my head!!" (The double exclamation marks are Dickens' own.)

"The Lamplighter" is early work, the narrative version of a farce that failed to reach the stage. "To Be Read at Dusk" I have chosen both because of the novelty of the narrative method and because of its strangeness as a ghost story. "Births. Mrs. Meek, of a Son" is something quite different, a rendering of one of the commonest of human situations, pride in paternity and the father's resentment of his dominating mother-in-law. It seems to me touching and funny — and also the nearest Dickens ever came to writing a short story in the modern sense. Am I, I wonder, alone in being reminded, while reading it, of the young Chekhov?

WALTER ALLEN

THE

BOARDING

HOUSE

1

IN TWO CHAPTERS

The Boarding House

CHAPTER THE FIRST

Mrs. Tibbs was, beyond all dispute, the most tidy, fidgety, thrifty little personage that ever inhaled the smoke of London; and the house of Mrs. Tibbs was, decidedly, the neatest in all Great Coram Street. The area and the area-steps, and the street-door and the street-door steps, and the brass handle, and the door-plate, and the knocker, and the fan-light, were all as clean and bright, as indefatigable white-washing, and hearth-stoning, and scrubbing and rubbing, could make them. The wonder was, that the brass door-plate, with the interesting inscription "Mrs. Tibbs," had never caught fire from constant friction, so perseveringly was it polished. There were meat-safe-looking blinds in the parlor-windows, blue and gold curtains in the drawing-room, and spring-roller blinds, as Mrs. Tibbs was wont in the pride of her heart to boast, "all the way up." The bell-lamp in the passage looked as clear as a soap-bubble; you could see yourself in all the tables, and French-polish yourself on any one of the stairs. The banisters were bees'-waxed; and the very stair-wires made your eyes wink, they were so glittering.

Mrs. Tibbs was somewhat short of stature, and Mr. Tibbs was by no means a large man. He had, moreover, very short legs, but, by way of indemnification, his face was peculiarly long. He was to his wife what the o is in 90 — he was of some importance *with* her — he was nothing without her. Mrs. Tibbs was always talking. Mr. Tibbs rarely spoke; but, if it were at any time possible to put in a word, when he should have said nothing at all, he had that talent.

3

Mrs. Tibbs detested long stories, and Mr. Tibbs had one, the conclusion of which had never been heard by his most intimate friends.
It always began, "I recollect when I was in the volunteer corps, in
eighteen hundred and six" — but, as he spoke very slowly and softly,
and his better half very quickly and loudly, he rarely got beyond
the introductory sentence. He was a melancholy specimen of the
story-teller. He was the wandering Jew of Joe Millerism.

Mr. Tibbs enjoyed a small independence from the pension-list —
about 43*l*. 15*s*. 10*d*. a year. His father, mother, and five interesting
scions from the same stock, drew a like sum from the revenue of a
grateful country, though for what particular service was never
known. But, as this said independence was not quite sufficient to
furnish two people with *all* the luxuries of this life, it had occurred
to the busy little spouse of Tibbs, that the best thing she could do
with a legacy of 700*l*., would be to take and furnish a tolerable
house — somewhere in that partially explored tract of country which
lies between the British Museum, and a remote village called Somers Town — for the reception of boarders. Great Coram Street was
the spot pitched upon. The house had been furnished accordingly;
two female servants and a boy engaged; and an advertisement inserted in the morning papers, informing the public that "Six individuals would meet with all the comforts of a cheerful musical home in
a select private family, residing within ten minutes' walk of" —
everywhere. Answers out of number were received, with all sorts of
initials; all the letters of the alphabet seemed to be seized with a sudden wish to go out boarding and lodging; voluminous was the correspondence between Mrs. Tibbs and the applicants; and most profound was the secrecy observed. "E." didn't like this; "I." couldn't
think of putting up with that; "I. O. U." didn't think the terms
would suit him; and "G. R." had never slept in a French bed. The
result, however, was that three gentlemen became inmates of Mrs.
Tibbs's house, on terms which were "agreeable to all parties." In
went the advertisement again, and a lady with her two daughters
proposed to increase — not their families, but Mrs. Tibbs's.

"Charming woman, that Mrs. Maplesone!" said Mrs. Tibbs, as she
and her spouse were sitting by the fire after breakfast; the gentlemen
having gone out on their several avocations. "Charming woman,
indeed!" repeated little Mrs. Tibbs, more by way of soliloquy than
anything else, for she never thought of consulting her husband. "And

the two daughters are delightful. We must have some fish today; they'll join us at dinner for the first time."

Mr. Tibbs placed the poker at right angles with the fire shovel, and essayed to speak, but recollected he had nothing to say.

"The young ladies," continued Mrs. T., "have kindly volunteered to bring their own piano."

Tibbs thought of the volunteer story, but did not venture it. A bright thought struck him —

"It's very likely — " said he.

"Pray don't lean your head against the paper," interrupted Mrs. Tibbs; "and don't put your feet on the steel fender; that's worse."

Tibbs took his head from the paper, and his feet from the fender, and proceeded. "It's very likely one of the young ladies may set her cap at young Mr. Simpson, and you know a marriage — "

"A what!" shrieked Mrs. Tibbs. Tibbs modestly repeated his former suggestion.

"I beg you won't mention such a thing," said Mrs. T. "A marriage, indeed! — to rob me of my boarders — no, not for the world."

Tibbs thought in his own mind that the event was by no means unlikely, but, as he never argued with his wife, he put a stop to the dialogue, by observing it was "time to go to business." He always went out at ten o'clock in the morning, and returned at five in the afternoon, with an exceedingly dirty face, and smelling moldy. Nobody knew what he was, or where he went; but Mrs. Tibbs used to say with an air of great importance, that he was engaged in the City.

The Miss Maplesones and their accomplished parent arrived in the course of the afternoon in a hackney-coach, and accompanied by a most astonishing number of packages. Trunks, bonnet-boxes, muff-boxes and parasols, guitar-cases, and parcels of all imaginable shapes, done up in brown paper, and fastened with pins, filled the passage. Then, there was such a running up and down with the luggage, such scampering for warm water for the ladies to wash in, and such a bustle, and confusion, and heating of servants, and curling-irons, as had never been known in Great Coram Street before. Little Mrs. Tibbs was quite in her element, bustling about, talking incessantly, and distributing towels and soap, like a head nurse in a hospital. The house was not restored to its usual state of quiet repose, until the ladies were safely shut up in their respective bedrooms, engaged in the important occupation of dressing for dinner.

"Are these gals 'andsome?" inquired Mr. Simpson of Mr. Septimus Hicks, another of the boarders, as they were amusing themselves in the drawing-room, before dinner, by lolling on sofas, and contemplating their pumps.

"Don't know," replied Mr. Septimus Hicks, who was a tallish, white-faced young man, with spectacles, and a black ribbon round his neck instead of a neckerchief — a most interesting person; a poetical walker of the hospitals, and a "very talented young man." He was fond of "lugging" into conversation all sorts of quotations from Don Juan, without fettering himself by the propriety of their application; in which particular he was remarkably independent. The other, Mr. Simpson, was one of those young men, who are in society what walking gentlemen are on the stage, only infinitely worse skilled in his vocation than the most indifferent artist. He was as empty-headed as the great bell of St. Paul's; always dressed according to the caricatures published in the monthly fashions; and spelled Character with a K.

"I saw a devilish number of parcels in the passage when I came home," simpered Mr. Simpson.

"Materials for the toilet, no doubt," rejoined the Don Juan reader.

> — "Much linen, lace, and several pair
> Of stockings, slippers, brushes, combs, complete;
> With other articles of ladies fair,
> To keep them beautiful, or leave them neat."

"Is that from Milton?" inquired Mr. Simpson.

"No — from Byron," returned Mr. Hicks, with a look of contempt. He was quite sure of his author, because he had never read any other. "Hush! Here come the gals," and they both commenced talking in a very loud key.

"Mrs. Maplesone and the Miss Maplesones, Mr. Hicks. Mr. Hicks — Mrs. Maplesone and the Miss Maplesones," said Mrs. Tibbs, with a very red face, for she had been superintending the cooking operations below stairs, and looked like a wax doll on a sunny day. "Mr. Simpson, I beg your pardon — Mrs. Maplesone and the Miss Maplesones" — and *vice versa*. The gentlemen immediately began to slide about with much politeness, and to look as if they wished their arms had been legs, so little did they know what to do with them. The ladies smiled, curtseyed, and glided into chairs, and dived for dropped pocket-handkerchiefs: the gentlemen leaned against two of the curtain-pegs; Mrs. Tibbs went through an admirable bit of serious pantomime with a servant who had come up to ask some question about the fish-sauce; and then the two young ladies looked at each other; and everybody else appeared to discover something very attractive in the pattern of the fender.

"Julia, my love," said Mrs. Maplesone to her youngest daughter, in a tone loud enough for the remainder of the company to hear — "Julia."

"Yes, Ma."

"Don't stoop." — This was said for the purpose of directing general attention to Miss Julia's figure, which was undeniable. Everybody looked at her, accordingly, and there was another pause.

"We had the most uncivil hackney-coachman today, you can imagine," said Mrs. Maplesone to Mrs. Tibbs, in a confidential tone.

"Dear me!" replied the hostess, with an air of great commiseration. She couldn't say more, for the servant again appeared at the door, and commenced telegraphing most earnestly to her "Missis."

"I think hackney-coachmen generally *are* uncivil," said Mr. Hicks, in his most insinuating tone.

"Positively I think they are," replied Mrs. Maplesone, as if the idea had never struck her before.

"And cabmen, too," said Mr. Simpson. This remark was a failure, for no one intimated, by word or sign, the slightest knowledge of the manners and customs of cabmen.

"Robinson, what *do* you want?" said Mrs. Tibbs to the servant, who, by way of making her presence known to her mistress, had been giving sundry hems and sniffs outside the door during the preceding five minutes.

"Please, ma'am, master wants his clean things," replied the servant, taken off her guard. The two young men turned their faces to the window, and "went off" like a couple of bottles of ginger-beer; the ladies put their handkerchiefs to their mouths; and little Mrs. Tibbs bustled out of the room to give Tibbs his clean linen — and the servant warning.

Mr. Calton, the remaining boarder, shortly afterwards made his appearance, and proved a surprising promoter of the conversation. Mr. Calton was a superannuated beau — an old boy. He used to say of himself that although his features were not regularly handsome, they were striking. They certainly were. It was impossible to look at his face without being reminded of a chubby street-door knocker, half-lion half-monkey; and the comparison might be extended to his whole character and conversation. He had stood still, while everything else had been moving. He never originated a conversation, or started an idea; but if any commonplace topic were broached, or, to pursue the comparison, if anybody *lifted him up*, he would hammer away with surprising rapidity. He had the tic-douloureux occasionally, and then he might be said to be muffled, because he did not make quite as much noise as at other times, when he would go on prosing, rat-tat-tat the same thing over and over again. He had never been married; but he was still on the lookout for a wife with money. He had a life interest worth about 300*l.* a year — he was exceedingly vain, and inordinately selfish. He had acquired the reputation of being the very pink of politeness, and he walked round the park, and up Regent Street, every day.

This respectable personage had made up his mind to render himself exceedingly agreeable to Mrs. Maplesone — indeed, the desire of being as amiable as possible extended itself to the whole party; Mrs. Tibbs having considered it an admirable little bit of management to represent to the gentlemen that she had *some* reason to believe the ladies were fortunes, and to hint to the ladies, that all the gentlemen were "eligible." A little flirtation, she thought, might keep her house full, without leading to any other result.

Mrs. Maplesone was an enterprising widow of about fifty: shrewd, scheming, and good-looking. She was amiably anxious on behalf of her daughters; in proof whereof she used to remark, that she would have no objection to marry again, if it would benefit her dear girls — she could have no other motive. The "dear girls" themselves were not at all insensible to the merits of "a good establishment." One of them was twenty-five; the other, three years younger. They had been at different watering-places, for four seasons; they had gambled at libraries, read books in balconies, sold at fancy fairs, danced at assemblies, talked sentiment — in short, they had done all that industrious girls could do — but, as yet, to no purpose.

"What a magnificent dresser Mr. Simpson is!" whispered Matilda Maplesone to her sister Julia.

"Splendid!" returned the youngest. The magnificent individual alluded to wore a maroon-colored dress-coat, with a velvet collar and cuffs of the same tint — very like that which usually invests the form of the distinguished unknown who condescends to play the "swell" in the pantomime at "Richardson's Show."

"What whiskers!" said Miss Julia.

"Charming!" responded her sister; "and what hair!" His hair was like a wig, and distinguished by that insinuating wave which graces the shining locks of those *chefs-d'œuvre* of art surmounting the waxen images in Bartellot's window in Regent Street; his whiskers meeting beneath his chin, seemed strings wherewith to tie it on, ere science had rendered them unnecessary by her patent invisible springs.

"Dinner's on the table, ma'am, if you please," said the boy, who now appeared for the first time, in a revived black coat of his master's.

"Oh! Mr. Calton, will you lead Mrs. Maplesone? — Thank you." Mr. Simpson offered his arm to Miss Julia; Mr. Septimus Hicks escorted the lovely Matilda; and the procession proceeded to the dining-room. Mr. Tibbs was introduced, and Mr. Tibbs bobbed up and down to the three ladies like a figure in a Dutch clock, with a powerful spring in the middle of his body, and then dived rapidly into his seat at the bottom of the table, delighted to screen himself behind a soup-tureen, which he could just see over, and that was all. The boarders were seated, a lady and gentleman alternately, like the layers of bread and meat in a plate of sandwiches; and then Mrs. Tibbs directed James to take off the covers. Salmon, lobster-sauce, giblet-soup, and the usual accompaniments were *dis*-covered: potatoes like petrifactions, and bits of toasted bread, the shape and size of blank dice.

"Soup for Mrs. Maplesone, my dear," said the bustling Mrs. Tibbs. She always called her husband "my dear" before company. Tibbs, who had been eating his bread, and calculating how long it would be before he should get any fish, helped the soup in a hurry, made a small island on the tablecloth, and put his glass upon it to hide it from his wife.

"Miss Julia, shall I assist you to some fish?"

"If you please — very little — oh! plenty, thank you" (a bit about the size of a walnut put upon the plate).

"Julia is a *very* little eater," said Mrs. Maplesone to Mr. Calton.

The knocker gave a single rap. He was busy eating the fish with his eyes: so he only ejaculated, "Ah!"

"My dear," said Mrs. Tibbs to her spouse after every one else had been helped, "what do *you* take?" The inquiry was accompanied with a look intimating that he mustn't say fish, because there was not much left. Tibbs thought the frown referred to the island on the tablecloth; he therefore coolly replied, "Why — I'll take a little — fish, I think."

"Did you say fish, my dear?" (another frown).

"Yes, dear," replied the villain, with an expression of acute hunger depicted in his countenance. The tears almost started to Mrs. Tibbs's eyes, as she helped her "wretch of a husband," as she inwardly called him, to the last eatable bit of salmon on the dish.

"James, take this to your master, and take away your master's knife." This was deliberate revenge, as Tibbs never could eat fish without one. He was, however, constrained to chase small particles of salmon round and round his plate with a piece of bread and a fork, the number of successful attempts being about one in seventeen.

"Take away, James," said Mrs. Tibbs, as Tibbs swallowed the fourth mouthful — and away went the plates like lightning.

"I'll take a bit of bread, James," said the poor "master of the house," more hungry than ever.

"Never mind your master now, James," said Mrs. Tibbs, "see about the meat." This was conveyed in the tone in which ladies usually give admonitions to servants in company, that is to say, a low one; but which, like a stage whisper, from its peculiar emphasis, is most distinctly heard by everybody present.

A pause ensued, before the table was replenished — a sort of parenthesis in which Mr. Simpson, Mr. Calton, and Mr. Hicks, produced respectively a bottle of sauterne, bucellas, and sherry, and took wine with everybody — except Tibbs. No one ever thought of him.

Between the fish and an intimated sirloin, there was a prolonged interval.

Here was an opportunity for Mr. Hicks. He could not resist the singularly appropriate quotation—

"But beef is rare within these oxless isles;
Goats' flesh there is, no doubt, and kid, and mutton,

And when a holiday upon them smiles,
A joint upon their barbarous spits they put on."

"Very ungentlemanly behavior," thought little Mrs. Tibbs, "to talk in that way."

"Ah," said Mr. Calton, filling his glass. "Tom Moore is my poet."

"And mine," said Mrs. Maplesone.

"And mine," said Miss Julia.

"And mine," added Mr. Simpson.

"Look at his compositions," resumed the knocker.

"To be sure," said Simpson, with confidence.

"Look at Don Juan," replied Mr. Septimus Hicks.

"Julia's letter," suggested Miss Matilda.

"Can anything be grander than the Fire Worshippers?" inquired Miss Julia.

"To be sure," said Simpson.

"Or Paradise and the Peri," said the old beau.

"Yes; or Paradise and the Peer," repeated Simpson, who thought he was getting through it capitally.

"It's all very well," replied Mr. Septimus Hicks, who, as we have before hinted, never had read anything but Don Juan. "Where will you find anything finer than the description of the siege, at the commencement of the seventh canto?"

"Talking of a siege," said Tibbs, with a mouthful of bread — "when I was in the volunteer corps, in eighteen hundred and six, our commanding officer was Sir Charles Rampart; and one day, when we were exercising on the ground on which the London University now stands, he says, says he, Tibbs (calling me from the ranks), Tibbs — "

"Tell your master, James," interrupted Mrs. Tibbs, in an awfully distinct tone, "tell your master if he *won't* carve those fowls, to send them to me." The discomfited volunteer instantly set to work, and carved the fowls almost as expeditiously as his wife operated on the haunch of mutton. Whether he ever finished the story is not known; but, if he did, nobody heard it.

As the ice was now broken, and the new inmates more at home, every member of the company felt more at ease. Tibbs himself most certainly did, because he went to sleep immediately after dinner. Mr. Hicks and the ladies discoursed most eloquently about poetry, and the theaters, and Lord Chesterfield's Letters; and Mr. Calton followed up what everybody said, with continuous double knocks. Mrs. Tibbs highly approved of every observation that fell from Mrs. Maplesone; and as Mr. Simpson sat with a smile upon his face and said "Yes," or "Certainly," at intervals of about four minutes each, he received full credit for understanding what was going forward. The gentlemen rejoined the ladies in the drawing-room very shortly after they had left the dining-parlor. Mrs. Maplesone and Mr. Calton played cribbage, and the "young people" amused themselves with music and conversation. The Miss Maplesones sang the most fascinating duets, and accompanied themselves on guitars, ornamented with bits of ethereal blue ribbon. Mr. Simpson put on a pink waistcoat, and said he was in raptures; and Mr. Hicks felt in the seventh heaven of poetry or the seventh canto of Don Juan — it was the same thing to him. Mrs. Tibbs was quite charmed with the newcomers; and Mr. Tibbs spent the evening in his usual way — he went to sleep, and woke up, and went to sleep again, and woke at supper-time.

*　　　　*　　　　*

We are not about to adopt the license of novel-writers, and to let "years roll on"; but we will take the liberty of requesting the reader to suppose that six months have elapsed, since the dinner we have described, and that Mrs. Tibbs's boarders have, during that period, sang, and danced, and gone to theaters and exhibitions, together, as ladies and gentlemen, wherever they board, often do. And we will beg them, the period we have mentioned having elapsed, to imagine farther that Mr. Septimus Hicks received, in his own bedroom (a front attic), at an early hour one morning, a note from Mr. Calton, requesting the favor of seeing him, as soon as convenient to himself, in his (Calton's) dressing-room on the second-floor back.

"Tell Mr. Calton I'll come down directly," said Mr. Septimus to the boy. "Stop — is Mr. Calton unwell?" inquired this excited walker of hospitals, as he put on a bed-furniture-looking dressing-gown.

"Not as I knows on, sir," replied the boy. "Please, sir, he looked rather rum, as it might be."

"Ah, that's no proof of his being ill," returned Hicks, unconsciously. "Very well: I'll be down directly." Downstairs ran the boy with the message, and down went the excited Hicks himself, almost

A GAME OF CRIBBAGE

as soon as the message was delivered. "Tap, tap." "Come in." — Door opens, and discovers Mr. Calton sitting in an easy chair. Mutual shakes of the hand exchanged, and Mr. Septimus Hicks motioned to a seat. A short pause. Mr. Hicks coughed, and Mr. Calton took a pinch of snuff. It was one of those interviews where neither party knows what to say. Mr. Septimus Hicks broke silence.

"I received a note — " he said, very tremulously, in a voice like a Punch with a cold.

"Yes," returned the other, "you did."

"Exactly."

"Yes."

Now, although this dialogue must have been satisfactory, both gentlemen felt there was something more important to be said; therefore they did as most men in such a situation would have done — they looked at the table with a determined aspect. The conversation had been opened, however, and Mr. Calton had made up his mind to continue it with a regular double knock. He always spoke very pompously.

"Hicks," said he, "I have sent for you, in consequence of certain arrangements which are pending in this house, connected with a marriage."

"With a marriage!" gasped Hicks, compared with whose expression of countenance, Hamlet's, when he sees his father's ghost, is pleasing and composed.

"With a marriage," returned the knocker. "I have sent for you to prove the great confidence I can repose in you."

"And will you betray me?" eagerly inquired Hicks, who in his alarm had even forgotten to quote.

"*I* betray *you!* Won't *you* betray *me?*"

"Never: no one shall know, to my dying day, that you had a hand in the business," responded the agitated Hicks, with an inflamed countenance, and his hair standing on end as if he were on the stool of an electrifying machine in full operation.

"People must know that, some time or other — within a year, I imagine," said Mr. Calton, with an air of great self-complacency, "we *may* have a family."

"*We!* — That won't affect you, surely?"

"The devil it won't!"

"No! how can it?" said the bewildered Hicks. Calton was too much inwrapped in the contemplation of his happiness to see the equivoque between Hicks and himself; and threw himself back in his chair. "Oh, Matilda!" sighed the antique beau, in a lackadaisical voice, and applying his right hand a little to the left of the fourth button of his waistcoat, counting from the bottom. "Oh, Matilda!"

"What Matilda?" inquired Hicks, starting up.

"Matilda Maplesone," responded the other, doing the same.

"I marry her tomorrow morning," said Hicks.

"It's false," rejoined his companion: "I marry her!"

"You marry her?"

"I marry her!"

"You marry Matilda Maplesone?"

"Matilda Maplesone."

"*Miss* Maplesone marry *you?*"

"Miss Maplesone! No: Mrs. Maplesone."

"Good Heaven!" said Hicks, falling into his chair: "You marry the mother, and I the daughter!"

"Most extraordinary circumstance!" replied Mr. Calton, "and rather inconvenient too; for the fact is, that owing to Matilda's wishing to keep her intention secret from her daughters until the ceremony had taken place, she doesn't like applying to any of her friends to give her away. I entertain an objection to making the affair known to my acquaintance just now; and the consequence is, that I sent to you to know whether you'd oblige me by acting as father."

"I should have been most happy, I assure you," said Hicks, in a tone of condolence; "but, you see, I shall be acting as bridegroom. One character is frequently a consequence of the other; but it is not usual to act in both at the same time. There's Simpson — I have no doubt he'll do it for you."

"I don't like to ask him," replied Calton, "he's such a donkey."

Mr. Septimus Hicks looked up at the ceiling, and down at the floor; at last an idea struck him. "Let the man of the house, Tibbs, be the father," he suggested; and then he quoted, as peculiarly applicable to Tibbs and the pair —

"Oh Powers of Heaven! what dark eyes meets she there?
'Tis — 'tis her father's — fixed upon the pair."

"The idea has struck me already," said Mr. Calton: "but, you see, Matilda, for what reason I know not, is very anxious that Mrs. Tibbs should know nothing about it, till it's all over. It's a natural delicacy, after all, you know."

"He's the best-natured little man in existence, if you manage him properly," said Mr. Septimus Hicks. "Tell him not to mention it to his wife, and assure him she won't mind it, and he'll do it directly. My marriage is to be a secret one, on account of the mother and *my* father; therefore he must be enjoined to secrecy."

A small double knock, like a presumptuous single one, was that instant heard at the street-door. It was Tibbs; it could be no one else; for no one else occupied five minutes in rubbing his shoes. He had been out to pay the baker's bill.

"Mr. Tibbs," called Mr. Calton in a very bland tone, looking over the banisters.

"Sir!" replied he of the dirty face.

"Will you have the kindness to step up-stairs for a moment?"

"Certainly, sir," said Tibbs, delighted to be taken notice of. The bedroom door was carefully closed, and Tibbs, having put his hat on the floor (as most timid men do), and been accommodated with a seat, looked as astounded as if he were suddenly summoned before the familiars of the Inquisition.

"A rather unpleasant occurrence, Mr. Tibbs," said Calton, in a very portentous manner, "obliges me to consult you, and to beg you will not communicate what I am about to say, to your wife."

Tibbs acquiesced, wondering in his own mind what the deuce the other could have done, and imagining that at least he must have broken the best decanters.

Mr. Calton resumed; "I am placed, Mr. Tibbs, in rather an unpleasant situation."

Tibbs looked at Mr. Septimus Hicks, as if he thought Mr. H.'s being in the immediate vicinity of his fellow-boarder might constitute the unpleasantness of his situation; but as he did not exactly know what to say, he merely ejaculated the monosyllable "Lor!"

"Now," continued the knocker, "let me beg you will exhibit no manifestations of surprise, which may be overheard by the domestics, when I tell you — command your feelings of astonishment — that two inmates of this house intend to be married tomorrow morning." And he drew back his chair several feet, to perceive the effect of the unlooked-for announcement.

If Tibbs had rushed from the room, staggered down-stairs, and fainted in the passage — if he had instantaneously jumped out of the window into the mews behind the house, in an agony of surprise — his behavior would have been much less inexplicable to Mr. Calton than it was, when he put his hands into his inexpressible-pockets, and said with a half-chuckle, "Just so."

"You are not surprised, Mr. Tibbs?" inquired Mr. Calton.

"Bless you, no, sir," returned Tibbs; "after all, it's very natural. When two young people get together, you know — "

"Certainly, certainly," said Calton, with an indescribable air of self-satisfaction.

"You don't think it's at all an out-of-the-way affair then?" asked Mr. Septimus Hicks, who had watched the countenance of Tibbs in mute astonishment.

"No, sir," replied Tibbs; "I was just the same at his age." He actually smiled when he said this.

"How devilish well I must carry my years!" thought the delighted old beau, knowing he was at least ten years older than Tibbs at that moment.

"Well, then, to come to the point at once," he continued, "I have to ask you whether you will object to act as father on the occasion?"

"Certainly not," replied Tibbs; still without evincing an atom of surprise.

"You will not?"

"Decidedly not," reiterated Tibbs, still as calm as a pot of porter with the head off.

Mr. Calton seized the hand of the petticoat-governed little man, and vowed eternal friendship from that hour. Hicks, who was all admiration and surprise, did the same.

"Now, confess," asked Mr. Calton of Tibbs, as he picked up his hat, "were you not a little surprised?"

"I b'lieve you!" replied that illustrious person, holding up one hand; "I b'lieve you! When I first heard of it."

"So sudden," said Septimus Hicks.

"So strange to ask *me*, you know," said Tibbs.

"So odd altogether!" said the superannuated love-maker; and then all three laughed.

"I say," said Tibbs, shutting the door which he had previously opened, and giving full vent to a hitherto corked-up giggle, "what bothers me is, what *will* his father say?"

Mr. Septimus Hicks looked at Mr. Calton.

"Yes; but the best of it is," said the latter, giggling in his turn, "I haven't got a father — he! he! he!"

"*You* haven't got a father. No; but *he* has," said Tibbs.

"*Who* has?" inquired Septimus Hicks.

"Why, *him.*"

"Him, who? Do you know my secret? Do you mean me?"

"You! No; you know who I mean," returned Tibbs with a knowing wink.

"For Heaven's sake, whom *do* you mean?" inquired Mr. Calton, who, like Septimus Hicks, was all but out of his senses at the strange confusion.

"Why, Mr. Simpson, of course," replied Tibbs; "who else could I mean?"

"I see it all," said the Byron-quoter; "Simpson marries Julia Maplesone to-morrow morning!"

"Undoubtedly," replied Tibbs, thoroughly satisfied, "of course he does."

It would require the pencil of Hogarth to illustrate — our feeble pen is inadequate to describe — the expression which the countenances of Mr. Calton and Mr. Septimus Hicks respectively assumed, at this unexpected announcement. Equally impossible is it to describe, although perhaps it is easier for our lady readers to imagine, what arts the three ladies could have used, so completely to entangle their separate partners. Whatever they were, however, they were successful. The mother was perfectly aware of the intended marriage of both daughters; and the young ladies were equally acquainted with the intention of their estimable parent. They agreed, however, that it would have a much better appearance if each feigned ignorance of the other's engagement; and it was equally desirable that all the marriages should take place on the same day, to prevent the discovery of one clandestine alliance, operating prejudicially on the others. Hence, the mystification of Mr. Calton and Mr. Septimus Hicks, and the pre-engagement of the unwary Tibbs.

On the following morning, Mr. Septimus Hicks was united to Miss Matilda Maplesone. Mr. Simpson also entered into a "holy alliance" with Miss Julia; Tibbs acting as father, "his first appearance in that character." Mr. Calton, not being quite so eager as the two young men, was rather struck by the double discovery; and as he had found some difficulty in getting any one to give the lady away, it occurred to him that the best mode of obviating the inconvenience would be not to take her at all. The lady, however, "appealed," as her counsel said on the trial of the cause, *Maplesone* v. *Calton,* for a breach of promise, "with a broken heart, to the outraged laws of her country." She recovered damages to the amount of 1,000*l.* which the unfortunate knocker was compelled to pay. Mr. Septimus Hicks having walked the hospitals, took it into his head to walk off altogether. His injured wife is at present residing with her mother at Boulogne. Mr. Simpson, having the misfortune to lose his wife six weeks after marriage (by her eloping with an officer during his temporary sojourn in the Fleet Prison, in consequence of his inability to discharge her little mantua-maker's bill), and being disinherited by his father, who died soon afterwards, was fortunate enough to obtain a permanent engagement at a fashionable haircutter's; hairdressing being a science to which he had frequently directed his attention. In this situation he had necessarily many opportunities of making himself acquainted with the habits, and style of thinking, of the exclusive portion of the nobility of this kingdom. To this fortunate circumstance are we indebted for the production of those brilliant efforts of genius, his fashionable novels, which so long as good taste, unsullied by exaggeration, cant, and quackery, continues to exist, cannot fail to instruct and amuse the thinking portion of the community.

It only remains to add, that this complication of disorders completely deprived poor Mrs. Tibbs of all her inmates, except the one whom she could have best spared — her husband. That wretched little man returned home, on the day of the wedding, in a state of partial intoxication; and, under the influence of wine, excitement, and despair, actually dared to brave the anger of his wife. Since that ill-fated hour he has constantly taken his meals in the kitchen, to which apartment, it is understood, his witticisms will be in future confined: a turn-up bedstead having been conveyed there by Mrs. Tibbs's order for his exclusive accommodation. It is possible that he will be enabled to finish, in that seclusion, his story of the volunteers.

The advertisement has again appeared in the morning papers. Results must be reserved for another chapter.

CHAPTER THE SECOND

"Well!" said little Mrs. Tibbs to herself, as she sat in the front parlor of the Coram Street mansion one morning, mending a piece of stair-carpet off the first landing; "Things have not turned out so badly, either, and if I only get a favorable answer to the advertisement, we shall be full again."

Mrs. Tibbs resumed her occupation of making worsted lattice-work in the carpet, anxiously listening to the two-penny postman, who was hammering his way down the street, at the rate of a penny a knock. The house was as quiet as possible. There was only one low sound to be heard — it was the unhappy Tibbs cleaning the gentle-men's boots in the back kitchen, and accompanying himself with a buzzing noise, in wretched mockery of humming a tune.

The postman drew near the house. He paused — so did Mrs. Tibbs. A knock — a bustle — a letter — post-paid.

"T. I. presents compt. to I. T. and T. I. begs To say that i see the advertisement And she will Do Herself the pleasure of calling On you at 12 o'clock tomorrow morning.

"T. I. as To apologize to I. T. for the shortness Of the notice But i hope it will not unconvenience you.

"I remain yours Truly

"Wednesday evening"

Little Mrs. Tibbs perused the document, over and over again; and the more she read it, the more was she confused by the mixture of the first and third person; the substitution of the "i" for the "T. I."; and the transition from the "I. T." to the "you." The writing looked like a skein of thread in a tangle, and the note was ingeniously folded into a perfect square, with the direction squeezed up into the right-hand corner, as if it were ashamed of itself. The back of the epistle was pleasingly ornamented with a large red wafer, which, with the addition of divers ink-stains, bore a marvellous resemblance to a black beetle trodden upon. One thing, however, was perfectly clear to the perplexed Mrs. Tibbs. Somebody was to call at twelve. The drawing-room was forthwith dusted for the third time that morning; three or four chairs were pulled out of their places, and a corresponding number of books carefully upset, in order that there might be a due absence of formality. Down went the piece of stair-carpet before noticed, and up ran Mrs. Tibbs "to make herself tidy."

The clock of New Saint Pancras Church struck twelve, and the Foundling, with laudable politeness, did the same ten minutes afterwards. Saint something else struck the quarter, and then there arrived a single lady with a double knock, in a pelisse the color of the interior of a damson pie; a bonnet of the same, with a regular conservatory of artificial flowers; a white veil, and a green parasol, with a cobweb border.

The visitor (who was very fat and red-faced) was shown into the drawing-room; Mrs. Tibbs presented herself, and the negotiation commenced.

"I called in consequence of an advertisement," said the stranger, in a voice as if she had been playing a set of Pan's pipes for a fortnight without leaving off.

"Yes!" said Mrs. Tibbs, rubbing her hands very slowly, and looking the applicant full in the face — two things she always did on such occasions.

"Money isn't no object whatever to me," said the lady, "so much as living in a state of retirement and obtrusion."

Mrs. Tibbs, as a matter of course, acquiesced in such an exceedingly natural desire.

"I am constantly attended by a medical man," resumed the pelisse wearer; "I have been a shocking unitarian for some time — I, indeed, have had very little peace since the death of Mr. Bloss."

Mrs. Tibbs looked at the relict of the departed Bloss, and thought he must have had very little peace in his time. Of course she could not say so; so she looked very sympathizing.

"I shall be a good deal of trouble to you," said Mrs. Bloss; "but for that trouble I am willing to pay. I am going through a course of treatment which renders attention necessary. I have one mutton-chop in bed at half-past eight, and another at ten, every morning."

Mrs. Tibbs, as in duty bound, expressed the pity she felt for anybody placed in such a distressing situation; and the carnivorous Mrs. Bloss proceeded to arrange the various preliminaries with wonderful despatch. "Now mind," said that lady, after terms were arranged; "I am to have the second-floor front, for my bedroom?"

"Yes, ma'am."

"And you'll find room for my little servant Agnes?"

"Oh! certainly."

"And I can have one of the cellars in the area for my bottled porter?"

"With the greatest pleasure; James shall get it ready for you by Saturday."

"And I'll join the company at the breakfast-table on Sunday morning," said Mrs. Bloss. "I shall get up on purpose."

"Very well," returned Mrs. Tibbs, in her most amiable tone; for satisfactory references had "been given and required," and it was quite certain that the newcomer had plenty of money. "It's rather singular," continued Mrs. Tibbs, with what was meant for a most bewitching smile, "that we have a gentleman now with us, who is in a very delicate state of health — a Mr. Gobler. His apartment is the back drawing-room."

"The next room?" inquired Mrs. Bloss.

"The next room," repeated the hostess.

"How very promiscuous!" ejaculated the widow.

"He hardly ever gets up," said Mrs. Tibbs in a whisper.

"Lor!" cried Mrs. Bloss, in an equally low tone.

"And when he is up," said Mrs. Tibbs, "we never can persuade him to go to bed again."

"Dear me!" said the astonished Mrs. Bloss, drawing her chair nearer Mrs. Tibbs. "What is his complaint?"

"Why, the fact is," replied Mrs. Tibbs, with a most communicative air, "he has no stomach whatever."

"No what?" inquired Mrs. Bloss, with a look of the most indescribable alarm.

"No stomach," repeated Mrs. Tibbs, with a shake of the head.

"Lord bless us! what an extraordinary case!" gasped Mrs. Bloss, as if she understood the communication in its literal sense, and was astonished at a gentleman without a stomach finding it necessary to board anywhere.

"When I say he has no stomach," explained the chatty little Mrs. Tibbs, "I mean that his digestion is so much impaired, and his interior so deranged, that his stomach is not of the least use to him; in fact, it's an inconvenience."

"Never heard such a case in my life!" exclaimed Mrs. Bloss. "Why, he's worse than I am."

"Oh, yes!" replied Mrs. Tibbs; "certainly." She said this with great confidence, for the damson pelisse suggested that Mrs. Bloss, at all events, was not suffering under Mr. Gobler's complaint.

"You have quite incited my curiosity," said Mrs. Bloss, as she rose to depart. "How I long to see him!"

"He generally comes down once a week," replied Mrs. Tibbs; "I dare say you'll see him on Sunday." With this consolatory promise Mrs. Bloss was obliged to be contented. She accordingly walked slowly down the stairs, detailing her complaints all the way; and Mrs. Tibbs followed her, uttering an exclamation of compassion at every step. James (who looked very gritty, for he was cleaning the knives) fell up the kitchen-stairs, and opened the street-door; and, after mutual farewells, Mrs. Bloss slowly departed, down the shady side of the street.

It is almost superfluous to say, that the lady whom we have just shown out at the street-door (and whom the two female servants are now inspecting from the second-floor windows) was exceedingly vulgar, ignorant, and selfish. Her deceased better-half had been an eminent cork-cutter, in which capacity he had amassed a decent fortune. He had no relative but his nephew, and no friend but his cook. The former had the insolence one morning to ask for the loan of fifteen pounds; and, by way of retaliation, he married the latter next day; he made a will immediately afterwards, containing a burst of honest indignation against his nephew (who supported himself and two sisters on 100l. a year), and a bequest of his whole property to his wife. He felt ill after breakfast, and died after dinner. There is a mantelpiece-looking tablet in a civic parish church, setting forth his virtues, and deploring his loss. He never dishonored a bill, or gave away a halfpenny.

The relict and sole executrix of this noble-minded man was an odd mixture of shrewdness and simplicity, liberality and meanness. Bred up as she had been, she knew no mode of living so agreeable as a boarding house; and having nothing to do, and nothing to wish for, she naturally imagined she must be very ill — an impression which was most assiduously promoted by her medical attendant, Dr. Wosky, and her handmaid Agnes: both of whom, doubtless for good reasons, encouraged all her extravagant notions.

Since the catastrophe recorded in the last chapter, Mrs. Tibbs had been very shy of young-lady boarders. Her present inmates were all lords of the creation, and she availed herself of the opportunity of their assemblage at the dinner-table, to announce the expected arrival of Mrs. Bloss. The gentlemen received the communication with stoical indifference, and Mrs. Tibbs devoted all her energies to prepare for the reception of the valetudinarian. The second-floor front was scrubbed, and washed, and flannelled, till the wet went through to the drawing-room ceiling. Clean white counterpanes, and curtains, and napkins, water-bottles as clear as crystal, blue jugs, and mahogany furniture, added to the splendor, and increased the comfort, of the apartment. The warming-pan was in constant requisition, and a fire lighted in the room every day. The chattels of Mrs. Bloss were forwarded by installments. First, there came a large hamper of Guinness's stout, and an umbrella; then, a train of trunks; then, a pair of clogs and a bandbox; then, an easy chair with an air-cushion; then, a variety of suspicious-looking packages; and — "though last not least" — Mrs. Bloss and Agnes: the latter in a cherry-colored merino dress, open-work stockings, and shoes with sandals: like a disguised Columbine.

The installation of the Duke of Wellington as Chancellor of the University of Oxford was nothing, in point of bustle and turmoil, to the installation of Mrs. Bloss in her new quarters. True, there was no bright doctor of civil law to deliver a classical address on the occasion; but there were several other old women present, who spoke quite as much to the purpose, and understood themselves equally well. The chop-eater was so fatigued with the process of removal that she declined leaving her room until the following morning; so a mutton-chop, pickle, a pill, a pint bottle of stout, and other medicines, were carried upstairs for her consumption.

"Why, what *do* you think, ma'am?" inquired the inquisitive Agnes of her mistress, after they had been in the house some three hours; "what *do* you think, ma'am? the lady of the house is married."

"Married!" said Mrs. Bloss, taking the pill and a draught of Guinness — "married! Unpossible!"

"She is indeed, ma'am," returned the Columbine; "and her husband, ma'am, lives — he — he — he — lives in the kitchen, ma'am."

"In the kitchen!"

"Yes, ma'am: and he — he — he — the housemaid says, he never goes into the parlor except on Sundays; and that Mrs. Tibbs makes him clean the gentlemen's boots; and that he cleans the windows, too, sometimes; and that one morning early, when he was in the front balcony cleaning the drawing-room windows, he called out to a gentleman on the opposite side of the way, who used to live here — 'Ah! Mr. Calton, sir, how are you?' " Here the attendant laughed till Mrs. Bloss was in serious apprehension of her chuckling herself into a fit.

"Well, I never!" said Mrs. Bloss.

"Yes. And please, ma'am, the servants gives him gin-and-water sometimes; and then he cries, and says he hates his wife and the boarders, and wants to tickle them."

"Tickle the boarders!" exclaimed Mrs. Bloss, seriously alarmed.

"No, ma'am, not the boarders, the servants."

"Oh, is that all!" said Mrs. Bloss, quite satisfied.

"He wanted to kiss me as I came up the kitchen-stairs, just now," said Agnes, indignantly; "but I gave it him — a little wretch!"

This intelligence was but too true. A long course of snubbing and neglect; his days spent in the kitchen, and his nights in the turn-up bedstead, had completely broken the little spirit that the unfortunate volunteer had ever possessed. He had no one to whom he could detail his injuries but the servants, and they were almost of necessity his chosen confidants. It is no less strange than true, however, that the little weaknesses which he had incurred, most probably during his military career, seemed to increase as his comforts diminished. He was actually a sort of journeyman Giovanni of the basement story.

The next morning, being Sunday, breakfast was laid in the front parlor at ten o'clock. Nine was the usual time, but the family always breakfasted an hour later on Sabbath. Tibbs enrobed himself in his Sunday costume — a black coat, and exceedingly short, thin trousers; with a very large white waistcoat, white stockings and cravat, and Blucher boots — and mounted to the parlor aforesaid. Nobody had come down, and he amused himself by drinking the contents of the milkpot with a teaspoon.

A pair of slippers were heard descending the stairs. Tibbs flew to a chair; and a stern-looking man, of about fifty, with very little hair on his head, and a Sunday paper in his hand, entered the room.

"Good morning, Mr. Evenson," said Tibbs, very humbly, with something between a nod and a bow.

"How do you do, Mr. Tibbs?" replied he of the slippers, as he sat himself down, and began to read his paper without saying another word.

"Is Mr. Wisbottle in town to-day, do you know, sir?" inquired Tibbs, just for the sake of saying something.

"I should think he was," replied the stern gentleman. "He was whistling 'The Light Guitar,' in the next room to mine, at five o'clock this morning."

"He's very fond of whistling," said Tibbs, with a slight smirk.

"Yes — I ain't," was the laconic reply.

Mr. John Evenson was in the receipt of an independent income, arising chiefly from various houses he owned in the different suburbs. He was very morose and discontented. He was a thorough radical, and used to attend a great variety of public meetings, for the express purpose of finding fault with everything that was proposed. Mr. Wisbottle, on the other hand, was a high Tory. He was a clerk in the Woods and Forests Office, which he considered rather an aristocratic employment; he knew the peerage by heart, and could tell you, offhand, where any illustrious personage lived. He had a good set of teeth, and a capital tailor. Mr. Evenson looked on all these qualifications with profound contempt; and the consequence was that the two were always disputing, much to the edification of the rest of the house. It should be added, that, in addition to his partiality for whistling, Mr. Wisbottle had a great idea of his singing powers. There were two other boarders, besides the gentleman in the back drawing-room — Mr. Alfred Tomkins and Mr. Frederick O'Bleary. Mr. Tomkins was a clerk in a wine-house; he was a connoisseur in paintings, and had a wonderful eye for the picturesque. Mr. O'Bleary was an Irishman, recently imported; he was in a perfectly wild state; and had come over to England to be an apothecary, a clerk in a government office, an actor, a reporter, or anything else that turned up — he was not particular. He was on familiar terms with two small Irish members, and got franks for everybody in the house. He felt convinced that his intrinsic merits must procure him a high destiny. He wore shepherd's-plaid inexpressibles, and used to look under all the ladies' bonnets as he walked along the streets. His manners and appearance reminded one of Orson.

"Here comes Mr. Wisbottle," said Tibbs; and Mr. Wisbottle forthwith appeared in blue slippers, and a shawl dressing-gown, whistling *"Di piacer."*

"Good morning, sir," said Tibbs again. It was almost the only thing he ever said to anybody.

"How are you, Tibbs?" condescendingly replied the amateur; and he walked to the window, and whistled louder than ever.

"Pretty air, that!" said Evenson, with a snarl, and without taking his eyes off the paper.

"Glad you like it," replied Wisbottle, highly gratified.

"Don't you think it would sound better, if you whistled it a little louder?" inquired the mastiff.

"No; I don't think it would," rejoined the unconscious Wisbottle.

"I'll tell you what, Wisbottle," said Evenson, who had been bottling up his anger for some hours — "the next time you feel disposed to whistle 'The Light Guitar' at five o'clock in the morning, I'll trouble you to whistle it with your head out o' window. If you don't, I'll learn the triangle — I will, by — "

The entrance of Mrs. Tibbs (with the keys in a little basket) interrupted the threat, and prevented its conclusion.

Mrs. Tibbs apologized for being down rather late; the bell was rung; James brought up the urn, and received an unlimited order for dry toast and bacon. Tibbs sat down at the bottom of the table, and began eating water-cresses like a Nebuchadnezzar. Mr. O'Bleary appeared, and Mr. Alfred Tomkins. The compliments of the morning were exchanged, and the tea was made.

"God bless me!" exclaimed Tomkins, who had been looking out at the window. "Here — Wisbottle — pray come here — make haste."

Mr. Wisbottle started from the table, and every one looked up.

"Do you see," said the connoisseur, placing Wisbottle in the right position — "a little more this way: there — do you see how splendidly the light falls upon the left side of that broken chimney-pot at No. 48?"

"Dear me! I see," replied Wisbottle, in a tone of admiration.

"I never saw an object stand out so beautifully against the clear sky in my life," ejaculated Alfred. Everybody (except John Evenson) echoed the sentiment; for Mr. Tomkins had a great character for finding out beauties which no one else could discover — he certainly deserved it.

"I have frequently observed a chimney-pot in College Green, Dublin, which has a much better effect," said the patriotic O'Bleary, who never allowed Ireland to be outdone on any point.

The assertion was received with obvious incredulity, for Mr. Tomkins declared that no other chimney-pot in the United Kingdom, broken or unbroken, could be so beautiful as the one at No. 48.

The room-door was suddenly thrown open, and Agnes appeared, leading in Mrs. Bloss, who was dressed in a geranium-colored muslin gown, and displayed a gold watch of huge dimensions; a chain to match; and a splendid assortment of rings, with enormous stones. A general rush was made for a chair, and a regular introduction took place. Mr. John Evenson made a slight inclination of the head; Mr. Frederick O'Bleary, Mr. Alfred Tomkins, and Mr. Wisbottle, bowed like the mandarins in a grocer's shop; Tibbs rubbed hands, and went round in circles. He was observed to close one eye, and to assume a clockwork sort of expression with the other; this has been considered as a wink, and it has been reported that Agnes was its object. We repel the calumny, and challenge contradiction.

Mrs. Tibbs inquired after Mrs. Bloss's health in a low tone. Mrs. Bloss, with a supreme contempt for the memory of Lindley Murray, answered the various questions in a most satisfactory manner; and a pause ensued, during which the eatables disappeared with awful rapidity.

"You must have been very much pleased with the appearance of the ladies going to the Drawing-room the other day, Mr. O'Bleary?" said Mrs. Tibbs, hoping to start a topic.

"Yes," replied Orson, with a mouthful of toast.

"Never saw anything like it before, I suppose?" suggested Wisbottle.

"No — except the Lord Lieutenant's levees," replied O'Bleary.

"Are they at all equal to our drawing-rooms?"

"Oh, infinitely superior!"

"God! I don't know," said the aristocratic Wisbottle, "the Dowager Marchioness of Publiccash was most magnificently dressed, and so was the Baron Slappenbachenhausen."

"What was he presented on?" inquired Evenson.

"On his arrival in England."

"I thought so," growled the radical; "you never hear of these fellows being presented on their going away again. They know better than that."

"Unless somebody pervades them with an apintment," said Mrs. Bloss, joining in the conversation in a faint voice.

"Well," said Wisbottle, evading the point, "it's a splendid sight."

"And did it never occur to you," inquired the radical, who never would be quiet; "did it never occur to you, that you pay for these precious ornaments of society?"

"It certainly *has* occurred to me," said Wisbottle, who thought this answer was a poser; "it *has* occurred to me, and I am willing to pay for them."

"Well, and it has occurred to me too," replied John Evenson, "and I ain't willing to pay for 'em. Then why should I? — I say, why should I?" continued the politician, laying down the paper, and knocking his knuckles on the table. "There are two great principles — demand — "

"A cup of tea if you please, dear," interrupted Tibbs.

"And supply — "

"May I trouble you to hand this tea to Mr. Tibbs?" said Mrs. Tibbs, interrupting the argument, and unconsciously illustrating it.

The thread of the orator's discourse was broken. He drank his tea and resumed the paper.

"If it's very fine," said Mr. Alfred Tomkins, addressing the company in general, "I shall ride down to Richmond to-day, and come back by the steamer. There are some splendid effects of light and shade on the Thames; the contrast between the blueness of the sky and the yellow water is frequently exceedingly beautiful." Mr. Wisbottle hummed, "Flow on, thou shining river."

"We have some splendid steam-vessels in Ireland," said O'Bleary.

"Certainly," said Mrs. Bloss, delighted to find a subject broached in which she could take part.

"The accommodations are extraordinary," said O'Bleary.

"Extraordinary indeed," returned Mrs. Bloss. "When Mr. Bloss was alive, he was promiscuously obligated to go to Ireland on business. I went with him, and raly the manner in which the ladies and gentlemen were accommodated with berths, is not creditable."

Tibbs, who had been listening to the dialogue, looked aghast, and evinced a strong inclination to ask a question, but was checked by a look from his wife. Mr. Wisbottle laughed, and said Tomkins had made a pun; and Tomkins laughed too, and said he had not.

The remainder of the meal passed off as breakfasts usually do. Con-

versation flagged, and people played with their teaspoons. The gentlemen looked out at the window; walked about the room; and, when
they got near the door, dropped off one by one. Tibbs retired to the
back parlor by his wife's orders, to check the greengrocer's weekly account; and ultimately Mrs. Tibbs and Mrs. Bloss were left alone
together.

"Oh dear!" said the latter, "I feel alarmingly faint; it's very singular." (It certainly was, for she had eaten four pounds of solids that
morning.) "By-the-bye," said Mrs. Bloss, "I have not seen Mr. What's-
his-name yet."

"Mr. Gobler?" suggested Mrs. Tibbs.

"Yes."

"Oh!" said Mrs. Tibbs, "he is a most mysterious person. He has his
meals regularly sent up-stairs, and sometimes don't leave his room for
weeks together."

"I haven't seen or heard nothing of him," repeated Mrs. Bloss.

"I dare say you'll hear him to-night," replied Mrs. Tibbs; "he
generally groans a good deal on Sunday evenings."

"I never felt such an interest in any one in my life," ejaculated
Mrs. Bloss. A little double-knock interrupted the conversation; Dr.
Wosky was announced, and duly shown in. He was a little man with
a red face — dressed of course in black, with a stiff white neckerchief.
He had a very good practice, and plenty of money, which he had
amassed by invariably humoring the worst fancies of all the females
of all the families he had ever been introduced into. Mrs. Tibbs offered to retire, but was entreated to stay.

"Well, my dear ma'am, and how are we?" inquired Wosky, in a
soothing tone.

"Very ill, doctor — very ill," said Mrs. Bloss, in a whisper.

"Ah! we must take care of ourselves; we must, indeed," said the
obsequious Wosky, as he felt the pulse of his interesting patient.
"How is your appetite?"

Mrs. Bloss shook her head.

"Our friend requires great care," said Wosky, appealing to Mrs.
Tibbs, who of course assented. "I hope, however, with the blessing of
Providence, that we shall be enabled to make her quite stout again."
Mrs. Tibbs wondered in her own mind what the patient would be
when she was made quite stout.

"We must take stimulants," said the cunning Wosky — "plenty of nourishment, and above all, we must keep our nerves quiet; we positively must not give way to our sensibilities. We must take all we can get," concluded the doctor, as he pocketed his fee, "and we must keep quiet."

"Dear man!" exclaimed Mrs. Bloss, as the doctor stepped into his carriage.

"Charming creature indeed — quite a lady's man!" said Mrs. Tibbs, and Dr. Wosky rattled away to make fresh gulls of delicate females, and pocket fresh fees.

As we had occasion, in a former paper, to describe a dinner at Mrs. Tibbs's; and as one meal went off very like another on all ordinary occasions; we will not fatigue our readers by entering into any other detailed account of the domestic economy of the establishment. We will therefore proceed to events, merely premising that the mysterious tenant of the back drawing-room was a lazy, selfish hypochondriac; always complaining and never ill. As his character in many respects closely assimilated to that of Mrs. Bloss, a very warm friendship soon sprung up between them. He was tall, thin, and pale; he always fancied he had a severe pain somewhere or other, and his face invariably wore a pinched, screwed-up expression; he looked, indeed, like a man who had got his feet in a tub of exceedingly hot water, against his will.

For two or three months after Mrs. Bloss's first appearance in Coram Street, John Evenson was observed to become, every day, more sarcastic and more ill-natured; and there was a degree of additional importance in his manner, which clearly showed that he fancied he had discovered something, which he only wanted a proper opportunity of divulging. He found it at last.

One evening, the different inmates of the house were assembled in the drawing-room engaged in their ordinary occupations. Mr. Gobler and Mrs. Bloss were sitting at a small card-table near the center window, playing cribbage; Mr. Wisbottle was describing semicircles on the music-stool, turning over the leaves of a book on the piano, and humming most melodiously; Alfred Tomkins was sitting at the round table, with his elbows duly squared, making a pencil sketch of a head considerably larger than his own; O'Bleary was reading Horace, and trying to look as if he understood it; and John Evenson had drawn his chair close to Mrs. Tibbs's work-table, and was talking to her very earnestly in a low tone.

"I can assure you, Mrs. Tibbs," said the radical, laying his forefinger on the muslin she was at work on; "I can assure you, Mrs. Tibbs, that nothing but the interest I take in your welfare would induce me to make this communication. I repeat, I fear Wisbottle is endeavoring to gain the affections of that young woman, Agnes, and that he is in the habit of meeting her in the store-room on the first floor, over the leads. From my bedroom I distinctly heard voices there, last night. I opened my door immediately, and crept very softly on to the landing; there I saw Mr. Tibbs, who, it seems, had been disturbed also. — Bless me, Mrs. Tibbs, you change color!"

"No, no — it's nothing," returned Mrs. T. in a hurried manner; "it's only the heat of the room."

"A flush!" ejaculated Mrs. Bloss from the card-table; "that's good for four."

"If I thought it was Mr. Wisbottle," said Mrs. Tibbs, after a pause, "he should leave this house instantly."

"Go!" said Mrs. Bloss again.

"And if I thought," continued the hostess with a most threatening air, "if I thought he was assisted by Mr. Tibbs — "

"One for his nob!" said Gobler.

"Oh," said Evenson, in a most soothing tone — he liked to make mischief — "I should hope Mr. Tibbs was not in any way implicated. He always appeared to me very harmless."

"I have generally found him so," sobbed poor little Mrs. Tibbs; crying like a watering-pot.

"Hush! hush! pray — Mrs. Tibbs — consider — we shall be observed — pray, don't!" said John Evenson, fearing his whole plan would be interrupted. "We will set the matter at rest with the utmost care, and I shall be most happy to assist you in doing so."

Mrs. Tibbs murmured her thanks.

"When you think every one has retired to rest to-night," said Evenson very pompously, "if you'll meet me without a light, just outside my bedroom door, by the staircase window, I think we can ascertain who the parties really are, and you will afterwards be enabled to proceed as you think proper."

Mrs. Tibbs was easily persuaded; her curiosity was excited, her jealousy was roused, and the arrangement was forthwith made. She resumed her work, and John Evenson walked up and down the room with his hands in his pockets, looking as if nothing had happened.

The game of cribbage was over, and conversation began again.

"Well, Mr. O'Bleary," said the humming-top, turning round on his pivot, and facing the company, "what did you think of Vauxhall the other night?"

"Oh, it's very fair," replied Orson, who had been enthusiastically delighted with the whole exhibition.

"Never saw anything like that Captain Ross's set-out — eh?"

"No," returned the patriot, with his usual reservation — "except in Dublin."

"I saw the Count de Canky and Captain Fitzthompson in the Gardens," said Wisbottle; "they appeared much delighted."

"Then it *must* be beautiful," snarled Evenson.

"I think the white bears is partickerlerly well done," suggested Mrs. Bloss. "In their shaggy white coats, they look just like Polar bears — don't you think they do, Mr. Evenson?"

"I think they look a great deal more like omnibus cads on all fours," replied the discontented one.

"Upon the whole, I should have liked our evening very well," gasped Gobler; "only I caught a desperate cold which increased my pain dreadfully! I was obliged to have several shower-baths before I could leave my room."

"Capital things those shower-baths!" ejaculated Wisbottle.

"Excellent!" said Tomkins.

"Delightful!" chimed in O'Bleary. (He had once seen one, outside a tinman's.)

"Disgusting machines!" rejoined Evenson, who extended his dislike to almost every created object, masculine, feminine, or neuter.

"Disgusting, Mr. Evenson!" said Gobler, in a tone of strong indignation. — "Disgusting! Look at their utility — consider how many lives they have saved by promoting perspiration."

"Promoting perspiration, indeed," growled John Evenson, stopping short in his walk across the large squares in the pattern of the carpet — "I was ass enough to be persuaded some time ago to have one in my bedroom. 'Gad, I was in it once, and it effectually cured *me*, for the mere sight of it threw me into a profuse perspiration for six months afterwards."

A titter followed this announcement, and before it had subsided James brought up "the tray," containing the remains of a leg of lamb which had made its *début* at dinner; bread; cheese; an atom of butter in a forest of parsley; one pickled walnut and the third of another; and so forth. The boy disappeared, and returned again with another tray, containing glasses and jugs of hot and cold water. The gentlemen brought in their spirit-bottles; the housemaid placed divers plated bedroom candlesticks under the card-table; and the servants retired for the night.

Chairs were drawn round the table, and the conversation proceeded in the customary manner. John Evenson, who never ate supper, lolled on the sofa, and amused himself by contradicting everybody. O'Bleary ate as much as he could conveniently carry, and Mrs. Tibbs felt a due degree of indignation thereat; Mr. Gobler and Mrs. Bloss conversed most affectionately on the subject of pill-taking, and other innocent amusements; and Tomkins and Wisbottle "got into an argument"; that is to say, they both talked very loudly and vehemently, each flattering himself that he had got some advantage about something, and neither of them having more than a very indistinct idea of what they were talking about. An hour or two passed away; and the boarders and the brass candlesticks retired in pairs to their respective bedrooms. John Evenson pulled off his boots, locked his door, and determined to sit up until Mr. Gobler had retired. He always sat in the drawing-room an hour after everybody else had left it, taking medicine, and groaning.

Great Coram Street was hushed into a state of profound repose: it was nearly two o'clock. A hackney-coach now and then rumbled slowly by; and occasionally some stray lawyer's clerk, on his way home to Somers Town, struck his iron heel on the top of the coal-cellar with a noise resembling the click of a smoke-jack. A low, monotonous, gushing sound was heard, which added considerably to the romantic dreariness of the scene. It was the water "coming in" at number eleven.

"He must be asleep by this time," said John Evenson to himself, after waiting with exemplary patience for nearly an hour after Mr. Gobler had left the drawing-room. He listened for a few moments; the house was perfectly quiet; he extinguished his rushlight, and opened his bedroom door. The staircase was so dark that it was impossible to see anything.

"S—s—s!" whispered the mischief-maker, making a noise like the first indication a catherine-wheel gives of the probability of its going off.

"Hush!" whispered somebody else.

"Is that you, Mrs. Tibbs?"

"Yes, sir."

"Where?"

"Here"; and the misty outline of Mrs. Tibbs appeared at the staircase window, like the ghost of Queen Anne in the tent scene in Richard.

"This way, Mrs. Tibbs," whispered the delighted busybody: "give me your hand — there! Whoever these people are, they are in the store-room now, for I have been looking down from my window, and I could see that they accidentally upset their candlestick, and are now in darkness. You have no shoes on, have you?"

"No," said little Mrs. Tibbs, who could hardly speak for trembling.

"Well; I have taken my boots off, so we can go down, close to the store-room door, and listen over the banisters"; and down-stairs they both crept accordingly, every board creaking like a patent mangle on a Saturday afternoon.

"It's Wisbottle and somebody, I'll swear," exclaimed the radical in an energetic whisper, when they had listened for a few moments.

"Hush — pray let's hear what they say!" exclaimed Mrs. Tibbs, the gratification of whose curiosity was now paramount to every other consideration.

"Ah! if I could but believe you," said a female voice coquettishly, "I'd be bound to settle my missis for life."

"What does she say?" inquired Mr. Evenson, who was not quite so well situated as his companion.

"She says she'll settle her missis's life," replied Mrs. Tibbs. "The wretch! they're plotting murder."

"I know you want money," continued the voice, which belonged to Agnes; "and if you'd secure me the five hundred pound, I warrant she should take fire soon enough."

"What's that?" inquired Evenson again. He could just hear enough to want to hear more.

"I think she says she'll set the house on fire," replied the affrighted Mrs. Tibbs. "But, thank God, I'm insured in the Phœnix!"

"The moment I have secured your mistress, my dear," said a man's voice in a strong Irish brogue, "you may depend on having the money."

"Bless my soul, it's Mr. O'Bleary!" exclaimed Mrs. Tibbs, in a parenthesis.

"The villain!" said the indignant Mr. Evenson.

"The first thing to be done," continued the Hibernian, "is to poison Mr. Gobler's mind."

"Oh, certainly," returned Agnes.

"What's that?" inquired Evenson again, in an agony of curiosity and a whisper.

"He says she's to mind and poison Mr. Gobler," replied Mrs. Tibbs, aghast at this sacrifice of human life.

"And in regard of Mrs. Tibbs," continued O'Bleary. — Mrs. Tibbs shuddered.

"Hush!" exclaimed Agnes, in a tone of the greatest alarm, just as Mrs. Tibbs was on the extreme verge of a fainting fit. "Hush!"

"Hush!" exclaimed Evenson, at the same moment, to Mrs. Tibbs.

"There's somebody coming *up*-stairs," said Agnes to O'Bleary.

"There's somebody coming *down*-stairs," whispered Evenson to Mrs. Tibbs.

"Go into the parlor, sir," said Agnes to her companion. "You will get there before whoever it is gets to the top of the kitchen stairs."

"The drawing-room, Mrs. Tibbs!" whispered the astonished Evenson to his equally astonished companion; and for the drawing-room they both made, plainly hearing the rustling of two persons, one coming down-stairs, and one coming up.

"What can it be?" exclaimed Mrs. Tibbs. "It's like a dream. I wouldn't be found in this situation for the world!"

"Nor I," returned Evenson, who could never bear a joke at his own expense. "Hush! here they are at the door."

"What fun!" whispered one of the newcomers. — It was Wisbottle.

"Glorious!" replied his companion, in an equally low tone. — This was Alfred Tomkins. "Who would have thought it?"

"I told you so," said Wisbottle, in a most knowing whisper. "Lord bless you, he has paid her most extraordinary attention for the last two months. I saw 'em when I was sitting at the piano to-night."

"Well, do you know I didn't notice it?" interrupted Tomkins.

"Not notice it!" continued Wisbottle. "Bless you; I saw him whispering to her, and she crying; and then I'll swear I heard him say something about to-night when we were all in bed."

"They're talking of *us!*" exclaimed the agonized Mrs. Tibbs, as the painful suspicion, and a sense of their situation, flashed upon her mind.

"I know it — I know it," replied Evenson, with a melancholy consciousness that there was no mode of escape.

"What's to be done? we cannot both stop here!" ejaculated Mrs. Tibbs, in a state of partial derangement.

"I'll get up the chimney," replied Evenson, who really meant what he said.

"You can't," said Mrs. Tibbs, in despair. "You can't — it's a register stove."

"Hush!" repeated John Evenson.

"Hush — hush!" cried somebody down-stairs.

"What a d——d hushing!" said Alfred Tomkins, who began to get rather bewildered.

"There they are!" exclaimed the sapient Wisbottle, as a rustling noise was heard in the store-room.

"Hark!" whispered both the young men.

"Hark!" repeated Mrs. Tibbs and Evenson.

"Let me alone, sir," said a female voice in the store-room.

"Oh, Hagnes!" cried another voice, which clearly belonged to Tibbs, for nobody else ever owned one like it. "Oh, Hagnes — lovely creature!"

"Be quiet, sir!" (A bounce.)

"Hag — "

"Be quiet, sir — I am ashamed of you. Think of your wife, Mr. Tibbs. Be quiet, sir!"

"My wife!" exclaimed the valorous Tibbs, who was clearly under the influence of gin-and-water, and a misplaced attachment; "I ate her! Oh, Hagnes! when I was in the volunteer corps, in eighteen hundred and — "

"I declare I'll scream. Be quiet, sir, will you?" (Another bounce and a scuffle.)

"What's that?" exclaimed Tibbs, with a start.

"What's what?" said Agnes, stopping short.

"Why, that!"

"Ah! you have done it nicely now, sir," sobbed the frightened Agnes, as a tapping was heard at Mrs. Tibbs's bedroom door, which would have beaten any dozen woodpeckers hollow.

"Mrs. Tibbs! Mrs. Tibbs!" called out Mrs. Bloss. "Mrs. Tibbs, pray get up." (Here the imitation of a woodpecker was resumed with tenfold violence.)

"Oh, dear — dear!" exclaimed the wretched partner of the depraved Tibbs. "She's knocking at my door. We must be discovered! What will they think?"

"Mrs. Tibbs! Mrs. Tibbs!" screamed the woodpecker again.

"What's the matter!" shouted Gobler, bursting out of the back drawing-room, like the dragon at Astley's.

"Oh, Mr. Gobler!" cried Mrs. Bloss, with a proper approximation to hysterics; "I think the house is on fire, or else there's thieves in it. I have heard the most dreadful noises!"

"The devil you have!" shouted Gobler again, bouncing back into his den, in happy imitation of the aforesaid dragon, and returning immediately with a lighted candle. "Why, what's this? Wisbottle! Tomkins! O'Bleary! Agnes! What the deuce! all up and dressed?"

"Astonishing!" said Mrs. Bloss, who had run down-stairs, and taken Mr. Gobler's arm.

"Call Mrs. Tibbs directly, somebody," said Gobler, turning into the front drawing-room. — "What! Mrs. Tibbs and Mr. Evenson! !"

"Mrs. Tibbs and Mr. Evenson!" repeated everybody, as that unhappy pair were discovered: Mrs. Tibbs seated in an arm-chair by the fireplace, and Mr. Evenson standing by her side.

We must leave the scene that ensued to the reader's imagination. We could tell how Mrs. Tibbs forthwith fainted away, and how it required the united strength of Mr. Wisbottle and Mr. Alfred Tomkins to hold her in her chair; how Mr. Evenson explained, and how his explanation was evidently disbelieved; how Agnes repelled the accusations of Mrs. Tibbs by proving that she was negotiating with Mr. O'Bleary to influence her mistress's affections in his behalf; and how Mr. Gobler threw a damp counterpane on the hopes of Mr. O'Bleary by avowing that he (Gobler) had already proposed to, and been accepted by, Mrs. Bloss; how Agnes was discharged from that lady's service; how Mr. O'Bleary discharged himself from Mrs. Tibbs's house, without going through the form of previously discharging his bill; and how that disappointed young gentleman rails against England and the English, and vows there is no virtue or fine feeling extant, "except in Ireland." We repeat that we *could* tell all this, but we love to exercise our self-denial, and we therefore prefer leaving it to be imagined.

The lady whom we have hitherto described as Mrs. Bloss, is no more. Mrs. Gobler exists: Mrs. Bloss has left us forever. In a secluded retreat in Newington Butts, far, far removed from the noisy strife of that great boarding house, the world, the enviable Gobler and his pleasing wife revel in retirement: happy in their complaints, their table, and their medicine; wafted through life by the grateful prayers of all the purveyors of animal food within three miles round.

We would willingly stop here, but we have a painful duty imposed upon us, which we must discharge. Mr. and Mrs. Tibbs have separated by mutual consent, Mrs. Tibbs receiving one moiety of 43*l.* 15*s.* 10*d.*, which we before stated to be the amount of her husband's annual income, and Mr. Tibbs the other. He is spending the evening of his days in retirement; and he is spending also, annually, that small but honorable independence. He resides among the original settlers at Walworth; and it has been stated, on unquestionable authority, that the conclusion of the volunteer story has been heard in a small tavern in that respectable neighborhood.

The unfortunate Mrs. Tibbs has determined to dispose of the whole of her furniture by public auction, and to retire from a residence in which she has suffered so much. Mr. Robins has been applied to, to conduct the sale, and the transcendent abilities of the literary gentlemen connected with his establishment are now devoted to the task of drawing up the preliminary advertisement. It is to contain, among a variety of brilliant matter, seventy-eight words in large capitals, and six original quotations in inverted commas.

HORATIO

SPARKINS

Horatio

Sparkins

"Indeed, my love, he paid Teresa very great attention on the last assembly night," said Mrs. Malderton, addressing her spouse, who, after the fatigues of the day in the City, was sitting with a silk handkerchief over his head, and his feet on the fender, drinking his port; "very great attention; and I say again, every possible encouragement ought to be given him. He positively must be asked down here to dine."

"Who must?" inquired Mr. Malderton.

"Why, you know whom I mean, my dear — the young man with the black whiskers and the white cravat, who has just come out at our assembly, and whom all the girls are talking about. Young — dear me! what's his name? — Marianne, what *is* his name?" continued Mrs. Malderton, addressing her youngest daughter, who was engaged in netting a purse, and looking sentimental.

"Mr. Horatio Sparkins, ma," replied Miss Marianne, with a sigh.

"Oh! yes, to be sure — Horatio Sparkins," said Mrs. Malderton. "Decidedly the most gentleman-like young man I ever saw. I am sure in the beautifully made coat he wore the other night, he looked like — like — "

"Like Prince Leopold, ma — so noble, so full of sentiment!" suggested Marianne, in a tone of enthusiastic admiration.

"You should recollect, my dear," resumed Mrs. Malderton, "that Teresa is now eight-and-twenty; and that it really is very important that something should be done."

Miss Teresa Malderton was a very little girl, rather fat, with vermilion cheeks, but good-humored, and still disengaged, although, to do her justice, the misfortune arose from no lack of perseverance on her part. In vain had she flirted for ten years; in vain had Mr. and Mrs. Malderton assiduously kept up an extensive acquaintance among the young eligible bachelors of Camberwell, and even of Wandsworth and Brixton; to say nothing of those who "dropped in" from town. Miss Malderton was as well known as the lion on the top of Northumberland House, and had an equal chance of "going off."

"I am quite sure you'd like him," continued Mrs. Malderton, "he is so gentlemanly!"

"So clever!" said Miss Marianne.

"And has such a flow of language!" added Miss Teresa.

"He has a great respect for you, my dear," said Mrs. Malderton to her husband. Mr. Malderton coughed, and looked at the fire.

"Yes, I'm sure he's very much attached to pa's society," said Miss Marianne.

"No doubt of it," echoed Miss Teresa.

"Indeed, he said as much to me in confidence," observed Mrs. Malderton.

"Well, well," returned Mr. Malderton, somewhat flattered; "if I see him at the assembly to-morrow, perhaps I'll ask him down. I hope he knows we live at Oak Lodge, Camberwell, my dear?"

"Of course — and that you keep a one-horse carriage."

"I'll see about it," said Mr. Malderton, composing himself for a nap; "I'll see about it."

Mr. Malderton was a man whose whole scope of ideas was limited to Lloyd's, the Exchange, the India House, and the Bank. A few successful speculations had raised him from a situation of obscurity and comparative poverty, to a state of affluence. As frequently happens in such cases, the ideas of himself and his family became elevated to an extraordinary pitch as their means increased; they affected fashion, taste, and many other fooleries, in imitation of their betters, and had a very decided and becoming horror of anything which could, by possibility, be considered *low*. He was hospitable from ostentation, illiberal from ignorance, and prejudiced from conceit. Egotism and the love of display induced him to keep an excellent table: convenience, and a love of good things of this life, ensured him plenty of guests. He liked to have clever men, or what he considered such, at his table, because it was a great thing to talk about;

but he never could endure what he called "sharp fellows." Probably he cherished this feeling out of compliment to his two sons, who gave their respected parent no uneasiness in that particular. The family were ambitious of forming acquaintances and connections in some sphere of society superior to that in which they themselves moved; and one of the necessary consequences of this desire, added to their utter ignorance of the world beyond their own small circle, was, that any one who could lay claim to an acquaintance with people of rank and title, had a sure passport to the table at Oak Lodge, Camberwell.

The appearance of Mr. Horatio Sparkins at the assembly had excited no small degree of surprise and curiosity among its regular frequenters. Who could he be? He was evidently reserved, and apparently melancholy. Was he a clergyman? — He danced too well. A barrister? — He said he was not called. He used very fine words, and talked a great deal. Could he be a distinguished foreigner, come to England for the purpose of describing the country, its manners and customs; and frequenting public balls and public dinners, with the view of becoming acquainted with high life, polished etiquette, and English refinement? — No, he had not a foreign accent. Was he a surgeon, a contributor to the magazines, a writer of fashionable novels, or an artist? — No; to each and all of these surmises, there existed some valid objection. — "Then," said everybody, "he must be *somebody*." — "I should think he must be," reasoned Mr. Malderton, within himself, "because he perceives our superiority, and pays us so much attention."

The night succeeding the conversation we have just recorded, was "assembly night." The double-fly was ordered to be at the door of Oak Lodge at nine o'clock precisely. The Miss Maldertons were dressed in sky-blue satin trimmed with artificial flowers; and Mrs. M. (who was a little fat woman), in ditto ditto, looked like her eldest daughter multiplied by two. Mr. Frederick Malderton, the eldest son, in full-dress costume, was the very *beau idéal* of a smart waiter; and Mr. Thomas Malderton, the youngest, with his white dress-stock, blue coat, bright buttons, and red watch-ribbon, strongly resembled the portrait of that interesting but rash young gentleman, George Barnwell. Every member of the party had made up his or her mind to cultivate the acquaintance of Mr. Horatio Sparkins. Miss Teresa, of course, was to be as amiable and interesting as ladies of eight-and-twenty on the lookout for a husband, usually are. Mrs. Malderton would be all smiles and graces. Miss Marianne would request the favor of some verses for her album. Mr. Malderton would patronize the great unknown by asking him to dinner. Tom intended to ascertain the extent of his information on the interesting topics of snuff and cigars. Even Mr. Frederick Malderton himself, the family authority on all points of taste, dress, and fashionable arrangement; who had lodgings of his own in town; who had a free admission to Covent Garden Theatre; who always dressed according to the fashions of the months; who went up the water twice a week in the season; and who actually had an intimate friend who once knew a gentleman who formerly lived in the Albany — even he had determined that Mr. Horatio Sparkins must be a devilish good fellow, and that he would do him the honor of challenging him to a game of billiards.

The first object that met the anxious eyes of the expectant family on their entrance into the ballroom, was the interesting Horatio, with his hair brushed off his forehead, and his eyes fixed on the ceiling, reclining in a contemplative attitude on one of the seats.

"There he is, my dear," whispered Mrs. Malderton to Mr. Malderton.

"How like Lord Byron!" murmured Miss Teresa.

"Or Montgomery!" whispered Miss Marianne.

"Or the portraits of Captain Cook!" suggested Tom.

"Tom — don't be an ass!" said his father, who checked him on all occasions, probably with a view to prevent his becoming "sharp" — which was very unnecessary.

The elegant Sparkins attitudinized with admirable effect, until the family had crossed the room. He then started up, with the most natural appearance of surprise and delight; accosted Mrs. Malderton with the utmost cordiality; saluted the young ladies in the most enchanting manner; bowed to, and shook hands with, Mr. Malderton, with a degree of respect amounting almost to veneration; and returned the greetings of the two young men in a half-gratified, half-patronizing manner, which fully convinced them that he must be an important, and, at the same time, condescending personage.

"Miss Malderton," said Horatio, after the ordinary salutations, and bowing very low, "may I be permitted to presume to hope that you will allow me to have the pleasure — "

"I don't *think* I am engaged," said Miss Teresa, with a dreadful affectation of indifference — "but, really — so many — "

Horatio looked handsomely miserable.

"I shall be most happy," simpered the interesting Teresa, at last. Horatio's countenance brightened up, like an old hat in a shower of rain.

"A very genteel young man, certainly!" said the gratified Mr. Malderton, as the obsequious Sparkins and his partner joined the quadrille which was just forming.

"He has a remarkably good address," said Mr. Frederick.

"Yes, he is a prime fellow," interposed Tom, who always managed to put his foot in it — "he talks just like an auctioneer."

"Tom!" said his father solemnly, "I think I desired you, before, not to be a fool." Tom looked as happy as a cock on a drizzly morning.

"How delightful!" said the interesting Horatio to his partner, as they promenaded the room at the conclusion of the set — "how delightful, how refreshing it is, to retire from the cloudy storms, the vicissitudes, and the troubles of life, even if it be but for a few short fleeting moments: and to spend those moments, fading and evanescent though they be, in the delightful, the blessed society of one individual — whose frowns would be death, whose coldness would be madness, whose falsehood would be ruin, whose constancy would be bliss; the possession of whose affection would be the brightest and best reward that Heaven could bestow on man!"

"What feeling! what sentiment!" thought Miss Teresa, as she leaned more heavily on her companion's arm.

"But enough — enough!" resumed the elegant Sparkins, with a theatrical air. "What have I said? what have I — I — to do with sentiments like these? Miss Malderton" — here he stopped short — "may I hope to be permitted to offer the humble tribute of — "

"Really, Mr. Sparkins," returned the enraptured Teresa, blushing in the sweetest confusion, "I must refer you to papa. I never can, without his consent, venture to — "

"Surely he cannot object — "

"Oh, yes. Indeed, indeed, you know him not!" interrupted Miss Teresa, well knowing there was nothing to fear, but wishing to make the interview resemble a scene in some romantic novel.

"He cannot object to my offering you a glass of negus," returned the adorable Sparkins, with some surprise.

"Is that all?" thought the disappointed Teresa. "What a fuss about nothing!"

"It will give me the greatest pleasure, sir, to see you to dinner at Oak Lodge, Camberwell, on Sunday next at five o'clock, if you have no better engagement," said Mr. Malderton, at the conclusion of the evening, as he and his sons were standing in conversation with Mr. Horatio Sparkins.

Horatio bowed his acknowledgments, and accepted the flattering invitation.

"I must confess," continued the father, offering his snuff-box to his new acquaintance, "that I don't enjoy these assemblies half so much as the comfort — I had almost said the luxury — of Oak Lodge. They have no great charms for an elderly man."

"And after all, sir, what is man?" said the metaphysical Sparkins. "I say, what is man?"

"Ah! very true," said Mr. Malderton; "very true."

"We know that we live and breathe," continued Horatio; "that we have wants and wishes, desires and appetites — "

"Certainly," said Mr. Frederick Malderton, looking profound.

"I say, we know that we exist," repeated Horatio, raising his voice, "but there we stop; there, is an end to our knowledge; there, is the summit of our attainments; there, is the termination of our ends. What more do we know?"

"Nothing," replied Mr. Frederick — than whom no one was more capable of answering for himself in that particular. Tom was about to hazard something, but, fortunately for his reputation, he caught his father's angry eye, and slunk off like a puppy convicted of petty larceny.

"Upon my word," said Mr. Malderton the elder, as they were returning home in the fly, "that Mr. Sparkins is a wonderful young man. Such surprising knowledge! such extraordinary information! and such a splendid mode of expressing himself!"

"I think he must be somebody in disguise," said Miss Marianne. "How charmingly romantic!"

"He talks very loud and nicely," timidly observed Tom, "but I don't exactly understand what he means."

"I almost begin to despair of *your* understanding anything, Tom," said his father, who, of course, had been much enlightened by Mr. Horatio Sparkins's conversation.

"It strikes me, Tom," said Miss Teresa, "that you have made yourself very ridiculous this evening."

"No doubt of it," cried everybody — and the unfortunate Tom reduced himself into the least possible space. That night, Mr. and Mrs. Malderton had a long conversation respecting their daughter's prospects and future arrangements. Miss Teresa went to bed, considering whether, in the event of her marrying a title, she could conscientiously encourage the visits of her present associates; and dreamed, all night, of disguised noblemen, large routs, ostrich plumes, bridal favors, and Horatio Sparkins.

Various surmises were hazarded on the Sunday morning, as to the mode of conveyance which the anxiously expected Horatio would adopt. Did he keep a gig? — was it possible he could come on horseback? — or would he patronize the stage? These, and other various conjectures of equal importance, engrossed the attention of Mrs. Malderton and her daughters during the whole morning after church.

"Upon my word, my dear, it's a most annoying thing that that vulgar brother of yours should have invited himself to dine here today," said Mr. Malderton to his wife. "On account of Mr. Sparkins's coming down, I purposely abstained from asking any one but Flamwell. And then to think of your brother — a tradesman — it's insufferable! I declare I wouldn't have him mention his shop, before our new guest — no, not for a thousand pounds! I wouldn't care if he had the good sense to conceal the disgrace he is to the family; but he's so fond of his horrible business, that he *will* let people know what he is."

Mr. Jacob Barton, the individual alluded to, was a large grocer; so vulgar, and so lost to all sense of feeling, that he actually never scrupled to avow that he wasn't above his business: "he'd made his money by it, and he didn't care who know'd it."

"Ah! Flamwell, my dear fellow, how d'ye do?" said Mr. Malderton, as a little spoffish man, with green spectacles, entered the room. "You got my note?"

"Yes, I did; and here I am in consequence."

"You don't happen to know this Mr. Sparkins by name? You know everybody!"

Mr. Flamwell was one of those gentlemen of remarkably extensive information whom one occasionally meets in society, who pretend to know everybody but in reality know nobody. At Malderton's where any stories about great people were received with a greedy ear, he was an especial favorite; and, knowing the kind of people he had to deal with, he carried his passion of claiming acquaintance with everybody, to the most immoderate length. He had rather a singular way of telling his greatest lies in a parenthesis, and with an air of self-denial, as if he feared being thought egotistical.

"Why, no, I don't know him by that name," returned Flamwell, in a low tone, and with an air of immense importance. "I have no doubt I know him, though. Is he tall?"

"Middle-sized," said Miss Teresa.

"With black hair?" inquired Flamwell, hazarding a bold guess.

"Yes," returned Miss Teresa, eagerly.

"Rather a snub nose?"

"No," said the disappointed Teresa, "he has a Roman nose."

"I said a Roman nose, didn't I?" inquired Flamwell. "He's an elegant young man?"

"Oh, certainly."

"With remarkably prepossessing manners?"

"Oh, yes!" said all the family together. "You must know him."

"Yes, I thought you knew him, if he was anybody," triumphantly exclaimed Mr. Malderton. "Who d'ye think he is?"

"Why, from your description," said Flamwell, ruminating, and sinking his voice almost to a whisper, "he bears a strong resemblance to the Honorable Augustus Fitz-Edward Fitz-John Fitz-Osborne. He's a very talented young man, and rather eccentric. It's extremely probable he may have changed his name for some temporary purpose."

Teresa's heart beat high. Could he be the Honorable Augustus Fitz-Edward Fitz-John Fitz-Osborne! What a name to be elegantly engraved upon two glazed cards, tied together with a piece of white satin ribbon! "The Honorable Mrs. Augustus Fitz-Edward Fitz-John Fitz-Osborne!" The thought was transport.

"It's five minutes to five," said Mr. Malderton, looking at his watch: "I hope he's not going to disappoint us."

"There he is!" exclaimed Miss Teresa, as a loud double-knock was heard at the door. Everybody endeavored to look — as people when they particularly expect a visitor always do — as if they were perfectly unsuspicious of the approach of anybody.

The room-door opened — "Mr. Barton!" said the servant.

"Confound the man!" murmured Malderton. "Ah! my dear sir, how d'ye do! Any news?"

"Why no," returned the grocer, in his usual bluff manner. "No, none partickler. None that I am much aware of. How d'ye do, gals and boys? Mr. Flamwell, sir — glad to see you."

"Here's Mr. Sparkins!" said Tom, who had been looking out at the window, "on *such* a black horse!" There was Horatio, sure enough, on a large black horse, curvetting and prancing along, like an Astley's supernumerary. After a great deal of reining in, and pulling up, with the accompaniments of snorting, rearing, and kicking, the animal consented to stop at about a hundred yards from the gate, where Mr. Sparkins dismounted, and confided him to the care of Mr. Malderton's groom. The ceremony of introduction was gone through, in all due form. Mr. Flamwell looked from behind his green spectacles at Horatio with an air of mysterious importance; and the gallant Horatio looked unutterable things at Teresa.

"Is he the Honorable Mr. Augustus What's-his-name?" whispered Mrs. Malderton to Flamwell, as he was escorting her to the dining room.

"Why, no — at least not exactly," returned that great authority — "not exactly."

"Who *is* he then?"

"Hush!" said Flamwell, nodding his head with a grave air, importing that he knew very well; but was prevented, by some grave reasons of state, from disclosing the important secret. It might be one of the ministers making himself acquainted with the views of the people.

"Mr. Sparkins," said the delighted Mrs. Malderton, "pray divide the ladies. John, put a chair for the gentleman between Miss Teresa and Miss Marianne." This was addressed to a man who, on ordinary occasions, acted as half-groom, half-gardener; but who, as it was important to make an impression on Mr. Sparkins, had been forced into a white neckerchief and shoes, and touched up, and brushed, to look like a second footman.

The dinner was excellent; Horatio was most attentive to Miss Teresa, and every one felt in high spirits, except Mr. Malderton, who, knowing the propensity of his brother-in-law, Mr. Barton, endured that sort of agony which the newspapers inform us is experienced by the surrounding neighborhood when a pot-boy hangs himself in a hayloft, and which is "much easier to be imagined than described."

"Have you seen your friend, Sir Thomas Noland, lately, Flamwell?" inquired Mr. Malderton, casting a sidelong look at Horatio, to see what effect the mention of so great a man had upon him.

"Why, no — not very lately. I saw Lord Gubbleton the day before yesterday."

"Ah! I hope his lordship is very well?" said Malderton, in a tone of the greatest interest. It is scarcely necessary to say that, until that moment, he had been quite innocent of the existence of such a person.

"Why, yes; he was very well — very well indeed. He's a devilish good fellow. I met him in the City, and had a long chat with him. Indeed, I'm rather intimate with him. I couldn't stop to talk to him as long as I could wish, though, because I was on my way to a banker's, a very rich man, and a member of Parliament, with whom I am also rather, indeed I may say very, intimate."

"I know whom you mean," returned the host, consequentially — in reality knowing as much about the matter as Flamwell himself. "He has a capital business."

This was touching on a dangerous topic.

"Talking of business," interposed Mr. Barton, from the center of the table. "A gentleman whom you knew very well, Malderton, before you made that first lucky spec of yours, called at our shop the other day, and — "

"Barton, may I trouble you for a potato?" interrupted the wretched master of the house, hoping to nip the story in the bud.

"Certainly," returned the grocer, quite insensible of his brother-in-law's object — "and he said in a very plain manner — "

"*Floury,* if you please," interrupted Malderton again; dreading the termination of the anecdote, and fearing a repetition of the word "shop."

"He said, says he," continued the culprit, after dispatching the potato; "says he, how goes on your business? So I said, jokingly — you know my way — says I, I'm never above my business, and I hope my business will never be above me. Ha, ha!"

"Mr. Sparkins," said the host, vainly endeavoring to conceal his dismay, "a glass of wine?"

HORATIO SPARKINS PAYS A VISIT

"With the utmost pleasure, sir."

"Happy to see you."

"Thank you."

"We were talking the other evening," resumed the host, addressing Horatio, partly with the view of displaying the conversational powers of his new acquaintance, and partly in the hope of drowning the grocer's stories — "we were talking the other night about the nature of man. Your argument struck me very forcibly."

"And me," said Mr. Frederick. Horatio made a graceful inclination of the head.

"Pray, what is your opinion of woman, Mr. Sparkins?" inquired Mrs. Malderton. The young ladies simpered.

"Man," replied Horatio, "man, whether he ranged the bright, gay, flowery plains of a second Eden, or the more sterile, barren, and I may say, commonplace regions, to which we are compelled to accustom ourselves, in times such as these; man, under any circumstances, or in any place — whether he were bending beneath the withering blasts of the frigid zone, or scorching under the rays of a vertical sun — man, without woman, would be — alone."

"I am very happy to find you entertain such honorable opinions, Mr. Sparkins," said Mrs. Malderton.

"And I," added Miss Teresa. Horatio looked his delight, and the young lady blushed.

"Now, it's my opinion — " said Mr. Barton.

"I know what you're going to say," interposed Malderton, determined not to give his relation another opportunity, "and I don't agree with you."

"What!" inquired the astonished grocer.

"I am sorry to differ from you, Barton," said the host, in as positive a manner as if he really were contradicting a position which the other had laid down, "but I cannot give my assent to what I consider a very monstrous proposition."

"But I meant to say —"

"You never can convince me," said Malderton, with an air of obstinate determination. "Never."

"And I," said Mr. Frederick, following up his father's attack, "cannot entirely agree in Mr. Sparkins's argument."

"What!" said Horatio, who became more metaphysical, and more argumentative, as he saw the female part of the family listening in wondering delight — "what! Is effect the consequence of cause? Is cause the precursor of effect?"

"That's the point," said Flamwell.

"To be sure," said Mr. Malderton.

"Because, if effect is the consequence of cause, and if cause does precede effect, I apprehend you are wrong," added Horatio.

"Decidedly," said the toad-eating Flamwell.

"At least, I apprehend that to be the just and logical deduction?" said Sparkins, in a tone of interrogation.

"No doubt of it," chimed in Flamwell again. "It settles the point."

"Well, perhaps it does," said Mr. Frederick; "I didn't see it before."

"I don't exactly see it now," thought the grocer; "but I suppose it's all right."

"How wonderfully clever he is!" whispered Mrs. Malderton to her daughters, as they retired to the drawing-room.

"Oh, he's quite a love!" said both the young ladies together; "he talks like an oracle. He must have seen a great deal of life."

The gentlemen being left to themselves, a pause ensued, during which everybody looked very grave, as if they were quite overcome by the profound nature of the previous discussion. Flamwell, who had made up his mind to find out who and what Mr. Horatio Sparkins really was, first broke silence.

"Excuse me, sir," said that distinguished personage, "I presume you have studied for the bar? I thought of entering once, myself — indeed, I'm rather intimate with some of the highest ornaments of that distinguished profession."

"N — no!" said Horatio, with a little hesitation; "not exactly."

"But you have been much among the silk gowns, or I mistake?" inquired Flamwell, deferentially.

"Nearly all my life," returned Sparkins.

The question was thus pretty well settled in the mind of Mr. Flamwell. He was a young gentleman "about to be called."

"I shouldn't like to be a barrister," said Tom, speaking for the first time, and looking round the table to find somebody who would notice the remark.

No one made any reply.

"I shouldn't like to wear a wig," said Tom, hazarding another observation.

"Tom, I beg you will not make yourself ridiculous," said his father. "Pray listen, and improve yourself by the conversation you hear, and don't be constantly making these absurd remarks."

"Very well, father," replied the unfortunate Tom, who had not spoken a word since he had asked for another slice of beef at a quarter past five o'clock P.M., and it was then eight.

"Well, Tom," observed his good-natured uncle, "never mind! *I* think with you. *I* shouldn't like to wear a wig. I'd rather wear an apron."

Mr. Malderton coughed violently. Mr. Barton resumed — "For if a man's above his business — "

The cough returned with tenfold violence, and did not cease until the unfortunate cause of it, in his alarm, had quite forgotten what he intended to say.

"Mr. Sparkins," said Flamwell, returning to the charge, "do you happen to know Mr. Delafontaine, of Bedford Square?"

"I have exchanged cards with him; since which, indeed, I have had an opportunity of serving him considerably," replied Horatio, slightly coloring; no doubt, at having been betrayed into making the acknowledgment.

"You are very lucky, if you have had an opportunity of obliging that great man," observed Flamwell, with an air of profound respect.

"I don't know who he is," he whispered to Mr. Malderton, confidentially, as they followed Horatio up to the drawing room. "It's quite clear, however, that he belongs to the law, and that he is somebody of great importance, and very highly connected."

"No doubt, no doubt," returned his companion.

The remainder of the evening passed away most delightfully. Mr. Malderton, relieved from his apprehensions by the circumstance of Mr. Barton's falling into a profound sleep, was as affable and gracious as possible. Miss Teresa played the "Fall of Paris," as Mr. Sparkins declared, in a most masterly manner, and both of them, assisted by Mr. Frederick, tried over glees and trios without number; they having made the pleasing discovery that their voices harmonized beautifully. To be sure, they all sang the first part; and Horatio, in addition to the slight drawback of having no ear, was perfectly innocent of knowing a note of music; still, they passed the time very agreeably, and it was past twelve o'clock before Mr. Sparkins ordered the mourning-coach-looking steed to be brought out — an order which was only complied with on the distinct understanding that he was to repeat his visit on the following Sunday.

"But perhaps Mr. Sparkins will form one of our party tomorrow evening?" suggested Mrs. M. "Mr. Malderton intends taking the girls to see the pantomime." Mr. Sparkins bowed, and promised to join the party in box 48, in the course of the evening.

"We will not tax you for the morning," said Miss Teresa, bewitchingly; "for ma is going to take us to all sorts of places, shopping. I know that gentlemen have a great horror of that employment." Mr. Sparkins bowed again, and declared that he should be delighted, but business of importance occupied him in the morning. Flamwell looked at Malderton significantly. "It's term time!" he whispered.

At twelve o'clock on the following morning, the "fly" was at the door of Oak Lodge, to convey Mrs. Malderton and her daughters on their expedition for the day. They were to dine and dress for the play at a friend's house. First, driving thither with their band-boxes, they departed on their first errand to make some purchases at Messrs. Jones, Spruggins, and Smith's, of Tottenham Court Road; after which, they were to go to Redmayne's in Bond Street; thence, to innumerable places that no one ever heard of. The young ladies beguiled the tediousness of the ride by eulogizing Mr. Horatio Sparkins, scolding their mamma for taking them so far to save a shilling, and wondering whether they should ever reach their destination. At length, the vehicle stopped before a dirty-looking ticketed linen-draper's shop, with goods of all kinds, and labels of all sorts and sizes, in the window. There were dropsical figures of seven with a little three-farthings in the corner, "perfectly invisible to the naked eye"; three hundred and fifty thousand ladies' boas, *from* one shilling and a penny halfpenny; real French kid shoes, at two and ninepence per pair; green parasols, at an equally cheap rate; and "every description of goods," as the proprietors said — and they must know best — "fifty per cent under cost price."

"Lor! ma, what a place you have brought us to!" said Miss Teresa; "what *would* Mr. Sparkins say if he could see us!"

"Ah! what, indeed!" said Miss Marianne, horrified at the idea.

"Pray be seated, ladies. What is the first article?" inquired the obsequious master of the ceremonies of the establishment, who, in his large white neckcloth and formal tie, looked like a bad "portrait of a gentleman" in the Somerset House exhibition.

"I want to see some silks," answered Mrs. Malderton.

"Directly, ma'am — Mr. Smith! Where *is* Mr. Smith?"

"Here, sir," cried a voice at the back of the shop.

"Pray make haste, Mr. Smith," said the M.C. "You never are to be found when you're wanted, sir."

Mr. Smith, thus enjoined to use all possible dispatch, leaped over the counter with great agility, and placed himself before the newly arrived customers. Mrs. Malderton uttered a faint scream; Miss Teresa, who had been stooping down to talk to her sister, raised her head, and beheld — Horatio Sparkins!

"We will draw a veil," as novel-writers say, over the scene that ensued. The mysterious, philosophical, romantic, metaphysical Sparkins — he who, to the interesting Teresa, seemed like the embodied idea of the young dukes and poetical exquisites in blue silk dressing gowns, and ditto ditto slippers, of whom she had read and dreamed, but had never expected to behold, was suddenly converted into Mr. Samuel Smith, the assistant at a "cheap shop"; the junior partner in a slippery firm of some three weeks' existence. The dignified evanishment of the hero of Oak Lodge, on this unexpected recognition, could only be equalled by that of a furtive dog with a considerable kettle at his tail. All the hopes of the Maldertons were destined at once to melt away, like the lemon ices at a Company's dinner; Almack's was still to them as distant as the North Pole; and Miss Teresa had as much chance of a husband as Captain Ross had of the northwest passage.

Years have elapsed since the occurrence of this dreadful morning. The daisies have thrice bloomed on Camberwell Green; the sparrows have thrice repeated their vernal chirps in Camberwell Grove; but the Miss Maldertons are still unmated. Miss Teresa's case is more desperate than ever; but Flamwell is yet in the zenith of his reputation; and the family have the same predilection for aristocratic personages, with an increased aversion to anything *low*.

THE
BLOOMSBURY
CHRISTENING

The Bloomsbury Christening

Mr. Nicodemus Dumps, or, as his acquaintance called him, "long Dumps," was a bachelor, six feet high, and fifty years old: cross, cadaverous, odd, and ill-natured. He was never happy but when he was miserable; and always miserable when he had the best reason to be happy. The only real comfort of his existence was to make everybody about him wretched — then he might be truly said to enjoy life. He was afflicted with a situation in the Bank worth five hundred a year, and he rented a "first-floor furnished," at Pentonville, which he originally took because it commanded a dismal prospect of an adjacent churchyard. He was familiar with the face of every tombstone, and the burial service seemed to excite his strongest sympathy. His friends said he was surly — he insisted he was nervous; they thought him a lucky dog, but he protested that he was "the most unfortunate man in the world." Cold as he was, and wretched as he declared himself to be, he was not wholly unsusceptible of attachments. He revered the memory of Hoyle, as he was himself an admirable and imperturbable whist player, and he chuckled with delight at a fretful and impatient adversary. He adored King Herod for his massacre of the innocents; and if he hated one thing more than another, it was a child. However, he could hardly be said to hate anything in particular, because he disliked everything in general; but perhaps his greatest antipathies were cabs, old women, doors that would not shut, musical amateurs, and omnibus cads. He subscribed to the "Society for the Suppression of Vice" for the pleasure of putting a stop to any harmless amusements; and he contributed largely towards the support of two itinerant Methodist parsons, in the amiable hope that if circumstances rendered any people happy in this world, they might perchance be rendered miserable by fears for the next.

Mr. Dumps had a nephew who had been married about a year, and who was somewhat of a favorite with his uncle, because he was an admirable subject to exercise his misery-creating powers upon. Mr. Charles Kitterbell was a small, sharp, spare man, with a very large head, and a broad, good-humored countenance. He looked like a faded giant, with the head and face partially restored; and he had a cast in his eye which rendered it quite impossible for any one with whom he conversed to know where he was looking. His eyes appeared fixed on the wall, and he was staring you out of countenance; in short, there was no catching his eye, and perhaps it is a merciful dispensation of Providence that such eyes are not catching. In addition to these characteristics, it may be added that Mr. Charles Kitterbell was one of the most credulous and matter-of-fact little personages that ever took *to* himself a wife, and *for* himself a house in Great Russell Street, Bedford Square. (Uncle Dumps always dropped the "Bedford Square," and inserted in lieu thereof the dreadful words "Tottenham Court Road.")

"No, but, uncle, 'pon my life you must — you must promise to be godfather," said Mr. Kitterbell, as he sat in conversation with this respected relative one morning.

"I cannot, indeed I cannot," returned Dumps.

"Well, but why not? Jemima will think it very unkind. It's very little trouble."

"As to the trouble," rejoined the most unhappy man in existence, "I don't mind that; but my nerves are in that state — I cannot go through the ceremony. You know I don't like going out. For God's sake, Charles, don't fidget with that stool so; you'll drive me mad." Mr. Kitterbell, quite regardless of his uncle's nerves, had occupied himself for some ten minutes in describing a circle on the floor with one leg of the office stool on which he was seated, keeping the other three up in the air, and holding fast on by the desk.

"I beg your pardon, uncle," said Kitterbell, quite abashed, suddenly releasing his hold of the desk, and bringing the three wandering legs back to the floor, with a force sufficient to drive them through it.

"But come, don't refuse. If it's a boy, you know, we must have two godfathers."

"*If* it's a boy!" said Dumps; "why can't you say at once whether it *is* a boy or not?"

"I should be very happy to tell you, but it's impossible I can undertake to say whether it's a girl or a boy, if the child isn't born yet."

"Not born yet!" echoed Dumps, with a gleam of hope lighting up his lugubrious visage. "Oh, well, it *may* be a girl, and then you won't want me; or if it is a boy, it *may* die before it is christened."

"I hope not," said the father that expected to be, looking very grave.

"I hope not," acquiesced Dumps, evidently pleased with the subject. He was beginning to get happy. "*I* hope not, but distressing cases frequently occur during the first two or three days of a child's life; fits, I am told, are exceedingly common, and alarming convulsions are almost matters of course."

"Lord, uncle!" ejaculated little Kitterbell, gasping for breath.

"Yes; my landlady was confined — let me see — last Tuesday: an uncommonly fine boy. On the Thursday night the nurse was sitting with him upon her knee before the fire, and he was as well as possible. Suddenly he became black in the face, and alarmingly spasmodic. The medical man was instantly sent for, and every remedy was tried, but — "

"How frightful!" interrupted the horror-stricken Kitterbell.

"The child died, of course. However, your child *may* not die; and if it should be a boy, and should *live* to be christened, why I suppose I must be one of the sponsors." Dumps was evidently good natured on the faith of his anticipations.

"Thank you, uncle," said his agitated nephew, grasping his hand as warmly as if he had done him some essential service. "Perhaps I had better not tell Mrs. K. what you have mentioned."

"Why, if she's low-spirited, perhaps you had better not mention the melancholy case to her," returned Dumps, who of course had invented the whole story; "though perhaps it would be but doing your duty as a husband to prepare her for the *worst*."

A day or two afterward, as Dumps was perusing a morning paper at the chop-house which he regularly frequented, the following paragraph met his eyes:

"*Births.* — On Saturday, the 18th inst., in Great Russell Street, the lady of Charles Kitterbell, Esq., of a son."

"It *is* a boy!" he exclaimed, dashing down the paper, to the astonishment of the waiters. "It *is* a boy!" But he speedily regained his composure as his eye rested on a paragraph quoting the number of infant deaths from the bills of mortality.

Six weeks passed away, and as no communication had been received from the Kitterbells, Dumps was beginning to flatter himself that the child was dead, when the following note painfully resolved his doubts:

"*Great Russell Street,*

"*Monday morning*

"DEAR UNCLE — You will be delighted to hear that my dear Jemima has left her room, and that your future godson is getting on capitally. He was very thin at first, but he is getting much larger, and nurse says he is filling out every day. He cries a good deal, and is a very singular color, which made Jemima and me rather uncomfortable; but as nurse says it's natural, and as of course we know nothing about these things yet, we are quite satisfied with what nurse says. We think he will be a sharp child; and nurse says she's sure he will, because he never goes to sleep. You will readily believe that we are all very happy, only we're a little worn out for want of rest, as he keeps us awake all night; but this we must expect, nurse says, for the first six or eight months. He has been vaccinated, but in consequence of the operation being rather awkwardly performed, some small particles of glass were introduced into the arm with the matter. Perhaps this may in some degree account for his being rather fractious; at least, so nurse says. We propose to have him christened at twelve o'clock on Friday, at Saint George's church, in Hart Street, by the name of Frederick Charles William. Pray don't be later than a quarter before twelve. We shall have a very few friends in the evening, when of course we shall see you. I am sorry to say that the dear boy appears rather restless and uneasy today: the cause, I fear, is fever.

"Believe me, dear Uncle,

"Yours affectionately,

"CHARLES KITTERBELL

"P.S. — I open this note to say that we have just discovered the cause of little Frederick's restlessness. It is not fever, as I apprehended, but a small pin, which nurse accidentally stuck in his leg yesterday evening. We have taken it out, and he appears more composed, though he still sobs a good deal."

It is almost unnecessary to say that the perusal of the above interesting statement was no great relief to the mind of the hypochondriacal Dumps. It was impossible to recede, however, and so he put the best face — that is to say, an uncommonly miserable one — upon the matter; and purchased a handsome silver mug for the infant Kitterbell, upon which he ordered the initials "F. C. W. K.," with the customary untrained grape-vine-looking flourishes, and a large full stop, to be engraved forthwith.

Monday was a fine day, Tuesday was delightful, Wednesday was equal to either, and Thursday was finer than ever; four successive fine days in London! Hackney coachmen became revolutionary, and crossing-sweepers began to doubt the existence of a First Cause. The *Morning Herald* informed its readers that an old woman in Camden Town had been heard to say that the fineness of the season was "unprecedented in the memory of the oldest inhabitant"; and Islington clerks, with large families and small salaries, left off their black gaiters, disdained to carry their once green cotton umbrellas, and walked to town in the conscious pride of white stockings and cleanly brushed Bluchers. Dumps beheld all this with an eye of supreme contempt — his triumph was at hand. He knew that if it had been fine for four weeks instead of four days, it would rain when he went out; he was lugubriously happy in the conviction that Friday would be a wretched day — and so it was. "I knew how it would be," said Dumps, as he turned round opposite the Mansion House at half-past eleven o'clock on the Friday morning. "I knew how it would be. *I* am concerned, and that's enough"; and certainly the appearance of the day was sufficient to depress the spirits of a much more buoyant-hearted individual than himself. It had rained, without a moment's cessation, since eight o'clock; everybody that passed up Cheapside, and down Cheapside, looked wet, cold, and dirty. All sorts of forgotten and long-concealed umbrellas had been put into requisition. Cabs whisked about, with the "fare" as carefully boxed up behind two glazed calico curtains as any mysterious picture in any one of

Mrs. Radcliffe's castles; omnibus horses smoked like steam-engines; nobody thought of "standing up" under doorways or arches; they were painfully convinced it was a hopeless case; and so everybody went hastily along, jumbling and jostling, and swearing and perspiring, and slipping about, like amateur skaters behind wooden chairs on the Serpentine on a frosty Sunday.

Dumps paused; he could not think of walking, being rather smart for the christening. If he took a cab he was sure to be spilt, and a hackney coach was too expensive for his economical ideas. An omnibus was waiting at the opposite corner — it was a desperate case — he had never heard of an omnibus upsetting or running away, and if the cad did knock him down, he could "pull him up" in return.

"Now, sir!" cried the young gentleman who officiated as "cad" to the "Lads of the Village," which was the name of the machine just noticed. Dumps crossed.

"This vay, sir!" shouted the driver of the "Hark-away," pulling up his vehicle immediately across the door of the opposition — "This vay, sir — he's full." Dumps hesitated, whereupon the "Lads of the Village" commenced pouring out a torrent of abuse against the "Hark-away"; but the conductor of the "Admiral Napier" settled the contest in a most satisfactory manner for all parties by seizing Dumps round the waist, and thrusting him into the middle of his vehicle, which had just come up and only wanted the sixteenth inside.

"All right," said the "Admiral," and off the thing thundered, like a fire engine at full gallop, with the kidnapped customer inside, standing in the position of a half doubled-up bootjack, and falling about with every jerk of the machine, first on the one side, and then on the other, like a "Jack-in-the-green," on May day, setting to the lady with a brass ladle.

"For Heaven's sake, where am I to sit?" inquired the miserable man of an old gentleman, into whose stomach he had just fallen for the fourth time.

"Anywhere but on my *chest*, sir," replied the old gentleman in a surly tone.

"Perhaps the *box* would suit the gentleman better," suggested a very damp lawyer's clerk, in a pink shirt, and a smirking countenance.

After a great deal of struggling and falling about, Dumps at last managed to squeeze himself into a seat, which, in addition to the slight disadvantage of being between a window that would not shut, and a door that must be open, placed him in close contact with a passenger, who had been walking about all the morning without an umbrella, and who looked as if he had spent the day in a full water-butt — only wetter.

"Don't bang the door so," said Dumps to the conductor, as he shut it after letting out four of the passengers; "I am very nervous — it destroys me."

"Did any gen'lm'n say anythink?" replied the cad, thrusting in his head, and trying to look as if he didn't understand the request.

"I told you not to bang the door so!" repeated Dumps, with an expression of countenance like the knave of clubs, in convulsions.

"Oh! vy, it's rather a sing'ler circumstance about this here door, sir, that it von't shut without banging," replied the conductor; and he opened the door very wide, and shut it again with a terrific bang, in proof of the assertion.

"I beg your pardon, sir," said a little prim, wheezing old gentleman, sitting opposite Dumps, "I beg your pardon; but have you ever observed, when you have been in an omnibus on a wet day, that four people out of five always come in with large cotton umbrellas, without a handle at the top, or the brass spike at the bottom?"

"Why, sir," returned Dumps, as he heard the clock strike twelve, "it never struck me before; but now you mention it, I — Hollo! hollo!" shouted the persecuted individual, as the omnibus dashed past Drury Lane, where he had directed to be set down — "Where is the cad?"

"I think he's on the box, sir," said the young gentleman before noticed in the pink shirt, which looked like a white one ruled with red ink.

"I want to be set down!" said Dumps in a faint voice, overcome by his previous efforts.

"I think these cads want to be *set down*," returned the attorney's clerk, chuckling at his sally.

"Hollo!" cried Dumps again.

"Hollo!" echoed the passengers. The omnibus passed St. Giles's church.

"Hold hard!" said the conductor; "I'm blowed if we ha'n't forgot the gen'lm'n as vas to be set down at Doory Lane. — Now, sir, make haste, if you please," he added, opening the door, and assisting Dumps out with as much coolness as if it was "all right." Dumps's indignation was for once getting the better of his cynical equanimity. "Drury Lane!" he gasped, with the voice of a boy in a cold bath for the first time.

"Doory Lane, sir? — yes, sir — third turning on the right-hand side, sir."

Dumps's passion was paramount: he clutched his umbrella, and was striding off with the firm determination of not paying the fare. The cad, by a remarkable coincidence, happened to entertain a directly contrary opinion, and Heaven knows how far the altercation would have proceeded, if it had not been most ably and satisfactorily brought to a close by the driver.

"Hollo!" said that respectable person, standing up on the box, and leaning with one hand on the roof of the omnibus. "Hollo, Tom! tell the gentleman if so be as he feels aggrieved, we will take him up to the Edge-er (Edgeware) Road for nothing, and set him down at Doory Lane when we comes back. He can't reject that, anyhow."

The argument was irresistible: Dumps paid the disputed sixpence, and in a quarter of an hour was on the staircase of No. 14, Great Russell Street.

Everything indicated that preparations were making for the reception of "a few friends" in the evening. Two dozen extra tumblers, and four ditto wine glasses — looking anything but transparent, with little bits of straw in them — were on the slab in the passage, just arrived. There was a great smell of nutmeg, port wine, and almonds, on the staircase; the covers were taken off the stair carpet, and the figure of Venus on the first landing looked as if she were ashamed of the composition candle in her right hand, which contrasted beautifully with the lamp-blacked drapery of the goddess of love. The female servant (who looked very warm and bustling) ushered Dumps into a front drawing-room, very prettily furnished, with a plentiful sprinkling of little baskets, paper table mats, china watchmen, pink and gold albums, and rainbow-bound little books on the different tables.

"Ah, uncle!" said Mr. Kitterbell, "how d'ye do? Allow me — Jemima, my dear — my uncle. I think you've seen Jemima before, sir?"

"Have had the *pleasure*," returned big Dumps, his tone and look making it doubtful whether in his life he had ever experienced the sensation.

"I'm sure," said Mrs. Kitterbell, with a languid smile, and a slight cough. "I'm sure — hem — any friend — of Charles's — hem — much less a relation, is — "

"I knew you'd say so, my love," said little Kitterbell, who, while he appeared to be gazing on the opposite houses, was looking at his wife with a most affectionate air: "Bless you!" The last two words were accompanied with a simper, and a squeeze of the hand, which stirred up all Uncle Dumps's bile.

"Jane, tell nurse to bring down baby," said Mrs. Kitterbell, addressing the servant. Mrs. Kitterbell was a tall, thin young lady, with very light hair, and a particularly white face — one of those young women who almost invariably, though one hardly knows why, recall to one's mind the idea of a cold fillet of veal. Out went the servant, and in came the nurse, with a remarkably small parcel in her arms, packed up in a blue mantle trimmed with white fur. — This was the baby.

"Now, uncle," said Mr. Kitterbell, lifting up that part of the mantle which covered the infant's face, with an air of great triumph, *"who* do you think he's like?"

"He! he! Yes, who?" said Mrs. K., putting her arm through her husband's, and looking up into Dumps's face with an expression of as much interest as she was capable of displaying.

"Good God, how small he is!" cried the amiable uncle, starting back with well-feigned surprise; *"remarkably* small indeed."

"Do you think so?" inquired poor little Kitterbell, rather alarmed. "He's a monster to what he was — ain't he, nurse?"

"He's a dear," said the nurse, squeezing the child, and evading the question — not because she scrupled to disguise the fact, but because she couldn't afford to throw away the chance of Dumps's half-crown.

"Well, but who is he like?" inquired little Kitterbell.

Dumps looked at the little pink heap before him, and only thought at the moment of the best mode of mortifying the youthful parents.

"I really don't know *who* he's like," he answered, very well knowing the reply expected of him.

"Don't you think he's like *me?*" inquired his nephew with a knowing air.

"Oh, *decidedly* not!" returned Dumps, with an emphasis not to be misunderstood. "Decidedly not like you. — Oh, certainly not."

"Like Jemima?" asked Kitterbell, faintly.

"Oh, dear no; not in the least. I'm no judge, of course, in such cases; but I really think he's more like one of those little carved representations that one sometimes sees blowing a trumpet on a tombstone!" The nurse stooped down over the child, and with great difficulty prevented an explosion of mirth. Pa and ma looked almost as miserable as their amiable uncle.

"Well!" said the disappointed little father, "you'll be better able to tell what he's like by-and-bye. You shall see him this evening with his mantle off."

"Thank you," said Dumps, feeling particularly grateful.

"Now, my love," said Kitterbell to his wife, "it's time we were off. We're to meet the other godfather and the godmother at the church, uncle — Mr. and Mrs. Wilson from over the way — uncommonly nice people. My love, are you well wrapped up?"

"Yes, dear."

"Are you sure you won't have another shawl?" inquired the anxious husband.

"No, sweet," returned the charming mother, accepting Dumps's proffered arm; and the little party entered the hackney coach that was to take them to the church; Dumps amusing Mrs. Kitterbell by expatiating largely on the danger of measles, thrush, teeth-cutting, and other interesting diseases to which children are subject.

The ceremony (which occupied about five minutes) passed off without anything particular occurring. The clergyman had to dine some distance from town, and had two churchings, three christenings, and a funeral to perform in something less than an hour. The godfathers and godmother, therefore, promised to renounce the devil and all his works — "and all that sort of thing" — as little Kitterbell said — "in less than no time"; and with the exception of Dumps nearly letting the child fall into the font when he handed it to the clergyman, the whole affair went off in the usual business-like and matter-of-course manner, and Dumps reentered the Bank gates at two o'clock with a heavy heart, and the painful conviction that he was regularly booked for an evening party.

THE BLOOMSBURY CHRISTENING

Evening came — and so did Dumps's pumps, black silk stockings, and white cravat which he had ordered to be forwarded, per boy, from Pentonville. The depressed godfather dressed himself at a friend's counting house, from whence, with his spirits fifty degrees below proof, he sallied forth — as the weather had cleared up, and the evening was tolerably fine — to walk to Great Russell Street. Slowly he paced up Cheapside, Newgate Street, down Snow Hill, and up Holborn ditto, looking as grim as the figurehead of a man-of-war, and finding out fresh causes of misery at every step. As he was crossing the corner of Hatton Garden, a man, apparently intoxicated, rushed against him, and would have knocked him down, had he not been providentially caught by a very genteel young man, who happened to be close to him at the time. The shock so disarranged Dumps's nerves, as well as his dress, that he could hardly stand. The gentleman took his arm, and in the kindest manner walked with him as far as Furnival's Inn. Dumps, for about the first time in his life, felt grateful and polite; and he and the gentlemanly-looking young man parted with mutual expressions of goodwill.

"There are at least some well-disposed men in the world," ruminated the misanthropical Dumps, as he proceeded towards his destination.

Rat — tat — ta-ra-ra-ra-ra-rat — knocked a hackney-coachman at Kitterbell's door, in imitation of a gentleman's servant, just as Dumps reached it; and out came an old lady in a large toque, and an old gentleman in a blue coat, and three female copies of the old lady in pink dresses, and shoes to match.

"It's a large party," sighed the unhappy godfather, wiping the perspiration from his forehead, and leaning against the area-railings. It was some time before the miserable man could muster up courage to knock at the door, and when he did, the smart appearance of a neighboring greengrocer (who had been hired to wait for seven and sixpence, and whose calves alone were worth double the money), the lamp in the passage, and the Venus on the landing, added to the hum of many voices, and the sound of a harp and two violins, painfully convinced him that his surmises were but too well founded.

"How are you?" said little Kitterbell, in a greater bustle than ever, bolting out of the little back parlor with a corkscrew in his hand, and various particles of sawdust, looking like so many inverted commas, on his inexpressibles.

"Good God!" said Dumps, turning into the aforesaid parlor to put his shoes on, which he had brought in his coat-pocket, and still more appalled by the sight of seven fresh-drawn corks, and a corresponding number of decanters. "How many people are there upstairs?"

"Oh, not above thirty-five. We've had the carpet taken up in the back drawing-room, and the piano and the card-tables are in the front. Jemima thought we'd better have a regular sit-down supper in the front parlor, because of the speechifying, and all that. But, Lord! uncle, what's the matter?" continued the excited little man, as Dumps stood with one shoe on, rummaging his pockets with the most frightful distortion of visage. "What have you lost? Your pock etbook?"

"No," returned Dumps, diving first into one pocket and then into the other, and speaking in a voice like Desdemona with the pillow over her mouth.

"Your card-case? snuff-box? the key of your lodgings?" continued Kitterbell, pouring question on question with the rapidity of lightning.

"No! no!" ejaculated Dumps, still diving eagerly into his empty pockets.

"Not — not — the *mug* you spoke of this morning?"

"Yes, the *mug!*" replied Dumps, sinking into a chair.

"How *could* you have done it?" inquired Kitterbell. "Are you sure you brought it out?"

"Yes! yes! I see it all!" said Dumps, starting up as the idea flashed across his mind; "miserable dog that I am — I was born to suffer. see it all: it was the gentlemanly-looking young man!"

"Mr. Dumps!" shouted the greengrocer in a stentorian voice, as he ushered the somewhat recovered godfather into the drawing room half an hour after the above declaration. "Mr. Dumps!" — everybody looked at the door, and in came Dumps, feeling about as much out of place as a salmon might be supposed to be on a gravel walk.

"Happy to see you again," said Mrs. Kitterbell, quite unconscious of the unfortunate man's confusion and misery; "you must allow me to introduce you to a few of our friends: my mamma, Mr. Dump — my papa and sisters." Dumps seized the hand of the mother as warmly as if she was his own parent, bowed *to* the young ladies, and *against* a gentleman behind him, and took no notice whatever of the father, who had been bowing incessantly for three minutes and a quarter.

"Uncle," said little Kitterbell, after Dumps had been introduced to a select dozen or two, "you must let me lead you to the other end of the room, to introduce you to my friend Danton. Such a splendid fellow! — I'm sure you'll like him — this way." — Dumps followed as tractably as a tame bear.

Mr. Danton was a young man of about five-and-twenty, with a considerable stock of impudence, and a very small share of ideas: he was a great favorite, especially with young ladies of from sixteen to twenty-six years of age, both inclusive. He could imitate the French horn to admiration, sang comic songs most inimitably, and had the most insinuating way of saying impertinent nothings to his doting female admirers. He had acquired, somehow or other, the reputation of being a great wit, and, accordingly, whenever he opened his mouth, everybody who knew him laughed very heartily.

The introduction took place in due form. Mr. Danton bowed, and twirled a lady's handkerchief, which he held in his hand, in a most comic way. Everybody smiled.

"Very warm," said Dumps, feeling it necessary to say something.

"Yes. It was warmer yesterday," returned the brilliant Mr. Danton. — A general laugh.

"I have great pleasure in congratulating you on your first appearance in the character of a father, sir," he continued, addressing Dumps — "godfather, I mean." — The young ladies were convulsed, and the gentlemen in ecstasies.

A general hum of admiration interrupted the conversation and announced the entrance of nurse with the baby. An universal rush of the young ladies immediately took place. (Girls are always *so* fond of babies in company.)

"Oh, you dear!" said one.

"How sweet!" cried another, in a low tone of the most enthusiastic admiration.

"Heavenly!" added a third.

"Oh! what dear little arms!" said a fourth, holding up an arm and fist about the size and shape of the leg of a fowl cleanly picked.

"Did you ever!" — said a little coquette with a large bustle, who looked like a French lithograph, appealing to a gentleman in three waistcoats — "Did you ever!"

"Never, in my life," returned her admirer, pulling up his collar.

"Oh! *do* let me take it, nurse!" cried another young lady. "The love."

"Can it open its eyes, nurse?" inquired another, affecting the utmost innocence. Suffice it to say, that the single ladies unanimously voted him an angel, and that the married ones, *nem. con.*, agreed that he was decidedly the finest baby they had ever beheld — except their own.

The quadrilles were resumed with great spirit. Mr. Danton was universally admitted to be beyond himself; several young ladies enchanted the company and gained admirers by singing "We met" — "I saw her at the Fancy Fair" — and other equally sentimental and interesting ballads. "The young men," as Mrs. Kitterbell said, "made themselves very agreeable"; the girls did not lose their opportunity; and the evening promised to go off excellently. Dumps didn't mind it: he had devised a plan for himself — a little bit of fun in his own way — and he was almost happy! He played a rubber and lost every point. Mr. Danton said he could not have lost every point, because he made a point of losing: everybody laughed tremendously. Dumps retorted with a better joke, and nobody smiled, with the exception of the host, who seemed to consider it his duty to laugh till he was black in the face, at everything. There was only one drawback — the musicians did not play with quite as much spirit as could have been wished. The cause, however, was satisfactorily explained; for it appeared, on the testimony of a gentleman who had come up from Gravesend in the afternoon, that they had been engaged on board a steamer all day, and had played almost without cessation all the way to Gravesend, and all the way back again.

The "sit-down supper" was excellent; there were four barley-sugar temples on the table, which would have looked beautiful if they had not melted away when the supper began; and a water-mill, whose only fault was that instead of going round, it ran over the tablecloth. Then there were fowls, and tongue, and trifle, and sweets, and lobster salad, and potted beef — and everything. And little Kitterbell kept calling out for clean plates, and the clean plates did not come: and then the gentlemen who wanted the plates said they didn't mind, they'd take a lady's; and then Mrs. Kitterbell applauded their gallantry, and the greengrocer ran about till he thought his seven and sixpence was very hardly earned; and the young ladies didn't eat much for fear it shouldn't look romantic, and the married ladies ate as much as possible, for fear they shouldn't have enough; and a great deal of wine was drunk, and everybody talked and laughed considerably.

"Hush! hush!" said Mr. Kitterbell, rising and looking very important. "My love (this was addressed to his wife at the other end of the table), take care of Mrs. Maxwell, and your mamma, and the rest of the married ladies; the gentlemen will persuade the young ladies to fill their glasses, I am sure."

"Ladies and gentlemen," said long Dumps, in a very sepulchral voice and rueful accent, rising from his chair like the ghost in Don Juan, "will you have the kindness to charge your glasses? I am desirous of proposing a toast."

A dead silence ensued, and the glasses were filled — everybody looked serious.

"Ladies and gentlemen," slowly continued the ominous Dumps. "I" — (here Mr. Danton imitated two notes from the French horn, in a very loud key, which electrified the nervous toast-proposer, and convulsed his audience).

"Order! order!" said little Kitterbell, endeavoring to suppress his laughter.

"Order!" said the gentlemen.

"Danton, be quiet," said a particular friend on the opposite side of the table.

"Ladies and gentlemen," resumed Dumps, somewhat recovered, and not much disconcerted, for he was always a pretty good hand at a speech — "In accordance with what is, I believe, the established usage on these occasions, I, as one of the godfathers of Master Frederick Charles William Kitterbell — (here the speaker's voice faltered, for he remembered the mug) — venture to rise to propose a toast. I need hardly say that it is the health and prosperity of that young gentleman, the particular event of whose early life we are here met to celebrate — (applause). Ladies and gentlemen, it is impossible to suppose that our friends here, whose sincere well-wishers we all are, can pass through life without some trials, considerable suffering, severe affliction, and heavy losses!" — Here the arch-traitor paused, and slowly drew forth a long, white pocket-handkerchief — his example was followed by several ladies. "That these trials may be long spared them is my most earnest prayer, my most fervent wish (a distinct sob from the grandmother). I hope and trust, ladies and gentle-men, that the infant whose christening we have this evening met to celebrate, may not be removed from the arms of his parents by pre-mature decay (several cambrics were in requisition): that his young and now *apparently* healthy form may not be wasted by lingering disease. (Here Dumps cast a sardonic glance around, for a great sensation was manifest among the married ladies.) You, I am sure, will concur with me in wishing that he may live to be a comfort and a blessing to his parents. ('Hear, hear!' and an audible sob from Mr. Kitterbell.) But should he not be what we could wish — should he forget in after times the duty which he owes to them — should they unhappily experience that distracting truth, 'how sharper than a serpent's tooth it is to have a thankless child' " — Here Mrs. Kitter-bell, with her handkerchief to her eyes, and accompanied by several ladies, rushed from the room, and went into violent hysterics in the passage, leaving her better half in almost as bad a condition, and a general impression in Dumps's favor; for people like sentiment, after all.

It need hardly be added, that this occurrence quite put a stop to the harmony of the evening. Vinegar, hartshorn, and cold water, were now as much in request as negus, rout-cakes, and *bon-bons* had been a short time before. Mrs. Kitterbell was immediately conveyed to her apartment, the musicians were silenced, flirting ceased, and the company slowly departed. Dumps left the house at the com-mencement of the bustle, and walked home with a light step, and (for him) a cheerful heart. His landlady, who slept in the next room, has offered to make oath that she heard him laugh, in his peculiar man-ner, after he had locked his door. The assertion, however, is so im-probable, and bears on the face of it such strong evidence of un-truth, that it has never obtained credence to this hour.

The family of Mr. Kitterbell has considerably increased since the period to which we have referred; he has now two sons and a daughter; and as he expects, at no distant period, to have another addition to his blooming progeny, he is anxious to secure an eligible godfather for the occasion. He is determined, however, to impose upon him two conditions. He must bind himself, by a solemn obliga-tion, not to make any speech after supper; and it is indispensable that he should be in no way connected with "the most miserable man in the world."

MR. MINNS

AND

HIS COUSIN

Mr. Minns

and

His Cousin

Mr. Augustus Minns was a bachelor, of about forty as he said — of about eight-and-forty as his friends said. He was always exceedingly clean, precise, and tidy; perhaps somewhat priggish, and the most retiring man in the world. He usually wore a brown frock coat without a wrinkle, light inexplicables without a spot, a neat neckerchief with a remarkably neat tie, and boots without a fault; moreover, he always carried a brown silk umbrella with an ivory handle. He was a clerk in Somerset House, or, as he said himself, he held "a responsible situation under Government." He had a good and increasing salary, in addition to some 10,000*l.* of his own (invested in the funds), and he occupied a first floor in Tavistock Street, Covent Garden, where he had resided for twenty years, having been in the habit of quarreling with his landlord the whole time: regularly giving notice of his intention to quit on the first day of every quarter, and as regularly countermanding it on the second. There were two classes of created objects which he held in the deepest and most unmingled horror; these were dogs, and children. He was not unamiable, but he could, at any time, have viewed the execution of a dog, or the assassination of an infant, with the liveliest satisfaction. Their habits were at variance with his love of order; and his love of order was as powerful as his love of life. Mr. Augustus Minns had no relations in or near London, with the exception of his cousin, Mr. Octavius Budden, to whose son, whom he had never seen (for he disliked the father), he had consented to become godfather by proxy. Mr. Budden having realized a moderate fortune by exercising the trade or calling of a corn-chandler, and having a great predilection for the country, had purchased a cottage in the vicinity of Stamford Hill, whither he retired with the wife of his bosom, and his only son, Master Alexander Augustus Budden. One evening, as Mr. and Mrs. B. were admiring their son, discussing his various merits, talking over his education, and disputing whether the classics should be made an essential part thereof, the lady pressed so strongly upon her husband the propriety of cultivating the friendship of Mr. Minns in behalf of their son, that Mr. Budden at last made up his mind, that it should not be his fault if he and his cousin were not in future more intimate.

"I'll break the ice, my love," said Mr. Budden, stirring up the sugar at the bottom of his glass of brandy-and-water, and casting a sidelong look at his spouse to see the effect of the announcement of his determination, "by asking Minns down to dine with us on Sunday."

"Then pray, Budden, write to your cousin at once," replied Mrs. Budden. "Who knows, if we could only get him down here, but he might take a fancy to our Alexander, and leave him his property? — Alick, my dear, take your legs off the rail of the chair!"

"Very true," said Mr. Budden, musing, "very true indeed, my love!"

On the following morning, as Mr. Minns was sitting at his breakfast-table, alternately biting his dry toast and casting a look upon the columns of his morning paper, which he always read from the title to the printer's name, he heard a loud knock at the street door; which was shortly afterwards followed by the entrance of his servant, who put into his hands a particularly small card, on which was engraved in immense letters, "Mr. Octavius Budden, Amelia Cottage (Mrs. B.'s name was Amelia), Poplar Walk, Stamford Hill."

"Budden!" ejaculated Minns, "what can bring that vulgar man here! — say I'm asleep — say I'm out, and shall never be home again — anything to keep him down-stairs."

"But please, sir, the gentleman's coming up," replied the servant, and the fact was made evident by an appalling creaking of boots on the staircase accompanied by a pattering noise; the cause of which Minns could not, for the life of him, divine.

"Hem — show the gentleman in," said the unfortunate bachelor. Exit servant, and enter Octavius preceded by a large white dog, dressed in a suit of fleecy hosiery, with pink eyes, large ears, and no perceptible tail.

The cause of the pattering on the stairs was but too plain. Mr. Augustus Minns staggered beneath the shock of the dog's appearance.

"My dear fellow, how are you?" said Budden, as he entered.

He always spoke at the top of his voice, and always said the same thing half-a-dozen times.

"How are you, my hearty?"

"How do you do, Mr. Budden? — pray take a chair!" politely stammered the discomfited Minns.

"Thank you — thank you — well — how are you, eh?"

"Uncommonly well, thank you," said Minns, casting a diabolical look at the dog, who, with his hind legs on the floor, and his fore paws resting on the table, was dragging a bit of bread and butter out of a plate, preparatory to devouring it, with the buttered side next the carpet.

"Ah, you rogue!" said Budden to his dog; "you see, Minns, he's like me, always at home, eh, my boy? — Egad, I'm precious hot and hungry! I've walked all the way from Stamford Hill this morning."

"Have you breakfasted?" inquired Minns.

"Oh, no! — came to breakfast with you; so ring the bell, my dear fellow, will you? and let's have another cup and saucer, and the cold ham. — Make myself at home, you see!" continued Budden, dusting his boots with a table napkin. "Ha! — ha! — ha! — 'pon my life, I'm hungry."

Minns rang the bell, and tried to smile.

"I decidedly never was so hot in my life," continued Octavius, wiping his forehead; "well, but how are you, Minns? 'Pon my soul, you wear capitally!"

"D'ye think so?" said Minns; and he tried another smile.

"'Pon my life, I do!"

"Mrs. B. and — what's his name — quite well?"

"Alick — my son, you mean; never better — never better. But at such a place as we've got at Poplar Walk, you know, he couldn't be ill if he tried. When I first saw it, by Jove! it looked so knowing, with the front garden, and the green railings, and the brass knocker, and all that — I really thought it was a cut above me."

"Don't you think you'd like the ham better," interrupted Minns, "if you cut it the other way?" He saw, with feelings which it is impossible to describe, that his visitor was cutting, or rather maiming, the ham, in utter violation of all established rules.

"No, thank ye," returned Budden, with the most barbarous indifference to crime, "I prefer it this way, it eats short. But I say, Minns, when will you come down and see us? You will be delighted with the place; I know you will. Amelia and I were talking about you the other night, and Amelia said — another lump of sugar, please; thank ye — she said, don't you think you could contrive, my dear, to say to Mr. Minns, in a friendly way — come down, sir — damn the dog! he's spoiling your curtains, Minns — ha! — ha! — ha!" Minns leaped from his seat as though he had received the discharge from a galvanic battery.

"Come out, sir! — go out, hoo!" cried poor Augustus, keeping, nevertheless, at a very respectful distance from the dog; having read of a case of hydrophobia in the paper of that morning. By dint of great exertion, much shouting, and a marvelous deal of poking under the tables with a stick and umbrella, the dog was at last dislodged, and placed on the landing outside the door, where he immediately commenced a most appalling howling; at the same time vehemently scratching the paint off the two nicely varnished bottom panels, until they resembled the interior of a backgammon board.

"A good dog for the country that!" coolly observed Budden to the distracted Minns, "but he's not much used to confinement. But now, Minns, when will you come down? I'll take no denial, positively. Let's see, today's Thursday. — Will you come on Sunday? We dine at five, don't say no — do."

After a great deal of pressing, Mr. Augustus Minns, driven to despair, accepted the invitation, and promised to be at Poplar Walk on the ensuing Sunday, at a quarter before five to the minute.

"Now mind the direction," said Budden: "the coach goes from the Flower Pot, in Bishopsgate Street, every half-hour. When the coach stops at the Swan, you'll see, immediately opposite you, a white house."

"Which is your house — I understand," said Minns, wishing to cut short the visit, and the story, at the same time.

"No, no, that's not mine; that's Grogus's, the great ironmonger's. I was going to say — you turn down by the side of the white house till you can't go another step further — mind that! — and then you turn to your right, by some stables — well; close to you, you'll see a wall with 'Beware of the Dog' written on it in large letters — (Minns shuddered) — go along by the side of that wall for about a quarter of a mile — and anybody will show you which is my place."

"Very well — thank ye — good-bye."

"Be punctual."

"Certainly: good morning."

"I say, Minns, you've got a card."

"Yes, I have; thank ye." And Mr. Octavius Budden departed, leaving his cousin looking forward to his visit on the following Sunday, with the feelings of a penniless poet to the weekly visit of his Scotch landlady.

Sunday arrived; the sky was bright and clear; crowds of people were hurrying along the streets, intent on their different schemes of pleasure for the day; everything and everybody looked cheerful and happy except Mr. Augustus Minns.

The day was fine, but the heat was considerable; when Mr. Minns had fagged up the shady side of Fleet Street, Cheapside, and Threadneedle Street, he had become pretty warm, tolerably dusty, and it was getting late into the bargain. By the most extraordinary good fortune, however, a coach was waiting at the Flower Pot, into which Mr. Augustus Minns got, on the solemn assurance of the cad that the vehicle would start in three minutes — that being the very utmost extremity of time it was allowed to wait by Act of Parliament. A quarter of an hour elapsed, and there were no signs of moving. Minns looked at his watch for the sixth time.

"Coachman, are you going or not?" bawled Mr. Minns, with his head and half his body out of the coach window.

"Di—rectly, sir," said the coachman, with his hands in his pockets, looking as much unlike a man in a hurry as possible.

"Bill, take them cloths off." Five minutes more elapsed: at the end of which time the coachman mounted the box, from whence he looked down the street, and up the street, and hailed all the pedestrians for another five minutes.

"Coachman! if you don't go this moment, I shall get out," said Mr. Minns, rendered desperate by the lateness of the hour, and the impossibility of being in Poplar Walk at the appointed time.

"Going this minute, sir," was the reply; and, accordingly, the machine trundled on for a couple of hundred yards, and then stopped again. Minns doubled himself up in a corner of the coach, and abandoned himself to his fate, as a child, a mother, a bandbox and a parasol, became his fellow passengers.

The child was an affectionate and an amiable infant; the little dear mistook Minns for his other parent, and screamed to embrace him.

"Be quiet, dear," said the mamma, restraining the impetuosity of the darling, whose little fat legs were kicking, and stamping, and twining themselves into the most complicated forms, in an ecstasy of impatience. "Be quiet, dear, that's not your papa."

"Thank Heaven I am not!" thought Minns, as the first gleam of pleasure he had experienced that morning shone like a meteor through his wretchedness.

Playfulness was agreeably mingled with affection in the disposition of the boy. When satisfied that Mr. Minns was not his parent, he endeavored to attract his notice by scraping his drab trousers with his dirty shoes, poking his chest with his mamma's parasol, and other nameless endearments peculiar to infancy, with which he beguiled the tediousness of the ride, apparently very much to his own satisfaction.

When the unfortunate gentleman arrived at the Swan, he found to his great dismay, that it was a quarter past five. The white house, the stables, the "Beware of the Dog" — every landmark was passed, with a rapidity not unusual to a gentleman of a certain age when too late for dinner. After the lapse of a few minutes, Mr. Minns found himself opposite a yellow brick house with a green door, brass knocker, and door plate, green window-frames and ditto railings, with "a garden" in front, that is to say, a small loose bit of graveled ground, with one round and two scalene triangular beds, containing a fir tree, twenty or thirty bulbs, and an unlimited number of marigolds. The taste of Mr. and Mrs. Budden was further displayed by the appearance of a Cupid on each side of the door, perched upon a heap of large chalk flints, variegated with pink conch shells. His knock at the door was answered by a stumpy boy, in drab livery, cotton stockings and high-lows, who, after hanging his hat on one of the dozen brass pegs which ornamented the passage, denominated by courtesy "The Hall," ushered him into a front drawing-room commanding a very extensive view of the backs of the neighboring houses. The usual ceremony of introduction, and so forth, over, Mr. Minns took his seat: not a little agitated at finding that he was the last comer, and, somehow or other, the Lion of about a dozen people, sitting together in a small drawing-room, getting rid of that most tedious of all time, the time preceding dinner.

"Well, Brogson," said Budden, addressing an elderly gentleman in a black coat, drab knee-breeches, and long gaiters, who, under pretense of inspecting the prints in an Annual, had been engaged in satisfying himself on the subject of Mr. Minns's general appearance, by looking at him over the tops of the leaves — "Well, Brogson, what do Ministers mean to do? Will they go out, or what?"

"Oh — why — really, you know, I'm the last person in the world to ask for news. Your cousin, from his situation, is the most likely person to answer the question."

Mr. Minns assured the last speaker, that although he was in Somerset House, he possessed no official communication relative to the projects of his Majesty's Ministers. But his remark was evidently received incredulously; and no further conjectures being hazarded on the subject, a long pause ensued, during which the company occupied themselves in coughing and blowing their noses, until the entrance of Mrs. Budden caused a general rise.

The ceremony of introduction being over, dinner was announced, and down-stairs the party proceeded accordingly — Mr. Minns escorting Mrs. Budden as far as the drawing-room door, but being prevented, by the narrowness of the staircase, from extending his gallantry any farther. The dinner passed off as such dinners usually do. Ever and anon, amidst the clatter of knives and forks, and the hum of conversation, Mr. B.'s voice might be heard, asking a friend to take wine, and assuring him he was glad to see him; and a great deal of by-play took place between Mrs. B. and the servants, respecting the removal of the dishes, during which her countenance assumed all the variations of a weather-glass, from "stormy" to "set fair."

Upon the dessert and wine being placed on the table, the servant, in compliance with a significant look from Mrs. B., brought down "Master Alexander," habited in a sky-blue suit with silver buttons; and possessing hair of nearly the same color as the metal. After sundry praises from his mother, and various admonitions as to his behavior from his father, he was introduced to his godfather.

"Well, my little fellow — you are a fine boy, ain't you?" said Mr. Minns, as happy as a tomtit on birdlime.

"Yes."

"How old are you?"

"Eight, next We'nsday. How old are *you?*"

"Alexander," interrupted his mother, "how dare you ask Mr. Minns how old he is!"

"He asked me how old *I* was," said the precocious child, to whom Minns had from that moment internally resolved that he never would bequeath one shilling. As soon as the titter occasioned by the observation had subsided, a little smirking man with red whiskers, sitting at the bottom of the table, who during the whole of dinner had been endeavoring to obtain a listener to some stories about Sheridan, called out, with a very patronizing air, "Alick, what part of speech is *be?*"

"A verb."

"That's a good boy," said Mrs. Budden, with all a mother's pride. "Now, you know what a verb is?"

"A verb is a word which signifies to be, to do, or to suffer; as, I am — I rule — I am ruled. Give me an apple, Ma."

"I'll give you an apple," replied the man with the red whiskers, who was an established friend of the family, or in other words was always invited by Mrs. Budden, whether Mr. Budden liked it or not, "if you'll tell me what is the meaning of *be.*"

"Be?" said the prodigy, after a little hesitation — "an insect that gathers honey."

"No, dear," frowned Mrs. Budden; "B double E is the substantive."

"I don't think he knows much yet about *common* substantives," said the smirking gentleman, who thought this an admirable opportunity for letting off a joke. "It's clear he's not very well acquainted with *proper names.* He! he! he!"

"Gentlemen," called out Mr. Budden, from the end of the table, in a stentorian voice, and with a very important air, "will you have the goodness to charge your glasses? I have a toast to propose."

"Hear! hear!" cried the gentlemen, passing the decanters. After they had made the round of the table, Mr. Budden proceeded — "Gentlemen; there is an individual present — "

"Hear! hear!" said the little man with red whiskers.

"*Pray* be quiet, Jones," remonstrated Budden.

"I say, gentlemen, there is an individual present," resumed the host, "in whose society I am sure we must take great delight — and — and — the conversation of that individual must have afforded to every one present, the utmost pleasure." ["Thank Heaven, he does not mean me!" thought Minns, conscious that his diffidence and exclusiveness had prevented his saying above a dozen words since he entered the house.] "Gentlemen, I am but a humble individual myself, and I perhaps ought to apologize for allowing any individual feelings of friendship and affection for the person I allude to, to induce me to venture to rise, to propose the health of that person — a person that, I am sure — that is to say, a person whose virtues must endear him to those who know him — and those who have not the pleasure of knowing him, cannot dislike him."

"Hear! hear!" said the company, in a tone of encouragement and approval.

"Gentlemen," continued Budden, "my cousin is a man who — who is a relation of my own." (Hear! hear!) Minns groaned audibly. "Who I am most happy to see here, and who, if he were not here, would certainly have deprived us of the great pleasure we all feel in seeing him. (Loud cries of hear!) Gentlemen, I feel that I have already trespassed on your attention for too long a time. With every feeling — of — with every sentiment of — of — "

"Gratification" — suggested the friend of the family.

" — Of gratification, I beg to propose the health of Mr. Minns."

"Standing, gentlemen!" shouted the indefatigable little man with the whiskers — "and with the honors. Take your time from me, if you please. Hip! hip! hip! — Za! — Hip! hip! hip! — Za! —Hip! hip! — Za — a — a!"

All eyes were now fixed on the subject of the toast, who by gulping down port wine at the imminent hazard of suffocation, endeavored to conceal his confusion. After as long a pause as decency would admit, he rose, but, as the newspapers sometimes say in their reports, "we regret that we are quite unable to give even the substance of the honorable gentleman's observations." The words "present company — honor — present occasion," and "great happiness" — heard occasionally, and repeated at intervals, with a countenance expressive of the utmost confusion and misery, convinced the company that he was making an excellent speech; and, accordingly, on his resuming his seat, they cried "Bravo!" and manifested tumultuous applause. Jones, who had been long watching his opportunity, then darted up.

"Budden," said he, "will you allow *me* to propose a toast?"

"Certainly," replied Budden, adding in an undertone to Minns right across the table, "Devilish sharp fellow that: you'll be very much pleased with his speech. He talks equally well on any subject." Minns bowed, and Mr. Jones proceeded:

"It has on several occasions, in various instances, under many circumstances, and in different companies, fallen to my lot to propose a toast to those by whom, at the time, I have had the honor to be surrounded. I have sometimes, I will cheerfully own — for why should I deny it? — felt the overwhelming nature of the task I have undertaken, and my own utter incapability to do justice to the subject. If such have been my feelings, however, on former occasions, what must they be now — now — under the extraordinary circumstances in which I am placed. (Hear! hear!) To describe my feelings accurately, would be impossible; but I cannot give you a better idea of them, gentlemen, than by referring to a circumstance which happens, oddly enough, to occur to my mind at the moment. On one occasion, when that truly great and illustrious man, Sheridan, was — "

Now, there is no knowing what new villainy in the form of a joke would have been heaped on the grave of that very ill-used man, Mr. Sheridan, if the boy in drab had not at that moment entered the room in a breathless state, to report that, as it was a very wet night, the nine o'clock stage had come round, to know whether there was anybody going to town, as, in that case, he (the nine o'clock) had room for one inside.

Mr. Minns started up; and, despite countless exclamations of surprise and entreaties to stay, persisted in his determination to accept the vacant place. But the brown silk umbrella was nowhere to be found; and as the coachman couldn't wait, he drove back to the Swan, leaving word for Mr. Minns to "run round" and catch him. However, as it did not occur to Mr. Minns for some ten minutes or so, that he had left the brown silk umbrella with the ivory handle in the other coach, coming down; and, moreover, as he was by no means remarkable for speed, it is no matter of surprise that when he accomplished the feat of "running round" to the Swan, the coach — the last coach — had gone without him.

It was somewhere about three o'clock in the morning, when Mr. Augustus Minns knocked feebly at the street-door of his lodgings in

Tavistock Street, cold, wet, cross, and miserable. He made his will next morning, and his professional man informs us, in that strict confidence in which we inform the public, that neither the name of Mr. Octavius Budden, nor of Mrs. Amelia Budden, nor of Master Alexander Augustus Budden, appears therein.

NOBODY'S
STORY

Nobody's Story

HE LIVED on the bank of a mighty river, broad and deep, which was always silently rolling on to a vast undiscovered ocean. It had rolled on, ever since the world began. It had changed its course sometimes, and turned into new channels, leaving its old ways dry and barren; but it had ever been upon the flow, and ever was to flow until Time should be no more. Against its strong, unfathomable stream, nothing made head. No living creature, no flower, no leaf, no particle of animate or inanimate existence ever strayed back from the undiscovered ocean. The tide of the river set resistlessly towards it; and the tide never stopped, any more than the earth stops in its circling round the sun.

He lived in a busy place, and he worked very hard to live. He had no hope of ever being rich enough to live a month without hard work, but he was quite content, God knows, to labor with a cheerful will. He was one of an immense family, all of whose sons and daughters gained their daily bread by daily work, prolonged from their rising up betimes until their lying down at night. Beyond this destiny he had no prospect, and he sought none.

There was over-much drumming, trumpeting, and speech-making, in the neighborhood where he dwelt; but he had nothing to do with that. Such clash and uproar came from the Bigwig family, at the unaccountable proceedings of which race, he marveled much. They set up the strangest statues, in iron, marble, bronze, and brass, before his door; and darkened his house with the legs and tails of uncouth images of horses. He wondered what it all meant, smiled in a rough good-humored way he had, and kept at his hard work.

The Bigwig family (composed of all the stateliest people thereabouts, and all the noisiest) had undertaken to save him the trouble of thinking for himself, and to manage him and his affairs. "Why truly," said he, "I have little time upon my hands; and if you will be so good as to take care of me, in return for the money I pay over" — for the Bigwig family were not above his money — "I shall be relieved and much obliged, considering that you know best." Hence the drumming, trumpeting, and speech-making, and the ugly images of horses which he was expected to fall down and worship.

"I don't understand all this," said he, rubbing his furrowed brow confusedly. "But it *has* a meaning, maybe, if I could find it out."

"It means," returned the Bigwig family, suspecting something of what he said, "honor and glory in the highest, to the highest merit."

"Oh!" said he. And he was glad to hear that.

But, when he looked among the images in iron, marble, bronze, and brass, he failed to find a rather meritorious countryman of his, once the son of a Warwickshire wool-dealer, or any single countryman whomsoever of that kind. He could find none of the men whose knowledge had rescued him and his children from terrific and disfiguring disease, whose boldness had raised his forefathers from the condition of serfs, whose wise fancy had opened a new and high existence to the humblest, whose skill had filled the workingman's world with accumulated wonders. Whereas, he did find others whom he knew no good of, and even others whom he knew much ill of.

"Humph!" said he. "I don't quite understand it."

So, he went home, and sat down by his fireside to get it out of his mind.

Now, his fireside was a bare one, all hemmed in by blackened streets; but it was a precious place to him. The hands of his wife were hardened with toil, and she was old before her time; but she was dear to him. His children, stunted in their growth, bore traces of unwholesome nurture; but they had beauty in his sight. Above all other things, it was an earnest desire of this man's soul that his children should be taught. "If I am sometimes misled," said he, "for want of knowledge, at least let them know better, and avoid my mistakes. If it is hard to me to reap the harvest of pleasure and instruction that is stored in books, let it be easier to them."

But, the Bigwig family broke out into violent family quarrels concerning what it was lawful to teach to this man's children. Some of the family insisted on such a thing being primary and indispensable above all other things; and others of the family insisted on such another thing being primary and indispensable above all other things; and the Bigwig family, rent into factions, wrote pamphlets, held convocations, delivered charges, orations, and all varieties of discourses; impounded one another in courts Lay and courts Ecclesiastical; threw dirt, exchanged pummelings, and fell together by the ears in unintelligible animosity. Meanwhile, this man, in his short evening snatches at his fireside, saw the demon Ignorance arise there, and take his children to itself. He saw his daughter perverted into a heavy slatternly drudge; he saw his son go moping down the ways of low sensuality, to brutality and crime; he saw the dawning light of intelligence in the eyes of his babies so changing into cunning and suspicion, that he could have rather wished them idiots.

"I don't understand this any the better," said he; "but I think it cannot be right. Nay, by the clouded Heaven above me, I protest against this as my wrong!"

Becoming peaceable again (for his passion was usually short-lived, and his nature kind), he looked about him on his Sundays and holidays, and he saw how much monotony and weariness there was, and thence how drunkenness arose with all its train of ruin. Then he appealed to the Bigwig family, and said, "We are a laboring people, and I have a glimmering suspicion in me that laboring people of whatever condition were made — by a higher intelligence than yours, as I poorly understand it — to be in need of mental refreshment and recreation. See what we fall into, when we rest without it. Come! Amuse me harmlessly, show me something, give me an escape!"

But, here the Bigwig family fell into a state of uproar absolutely deafening. When some few voices were faintly heard, proposing to show him the wonders of the world, the greatness of creation, the mighty changes of time, the workings of nature and the beauties of art — to show him these things, that is to say, at any period of his life when he could look upon them — there arose among the Bigwigs such roaring and raving, such pulpiting and petitioning, such maundering and memorializing, such name-calling and dirt-throwing, such a shrill wind of parliamentary questioning and feeble replying — where "I dare not" waited on "I would" — that the poor fellow stood aghast, staring wildly around.

"Have I provoked all this," said he, with his hands to his affrighted ears, "by what was meant to be an innocent request, plainly arising out of my familiar experience, and the common knowledge of all men who choose to open their eyes? I don't understand, and I am not understood. What is to come of such a state of things?"

He was bending over his work, often asking himself the question, when the news began to spread that a pestilence had appeared among the laborers, and was slaying them by thousands. Going forth to look about him, he soon found this to be true. The dying and the dead were mingled in the close and tainted houses among which his life was passed. New poison was distilled into the always murky, always sickening air. The robust and the weak, old age and infancy, the father and the mother, all were stricken down alike.

What means of flight had he? He remained there, where he was, and saw those who were dearest to him die. A kind preacher came to him, and would have said some prayers to soften his heart in his gloom, but he replied:

"O what avails it, missionary, to come to me, a man condemned to residence in this fetid place, where every sense bestowed upon me for my delight becomes a torment, and where every minute of my numbered days is new mire added to the heap under which I lie oppressed! But, give me my first glimpse of Heaven, through a little of its light and air; give me pure water; help me to be clean; lighten this heavy atmosphere and heavy life, in which our spirits sink, and we become the indifferent and callous creatures you too often see us; gently and kindly take the bodies of those who die among us, out of the small room where we grow to be so familiar with the awful change that even ITS sanctity is lost to us; and, Teacher, then I will hear — none know better than you, how willingly — of Him whose thoughts were so much with the poor, and who had compassion for all human sorrow!"

He was at work again, solitary and sad, when his Master came and stood near to him dressed in black. He, also, had suffered heavily. His young wife, his beautiful and good young wife, was dead; so, too, his only child.

"Master, 'tis hard to bear — I know it — but be comforted. I would give you comfort, if I could."

The Master thanked him from his heart, but, said he, "O you laboring men! The calamity began among you. If you had but lived more healthily and decently, I should not be the widowed and bereft mourner that I am this day."

"Master," returned the other, shaking his head, "I have begun to understand a little that most calamities will come from us, as this one did, and that none will stop at our poor doors, until we are united with that great squabbling family yonder, to do the things that are right. We cannot live healthily and decently, unless they who undertook to manage us provide the means. We cannot be instructed unless they will teach us; we cannot be rationally amused, unless they will amuse us; we cannot but have some false gods of our own, while they set up so many of theirs in all the public places. The evil consequences of imperfect instruction, the evil consequences of pernicious neglect, the evil consequences of unnatural restraint and the denial of humanizing enjoyments, will all come from us, and none of them will stop with us. They will spread far and wide. They always do; they always have done — just like the pestilence. I understand so much, I think, at last."

But the Master said again, "O you laboring men! How seldom do we ever hear of you, except in connection with some trouble!"

"Master," he replied, "I am Nobody, and little likely to be heard of (nor yet much wanted to be heard of, perhaps), except when there *is* some trouble. But it never begins with me, and it never can end with me. As sure as Death, it comes down to me, and it goes up from me."

There was so much reason in what he said, that the Bigwig family, getting wind of it, and being horribly frightened by the late desolation, resolved to unite with him to do the things that were right — at all events, so far as the said things were associated with the direct prevention, humanly speaking, of another pestilence. But, as their fear wore off, which it soon began to do, they resumed their falling out among themselves, and did nothing. Consequently the scourge appeared again — low down as before — and spread avengingly upward as before, and carried off vast numbers of the brawlers. But not a man among them ever admitted, if in the least degree he ever perceived, that he had anything to do with it.

So Nobody lived and died in the old, old, old way; and this, in the main, is the whole of Nobody's story.

Had he no name, you ask? Perhaps it was Legion. It matters little what his name was. Let us call him Legion.

If you were ever in the Belgian villages near the field of Waterloo, you will have seen, in some quiet little church, a monument erected by faithful companions in arms to the memory of Colonel A, Major B, Captains C, D and E, Lieutenants F and G, Ensigns H, I and J, seven non-commissioned officers, and one hundred and thirty rank and file, who fell in the discharge of their duty on the memorable day. The story of Nobody is the story of the rank and file of the earth. They bear their share of the battle; they have their part in the victory; they fall; they leave no name but in the mass. The march of the proudest of us, leads to the dusty way by which they go. O! Let us think of them this year at the Christmas fire, and not forget them when it is burned out.

GOING INTO

SOCIETY

Going into Society

At ONE period of its reverses, the House fell into the occupation of a Showman. He was found registered as its occupier, on the parish books of the time when he rented the House, and there was therefore no need of any clue to his name. But, he himself was less easy to be found; for, he had led a wandering life, and settled people had lost sight of him, and people who plumed themselves on being respectable were shy of admitting that they had ever known anything of him. At last, among the marsh lands near the river's level, that lie about Deptford and the neighboring market-gardens, a Grizzled Personage in velveteen, with a face so cut up by varieties of weather that he looked as if he had been tattooed, was found smoking a pipe at the door of a wooden house on wheels. The wooden house was laid up in ordinary for the winter, near the mouth of a muddy creek; and everything near it, the foggy river, the misty marshes, and the steaming market-gardens, smoked in company with the grizzled man. In the midst of this smoking party, the funnel-chimney of the wooden house on wheels was not remiss, but took its pipe with the rest in a companionable manner.

On being asked if it were he who had once rented the House to Let, Grizzled Velveteen looked surprised, and said yes. Then his name was Magsman? That was it, Toby Magsman — which lawfully christened Robert; but called in the line, from a infant, Toby. There was nothing agin Toby Magsman, he believed? If there was suspicion of such — mention it!

There was no suspicion of such, he might rest assured. But, some inquiries were making about that House, and would he object to say why he left it?

Not at all; why should he? He left it, along of a Dwarf.

Along of a Dwarf?

Mr. Magsman repeated, deliberately and emphatically, Along of a Dwarf.

Might it be compatible with Mr. Magsman's inclination and convenience to enter, as a favor, into a few particulars?

Mr. Magsman entered into the following particulars.

It was a long time ago, to begin with; afore lotteries and a deal more was done away with. Mr. Magsman was looking about for a good pitch, and he see that house, and he says to himself, "I'll have you, if you're to be had. If money'll get you, I'll have you."

The neighbors cut up rough, and made complaints; but Mr. Magsman don't know what they *would* have had. It was a lovely thing. First of all, there was the canvas, representin the picter of the Giant, in Spanish trunks and a ruff, who was himself half the heighth of the house, and was run up with a line and pulley to a pole on the roof, so that his Ed was coeval with the parapet. Then, there was the canvas, representin the picter of the Albina lady, showing her white air to the Army and Navy in correct uniform. Then, there was the canvas, representin the picter of the Wild Indian a scalpin a member of some foreign nation. Then, there was the canvas, representin the picter of a child of a British Planter, seized by two Boa Constrictors — not that *we* never had no child, nor no Constrictors neither. Similarly, there was the canvas, representin the picter of the Wild Ass of the Prairies — not that *we* never had no wild asses, nor wouldn't have had 'em at a gift. Last, there was the canvas, representin the picter of the Dwarf, and like him too (considerin), with George the Fourth in such a state of astonishment at him as His Majesty couldn't with his utmost politeness and stoutness express. The front of the House was so covered with canvases, that there wasn't a spark of daylight ever visible on that side. "MAGSMAN'S AMUSEMENTS," fifteen foot long by two foot high, ran over the front door and parlor winders. The passage was a Arbor of green baize and gardenstuff. A barrel-organ performed there unceasing. And as to respectability — if threepence ain't respectable, what is?

But, the Dwarf is the principal article at present, and he was worth the money. He was wrote up as MAJOR TPSCHOFFKI, OF THE IMPE-

RIAL BULGRADERIAN BRIGADE. Nobody couldn't pronounce the name, and it never was intended anybody should. The public always turned it, as a regular rule, into Chopski. In the line he was called Chops; partly on that account, and partly because his real name, if he ever had any real name (which was very dubious), was Stakes.

He was a uncommon small man, he really was. Certainly not so small as he was made out to be, but where *is* your Dwarf as is? He was a most uncommon small man, with a most uncommon large Ed; and what he had inside that Ed, nobody never knowed but himself: even supposin himself to have ever took stock of it, which it would have been a stiff job for even him to do.

The kindest little man as never growed! Spirited, but not proud. When he travelled with the Spotted Baby — though he knowed himself to be a nat'ral Dwarf, and knowed the Baby's spots to be put upon him artificial, he nursed that Baby like a mother. You never heerd him give a ill-name to a Giant. He *did* allow himself to break out into strong language respectin the Fat Lady from Norfolk; but that was an affair of the 'art; and when a man's 'art has been trifled with by a lady, and the preference giv to a Indian, he ain't master of his actions.

He was always in love, of course; every human nat'ral phenomenon is. And he was always in love with a large woman; *I* never knowed the Dwarf as could be got to love a small one. Which helps to keep 'em the Curiosities they are.

One sing'ler idea he had in that Ed of his, which must have meant something, or it wouldn't have been there. It was always his opinion that he was entitled to property. He never would put his name to anything. He had been taught to write, by the young man without arms, who got his living with his toes (quite a writing-master *he* was, and taught scores in the line), but Chops would have starved to death, afore he'd have gained a bit of bread by putting his hand to a paper. This is the more curious to bear in mind, because HE had no property, nor hope of property, except his house and a sarser. When I say his house, I mean the box, painted and got up outside like a reg'lar six-roomer, that he used to creep into, with a diamond ring (or quite as good to look at) on his forefinger, and ring a little bell out of what the Public believed to be the Drawing-room winder. And when I say a sarser, I mean a Chaney sarser in which he made a collection for himself at the end of every Entertainment. His cue for that, he took from me; "Ladies and gentlemen, the little man will now walk three times round the Cairawan, and retire behind the curtain." When he said anything important, in private life, he mostly wound it up with this form of words, and they was generally the last thing he said to me at night afore he went to bed.

He had what I consider a fine mind — a poetic mind. His ideas respectin his property never come upon him so strong as when he sat upon a barrel-organ and had the handle turned. Arter the wibration had run through him a little time, he would screech out, "Toby, I feel my property coming — grind away! I'm counting my guineas by thousands, Toby — grind away! Toby, I shall be a man of fortun! I feel the Mint a jingling in me, Toby, and I'm swelling out into the Bank of England!" Such is the influence of music on a poetic mind. Not that he was partial to any other music but a barrel-organ; on the contrairy, hated it.

He had a kind of a everlasting grudge agin the Public: which is a thing you may notice in many phenomenons that get their living out of it. What riled him most in the nater of his occupation was, that it kep him out of Society. He was continiwally saying, "Toby, my ambition is, to go into Society. The curse of my position towards the public is, that it keeps me hout of Society. This don't signify to a low beast of a Indian; he an't formed for Society. This don't signify to a Spotted Baby; *he* an't formed for Society. — I am."

Nobody never could make out what Chops done with his money. He had a good salary, down on the drum every Saturday as the day came round, besides having the run of his teeth — and he was a Woodpecker to eat — but all Dwarfs are. The sarser was a little income, bringing him in so many halfpence that he'd carry 'em for a week together, tied up in a pocket-handkercher. And yet he never had money. And it couldn't be the Fat Lady from Norfolk, as was once supposed, because it stands to reason that when you have a animosity towards a Indian, which makes you grind your teeth at him to his face, and which can hardly hold you from Goosing him audible when he's going through his War-Dance — it stands to reason you wouldn't under them circumstances deprive yourself, to support that Indian in the lap of luxury.

Most unexpected, the mystery came out one day at Egham Races. The Public was shy of bein pulled in, and Chops was ringin his little bell out of his drawing-room winder, and was snarling to me over his

shoulder as he kneeled down with his legs out at the back-door —
for he couldn't be shoved into his house without kneeling down, and
the premises wouldn't accommodate his legs — was snarlin, "Here's
a precious Public for you; why the Devil don't they tumble up?"
when a man in the crowd holds up a carrier-pigeon, and cries out,
"If there's any person here as has got a ticket, the Lottery's just
drawed, and the number as has come up for the great prize is three,
seven, forty-two! Three, seven, forty-two!" I was givin the man to the
Furies myself, for calling off the Public's attention — for the Public
will turn away, at any time, to look at anything in preference to the
thing showed 'em; and if you doubt it, get 'em together for any
indiwidual purpose on the face of the earth, and send only two people in late, and see if the whole company an't far more interested in
takin particular notice of them two than of you — I say, I wasn't best
pleased with the man for callin out, and wasn't blessin him in my
own mind, when I see Chops's little bell fly out of winder at a old
lady, and he gets up and kicks his box over, exposin the whole
secret, and he catches hold of the calves of my legs and he says to
me, "Carry me into the wan, Toby, and throw a pail of water over
me or I'm a dead man, for I've come into my property!"

Twelve thousand odd hundred pound, was Chops's winnins. He
had bought a half-ticket for the twenty-five thousand prize, and it had
come up. The first use he made of his property, was to offer to fight
the Wild Indian for five hundred pound a side, him with a poisoned
darnin-needle and the Indian with a club; but the Indian being in
want of backers to that amount, it went no further.

Arter he had been mad for a week — in a state of mind, in short,
in which, if I had let him sit on the organ for only two minutes, I
believe he would have bust — but we kep the organ from him — Mr.
Chops come round, and behaved liberal and beautiful to all. He then
sent for a young man he knowed, as had a wery genteel appearance
and was a Bonnet at a gaming-booth (most respectable brought up,
father havin been imminent in the livery stable line but unfort'nate
in a commercial crisis, through paintin a old gray, ginger-bay, and
sellin him with a Pedigree), and Mr. Chops said to this Bonnet, who
said his name was Normandy, which it wasn't:

"Normandy, I'm a goin into Society. Will you go with me?"

Says Normandy: "Do I understand you, Mr. Chops, to hintimate
that the 'ole of the expenses of that move will be borne by yourself?"

"Correct," says Mr. Chops. "And you shall have a princely allowance too."

The Bonnet lifted Mr. Chops upon a chair, to shake hands with him, and replied in poetry, with his eyes seemingly full of tears:

> "My boat is on the shore,
> And my bark is on the sea,
> And I do not ask for more,
> But I'll Go: — along with thee."

They went into Society, in a chay and four grays with silk jackets. They took lodgings in Pall Mall, London, and they blazed away.

In consequence of a note that was brought to Bartlemy Fair in the autumn of next year by a servant, most wonderful got up in milk-white cords and tops, I cleaned myself and went to Pall Mall, one evening appinted. The gentlemen was at their wine arter dinner, and Mr. Chops's eyes was more fixed in that Ed of his than I thought good for him. There was three of 'em (in company, I mean), and I knowed the third well. When last met, he had on a white Roman shirt, and a bishop's mitre covered with leopard-skin, and played the clarionet all wrong, in a band at a Wild Beast Show.

This gent took on not to know me, and Mr. Chops said: "Gentlemen, this is a old friend of former days": and Normandy looked at me through a eye-glass, and said, "Magsman, glad to see you!" — which I'll take my oath he wasn't. Mr. Chops, to git him convenient to the table, had his chair on a throne (much of the form of George the Fourth's in the canvas), but he hardly appeared to me to be King there in any other pint of view, for his two gentlemen ordered about like Emperors. They was all dressed like May-Day — gorgeous! — and as to Wine, they swam in all sorts.

I made the round of the bottles, first separate (to say I had done it), and then mixed 'em all together (to say I had done it), and then tried two of 'em as half-and-half, and then t'other two. Altogether, I passed a pleasin evenin, but with a tendency to feel muddled, until I considered it good manners to get up and say, "Mr. Chops, the best of friends must part, I thank you for the wariety of foreign drains you have stood so 'ansome, I looks towards you in red wine, and I takes my leave." Mr. Chops replied, "If you'll just hitch me out of this over your right arm, Magsman, and carry me downstairs, I'll see you

AN EVENING IN PALL MALL

out." I said I couldn't think of such a thing, but he would have it, so I lifted him off his throne. He smelt strong of Maideary, and I couldn't help thinking as I carried him down that it was like carrying a large bottle full of wine, with a rayther ugly stopper, a good deal out of proportion.

When I set him on the door-mat in the hall, he kep me close to him by holding on to my coat-collar, and he whispers:

"I ain't 'appy, Magsman."

"What's on your mind, Mr. Chops?"

"They don't use me well. They ain't grateful to me. They puts me on the mantel-piece when I won't have in more Champagne-wine, and they locks me in the sideboard when I won't give up my property."

"Get rid of 'em, Mr. Chops."

"I can't. We're in Society together and what would Society say?"

"Come out of Society!" says I.

"I can't. You don't know what you're talking about. When you have once gone into Society, you mustn't come out of it."

"Then if you'll excuse the freedom, Mr. Chops," were my remark, shaking my head grave, "I think it's a pity you ever went in."

Mr. Chops shook that deep Ed of his, to a surprisin extent, and slapped it half-a-dozen times with his hand, and with more Wice than I thought were in him. Then, he says, "You're a good fellow, but you don't understand. Good night, go along. Magsman, the little man will now walk three times round the Cairawan, and retire behind the curtain." The last I see of him on that occasion was his tryin, on the extremest werge of insensibility, to climb up the stairs, one by one, with his hands and knees. They'd have been much too steep for him, if he had been sober; but he wouldn't be helped.

It warn't long after that, that I read in the newspaper of Mr. Chops's being presented at court. It was printed, "It will be recollected" — and I've noticed in my life, that it is sure to be printed that it *will* be recollected, whenever it won't — "that Mr. Chops is the individual of small stature, whose brilliant success in the last State Lottery attracted so much attention." Well, I says to myself, Such is Life! He has been and done it in earnest at last! He has astonished George the Fourth!

(On account of which, I had that canvas new-painted, him with a bag of money in his hand, a presentin it to George the Fourth, and a lady in Ostrich Feathers fallin in love with him in a bag-wig, sword, and buckles correct.)

I took the House as is the subject of present inquiries — though not the honor of bein acquainted — and I run Magsman's Amusements in it thirteen months — sometimes one thing, sometimes another, sometimes nothin particular, but always all the canvases outside. One night, when we had played the last company out, which was a shy company, through its raining Heavens hard, I was takin a pipe in the one pair back along with the young man with the toes, which I had taken on for a month (though he never drawed — except on paper), and I heard a kickin at the street door. "Halloa!" I says to the young man, "what's up?" He rubs his eyebrows with his toes, and he says, "I can't imagine, Mr. Magsman" — which he never could imagine nothin, and was monotonous company.

The noise not leavin off, I laid down my pipe, and I took up a candle, and I went down and opened the door. I looked out into the street; but nothin could I see, and nothin was I aware of, until I turned round quick, because some creetur run between my legs into the passage. There was Mr. Chops!

"Magsman," he says, "take me, on the old terms, and you've got me; if it's done, say done!"

I was all of a maze, but I said, "Done, Sir."

"Done to your done, and double done!" says he. "Have you got a bit of supper in the house?"

Bearin in mind them sparklin warieties of foreign drains as we'd guzzled away at in Pall Mall, I was ashamed to offer him cold sassages and gin-and-water; but he took 'em both and took 'em free; havin a chair for his table, and sittin down at it on a stool, like hold times. I, all of a maze all the while.

It was arter he had made a clean sweep of the sassages (beef, and to the best of my calculations two pound and a quarter), that the wisdom as was in that little man began to come out of him like perspiration.

"Magsman," he says, "look upon me! You see afore you, One as has both gone into Society and come out."

"O! You *are* out of it, Mr. Chops? How did you get out, Sir?"

"Sold out!" says he. You never saw the like of the wisdom as his Ed expressed, when he made use of them two words.

"My friend Magsman, I'll impart to you a discovery I've made.

It's wallable; it's cost twelve thousand five hundred pound; it may do you good in life. — The secret of this matter is, that it ain't so much that a person goes into Society, as that Society goes into a person."

Not exactly keepin up with his meanin, I shook my head, put on a deep look, and said, "You're right there, Mr. Chops."

"Magsman," he says, twitchin me by the leg, "Society has gone into me, to the tune of every penny of my property."

I felt that I went pale, and though nat'rally a bold speaker, I couldn't hardly say, "Where's Normandy?"

"Bolted. With the plate," said Mr. Chops.

"And t'other one?" meaning him as formerly wore the bishop's mitre.

"Bolted. With the jewels," said Mr. Chops.

I sat down and looked at him, and he stood up and looked at me.

"Magsman," he says, and he seemed to myself to get wiser as he got hoarser; "Society, taken in the lump, is all dwarfs. At the court of St. James's, they was all a doing my old business — all a goin three times round the Cairawan, in the hold court-suits and properties. Elsewheres, they was most of 'em ringin their little bells out of make-believes. Everywheres, the sarser was a goin round. Magsman, the sarser is the uniwersal Institution!"

I perceived, you understand, that he was soured by his misfortuns, and I felt for Mr. Chops.

"As to Fat Ladies," says he, giving his head a tremendious one agin the wall, "there's lots of *them* in Society, and worse than the original. *Hers* was a outrage upon Taste — simply a outrage upon Taste — awakenin contempt — carryin its own punishment in the form of a Indian!" Here he giv himself another tremendious one. "But *theirs*, Magsman, *theirs* is mercenary outrages. Lay in Cashmeer shawls, buy bracelets, strew 'em and a lot of 'andsome fans and things about your rooms, let it be known that you give away like water to all as come to admire, and the Fat Ladies that don't exhibit for so much down upon the drum, will come from all the pints of the compass to flock about you, whatever you are. They'll drill holes in your 'art, Magsman, like a Cullender. And when you've no more left to give, they'll laugh at you to your face, and leave you to have your bones picked dry by Wulturs, like the dead Wild Ass of the Prairies that you deserve to be!" Here he giv himself the most tremendious one of all, and dropped.

I thought he was gone. His Ed was so heavy, and he knocked it so hard, and he fell so stoney, and the sassagerial disturbance in him must have been so immense, that I thought he was gone. But, he soon come round with care, and he sat up on the floor, and he said to me, with wisdom comin out of his eyes, if ever it come:

"Magsman! The most material difference between the two states of existence through which your unappy friend has passed"; he reached out his poor little hand, and his tears dropped down on the moustachio which it was a credit to him to have done his best to grow, but it is not in mortals to command success — "the difference is this. When I was out of Society, I was paid light for being seen. When I went into Society, I paid heavy for being seen. I prefer the former, even if I wasn't forced upon it. Give me out through the trumpet, in the hold way, to-morrow."

Arter that, he slid into the line again as easy as if he had been iled all over. But the organ was kep from him, and no allusions was ever made, when a company was in, to his property. He got wiser every day; his views of Society and the Public was luminous, bewilderin, awful; and his Ed got bigger and bigger as his Wisdom expanded it.

He took well, and pulled 'em in most excellent for nine weeks. At the expiration of that period, when his Ed was a sight, he expressed one evenin, the last Company havin been turned out and the door shut, a wish to have a little music.

"Mr. Chops," I said (I never dropped the "Mr." with him; the world might do it, but not me); "Mr. Chops, are you sure as you are in a state of mind and body to sit upon the organ?"

His answer was this: "Toby, when next met with on the tramp, I forgive her and the Indian. And I am."

It was with fear and trembling that I began to turn the handle; but he sat like a lamb. It will be my belief to my dying day, that I see his Ed expand as he sat; you may therefore judge how great his thoughts was. He sat out all the changes, and then he come off.

"Toby," he says, with a quiet smile, "the little man will now walk three times round the Cairawan, and retire behind the curtain."

When we called him in the morning, we found him gone into a much better Society than mine or Pall Mall's. I giv Mr. Chops as comfortable a funeral as lay in my power, followed myself as Chief, and had the George the Fourth canvas carried first, in the form of a banner. But, the House was so dismal arterwards, that I giv it up, and took to the Wan again.

"I don't triumph," said Jarber, folding up the second manuscript, and looking hard at Trottle. "I don't triumph over this worthy creature. I merely ask him if he is satisfied now?"

"How can he be anything else?" I said, answering for Trottle, who sat obstinately silent. "This time, Jarber, you have not only read us a delightfully amusing story, but you have also answered the question about the House. Of course it stands empty now. Who would think of taking it after it had been turned into a caravan?" I looked at Trottle, as I said those last words, and Jarber waved his hand indulgently in the same direction.

"Let this excellent person speak," said Jarber. "You were about to say, my good man — ?"

"I only wished to ask, Sir," said Trottle doggedly, "if you could kindly oblige me with a date or two in connection with that last story?"

"A date!" repeated Jarber. "What does the man want with dates?"

"I should be glad to know, with great respect," persisted Trottle, "if the person named Magsman was the last tenant who lived in the House. It's my opinion — if I may be excused for giving it — that he most decidedly was not."

With those words, Trottle made a low bow, and quietly left the room.

There is no denying that Jarber, when we were left together, looked sadly discomposed. He had evidently forgotten to inquire about dates; and, in spite of his magnificent talk about his series of discoveries, it was quite as plain that the two stories he had just read, had really and truly exhausted his present stock. I thought myself bound, in common gratitude, to help him out of his embarrassment by a timely suggestion. So I proposed that he should come to tea again, on the next Monday evening, the thirteenth, and should make such inquiries in the meantime, as might enable him to dispose triumphantly of Trottle's objection.

He gallantly kissed my hand, made a neat little speech of acknowledgment, and took his leave. For the rest of the week I would not encourage Trottle by allowing him to refer to the House at all. I suspected he was making his own inquiries about dates, but I put no questions to him.

On Monday evening, the thirteenth, that dear unfortunate Jarber came, punctual to the appointed time. He looked so terribly harassed, that he was really quite a spectacle of feebleness and fatigue. I saw, at a glance, that the question of dates had gone against him, that Mr. Magsman had not been the last tenant of the House, and that the reason of its emptiness was still to seek.

"What I have gone through," said Jarber, "words are not eloquent enough to tell. O Sophonisba, I have begun another series of discoveries! Accept the last two as stories laid on your shrine; and wait to blame me for leaving your curiosity unappeased, until you have heard Number Three."

Number Three looked like a very short manuscript, and I said as much. Jarber explained to me that we were to have some poetry this time. In the course of his investigations he had stepped into the Circulating Library, to seek for information on the one important subject. All the Library-people knew about the House was, that a female relative of the last tenant, as they believed, had, just after that tenant left, sent a little manuscript poem to them which she described as referring to events that had actually passed in the House; and which she wanted the proprietor of the Library to publish. She had written no address on her letter; and the proprietor had kept the manuscript ready to be given back to her (the publishing of poems not being in his line) when she might call for it. She had never called for it; and the poem had been lent to Jarber, at his express request, to read to me.

Before he began, I rang the bell for Trottle; being determined to have him present at the new reading, as a wholesome check on his obstinacy. To my surprise Peggy answered the bell, and told me that Trottle had stepped out without saying where. I instantly felt the strongest possible conviction that he was at his old tricks: and that his stepping out in the evening, without leave, meant — Philandering.

Controlling myself on my visitor's account, I dismissed Peggy, stifled my indignation, and prepared, as politely as might be, to listen to Jarber.

SOMEBODY'S

LUGGAGE

IN FOUR CHAPTERS

Somebody's Luggage

I. HIS LEAVING IT TILL CALLED FOR

THE WRITER of these humble lines being a Waiter, and having come of a family of Waiters, and owning at the present time five brothers who are all Waiters, and likewise an only sister who is a Waitress, would wish to offer a few words respecting his calling; first having the pleasure of hereby in a friendly manner offering the Dedication of the same unto JOSEPH, much respected Head Waiter at the Slamjam Coffee-house, London, E.C., than which a individual more eminently deserving of the name of man, or a more amenable honor to his own head and heart, whether considered in the light of a Waiter or regarded as a human being, do not exist.

In case confusion should arise in the public mind (which it is open to confusion on many subjects) respecting what is meant or implied by the term Waiter, the present humble lines would wish to offer an explanation. It may not be generally known that the person as goes out to wait is *not* a Waiter. It may not be generally known that the hand as is called in extra, at the Freemasons' Tavern, or the London, or the Albion, or otherwise, is *not* a Waiter. Such hands may be took on for Public Dinners by the bushel (and you may know them by their breathing with difficulty when in attendance, and taking away the bottle ere yet it is half out); but such are *not* Waiters. For you cannot lay down the tailoring, or the shoemaking, or the brokering, or the green-grocering, or the pictorial-periodicalling, or the second-hand wardrobe, or the small fancy businesses — you cannot lay down those lines of life at your will and pleasure by the half-day or evening, and take up Waitering. You may suppose you can, but you cannot; or you may go so far as to say you do, but you do not. Nor yet can you lay down the gentleman's-service when stimulated by prolonged incompatibility on the part of Cooks (and here it may be remarked that Cooking and Incompatibility will be mostly found united), and take up Waitering. It has been ascertained that what a gentleman will sit meek under, at home, he will not bear out of doors, at the Slamjam or any similar establishment. Then, what is the inference to be drawn respecting true Waitering? You must be bred to it. You must be born to it.

Would you know how born to it, Fair Reader — if of the adorable female sex? Then learn from the biographical experience of one that is a Waiter in the sixty-first year of his age.

You were conveyed — ere yet your dawning powers were otherwise developed than to harbor vacancy in your inside — you were conveyed, by surreptitious means, into a pantry adjoining the Admiral Nelson, Civic and General Dining-Rooms, there to receive by stealth that healthful sustenance which is the pride and boast of the British female constitution. Your mother was married to your father (himself a distant Waiter) in the profoundest secrecy; for a Waitress known to be married would ruin the best of businesses — it is the same as on the stage. Hence your being smuggled into the pantry, and that — to add to the infliction — by an unwilling grandmother. Under the combined influence of the smells of roast and boiled, and soup, and gas, and malt liquors, you partook of your earliest nourishment; your unwilling grandmother sitting prepared to catch you when your mother was called and dropped you; your grandmother's shawl ever ready to stifle your natural complainings; your innocent mind surrounded by uncongenial cruets, dirty plates, dish-covers, and cold gravy; your mother calling down the pipe for veals and porks, instead of soothing you with nursery rhymes. Under these untoward circumstances you were early weaned. Your unwilling grandmother, ever growing more unwilling as your food assimilated less, then contracted habits of shaking you till your system curdled, and your food would not assimilate at all. At length she was no longer spared, and could have been thankfully spared much sooner. When your brothers began to appear in succession, your mother retired, left off her smart dressing (she had previously been a smart dresser), and her dark ringlets (which had previously been flowing), and haunted your father late of nights, lying in wait for him, through all weathers, up the shabby court which led to the back door of the Royal Old Dust-Bin (said to have been so named by George the Fourth), where your father was Head. But the Dust-Bin was going down then, and your father took but little — excepting from a liquid point of view. Your mother's object in those visits was of a housekeeping character, and you was set on to whistle your father out. Sometimes he came out, but generally not. Come or not come, however, all that part of his existence which was unconnected with open Waitering was kept a close secret, and was acknowledged by your mother to be a close secret, and you and your mother flitted about the court, close secrets both of you, and would scarcely have confessed under torture that you knew your father, or that your father had any name than Dick (which wasn't his name, though he was never known by any other), or that he had kith or kin or chick or child. Perhaps the attraction of this mystery, combined with your father's having a damp compartment to himself, behind a leaky cistern, at the Dust-Bin — a sort of a cellar compartment, with a sink in it, and a smell, and a plate rack, and a bottle rack, and three windows that didn't match each other or anything else, and no daylight — caused your young mind to feel convinced that you must grow up to be a Waiter too; but you did feel convinced of it, and so did all your brothers, down to your sister. Every one of you felt convinced that you was born to the Waitering. At this stage of your career, what was your feelings one day when your father came home to your mother in open broad daylight — of itself an act of Madness on the part of a Waiter — and took to his bed (leastwise, your mother and family's bed), with the statement that his eyes were devilled kidneys. Physicians being in vain, your father expired, after repeating at intervals for a day and a night, when gleams of reason and old business fitfully illuminated his being, "Two and two is five. And three is sixpence." Interred in the parochial department of the neighboring churchyard, and accompanied to the grave by as many Waiters of long standing as could spare the morning time from their soiled glasses (namely, one), your bereaved form was attired in a white neckankecher, and you was took on from motives of benevolence at The George and Gridiron, theatrical and supper. Here, supporting nature on what you found in the plates (which was as it happened, and but too often thoughtlessly, immersed in mustard), and on what you found in the glasses (which rarely went beyond driblets and lemon), by night you dropped asleep standing, till you was cuffed awake, and by day was set to polishing every individual article in the coffee-room. Your couch being sawdust; your counterpane being ashes of cigars. Here, frequently hiding a heavy heart under the smart tie of your white neckankecher (or correctly speaking lower down and more to the left), you picked up the rudiments of knowledge from an extra, by the name of Bishops, and by calling plate-washer, and gradually elevating your mind with chalk on the back of the corner-box partition, until such time as you used the inkstand when it was out of hand, attained to manhood, and to be the Waiter that you find yourself.

I could wish here to offer a few respectful words on behalf of the calling so long the calling of myself and family, and the public interest in which is but too often very limited. We are not generally understood. No, we are not. Allowance enough is not made for us. For, say that we ever show a little drooping listlessness of spirits, or what might be termed indifference or apathy. Put it to yourself what would your own state of mind be, if you was one of an enormous family every member of which except you was always greedy, and in a hurry. Put it to yourself that you was regularly replete with animal food at the slack hours of one in the day and again at nine P.M., and that the repleter you was, the more voracious all your fellow-creatures came in. Put it to yourself that it was your business, when your digestion was well on, to take a personal interest and sympathy in a hundred gentlemen fresh and fresh (say, for the sake of argument, only a hundred), whose imaginations was given up to grease and fat and gravy and melted butter, and abandoned to questioning you about cuts of this, and dishes of that — each of 'em going on as if him and you and the bill of fare was alone in the world. Then look what you are expected to know. You are never out, but they seem to think you regularly attend everywhere. "What's this, Christopher, that I hear about the smashed Excursion Train?" — "How are they doing at the Italian Opera, Christopher?" — "Christopher, what are the real particulars of this business at the Yorkshire Bank?" Similarly a ministry gives me more trouble than it gives the Queen. As to Lord Palmerston, the constant and wearing connection into which I have been brought with his lordship during the last few years is deserving of a pension. Then look at the Hypocrites we are made, and the lies (white, I hope) that are forced upon us! Why must a sedentary-pursuited Waiter be considered to be a judge of horseflesh, and to have a most tremenjous interest in horse training and racing? Yet it would be half our little incomes out of our pockets if we didn't take on to have those sporting tastes. It is the same (inconceivable why!) with Farming. Shooting, equally so. I am sure that so regular as the months of August, September, and October come round, I am ashamed of myself in my own private bosom for the way in which I make believe to care whether or not the grouse is strong on the wing (much their wings, or drumsticks either, signifies to me, uncooked!), and whether the partridges is plentiful among the turnips, and whether the pheasants is shy or bold, or anything else you please to mention. Yet you may see me, or any other Waiter of my standing, holding on by the back of the box, and leaning over a gentleman with his purse out and his bill before him, discussing these points in a confidential tone of voice, as if my happiness in life entirely depended on 'em.

I have mentioned our little incomes. Look at the most unreasonable point of all, and the point on which the greatest injustice is done us! Whether it is owing to our always carrying so much change in our right-hand trousers-pocket, and so many halfpence in our coat-tails, or whether it is human nature (which I were loth to believe), what is meant by the everlasting fable that Head Waiters is rich? How did that fable get into circulation? Who first put it about, and what are the facts to establish the unblushing statement? Come forth, thou slanderer, and refer the public to the Waiter's will in Doctors' Commons supporting thy malignant hiss! Yet this is so commonly dwelled upon — especially by the screws who give Waiters the least — that denial is vain; and we are obliged, for our credit's sake, to carry our heads as if we were going into a business, when of the two we are much more likely to go into a union. There was formerly a screw as frequented the Slamjam ere yet the present writer had quitted that establishment on a question of tea-ing his assistant staff out of his own pocket, which screw carried the taunt to its bitterest height. Never soaring above threepence, and as often as not grovelling on the earth a penny lower, he yet represented the present writer as a large holder of Consols, a lender of money on mortgage, a Capitalist. He has been overheard to dilate to other customers on the allegation that the present writer put out thousands of pounds at interest in Distilleries and Breweries. "Well, Christopher," he would say (having grovelled his lowest on the earth, half a moment before), "looking out for a House to open, eh? Can't find a business to be disposed of on a scale as is up to your resources, humph?" To such a dizzy precipice of falsehood has this misrepresentation taken wing, that the well-known and highly respected OLD CHARLES, long eminent at the West Country Hotel, and by some considered the Father of the Waitering, found himself under the obligation to fall into it through so many years that his own wife (for he had an unbeknown old lady in that capacity towards himself) believed it! And what was the consequence? When he was borne to his grave on the shoulders of six picked Waiters, with six more for change, six more acting as pall-bearers, all keeping step in a pouring shower without a dry eye visible, and a concourse only inferior to Royalty, his pantry and lodgings was equally ransacked high and low for property, and none was found! How could it be found, when, beyond his last monthly collection of walking-sticks, umbrellas, and pocket-handkerchiefs (which happened to have been not yet disposed of, though he had ever been through life punctual in clearing off his collections by the month), there was no property existing? Such, however, is the force of this universal libel, that the widow of Old Charles, at the present hour an inmate of the Almshouses of the Cork-Cutters' Company, in Blue Anchor Road (identified sitting at the door of one of 'em, in a clean cap and a Windsor arm-chair, only last Monday) expects John's hoarded wealth to be found hourly! Nay, ere yet he had succumbed to the grisly dart, and when his portrait was painted in oils life-size, by subscription of the frequenters of the West Country, to hang over the coffee-room chimneypiece, there were not wanting those who contended that what is termed the accessories of such a portrait ought to be the Bank of England out of window, and a strongbox on the table. And but for better-regulated minds contending for a bottle and screw and the attitude of drawing — and carrying their point — it would have been so handed down to posterity.

I am now brought to the title of the present remarks. Having, I hope without offense to any quarter, offered such observations as I felt it my duty to offer, in a free country which has ever dominated the seas, on the general subject, I will now proceed to wait on the particular question.

At a momentous period of my life, when I was off, so far as concerned notice given, with a House that shall be nameless — for the question on which I took my departing stand was a fixed charge for waiters, and no House as commits itself to that eminently un-English act of more than foolishness and baseness shall be advertised by me — I repeat, at a momentous crisis, when I was off with a House too mean for mention, and not yet on with that to which I have ever since had the honor of being attached in the capacity of Head,* I was casting about what to do next. Then it were that proposals were made to me on behalf of my present establishment. Stipulations were necessary on my part, emendations were necessary on my part: in the end, ratifications ensued on both sides, and I entered on a new career.

We are a bed business, and a coffee-room business. We are not a general dining business, nor do we wish it. In consequence, when diners drop in, we know what to give 'em as will keep 'em away another time. We are a Private Room or Family business also; but coffee-room principal. Me and the Directory and the Writing Materials and cetrer occupy a place to ourselves — a place fended off up a step or two at the end of the coffee-room, in what I call the good old-fashioned style. The good old-fashioned style is, that whatever you want, down to a wafer, you must be olely and solely dependent on the Head Waiter for. You must put yourself a new-born Child into his hands. There is no other way in which a business untinged with Continental Vice can be conducted. (It were bootless to add, that if languages is required to be jabbered and English is not good enough, both families and gentlemen had better go somewhere else.)

When I began to settle down in this right-principled and well-conducted House, I noticed, under the bed in No. 24 B (which it is up a angle off the staircase, and usually put off upon the lowly-minded), a heap of things in a corner. I asked our Head Chambermaid in the course of the day,

* Its name and address at length, with other full particulars, all editorially struck out.

"What are them things in 24 B?"

To which she answered with a careless air,

"Somebody's Luggage."

Regarding her with a eye not free from severity, I says,

"Whose Luggage?"

Evading my eye, she replied,

"Lor! How should *I* know!"

— Being, it may be right to mention, a female of some pertness, though acquainted with her business.

A Head Waiter must be either Head or Tail. He must be at one extremity or the other of the social scale. He cannot be at the waist of it, or anywhere else but the extremities. It is for him to decide which of the extremities.

On the eventful occasion under consideration, I give Mrs. Pratchett so distinctly to understand my decision, that I broke her spirit as towards myself, then and there, and for good. Let not inconsistency be suspected on account of my mentioning Mrs. Pratchett as "Mrs.," and having formerly remarked that a waitress must not be married. Readers are respectfully requested to notice that Mrs. Pratchett was not a waitress, but a chambermaid. Now a chambermaid *may* be married; if Head, generally is married — or says so. It comes to the same thing as expressing what is customary. (N.B. Mr. Pratchett is in Australia, and his address there is "the Bush.")

Having took Mrs. Pratchett down as many pegs as was essential to the future happiness of all parties, I requested her to explain herself.

"For instance," I says, to give her a little encouragement, "who is Somebody?"

"I give you my sacred honor, Mr. Christopher," answers Pratchett, "that I haven't the faintest notion."

But for the manner in which she settled her cap-strings, I should have doubted this; but in respect of positiveness it was hardly to be discriminated from an affidavit.

"Then you never saw him?" I followed her up with.

"Nor yet," said Mrs. Pratchett, shutting her eyes and making as if she had just took a pill of unusual circumference — which gave a remarkable force to her denial — "nor yet any servant in this house. All have been changed, Mr. Christopher, within five year, and Somebody left his Luggage here before then."

Inquiry of Miss Martin yielded (in the language of the Bard of A. 1.) "confirmation strong." So it had really and truly happened. Miss Martin is the young lady at the bar as makes out our bills; and though higher than I could wish considering her station, is perfectly well-behaved.

Farther investigations led to the disclosure that there was a bill against this Luggage to the amount of two sixteen six. The luggage had been lying under the bedstead of 24 B over six year. The bedstead is a four-poster, with a deal of old hanging and valance, and is, as I once said, probably connected with more than 24 Bs — which I remember my hearers was pleased to laugh at, at the time.

I don't know why — when DO we know why? — but this Luggage laid heavy on my mind. I fell a wondering about Somebody, and what he had got and been up to. I couldn't satisfy my thoughts why he should leave so much Luggage against so small a bill. For I had the Luggage out within a day or two and turned it over, and the following were the items: A black portmanteau, a black bag, a desk, a dressing-case, a brown-paper parcel, a hat-box, and an umbrella strapped to a walking-stick. It was all very dusty and fluey. I had our porter up to get under the bed and fetch it out; and though he habitually wallows in dust — swims in it from morning to night, and wears a close-fitting waistcoat with black calimanco sleeves for the purpose — it made him sneeze again, and his throat was that hot with it that it was obliged to be cooled with a drink of Allsopp's draft.

The Luggage so got the better of me, that instead of having it put back when it was well dusted and washed with a wet cloth — previous to which it was so covered with feathers that you might have thought it was turning into poultry, and would by and by begin to Lay — I say, instead of having it put back, I had it carried into one of my places downstairs. There from time to time I stared at it and stared at it, till it seemed to grow big and grow little, and come forward at me and retreat again, and go through all manner of performances resembling intoxication. When this had lasted weeks — I may say months, and not be far out — I one day thought of asking Miss Martin for the particulars of the Two sixteen six total. She was so obliging as to extract it from the books — it dating before her time — and here follows a true copy:

Coffee-Room.

1856.	No. 4	£	s.	d.
Feb. 2d,	Pen and Paper	0	0	6
	Port Negus	0	2	0
	Ditto	0	2	0
	Pen and Paper	0	0	6
	Tumbler broken	0	2	6
	Brandy	0	2	0
	Pen and paper	0	0	6
	Anchovy toast	0	2	6
	Pen and paper	0	0	6
	Bed	0	3	0
Feb. 3d,	Pen and paper	0	0	6
	Breakfast	0	2	6
	" Broiled ham	0	2	0
	" Eggs	0	1	0
	" Watercresses	0	1	0
	Breakfast — Shrimps	0	1	0
	Pen and paper	0	0	6
	Blotting paper	0	0	6
	Messenger to Paternoster-row and back	0	1	6
	Again, when No Answer	0	1	6
	Brandy 2s., Deviled Pork chop 2s.	0	4	0
	Pens and paper	0	1	0
	Messenger to Albemarle street and back	0	1	0
	Again (detained), when No Answer	0	1	6
	Salt-cellar broken	0	3	6
	Large Liqueur glass Orange Brandy	0	1	6
	Dinner, Soup, Fish, Joint, and bird	0	7	6
	Bottle old East India Brown	0	8	0
	Pen and paper	0	0	6
		£2	16	6

Mem.: January 1st, 1857. He went out after dinner, directing Luggage to be ready when he called for it. Never called.

So far from throwing a light upon the subject, this bill appeared to me, if I may so express my doubts, to involve it in a yet more lurid halo. Speculating it over with the Mistress, she informed me that the luggage had been advertised in the Master's time as being to be sold after such and such a day to pay expenses, but no farther steps had been taken. (I may here remark, that the Mistress is a widow in her fourth year. The Master was possessed of one of those unfortunate constitutions in which Spirits turns to Water, and rises in the ill-starred Victim.)

My speculating it over, not then only, but repeatedly, sometimes with the Mistress, sometimes with one, sometimes with another, led up to the Mistress's saying to me — whether at first in joke or in earnest, or half joke and half earnest, it matters not:

"Christopher, I am going to make you a handsome offer."

(If this should meet her eye — a lovely blue — may she not take it ill my mentioning that if I had been eight or ten year younger, I would have done as much by her! That is, I would have made her a offer. It is for others than me to denominate it a handsome one.)

"Christopher, I am going to make you a handsome offer."

"Put a name to it, ma'am."

"Look here, Christopher. Run over the articles of Somebody's Luggage. You've got it all by heart, I know."

"A black portmanteau, ma'am, a black bag, a desk, a dressing-case, a brown-paper parcel, a hat-box, and an umbrella strapped to a walking-stick."

"All just as they were left. Nothing opened, nothing tampered with."

"You are right, ma'am. All locked but the brown-paper parcel, and that sealed."

The Mistress was leaning on Miss Martin's desk at the bar-window, and she taps the open book that lays upon the desk — she has a pretty-made hand to be sure — and bobs her head over it and laughs.

"Come," says she, "Christopher. Pay me Somebody's bill, and you shall have Somebody's Luggage."

I rather took to the idea from the first moment; but,

"It mayn't be worth the money," I objected, seeming to hold back.

"That's a Lottery," says the Mistress, folding her arms upon the book — it ain't her hands alone that's pretty made, the observation extends right up her arms. "Won't you venture two pound sixteen shillings and sixpence in the Lottery? Why, there's no blanks!" says the Mistress, laughing and bobbing her head again, "you *must* win.

If you lose, you must win! All prizes in this Lottery! Draw a blank, and remember, Gentlemen-Sportsmen, you'll still be entitled to a black portmanteau, a black bag, a desk, a dressing-case, a sheet of brown paper, a hat-box, and an umbrella strapped to a walking-stick!"

To make short of it, Miss Martin come round me, and Mrs. Pratchett come round me, and the Mistress she was completely round me already, and all the women in the house come round me, and if it had been Sixteen two instead of Two sixteen, I should have thought myself well out of it. For what can you do when they do come round you?

So I paid the money — down — and such a laughing as there was among 'em! But I turned the tables on 'em regularly, when I said:

"My family-name is Blue-Beard. I'm going to open Somebody's Luggage all alone in the Secret Chamber, and not a female eye catches sight of the contents!"

Whether I thought proper to have the firmness to keep to this, don't signify, or whether any female eye, and if any, how many, was really present when the opening of the Luggage came off. Somebody's Luggage is the question at present: Nobody's eyes, nor yet noses.

What I still look at most, in connection with that Luggage, is the extraordinary quantity of writing-paper, and all written on! And not our paper neither — not the paper charged in the bill, for we know our paper — so he must have been always at it. And he had crumpled up this writing of his, everywhere, in every part and parcel of his luggage. There was writing in his dressing-case, writing in his boots, writing among his shaving-tackle, writing in his hat-box, writing folded away down among the very whalebones of his umbrella.

His clothes wasn't bad, what there was of 'em. His dressing-case was poor — not a particle of silver stopper — bottle apertures with nothing in 'em, like empty little dog kennels — and a most searching description of tooth-powder diffusing itself around, as under a deluded mistake that all the chinks in the fittings was divisions in teeth. His clothes I parted with, well enough, to a second-hand dealer not far from St. Clement's Danes, in the Strand — him as the officers in the Army mostly dispose of their uniforms to, when hard pressed with debts of honor, if I may judge from their coats and epaulets diversifying the window with their backs towards the public. The same party bought in one lot the portmanteau, the bag, the desk, the dressing-case, the hat-box, the umbrella, strap, and walking-stick. On my remarking that I should have thought those articles not quite in his line, he said: "No more ith a man'th grandmother, Mithter Chrithtopher; but if any man will bring hith grandmother here, and offer her at a fair trifle below what the'll feth with good luck when the'th thcoured and turned — I'll buy her!"

These transactions brought me home, and, indeed, more than home, for they left a goodish profit on the original investment. And now there remained the writings; and the writings I particular wish to bring under the candid attention of the reader.

I wish to do so without postponement, for this reason. This is to say, namely, viz. i.e., as follows, thus: Before I proceed to recount the mental sufferings of which I became the prey in consequence of the writings, and before following up that harrowing tale with a statement of the wonderful and impressive catastrophe, as thrilling in its nature as unlooked for in any other capacity, which crowned the ole and filled the cup of unexpectedness to overflowing, the writings themselves ought to stand forth to view. Therefore it is that they now come next. One word to introduce them, and I lay down my pen (I hope, my unassuming pen) until I take it up to trace the gloomy sequel of a mind with something on it.

He was a smeary writer, and wrote a dreadful bad hand. Utterly regardless of ink, he lavished it on every undeserving object — on his clothes, his desk, his hat, the handle of his toothbrush, his umbrella. Ink was found freely on the coffee-room carpet by No. 4 table, and two blots was on his restless couch. A reference to the document I have given entire will show that on the morning of the third of February, eighteen fifty-six, he procured his no less than fifth pen and paper. To whatever deplorable act of ungovernable composition he immolated those materials obtained from the bar, there is no doubt that the fatal deed was committed in bed, and that it left its evidences but too plainly, long afterwards, upon the pillow-case.

He had put no Heading to any of his writings. Alas! Was he likely to have a Heading without a Head, and where was *his* Head when he took such things into it? In some cases, such as his Boots, he would appear to have hid the writings; thereby involving his style in greater obscurity. But his boots was at least pairs — and no two of his writings can put in any claim to be so regarded. Here follows (not to give more specimens) what was found in —

CHAPTER II

HIS BOOTS

"Eh! well then, Monsieur Mutuel! What do I know, what can I say? I assure you that he calls himself Monsieur The Englishman."

"Pardon. But I think it is impossible," said Monsieur Mutuel — a spectacled, snuffy, stooping old gentleman in carpet shoes and a cloth cap with a peaked shade, a loose blue frock coat reaching to his heels, a large limp white shirt-frill, and cravat to correspond — that is to say, white was the natural color of his linen on Sundays, but it toned down with the week.

"It is," repeated Monsieur Mutuel, his amiable old walnut-shell countenance very walnut-shelly indeed as he smiled and blinked in the bright morning sunlight — "it is, my cherished Madame Bouclet, I think, impossible!"

"Hey!" (with a little vexed cry and a great many tosses of her head). "But it is not impossible that you are a Pig!" retorted Madame Bouclet, a compact little woman of thirty-five or so. "See then — look there — read! 'On the second floor Monsieur L'Anglais.' Is it not so?"

"It is so," said Monsieur Mutuel.

"Good. Continue your morning walk. Get out!" Madame Bouclet dismissed him with a lively snap of her fingers.

The morning walk of Monsieur Mutuel was in the brightest patch that the sun made in the Grande Place of a dull old fortified French town. The manner of his morning walk was with his hands crossed behind him; an umbrella, in figure the express image of himself, always in one hand; a snuff box in the other. Thus, with the shuffling gait of the Elephant (who really does deal with the very worst trousers-maker employed by the Zoological world, and who appeared to have recommended him to Monsieur Mutuel), the old gentleman sunned himself daily when sun was to be had — of course, at the same time sunning a red ribbon at his buttonhole; for was he not an ancient Frenchman?

Being told by one of the angelic sex to continue his morning walk and get out, Monsieur Mutuel laughed a walnut-shell laugh, pulled off his cap at arm's length with the hand that contained his snuff box, kept it off for a considerable period after he had parted from Madame Bouclet, and continued his morning walk and got out, like a man of gallantry as he was.

The documentary evidence to which Madame Bouclet had referred Monsieur Mutuel was the list of her lodgers, sweetly written forth by her own Nephew and Bookkeeper, who held the pen of an Angel, and posted up at the side of her gateway, for the information of the Police: "Au second, M. L'Anglais, Propriétaire." On the second floor, Mr. The Englishman, man of property. So it stood; nothing could be plainer.

Madame Bouclet now traced the line with her forefinger, as it were to confirm and settle herself in her parting snap at Monsieur Mutuel, and so placing her right hand on her hip with a defiant air, as if nothing should ever tempt her to unsnap that snap, strolled out into the Place to glance up at the windows of Mr. The Englishman. That worthy happening to be looking out of window at the moment, Madame Bouclet gave him a graceful salutation with her head, looked to the right and looked to the left to account to him for her being there, considered for a moment, like one who accounted to herself for somebody she had expected not being there, and re-entered her own gateway. Madame Bouclet let all her house giving on the Place in furnished flats or floors, and lived up the yard behind in company with Monsieur Bouclet her husband (great at billiards), an inherited brewing business, several fowls, two carts, a nephew, a little dog in a big kennel, a grape-vine, a counting-house, four horses, a married sister (with a share in the brewing business), the husband and two children of the married sister, a parrot, a drum (performed on by the little boy of the married sister), two billeted soldiers, a quantity of pigeons, a fife (played by the nephew in a ravishing manner), several domestics and supernumeraries, a perpetual flavor of coffee and soup, a terrific range of artificial rocks and wooden precipices at least four feet high, a small fountain, and half-a-dozen large sunflowers.

Now the Englishman, in taking his Appartement — or, as one might say on our side of the Channel, his set of chambers — had given his name, correct to the letter, LANGLEY. But as he had a British way of not opening his mouth very wide on foreign soil, except at meals, the Brewery had been able to make nothing of it but L'Anglais. So Mr. The Englishman he had become and he remained.

"Never saw such a people!" muttered Mr. The Englishman, as he now looked out of window. "Never did, in my life!"

This was true enough, for he had never before been out of his own country — a right little island, a tight little island, a bright little island, a show-fight little island, and full of merit of all sorts; but not the whole round world.

"These chaps," said Mr. The Englishman to himself, as his eye rolled over the Place, sprinkled with military here and there, "are no more like soldiers —" Nothing being sufficiently strong for the end of his sentence, he left it unended.

This again (from the point of view of his experience) was strictly correct; for though there was a great agglomeration of soldiers in the town and neighboring country, you might have held a grand Review and Field-day of them every one, and looked in vain among them all for a soldier choking behind his foolish stock, or a soldier lamed by his ill-fitting shoes, or a soldier deprived of the use of his limbs by straps and buttons, or a soldier elaborately forced to be self-helpless in all the small affairs of life. A swarm of brisk, bright, active, bustling, handy, odd, skirmishing fellows, able to turn cleverly at anything, from a siege to soup, from great guns to needles and thread, from the broadsword exercise to slicing an onion, from making war to making omelets, was all you would have found.

What a swarm! From the Great Place under the eye of Mr. The Englishman, where a few awkward squads from the last conscription were doing the goose-step — some members of those squads still as to their bodies, in the chrysalis peasant-state of Blouse, and only military butterflies as to their regimentally clothed legs — from the Great Place, away outside the fortifications, and away for miles along the dusty roads, soldiers swarmed. All day long, upon the grass-grown ramparts of the town, practicing soldiers trumpeted and bugled; all day long, down in angles of dry trenches, practicing soldiers drummed and drummed. Every forenoon, soldiers burst out of the great barracks into the sandy gymnasium-ground hard by, and flew over the wooden horse, and hung on to flying ropes, and dangled upside-down between parallel bars, and shot themselves off wooden platforms — splashes, sparks, coruscations, showers of soldiers. At every corner of the town wall, every guard-house, every gateway, every sentry-box, every drawbridge, every reedy ditch, and rushy dike, soldiers, soldiers, soldiers. And the town being pretty well all wall, guard-house, gateway, sentry-box, drawbridge, reedy ditch, and rushy dike, the town was pretty well all soldiers.

What would the sleepy old town have been without the soldiers, seeing that even with them it had so overslept itself as to have slept its echoes hoarse, its defensive bars and locks and bolts and chains all rusty, and its ditches stagnant! From the days when VAUBAN engineered it to that perplexing extent that to look at it was like being knocked on the head with it, the stranger becoming stunned and stertorous under the shock of its incomprehensibility — from the days when VAUBAN made it the express incorporation of every substantive and adjective in the art of military engineering, and not only twisted you into it and twisted you out of it, to the right, to the left, opposite, under here, over there, in the dark, in the dirt, by the gateway, archway, covered way, dry way, wet way, fosse, portcullis, drawbridge, sluice, squat tower, pierced wall, and heavy battery, but likewise took a fortifying dive under the neighboring country, and came to the surface three or four miles off, blowing out incomprehensible mounds and batteries among the quiet crops of chicory and beet-root — from those days to these the town had been asleep, and dust and rust and must had settled on its drowsy Arsenals and Magazines, and grass had grown up in its silent streets.

On market-days alone, its Great Place suddenly leaped out of bed. On market-days, some friendly enchanter struck his staff upon the stones of the Great Place, and instantly arose the liveliest booths and stalls, and sittings and standings, and a pleasant hum of chaffering and huckstering from many hundreds of tongues, and a pleasant, though peculiar, blending of colors — white caps, blue blouses, and green vegetables — and at last the Knight destined for the adventure seemed to have come in earnest, and all the Vaubanois sprang up awake. And now, by long, low-lying avenues of trees, jolting in white-hooded donkey-cart, and on donkey-back, and in tumbril and wagon, and cart and cabriolet, and afoot with barrow and burden — and along the dikes and ditches and canals, in little peak-prowed country boats — came peasant-men and women in flocks and crowds, bringing articles for sale. And here you had boots and shoes, and sweetmeats and stuffs to wear, and here (in the cool shade of the Town-hall) you had milk and cream and butter and cheese, and here you had fruits and onions and carrots, and all things needful for your soup, and here you had poultry and flowers and protesting pigs, and here new shovels, axes, spades, and bill hooks for your farming work, and here huge mounds of bread, and here your unground grain in sacks, and here your children's dolls, and here the cake-seller, announcing his wares by beat and roll of drum. And hark! fanfaronade of trumpets, and here into the Great Place, resplendent in an open carriage, with four gorgeously attired servitors up behind, playing horns, drums, and cymbals, rolled "the Daughter of a Physician" in massive golden chains and earrings, and blue-feathered hat, shaded from the admiring sun by two immense umbrellas of artificial roses, to dispense (from motives of philanthropy) that small and pleasant dose which had cured so many thousands! Toothache, earache, headache, heartache, stomachache, debility, nervousness, fits, fainting, fever, ague, all equally cured by the small and pleasant dose of the great Physician's great daughter! The process was this — she, the Daughter of a Physician, proprietress of the superb equipage you now admired with its confirmatory blasts of trumpet, drum, and cymbal, told you so: On the first day after taking the small and pleasant dose, you would feel no particular influence beyond a most harmonious sensation of indescribable and irresistible joy; on the second day you would be so astonishingly better that you would think yourself changed into somebody else; on the third day you would be entirely free from your disorder, whatever its nature and however long you had had it, and would seek out the Physician's Daughter to throw yourself at her feet, kiss the hem of her garment, and buy as many more of the small and pleasant doses as by the sale of all your few effects you could obtain; but she would be inaccessible — gone for herbs to the Pyramids of Egypt — and you would be (though cured) reduced to despair! Thus would the Physician's Daughter drive her trade (and briskly too), and thus would the buying and selling and mingling of tongues and colors continue, until the changing sunlight, leaving the Physician's Daughter in the shadow of high roofs, admonished her to jolt out westward, with a departing effect of gleam and glitter on the splendid equipage and brazen blast. And now the enchanter struck his staff upon the stones of the Great Place once more, and down went the booths, the sittings and standings, and vanished the merchandise, and with it the barrows, donkeys, donkey-carts, and tumbrils, and all other things on wheels and feet, except the slow scavengers with unwieldy carts and meager horses clearing up the rubbish, assisted by the sleek town pigeons, better plumped out than on non-market-days. While there was yet an hour or two to wane before the autumn sunset, the loiterer outside town-gate and drawbridge, and postern and double-ditch, would see the last white-hooded cart lessening in the avenue of lengthening shadows of trees, or the last country boat, paddled by the last market-woman on her way home, showing black upon the reddening, long, low, narrow dike between him and the mill; and as the paddle-parted scum and weed closed over the boat's track, he might be comfortably sure that its sluggish rest would be troubled no more until next market-day.

As it was not one of the Great Place's days for getting out of bed, when Mr. The Englishman looked down at the young soldiers practicing the goose-step there, his mind was left at liberty to take a military turn.

"These fellows are billeted everywhere about," said he; "and to see them lighting the people's fires, boiling the people's pots, minding the people's babies, rocking the people's cradles, washing the people's greens, and making themselves generally useful, in every sort of unmilitary way, is most ridiculous! Never saw such a set of fellows — never did in my life!"

All perfectly true again. Was there not Private Valentine in that very house, acting as sole housemaid, valet, cook, steward, and nurse, in the family of his captain, Monsieur le Capitaine de la Cour — cleaning the floors, making the beds, doing the marketing, dressing the captain, dressing the dinners, dressing the salads, and dressing the baby, all with equal readiness? Or, to put him aside, he being in loyal attendance on his Chief, was there not Private Hyppolite, billeted at the Perfumer's two hundred yards off, who, when not on duty, volunteered to keep shop while the fair Perfumeress stepped out to speak to a neighbor or so, and laughingly sold soap with his war sword girded on him? Was there not Emile, billeted at the Clock-maker's, perpetually turning to of an evening, with his coat off, winding up the stock? Was there not Eugène, billeted at the Tinman's, cultivating, pipe in mouth, a garden four feet square, for the Tinman, in the little court, behind the shop, and extorting the fruits of the earth from the same, on his knees, with the sweat of his brow? Not to multiply examples, was there not Baptiste, billeted on the poor Water-carrier, at that very instant sitting on the pavement in the sunlight, with his martial legs asunder, and one of the Water-carrier's spare pails between them, which (to the delight and glory of the heart of the Water-carrier coming across the Place from the fountain, yoked and burdened) he was painting bright-green outside and bright-red within? Or, to go no farther than the Barber's at the very next door, was there not Corporal Théophile —

"No," said Mr. The Englishman, glancing down at the Barber's, "he is not there at present. There's the child, though."

A mere mite of a girl stood on the steps of the Barber's shop, looking across the Place. A mere baby, one might call her, dressed in the close white linen cap which small French country children wear (like the children in Dutch pictures), and in a frock of homespun blue, that had no shape except where it was tied round her little fat throat. So that, being naturally short and round all over, she looked, behind, as if she had been cut off at her natural waist, and had had her head neatly fitted on it.

"There's the child, though."

To judge from the way in which the dimpled hand was rubbing the eyes, the eyes had been closed in a nap, and were newly opened. But they seemed to be looking so intently across the Place, that the Englishman looked in the same direction.

"O!" said he presently. "I thought as much. The Corporal's there."

The Corporal, a smart figure of a man of thirty, perhaps a thought under the middle size, but very neatly made — a sunburned Corporal with a brown peaked beard — faced about at the moment, addressing voluble words of instruction to the squad in hand. Nothing was amiss or awry about the Corporal. A lithe and nimble Corporal, quite complete, from the sparkling dark eyes under his knowing uniform cap to his sparkling white gaiters. The very image and presentment of a Corporal of his country's army, in the line of his shoulders, the line of his waist, the broadest line of his Bloomer trousers, and their narrowest line at the calf of his leg.

Mr. The Englishman looked on, and the child looked on, and the Corporal looked on (but the last-named at his men), until the drill ended a few minutes afterwards, and the military sprinkling dried up directly, and was gone. Then said Mr. The Englishman to himself, "Look here! By George!" And the Corporal, dancing towards the Barber's with his arms wide open, caught up the child, held her

CORPORAL THÉOPHILE IS OBSERVED

over his head in a flying attitude, caught her down again, kissed her, and made off with her into the Barber's house.

Now Mr. The Englishman had had a quarrel with his erring and disobedient and disowned daughter, and there was a child in that case too. Had not his daughter been a child, and had she not taken angel-flights above his head as this child had flown above the Corporal's?

"He's a" — National Participled — "fool!" said the Englishman, and shut his window.

But the windows of the house of Memory, and the windows of the house of Mercy, are not so easily closed as windows of glass and wood. They fly open unexpectedly; they rattle in the night; they must be nailed up. Mr. The Englishman had tried nailing them, but had not driven the nails quite home. So he passed but a disturbed evening and a worse night.

By nature a good-tempered man? No; very little gentleness, confounding the quality with weakness. Fierce and wrathful when crossed? Very, and stupendously unreasonable. Moody? Exceedingly so. Vindictive? Well; he *had* had scowling thoughts that he would formally curse his daughter, as he had seen it done on the stage. But remembering that the real Heaven is some paces removed from the mock one in the great chandelier of the Theater, he had given that up.

And he had come abroad to be rid of his repudiated daughter for the rest of his life. And here he was.

At bottom, it was for this reason, more than for any other, that Mr. The Englishman took it extremely ill that Corporal Théophile should be so devoted to little Bebelle, the child at the Barber's shop. In an unlucky moment he had chanced to say to himself, "Why, confound the fellow, he is not her father!" There was a sharp sting in the speech which ran into him suddenly, and put him in a worse mood. So he had National Participled the unconscious Corporal with most hearty emphasis, and had made up his mind to think no more about such a mountebank.

But it came to pass that the Corporal was not to be dismissed. If he had known the most delicate fibers of the Englishman's mind, instead of knowing nothing on earth about him, and if he had been the most obstinate Corporal in the Grand Army of France, instead of being the most obliging, he could not have planted himself with more determined immovability plump in the midst of all the English-man's thoughts. Not only so, but he seemed to be always in his view. Mr. The Englishman had but to look out of window, to look upon the Corporal with little Bebelle. He had but to go for a walk, and there was the Corporal walking with Bebelle. He had but to come home again, disgusted, and the Corporal and Bebelle were at home before him. If he looked out at his back windows early in the morning, the Corporal was in the Barber's back yard, washing and dressing and brushing Bebelle. If he took refuge at his front win-dows, the Corporal brought his breakfast out into the Place, and shared it there with Bebelle. Always Corporal and always Bebelle. Never Corporal without Bebelle. Never Bebelle without Corporal.

Mr. The Englishman was not particularly strong in the French language as a means of oral communication, though he read it very well. It is with languages as with people — when you only know them by sight, you are apt to mistake them; you must be on speaking terms before you can be said to have established an acquaintance.

For this reason, Mr. The Englishman had to gird up his loins considerably before he could bring himself to the point of exchang-ing ideas with Madame Bouclet on the subject of this Corporal and this Bebelle. But Madame Bouclet looking in apologetically one morning to remark, that, O Heaven! she was in a state of desolation because the lamp-maker had not sent home that lamp confided to him to repair, but that truly he was a lamp-maker against whom the whole world shrieked out, Mr. The Englishman seized the occa-sion. "Madame, that baby — "

"Pardon, monsieur. That lamp."

"No, no, that little girl."

"But, pardon!" said Madame Bouclet, angling for a clue, "one cannot light a little girl, or send her to be repaired?"

"The little girl — at the house of the barber."

"Ah-h-h!" cried Madame Bouclet, suddenly catching the idea with her delicate little line and rod. "Little Bebelle? Yes, yes, yes! And her friend the Corporal? Yes, yes, yes, yes! So genteel of him — is it not?"

"He is not — ?"

"Not at all; not at all! He is not one of her relations. Not at all!"

"Why, then, he — "

"Perfectly!" cried Madame Bouclet, "you are right, monsieur. It is so genteel of him. The less relation, the more genteel. As you say."

"Is she — ?"

"The child of the barber?" Madame Bouclet whisked up her skillful little line and rod again. "Not at all, not at all! She is the child of — in a word, of no one."

"The wife of the barber, then — ?"

"Indubitably. As you say. The wife of the barber receives a small stipend to take care of her. So much by the month. Eh, then! It is without doubt very little, for we are all poor here."

"You are not poor, madame."

"As to my lodgers," replied Madame Bouclet, with a smiling and a gracious bend of her head, "no. As to all things else, so-so."

"You flatter me, madame."

"Monsieur, it is you who flatter me in living here."

Certain fishy gasps on Mr. The Englishman's part, denoting that he was about to resume his subject under difficulties, Madame Bouclet observed him closely, and whisked up her delicate line and rod again with triumphant success.

"O no, monsieur, certainly not. The wife of the barber is not cruel to the poor child, but she is careless. Her health is delicate, and she sits all day, looking out at window. Consequently, when the Corporal first came, the poor little Bebelle was much neglected."

"It is a curious — " began Mr. The Englishman.

"Name? That Bebelle? Again you are right, monsieur. But it is a playful name for Gabrielle."

"And so the child is a mere fancy of the Corporal's?" said Mr. The Englishman, in a gruffly disparaging tone of voice.

"Eh, well!" returned Madame Bouclet, with a pleading shrug: "one must love something. Human nature is weak."

("Devilish weak," muttered the Englishman, in his own language.)

"And the Corporal," pursued Madame Bouclet, "being billeted at the barber's — where he will probably remain a long time, for he is attached to the General — and finding the poor unowned child in need of being loved, and finding himself in need of loving — why, there you have it all, you see!"

Mr. The Englishman accepted this interpretation of the matter with an indifferent grace, and observed to himself, in an injured manner, when he was again alone: "I shouldn't mind it so much, if these people were not such a" — National Participled — "sentimental people!"

There was a Cemetery outside the town, and it happened ill for the reputation of the Vaubanois, in this sentimental connection, that he took a walk there that same afternoon. To be sure there were some wonderful things in it (from the Englishman's point of view), and of a certainty in all Britain you would have found nothing like it. Not to mention the fanciful flourishes of hearts and crosses in wood and iron, that were planted all over the place, making it look very like a Firework-ground, where a most splendid pyrotechnic display might be expected after dark, there were so many wreaths upon the graves, embroidered, as it might be, "To my mother," "To my daughter," "To my father," "To my brother," "To my sister," "To my friend," and those many wreaths were in so many stages of elaboration and decay, from the wreath of yesterday, all fresh color and bright beads, to the wreath of last year, a poor moldering wisp of straw! There were so many little gardens and grottoes made upon graves, in so many tastes, with plants and shells and plaster figures and porcelain pitchers, and so many odds and ends! There were so many tributes of remembrance hanging up, not to be discriminated by the closest inspection from little round waiters, whereon were depicted in glowing hues either a lady or a gentleman with a white pocket-handkerchief out of all proportion, leaning, in a state of the most faultless mourning and most profound affliction, on the most architectural and gorgeous urn! There were so many surviving wives who had put their names on the tombs of their deceased husbands, with a blank for the date of their own departure from this weary world; and there were so many surviving husbands who had rendered the same homage to their deceased wives; and out of the number there must have been so many who had long ago married again! In fine, there was so much in the place that would have seemed mere frippery to a stranger, save for the consideration that the lightest paper flower that lay upon the poorest heap of earth was never touched by a rude hand, but perished there, a sacred thing!

"Nothing of the solemnity of Death here," Mr. The Englishman had been going to say, when this last consideration touched him with a mild appeal, and on the whole he walked out without saying it. "But these people are," he insisted, by way of compensation, when he was well outside the gate, "they are so" — Participled — "sentimental!"

His way back lay by the military gymnasium-ground. And there he passed the Corporal glibly instructing young soldiers how to swing themselves over rapid and deep watercourses on their way to Glory, by means of a rope, and himself deftly plunging off a platform, and flying a hundred feet or two, as an encouragement to them to begin. And there he also passed, perched on a crowning eminence (probably by the Corporal's careful hands), the small Bebelle, with her round eyes wide open, surveying the proceeding like a wondering sort of blue and white bird.

"If that child was to die," this was his reflection as he turned his back and went his way — "and it would almost serve the fellow right for making such a fool of himself — I suppose we should have *him* sticking up a wreath and a waiter in that fantastic burying ground."

Nevertheless, after another early morning or two of looking out of window, he strolled down into the Place, when the Corporal and Bebelle were walking there, and touching his hat to the Corporal (an immense achievement) wished him Good-day.

"Good-day, monsieur."

"This is a rather pretty child you have here," said Mr. The Englishman, taking her chin in his hand, and looking down into her astonished blue eyes.

"Monsieur, she is a very pretty child," returned the Corporal, with a stress on his polite correction of the phrase.

"And good?" said the Englishman.

"And very good. Poor little thing!"

"Hah!" The Englishman stooped down and patted her cheek, not without awkwardness, as if he were going too far in his conciliation. "And what is this medal round your neck, my little one?"

Bebelle having no other reply on her lips than her chubby right fist, the Corporal offered his services as interpreter.

"Monsieur demands, what is this, Bebelle?"

"It is the Holy Virgin," said Bebelle.

"And who gave it you?" asked the Englishman.

"Théophile."

"And who is Théophile?"

Bebelle broke into a laugh, laughed merrily and heartily, clapped her chubby hands, and beat her little feet on the stone pavement of the Place.

"He doesn't know Théophile! Why, he doesn't know any one! He doesn't know anything!" Then, sensible of a small solecism in her manners, Bebelle twisted her right hand in a leg of the Corporal's Bloomer trousers, and, laying her cheek against the place, kissed it.

"Monsieur Théophile, I believe?" said the Englishman to the Corporal.

"It is I, monsieur."

"Permit me." Mr. The Englishman shook him heartily by the hand and turned away. But he took it mighty ill that old Monsieur Mutuel in his patch of sunlight, upon whom he came as he turned, should pull off his cap to him with a look of pleased approval. And he muttered, in his own tongue, as he returned the salutation, "Well, walnut-shell! And what business is it of *yours?*"

Mr. The Englishman went on for many weeks passing but disturbed evenings and worse nights, and constantly experiencing that those aforesaid windows in the houses of Memory and Mercy rattled after dark, and that he had very imperfectly nailed them up. Likewise, he went on for many weeks daily improving the acquaintance of the Corporal and Bebelle. That is to say, he took Bebelle by the chin, and the Corporal by the hand, and offered Bebelle sous and the Corporal cigars, and even got the length of changing pipes with the Corporal and kissing Bebelle. But he did it all in a shamefaced way, and always took it extremely ill that Monsieur Mutuel in his patch of sunlight should note what he did. Whenever that seemed to be the case, he always growled in his own tongue, "There you are again, walnut-shell! What business is it of *yours?*"

In a word, it had become the occupation of Mr. The Englishman's life to look after the Corporal and little Bebelle, and to resent old Monsieur Mutuel's looking after *him.* An occupation only varied by a fire in the town one windy night, and much passing of water buckets from hand to hand (in which the Englishman rendered good service), and much beating of drums — when all of a sudden the Corporal disappeared.

Next, all of a sudden, Bebelle disappeared.

She had been visible a few days later than the Corporal — sadly deteriorated as to washing and brushing — but she had not spoken when addressed by Mr. The Englishman, and had looked scared and had run away. And now it would seem that she had run away for good. And there lay the Great Place under the windows, bare and barren.

In his shamefaced and constrained way, Mr. The Englishman asked no question of any one, but watched from his front windows and watched from his back windows, and lingered about the Place, and peeped in at the Barber's shop, and did all this and much more with a whistling and tune-humming pretense of not missing anything, until one afternoon when Monsieur Mutuel's patch of sunlight was in shadow, and when, according to all rule and precedent, he had no right whatever to bring his red ribbon out of doors, behold here he was, advancing with his cap already in his hand twelve paces off!

Mr. The Englishman had got as far into his usual objurgation as, "What bu—si — " when he checked himself.

"Ah, it is sad, it is sad! Hélas, it is unhappy, it is sad!" Thus old Monsieur Mutuel, shaking his grey head.

"What busin — at least, I would say, what do you mean, Monsieur Mutuel?"

"Our Corporal. Hélas, our dear Corporal!"

"What has happened to him?"

"You have not heard?"

"No."

"At the fire. But he was so brave, so ready. Ah, too brave, too ready!"

"May the Devil carry you away!" the Englishman broke in impatiently; "I beg your pardon — I mean me — I am not accustomed to speak French — go on, will you?"

"And a falling beam — "

"Good God!" exclaimed the Englishman. "It was a private soldier who was killed?"

"No. A Corporal, the same Corporal, our dear Corporal. Beloved by all his comrades. The funeral ceremony was touching — penetrating. Monsieur The Englishman, your eyes fill with tears."

"What bu—si — "

"Monsieur The Englishman, I honor those emotions. I salute you with profound respect. I will not obtrude myself upon your noble heart."

Monsieur Mutuel — a gentleman in every thread of his cloudy

linen, under whose wrinkled hand every grain in the quarter of an ounce of poor snuff in his poor little tin box became a gentleman's property — Monsieur Mutuel passed on, with his cap in his hand.

"I little thought," said the Englishman, after walking for several minutes, and more than once blowing his nose, "when I was looking round that cemetery — I'll go there!"

Straight he went there, and when he came within the gate he paused, considering whether he should ask at the lodge for some direction to the grave. But he was less than ever in a mood for asking questions, and he thought, "I shall see something on it to know it by."

In search of the Corporal's grave he went softly on, up this walk and down that, peering in, among the crosses and hearts and columns and obelisks and tombstones, for a recently disturbed spot. It troubled him now to think how many dead there were in the cemetery — he had not thought them a tenth part so numerous before — and after he had walked and sought for some time, he said to himself, as he struck down a new vista of tombs, "I might suppose that every one was dead but I."

Not every one. A live child was lying on the ground asleep. Truly he had found something on the Corporal's grave to know it by, and the something was Bebelle.

With such a loving will had the dead soldier's comrades worked at his resting place, that it was already a neat garden. On the green turf of the garden Bebelle lay sleeping, with her cheek touching it. A plain, unpainted little wooden Cross was planted in the turf, and her short arm embraced this little Cross, as it had many a time embraced the Corporal's neck. They had put a tiny flag (the flag of France) at his head, and a laurel garland.

Mr. The Englishman took off his hat, and stood for a while silent. Then, covering his head again, he bent down on one knee, and softly roused the child.

"Bebelle! My little one!"

Opening her eyes, on which the tears were still wet, Bebelle was at first frightened; but seeing who it was, she suffered him to take her in his arms, looking steadfastly at him.

"You must not lie here, my little one. You must come with me."

"No, no. I can't leave Théophile. I want the good dear Théophile."

"We will go and seek him, Bebelle. We will go and look for him in England. We will go and look for him at my daughter's, Bebelle."

"Shall we find him there?"

"We shall find the best part of him there. Come with me, poor forlorn little one. Heaven is my witness," said the Englishman, in a low voice, as, before he rose, he touched the turf above the gentle Corporal's breast, "that I thankfully accept this trust!"

It was a long way for the child to have come unaided. She was soon asleep again, with her embrace transferred to the Englishman's neck. He looked at her worn shoes, and her galled feet, and her tired face, and believed that she had come there every day.

He was leaving the grave with the slumbering Bebelle in his arms, when he stopped, looked wistfully down at it, and looked wistfully at the other graves around. "It is the innocent custom of the people," said Mr. The Englishman, with hesitation. "I think I should like to do it. No one sees."

Careful not to wake Bebelle as he went, he repaired to the lodge where such little tokens of remembrance were sold, and bought two wreaths. One, blue and white and glistening silver, "To my friend"; one of a soberer red and black and yellow, "To my friend." With these he went back to the grave, and so down on one knee again. Touching the child's lips with the brighter wreath, he guided her hand to hang it on the Cross; then hung his own wreath there. After all, the wreaths were not far out of keeping with the little garden. To my friend. To my friend.

Mr. The Englishman took it very ill when he looked round a street corner into the Great Place, carrying Bebelle in his arms, that old Mutuel should be there airing his red ribbon. He took a world of pains to dodge the worthy Mutuel, and devoted a surprising amount of time and trouble to skulking into his own lodging like a man pursued by Justice. Safely arrived there at last, he made Bebelle's toilet with as accurate a remembrance as he could bring to bear upon that work of the way in which he had often seen the poor Corporal make it, and having given her to eat and drink, laid her down on his own bed. Then he slipped out into the Barber's shop, and after a brief interview with the Barber's wife, and a brief recourse to his purse and card case, came back again with the whole of Bebelle's personal property in such a very little bundle that it was quite lost under his arm.

As it was irreconcilable with his whole course and character that he should carry Bebelle off in state, or receive any compliments or congratulations on that feat, he devoted the next day to getting his two portmanteaus out of the house by artfulness and stealth, and to comporting himself in every particular as if he were going to run away — except, indeed, that he paid his few debts in the town, and prepared a letter to leave for Madame Bouclet, enclosing a sufficient sum of money in lieu of notice. A railway train would come through at midnight, and by that train he would take away Bebelle to look for Théophile in England and at his forgiven daughter's.

At midnight, on a moonlight night, Mr. The Englishman came creeping forth like a harmless assassin, with Bebelle on his breast instead of a dagger. Quiet the Great Place, and quiet the never-stirring streets; closed the cafés; huddled together motionless their billiard balls; drowsy the guard or sentinel on duty here and there; lulled for the time, by sleep, even the insatiate appetite of the Office of Town dues.

Mr. The Englishman left the Place behind, and left the streets behind, and left the civilian-inhabited town behind, and descended down among the military works of Vauban, hemming all in. As the shadow of the first heavy arch and postern fell upon him and was left behind, as the shadow of the second heavy arch and postern fell upon him and was left behind, as his hollow tramp over the first drawbridge was succeeded by a gentler sound, as his hollow tramp over the second drawbridge was succeeded by a gentler sound, as he overcame the stagnant ditches one by one, and passed out where the flowing waters were and where the moonlight, so the dark shades and the hollow sounds and the unwholesomely locked currents of his soul were vanquished and set free. See to it, Vaubans of your own hearts, who gird them in with triple walls and ditches, and with bolt and chain and bar and lifted bridge — raze those fortifications, and lay them level with the all-absorbing dust, before the night cometh when no hand can work!

All went prosperously, and he got into an empty carriage in the train, where he could lay Bebelle on the seat over against him, as on a couch, and cover her from head to foot with his mantle. He had just drawn himself up from perfecting this arrangement, and had just leaned back in his own seat contemplating it with great satisfaction, when he became aware of a curious appearance at the open carriage window — a ghostly little tin box floating up in the moonlight, and hovering there.

He leaned forward, and put out his head. Down among the rails and wheels and ashes, Monsieur Mutuel, red ribbon and all!

"Excuse me, Monsieur The Englishman," said Monsieur Mutuel, holding up his box at arm's length, the carriage being so high and he so low; "but I shall reverence the little box forever, if your so generous hand will take a pinch from it at parting."

Mr. The Englishman reached out of the window before complying, and — without asking the old fellow what business it was of his — shook hands and said, "Adieu! God bless you!"

"And, Mr. The Englishman, God bless *you!*" cried Madame Bouclet, who was also there among the rails and wheels and ashes. "And God will bless you in the happiness of the protected child now with you. And God will bless you in your own child at home. And God will bless you in your own remembrances. And this from me!"

He had barely time to catch a bouquet from her hand, when the train was flying through the night. Round the paper that enfolded it was bravely written (doubtless by the nephew who held the pen of an Angel), "Homage to the friend of the friendless."

"Not bad people, Bebelle!" said Mr. The Englishman, softly drawing the mantle a little from her sleeping face, that he might kiss it, "though they are so — "

Too "sentimental" himself at the moment to be able to get out that word, he added nothing but a sob, and traveled for some miles, through the moonlight, with his hand before his eyes.

CHAPTER III

HIS BROWN-PAPER PARCEL

My works are well known. I am a young man in the Art line. You have seen my works many a time, though it's fifty thousand to one if you have seen me. You say you don't want to see me? You say your interest is in my works, and not in me? Don't be too sure about that. Stop a bit.

Let us have it down in black and white at the first go off, so that there may be no unpleasantness or wrangling afterwards. And this is looked over by a friend of mine, a ticket writer, that is up to literature. I am a young man in the Art line — in the Fine-Art line. You have seen my works over and over again, and you have been curious about me, and you think you have seen me. Now, as a safe rule, you never have seen me, and you never do see me, and you never will see me. I think that's plainly put — and it's what knocks me over.

If there's a blighted public character going, I am the party.

It has been remarked by a certain (or an uncertain) philosopher, that the world knows nothing of its greatest men. He might have put it plainer if he had thrown his eye in my direction. He might have put it, that while the world knows something of them that apparently go in and win, it knows nothing of them that really go in and don't win. There it is again in another form — and that's what knocks me over.

Not that it's only myself that suffers from injustice, but that I am more alive to my own injuries than to any other man's. Being, as I have mentioned, in the Fine-Art line, and not the Philanthropic line, I openly admit it. As to company in injury, I have company enough. Who are you passing every day at your Competitive Excruciations? The fortunate candidates whose heads and livers you have turned upside down for life? Not you. You are really passing the Crammers and Coaches. If your principle is right, why don't you turn out tomorrow morning with the keys of your cities on velvet cushions, your musicians playing, and your flags flying, and read addresses to the Crammers and Coaches on your bended knees, beseeching them to come out and govern you? Then, again, as to your public business of all sorts, your Financial statements and your Budgets; the Public knows much, truly, about the real doers of all that! Your Nobles and Right Honorables are first-rate men? Yes, and so is a goose a first-rate bird. But I'll tell you this about the goose; you'll find his natural flavor disappointing, without stuffing.

Perhaps I am soured by not being popular? But suppose I AM popular. Suppose my works never fail to attract. Suppose that, whether they are exhibited by natural light or by artificial, they inevitably draw the public. Then no doubt they are preserved in some Collection? No, they are not; they are not preserved in any Collection.

Copyright? No, nor yet copyright. Anyhow they must be some-where? Wrong again, for they are often nowhere.

Says you, "At all events, you are in a moody state of mind, my friend." My answer is, I have described myself as a public character with a blight upon him — which fully accounts for the curdling of the milk in *that* cocoa-nut.

Those that are acquainted with London are aware of a locality on the Surrey side of the river Thames, called the Obelisk, or, more generally, the Obstacle. Those that are not acquainted with London will also be aware of it, now that I have named it. My lodging is not far from that locality. I am a young man of that easy disposition, that I lie abed till it's absolutely necessary to get up and earn something, and then I lie abed again till I have spent it.

It was on an occasion when I had had to turn to with a view to victuals, that I found myself walking along the Waterloo Road, one evening after dark, accompanied by an acquaintance and fellow-lodger in the gas-fitting way of life. He is very good company, having worked at the theaters, and, indeed, he has a theatrical turn him-self, and wishes to be brought out in the character of Othello; but whether on account of his regular work always blacking his face and hands more or less, I cannot say.

"Tom," he says, "what a mystery hangs over you!"

"Yes, Mr. Click" — the rest of the house generally give him his name, as being first, front, carpeted all over, his own furniture, and if not mahogany, an out-and-out imitation — "yes, Mr. Click, a mystery does hang over me."

"Makes you low, you see, don't it?" says he, eyeing me sideways.

"Why, yes, Mr. Click, there are circumstances connected with it that have," I yielded to a sigh, "a lowering effect."

"Gives you a touch of the misanthrope too, don't it?" says he. "Well, I'll tell you what. If I was you, I'd shake it off."

"If I was you, I would, Mr. Click; but, if you was me, you wouldn't."

"Ah!" says he, "there's something in that."

When we had walked a little further, he took it up again by touching me on the chest. "You see, Tom, it seems to me as if, in the words of the poet who wrote the domestic drama of The Stranger, you had a silent sorrow there."

"I have, Mr. Click."

"I hope, Tom," lowering his voice in a friendly way, "it isn't coining, or smashing?"

"No, Mr. Click. Don't be uneasy."

"Nor yet forg — " Mr. Click checked himself, and added, "counterfeiting anything, for instance?"

"No, Mr. Click. I am lawfully in the Art line — Fine-Art line — but I can say no more."

"Ah! Under a species of star? A kind of malignant spell? A sort of a gloomy destiny? A cankerworm pegging away at your vitals in secret, as well as I make it out?" said Mr. Click, eyeing me with some admiration.

I told Mr. Click that was about it, if we came to particulars; and I thought he appeared rather proud of me.

Our conversation had brought us to a crowd of people, the greater part struggling for a front place from which to see something on the pavement, which proved to be various designs executed in colored chalks on the pavement stones, lighted by two candles stuck in mud sconces. The subjects consisted of a fine fresh salmon's head and shoulders, supposed to have been recently sent home from the fishmonger's; a moonlight night at sea (in a circle); dead game; scrollwork; the head of a hoary hermit engaged in devout contemplation; the head of a pointer smoking a pipe; and a cherubim, his flesh creased as in infancy, going on a horizontal errand against the wind. All these subjects appeared to me to be exquisitely done.

On his knees on one side of this gallery, a shabby person of modest appearance who shivered dreadfully (though it wasn't at all cold), was engaged in blowing the chalk-dust off the moon, toning the outline of the back of the hermit's head with a bit of leather, and fattening the down-stroke of a letter or two in the writing. I have forgotten to mention that writing formed a part of the composition, and that it also — as it appeared to me — was exquisitely done. It ran as follows, in fine round characters: "An honest man is the noblest work of God. 1 2 3 4 5 6 7 8 9 o. £ s. d. Employment in an office is humbly requested. Honor the Queen. Hunger is a o 9 8 7 6 5 4 3 2 1 sharp thorn. Chip chop, cherry chop, fol de rol de ri do. Astronomy and mathematics. I do this to support my family."

Murmurs of admiration at the exceeding beauty of this performance went about among the crowd. The artist, having finished his touching (and having spoiled those places), took his seat on the pavement, with his knees crouched up very nigh his chin; and halfpence began to rattle in.

"A pity to see a man of that talent brought so low; ain't it?" said one of the crowd to me.

"What he might have done in the coach-painting, or house decorating!" said another man, who took up the first speaker because I did not.

"Why, he writes — alone — like the Lord Chancellor!" said another man.

"Better," said another. "I know *his* writing. *He* couldn't support his family this way."

Then, a woman noticed the natural fluffiness of the hermit's hair, and another woman, her friend, mentioned of the salmon's gills that you could almost see him gasp. Then, an elderly country gentleman stepped forward and asked the modest man how he executed his work? And the modest man took some scraps of brown paper with colors in 'em out of his pockets, and showed them. Then a fair-complexioned donkey, with sandy hair and spectacles, asked if the hermit was a portrait? To which the modest man, casting a sorrowful glance upon it, replied that it was, to a certain extent, a recollection of his father. This caused a boy to yelp out, "Is the Pinter a smoking the pipe your mother?" who was immediately shoved out of view by a sympathetic carpenter with his basket of tools at his back.

At every fresh question or remark the crowd leaned forward more eagerly, and dropped the halfpence more freely, and the modest man gathered them up more meekly. At last, another elderly gentleman came to the front, and gave the artist his card, to come to his office to-morrow, and get some copying to do. The card was accompanied by sixpence, and the artist was profoundly grateful, and, before he put the card in his hat, read it several times by the light of his candles to fix the address well in his mind, in case he should lose it. The crowd was deeply interested by this last incident, and a man in the second row with a gruff voice growled to the artist, "You've got a chance in life now, ain't you?" The artist answered (sniffing in a very low-spirited way, however), "I'm thankful to hope so." Upon which there was a general chorus of "*You* are all right," and the halfpence slackened very decidedly.

I felt myself pulled away by the arm, and Mr. Click and I stood alone at the corner of the next crossing.

"Why, Tom," said Mr. Click, "what a horrid expression of face you've got!"

"Have I?" says I.

"Have you?" says Mr. Click. "Why, you looked as if you would have his blood?"

"Whose blood?"

"The artist's."

"The artist's?" I repeated. And I laughed, frantically, wildly, gloomily, incoherently, disagreeably. I am sensible that I did. I know I did.

Mr. Click stared at me in a scared sort of a way, but said nothing until we had walked a street's length. He then stopped short, and said, with excitement on the part of his forefinger:

"Thomas, I find it necessary to be plain with you. I don't like the envious man. I have identified the cankerworm that's pegging away at *your* vitals, and it's envy, Thomas."

"Is it?" says I.

"Yes, it is," says he. "Thomas, beware of envy. It is the green-eyed monster which never did and never will improve each shining hour, but quite the reverse. I dread the envious man, Thomas. I confess that I am afraid of the envious man, when he is so envious as you are. Whilst you contemplated the works of a gifted rival, and whilst you heard that rival's praises, and especially whilst you met his humble glance as he put that card away, your countenance was so malevolent as to be terrific. Thomas, I have heard of the envy of them that follows the Fine-Art line, but I never believed it could be what yours is. I wish you well, but I take my leave of you. And if you should ever get into trouble through knifeing — or say, garotting — a brother artist, as I believe you will, don't call me to character, Thomas, or I shall be forced to injure your case."

Mr. Click parted from me with those words, and we broke off our acquaintance.

I became enamored. Her name was Henrietta. Contending with my easy disposition, I frequently got up to go after her. She also dwelt in the neighborhood of the Obstacle, and I did fondly hope that no other would interpose in the way of our union.

To say that Henrietta was volatile is but to say that she was woman. To say that she was in the bonnet-trimming is feebly to express the taste which reigned predominant in her own.

THE PICCADILLY ARTIST AT WORK

She consented to walk with me. Let me do her the justice to say that she did so upon trial. "I am not," said Henrietta, "as yet prepared to regard you, Thomas, in any other light than as a friend; but as a friend I am willing to walk with you, on the understanding that softer sentiments may flow."

We walked.

Under the influence of Henrietta's beguilements, I now got out of bed daily. I pursued my calling with an industry before unknown, and it cannot fail to have been observed at that period, by those most familiar with the streets of London, that there was a larger supply. But hold! The time is not yet come!

One evening in October I was walking with Henrietta, enjoying the cool breezes wafted over Vauxhall Bridge. After several slow turns, Henrietta gaped frequently (so inseparable from woman is the love of excitement), and said, "Let's go home by Grosvenor Place, Piccadilly, and Waterloo" — localities, I may state for the information of the stranger and the foreigner, well known in London, and the last a Bridge.

"No. Not by Piccadilly, Henrietta," said I.

"And why not Piccadilly, for goodness' sake?" said Henrietta.

Could I tell her? Could I confess to the gloomy presentiment that overshadowed me? Could I make myself intelligible to her? No.

"I don't like Piccadilly, Henrietta."

"But I do," said she. "It's dark now, and the long rows of lamps in Piccadilly after dark are beautiful. I *will* go to Piccadilly!"

Of course we went. It was a pleasant night, and there were numbers of people in the streets. It was a brisk night, but not too cold, and not damp. Let me darkly observe, it was the best of all nights — FOR THE PURPOSE.

As we passed the garden wall of the Royal Palace, going up Grosvenor Place, Henrietta murmured, "I wish I was a Queen!"

"Why so, Henrietta?"

"I would make *you* Something," said she, and crossed her two hands on my arm, and turned away her head.

Judging from this that the softer sentiments alluded to above had begun to flow, I adapted my conduct to that belief. Thus happily we passed on into the detested thoroughfare of Piccadilly. On the right of that thoroughfare is a row of trees, the railing of the Green Park, and a fine broad eligible piece of pavement.

"Oh my!" cried Henrietta presently. "There's been an accident!"

I looked to the left, and said, "Where, Henrietta?"

"Not there, stupid!" said she. "Over by the Park railings. Where the crowd is. Oh no, it's not an accident, it's something else to look at! What's them lights?"

She referred to two lights twinkling low amongst the legs of the assemblage: two candles on the pavement.

"Oh, do come along!" cried Henrietta, skipping across the road with me. I hung back, but in vain. "Do let's look!"

Again, designs upon the pavement. Center compartment, Mount Vesuvius going it (in a circle), supported by four oval compartments, severally representing a ship in heavy weather, a shoulder of mutton attended by two cucumbers, a golden harvest with distant cottage of proprietor, and a knife and fork after nature; above the center compartment a bunch of grapes, and over the whole a rainbow. The whole, as it appeared to me, exquisitely done.

The person in attendance on these works of art was in all respects, shabbiness excepted, unlike the former personage. His whole appearance and manner denoted briskness. Though threadbare, he expressed to the crowd that poverty had not subdued his spirit, or tinged with any sense of shame this honest effort to turn his talents to some account. The writing which formed part of his composition was conceived in a similarly cheerful tone. It breathed the following sentiments: "The writer is poor, but not despondent. To a British 1 2 3 4 5 6 7 8 9 0 Public he £ s. d. appeals. Honor to our brave Army! And also 0 9 8 7 6 5 4 3 2 1 to our gallant Navy. BRITONS STRIKE the A B C D E F G writer in common chalks would be grateful for any suitable employment HOME! HURRAH!" The whole of this writing appeared to me to be exquisitely done.

But this man, in one respect like the last, though seemingly hard at it with a great show of brown paper and rubbers, was only really fattening the down-stroke of a letter here and there, or blowing the loose chalk off the rainbow, or toning the outside edge of the shoulder of mutton. Though he did this with the greatest confidence, he did it (as it struck me) in so ignorant a manner, and so spoiled everything he touched, that when he began upon the purple smoke from the chimney of the distant cottage of the proprietor of the golden harvest (which smoke was beautifully soft), I found myself saying aloud, without considering of it:

"Let that alone, will you?"

"Halloa!" said the man next me in the crowd, jerking me roughly from him with his elbow, "why didn't you send a telegram? If we had known you was coming, we'd have provided something better for you. You understand the man's work better than he does himself, don't you? Have you made your will? You're too clever to live long."

"Don't be hard upon the gentleman, Sir," said the person in attendance on the works of art, with a twinkle in his eye as he looked at me; "he may chance to be an artist himself. If so, Sir, he will have a fellow-feeling with me, Sir, when I" — he adapted his action to his words as he went on, and gave a smart slap of his hands between each touch, working himself all the time about and about the composition — "when I lighten the bloom of my grapes — shade off the orange in my rainbow — dot the i of my Britons — throw a yellow light into my cow-cum-*ber* — insinuate another morsel of fat into my shoulder of mutton — dart another zigzag flash of lightning at my ship in distress!"

He seemed to do this so neatly, and was so nimble about it, that the halfpence came flying in.

"Thanks, generous public, thanks!" said the professor. "You will stimulate me to further exertions! My name will be found in the list of British Painters yet. I shall do better than this, with encouragement. I shall indeed."

"You never can do better than that bunch of grapes," said Henrietta. "Oh, Thomas, them grapes!"

"Not better than *that*, lady? I hope for the time when I shall paint anything but your own bright eyes and lips equal to life."

"(Thomas, did you ever?) But it must take a long time, Sir," said Henrietta, blushing, "to paint equal to that."

"I was prenticed to it, Miss," said the young man, smartly touching up the composition — "prenticed to it in the caves of Spain and Portingale, ever so long and two year over."

There was a laugh from the crowd; and a new man who had worked himself in next me, said, "He's a smart chap, too; ain't he?"

"And what a eye!" exclaimed Henrietta softly.

"Ah! He need have a eye," said the man.

"Ah! He just need," was murmured among the crowd.

"He couldn't come that 'ere burning mountain without a eye," said the man. He had got himself accepted as an authority, somehow, and everybody looked at his finger as it pointed out Vesuvius. "To come that effect in a general illumination would require a eye; but to come it with two dips — why, it's enough to blind him!"

That impostor, pretending not to have heard what was said, now winked to any extent with both eyes at once, as if the strain upon his sight was too much, and threw back his long hair — it was very long — as if to cool his fevered brow. I was watching him doing it, when Henrietta suddenly whispered, "Oh, Thomas, how horrid you look!" and pulled me out by the arm.

Remembering Mr. Click's words, I was confused when I retorted, "What do you mean by horrid?"

"Oh gracious! Why, you looked," said Henrietta, "as if you would have his blood."

I was going to answer, "So I would, for twopence — from his nose," when I checked myself and remained silent.

We returned home in silence. Every step of the way, the softer sentiments that had flowed, ebbed twenty mile an hour. Adapting my conduct to the ebbing, as I had done to the flowing, I let my arm drop limp, so as she could scarcely keep hold of it, and I wished her such a cold good night at parting, that I keep within the bounds of truth when I characterize it as a Rasper.

In the course of the next day I received the following document:

"Henrietta informs Thomas that my eyes are open to you. I must ever wish you well, but walking and us is separated by an unfarmable abyss. One so malignant to superiority — Oh that look at him! — can never never conduct

"HENRIETTA

"P.S. — To the altar."

Yielding to the easiness of my disposition, I went to bed for a week, after receiving this letter. During the whole of such time, London was bereft of the usual fruits of my labor. When I resumed it, I found that Henrietta was married to the artist of Piccadilly.

Did I say to the artist? What fell words were those, expressive of what a galling hollowness, of what a bitter mockery! I — I — I — am the artist. I was the real artist of Piccadilly, I was the real artist of the Waterloo Road, I am the only artist of all those pavement-subjects which daily and nightly arouse your admiration. I do 'em, and

I let 'em out. The man you behold with the papers of chalks and the rubbers, touching up the down-strokes of the writing and shading off the salmon, the man you give the credit to, the man you give the money to, hires — yes! and I live to tell it! — hires those works of art of me, and brings nothing to 'em but the candles.

Such is genius in a commercial country. I am not up to the shivering, I am not up to the liveliness, I am not up to the wanting-employment-in-an-office move; I am only up to originating and executing the work. In consequence of which you never see me; you think you see me when you see somebody else, and that somebody else is a mere Commercial character. The one seen by self and Mr. Click in the Waterloo Road can only write a single word, and that I taught him, and it's MULTIPLICATION — which you may see him execute upside down, because he can't do it the natural way. The one seen by self and Henrietta by the Green Park railings can just smear into existence the two ends of a rainbow, with his cuff and a rubber — if very hard put upon making a show — but he could no more come the arch of the rainbow, to save his life, than he could come the moonlight, fish, volcano, shipwreck, mutton, hermit, or any of my most celebrated effects.

To conclude as I began: if there's a blighted public character going, I am the party. And often as you have seen, do see, and will see, my Works, it's fifty thousand to one if you'll ever see me, unless, when the candles are burned down and the Commercial character is gone, you should happen to notice a neglected young man perseveringly rubbing out the last traces of the pictures, so that nobody can renew the same. That's me.

CHAPTER IV

HIS WONDERFUL END

It will have been, ere now, perceived that I sold the foregoing writings. From the fact of their being printed in these pages, the inference will, ere now, have been drawn by the reader (may I add, the gentle reader?) that I sold them to One who never yet — *

Having parted with the writings on most satisfactory terms — for,

* The remainder of this complimentary sentence editorially struck out.

in opening negotiations with the present Journal, was I not placing myself in the hands of One of whom it may be said, in the words of Another,* — I resumed my usual functions. But I too soon discovered that peace of mind had fled from a brow which, up to that time, Time had merely took the hair off, leaving an unruffled expanse within.

It were superfluous to veil it — the brow to which I allude is my own.

Yes, over that brow uneasiness gathered like the sable wing of the fabled bird, as — as no doubt will be easily identified by all right-minded individuals. If not, I am unable, on the spur of the moment, to enter into particulars of him. The reflection that the writings must now inevitably get into print, and that He might yet live and meet with them, sat like the Hag of Night upon my jaded form. The elasticity of my spirits departed. Fruitless was the Bottle, whether Wine or Medicine. I had recourse to both, and the effect of both upon my system was witheringly lowering.

In this state of depression, into which I subsided when I first began to revolve what could I ever say if He — the unknown — was to appear in the Coffee-room and demand reparation, I one forenoon in this last November received a turn that appeared to be given me by the finger of Fate and Conscience, hand in hand. I was alone in the Coffee-room, and had just poked the fire into a blaze, and was standing with my back to it, trying whether heat would penetrate with soothing influence to the Voice within, when a young man in a cap, of an intelligent countenance, though requiring his hair cut, stood before me.

"Mr. Christopher, the Head Waiter?"

"The same."

The young man shook his hair out of his vision — which it impeded — took a packet from his breast, and handing it over to me, said, with his eye (or did I dream?) fixed with a lambent meaning on me, "The Proofs."

Although I smelled my coat-tails singeing at the fire, I had not the power to withdraw them. The young man put the packet in my faltering grasp, and repeated — let me do him the justice to add, with civility:

"The Proofs. A. Y. R."

---

* The remainder of this complimentary sentence editorially struck out.

With those words he departed.

A. Y. R.? And You Remember. Was that his meaning? At Your Risk. Were the letters short for *that* reminder? Anticipate Your Retribution. Did they stand for *that* warning? Out-dacious Youth Repent? But no; for that, a O was happily wanting, and the vowel here was a A.

I opened the packet, and found that its contents were the foregoing writings printed just as the reader (may I add the discerning reader?) peruses them. In vain was the reassuring whisper — A. Y. R., All the Year Round — it could not cancel the Proofs. Too appropriate name. The Proofs of my having sold the Writings.

My wretchedness daily increased. I had not thought of the risk I ran, and the defying publicity I put my head into, until all was done, and all was in print. Give up the money to be off the bargain and prevent the publication, I could not. My family was down in the world, Christmas was coming on, a brother in the hospital and a sister in he rheumatics could not be entirely neglected. And it was not only ins in the family that had told on the resources of one unaided Waitering; outs were not wanting. A brother out of a situation, and another brother out of money to meet an acceptance, and another brother out of his mind, and another brother out at New York (not the same, though it might appear so), had really and truly brought me to a stand till I could turn myself round. I got worse and worse in my meditations, constantly reflecting "The Proofs," and reflecting that when Christmas drew nearer, and the Proofs were published, there could be no safety from hour to hour but that He might confront me in the Coffee-room, and in the face of day and his country demand his rights.

The impressive and unlooked-for catastrophe towards which I dimly pointed the reader (shall I add, the highly intellectual reader?) in my first remarks now rapidly approaches.

It was November still, but the last echoes of the Guy Foxes had long ceased to reverberate. We was slack — several joints under our average mark, and wine, of course, proportionate. So slack had we become at last, that Beds Nos. 26, 27, 28, and 31, having took their six o'clock dinners, and dozed over their respective pints, had drove away in their respective Hansoms for their respective Night Mail-trains and left us empty.

I had took the evening paper to No. 6 table — which is warm and most to be preferred — and, lost in the all-absorbing topics of the day, had dropped into a slumber. I was recalled to consciousness by the well-known intimation, "Waiter!" and replying, "Sir!" found a gentleman standing at No. 4 table. The reader (shall I add, the observant reader?) will please to notice the locality of the gentleman, — *at No. 4 table.*

He had one of the new-fangled uncollapsible bags in his hand (which I am against, for I don't see why you shouldn't collapse, while you are about it, as your fathers collapsed before you), and he said:

"I want to dine, waiter. I shall sleep here to-night."

"Very good, Sir. What will you take for dinner, Sir?"

"Soup, bit of codfish, oyster sauce, and the joint."

"Thank you, Sir."

I rang the chambermaid's bell; and Mrs. Pratchett marched in, according to custom, demurely carrying a lighted flat candle before her, as if she was one of a long public procession, all the other members of which was invisible.

In the meanwhile the gentleman had gone up to the mantelpiece, right in front of the fire, and had laid his forehead against the mantelpiece (which it is a low one, and brought him into the attitude of leap-frog), and had heaved a tremenjous sigh. His hair was long and lightish; and when he laid his forehead against the mantelpiece, his hair all fell in a dusty fluff together over his eyes; and when he now turned round and lifted up his head again, it all fell in a dusty fluff together over his ears. This give him a wild appearance, similar to a blasted heath.

"O! The chambermaid. Ah!" He was turning something in his mind. "To be sure. Yes. I won't go upstairs now, if you will take my bag. It will be enough for the present to know my number. — Can you give me 24 B?"

(O Conscience, what a Adder art thou!)

Mrs. Pratchett allotted him the room, and took his bag to it. He then went back before the fire, and fell a biting his nails.

"Waiter!" biting between the words, "give me," bite, "pen and paper; and in five minutes," bite, "let me have, if you please," bite, "a," bite, "Messenger."

Unmindful of his waning soup, he wrote and sent off six notes before he touched his dinner. Three were City; three West-End. The

City letters were to Cornhill, Ludgate-hill, and Farringdon-street. The West-End letters were to Great Marlborough-street, New Burington-street, and Piccadilly. Everybody was systematically denied at every one of the six places, and there was not a vestige of any answer. Our light porter whispered to me, when he came back with that report, "All Booksellers."

But before then he had cleared off his dinner, and his bottle of wine. He now — mark the concurrence with the document formerly given in full! — knocked a plate of biscuits off the table with his agitated elber (but without breakage), and demanded boiling brandy-and-water.

Now fully convinced that it was Himself, I perspired with the utmost freedom. When he become flushed with the heated stimulant referred to, he again demanded pen and paper, and passed the succeeding two hours in producing a manuscript which he put in the fire when completed. He then went up to bed, attended by Mrs. Pratchett. Mrs. Pratchett (who was aware of my emotions) told me, on coming down, that she had noticed his eye rolling into every corner of the passages and staircase, as if in search of his Luggage, and that, looking back as she shut the door of 24 B, she perceived him with his coat already thrown off immersing himself bodily under the bedstead, like a chimley-sweep before the application of machinery.

The next day — I forbear the horrors of that night — was a very foggy day in our part of London, insomuch that it was necessary to light the Coffee-room gas. We was still alone, and no feverish words of mine can do justice to the fitfulness of his appearance as he sat at No. 4 table, increased by there being something wrong with the meter.

Having again ordered his dinner, he went out, and was out for the best part of two hours. Inquiring on his return whether any of the answers had arrived, and receiving an unqualified negative, his instant call was for Mulligatawny, the Cayenne Pepper, and Orange Brandy.

Feeling that the mortal struggle was now at hand, I also felt that I must be equal to him, and with that view resolved that whatever he took I would take. Behind my partition, but keeping my eye on him over the curtain, I therefore operated on Mulligatawny, Cayenne Pepper, and Orange Brandy. And at a later period of the day, when he again said, "Orange Brandy," I said so too, in a lower tone, to George, my Second Lieutenant (my First was absent on leave), who acts between me and the bar.

Throughout that awful day he walked about the Coffee-room continually. Often he came close up to my partition, and then his eye rolled within, too evidently in search of any signs of his Luggage. Half-past six came, and I laid his cloth. He ordered a bottle of Old Brown. I likewise ordered a bottle of Old Brown. He drank his. I drank mine (as nearly as my duties would permit) glass for glass against his. He topped with coffee and a small glass. I topped with coffee and a small glass. He dozed. I dozed. At last, "Waiter!" — and he ordered his bill. The moment was now at hand when we two must be locked in the deadly grapple.

Swift as the arrow from the bow, I had formed my resolution; in other words, I had hammered it out between nine and nine. It was, that I would be the first to open up the subject with a full acknowledgment, and would offer any gradual settlement within my power. He paid his bill (doing what was right by attendance) with his eye rolling about him to the last for any tokens of his Luggage. One only time our gaze then met, with the lustrous fixedness (I believe I am correct in imputing that character to it?) of the well-known Basilisk. The decisive moment had arrived.

With a tolerable steady hand, though with humility, I laid The Proofs before him.

"Gracious Heavens!" he cries out, leaping up, and catching hold of his hair. "What's this? Print!"

"Sir," I replied, in a calming voice, and bending forward, "I humbly acknowledge to being the unfortunate cause of it. But I hope, Sir, that when you have heard the circumstances explained, and the innocence of my intentions — "

To my amazement, I was stopped short by his catching me in both his arms, and pressing me to his breast-bone; where I must confess to my face (and particular, nose) having undergone some temporary vexation from his wearing his coat buttoned high up, and his buttons being uncommon hard.

"Ha, ha, ha!" he cries, releasing me with a wild laugh, and grasping my hand. "What is your name, my Benefactor?"

"My name, Sir" (I was crumpled, and puzzled to make him out), "is Christopher; and I hope, Sir, that, as such, when you've heard my ex — "

"In print!" he exclaims again, dashing the proofs over and over as if he was bathing in them. "In print!! O Christopher! Philanthropist! Nothing can recompense you — but what sum of money would be acceptable to you?"

I had drawn a step back from him, or I should have suffered from his buttons again.

"Sir, I assure you, I have been already well paid, and — "

"No, no, Christopher! Don't talk like that! What sum of money would be acceptable to you, Christopher? Would you find twenty pounds acceptable, Christopher?"

However great my surprise, I naturally found words to say, "Sir, I am not aware that the man was ever yet born without more than the average amount of water on the brain as would *not* find twenty pounds acceptable. But — extremely obliged to you, Sir, I'm sure"; for he had tumbled it out of his purse and crammed it in my hand in two bank-notes; "but I could wish to know, Sir, if not intruding, how I have merited this liberality?"

"Know then, my Christopher," he says, "that from boyhood's hour I have unremittingly and unavailingly endeavored to get into print. Know, Christopher, that all the Booksellers alive — and several dead — have refused to put me into print. Know, Christopher, that I have written unprinted Reams. But they shall be read to you, my friend and brother. You sometimes have a holiday?"

Seeing the great danger I was in, I had the presence of mind to answer, "Never!" To make it more final, I added, "Never! Not from the cradle to the grave."

"Well," says he, thinking no more about that, and chuckling at his proofs again. "But I am in print! The first flight of ambition emanating from my father's lowly cot is realized at length! The golden bow" — he was getting on — "struck by the magic hand, has emitted a complete and perfect sound! When did this happen, my Christopher?"

"Which happen, Sir?"

"This," he held it out at arm's length to admire it — "this Perrint."

When I had given him my detailed account of it, he grasped me by the hand again, and said:

"Dear Christopher, it should be gratifying to you to know that you are an instrument in the hands of Destiny. Because you *are*."

A passing Something of a melancholy cast put it into my head to shake it, and to say, "Perhaps we all are."

"I don't mean that," he answered; "I don't take that wide range; I confine myself to the special case. Observe me well, my Christopher! Hopeless of getting rid, through any effort of my own, of any of the manuscripts among my Luggage — all of which, send them where I would, were always coming back to me — it is now some seven years since I left that Luggage here, on the desperate chance, either that the too, too faithful manuscripts would come back to me no more, or that some one less accursed than I might give them to the world. You follow me, my Christopher?"

"Pretty well, Sir." I followed him so far as to judge that he had a weak head, and that the Orange, the Boiling, and Old Brown combined was beginning to tell. (The Old Brown, being heady, is best adapted to seasoned cases.)

"Years elapsed, and those compositions slumbered in dust. At length, Destiny, choosing her agent from all mankind, sent You here, Christopher, and lo! the Casket was burst asunder, and the Giant was free!"

He made hay of his hair after he said this, and he stood a-tiptoe.

"But," he reminded himself in a state of excitement, "we must sit up all night, my Christopher. I must correct these Proofs for the press. Fill all the inkstands, and bring me several new pens."

He smeared himself and he smeared the Proofs, the night through, to that degree that when Sol gave him warning to depart (in a four-wheeler), few could have said which was them, and which was him, and which was blots. His last instructions was, that I should instantly run and take his corrections to the office of the present Journal. I did so. They most likely will not appear in print, for I noticed a message being brought round from Beauford Printing House, while I was a throwing this concluding statement on paper, that the ole resources of that establishment was unable to make out what they meant. Upon which a certain gentleman in company, as I will not more particularly name — but of whom it will be sufficient to remark, standing on the broad basis of a wave-girt isle, that whether we regard him in the light of — * laughed, and put the corrections in the fire.

* The remainder of this complimentary parenthesis editorially struck out.

MRS.

LIRRIPER'S

LODGINGS

IN TWO CHAPTERS

Mrs. Lirriper's Lodgings

I. HOW MRS. LIRRIPER CARRIED ON THE BUSINESS

W<small>HOEVER</small> would begin to be worried with letting Lodgings that wasn't a lone woman with a living to get is a thing inconceivable to me, my dear; excuse the familiarity, but it comes natural to me in my own little room, when wishing to open my mind to those that I can trust, and I should be truly thankful if they were all mankind, but such is not so, for have but a Furnished bill in the window and your watch on the mantelpiece, and farewell to it if you turn your back for but a second, however gentlemanly the manners; nor is being of your own sex any safeguard, as I have reason, in the form of sugar-tongs to know, for that lady (and a fine woman she was) got me to run for a glass of water, on the plea of going to be confined, which certainly turned out true, but it was in the Station-house.

Number Eighty-one Norfolk Street, Strand — situated midway between the City and St. James's, and within five minutes' walk of the principal places of public amusement — is my address. I have rented this house many years, as the parish rate-books will testify; and I could wish my landlord was as alive to the fact as I am myself; but no, bless you, not a half a pound of paint to save his life, nor so much, my dear, as a tile upon the roof, though on your bended knees.

My dear, you never have found Number Eighty-One Norfolk Street, Strand, advertised in Bradshaw's *Railway Guide,* and with the blessing of Heaven you never will or shall so find it. Some there are who do not think it lowering themselves to make their names that cheap, and even going the lengths of a portrait of the house not like it with a blot in every window and a coach and four at the door, but what will suit Wozenham's lower down on the other side of the way will not suit me, Miss Wozenham having her opinions and me having mine, though when it comes to systematic underbidding capable of being proved on oath in a court of justice and taking the form of "If Mrs. Lirriper names eighteen shillings a week, I name fifteen and six," it then comes to a settlement between yourself and your conscience, supposing for the sake of argument your name to be Wozenham, which I am well aware it is not or my opinion of you would be greatly lowered, and as to airy bedrooms and a night-porter in constant attendance the less said the better, the bedrooms being stuffy and the porter stuff.

It is forty years ago since me and my poor Lirriper got married at St. Clement's Danes, where I now have a sitting in a very pleasant pew with genteel company and my own hassock, and being partial to evening service not too crowded. My poor Lirriper was a handsome figure of a man, with a beaming eye and a voice as mellow as a musical instrument made of honey and steel, but he had ever been a free liver being in the commercial travelling line and travelling what he called a limekiln road — "a dry road, Emma my dear," my poor Lirriper says to me, "where I have to lay the dust with one drink or another all day long and half the night, and it wears me, Emma" — and this led to his running through a good deal and might have run through the turnpike too when that dreadful horse that never would stand still for a single instant set off, but for its being night and the gate shut, and consequently took his wheel, my poor Lirriper and the gig smashed to atoms and never spoke afterwards. He was a handsome figure of a man, and a man with a jovial heart and a sweet temper; but if they had come up then they never could have given you the mellowness of his voice, and indeed I consider photographs wanting in mellowness as a general rule and making you look like a new-ploughed field.

My poor Lirriper being behindhand with the world and being buried at Hatfield church in Hertfordshire, not that it was his native place but that he had a liking for the Salisbury Arms where we went upon our wedding-day and passed as happy a fortnight as ever happy was, I went round to the creditors and I says "Gentlemen I am acquainted with the fact that I am not answerable for my late husband's debts but I wish to pay them for I am his lawful wife and his good name is dear to me. I am going into the Lodgings gentlemen as a business and if I prosper every farthing that my late husband owed shall be paid for the sake of the love I bore him, by this right hand." It took a long time to do but it was done, and the silver cream-jug which is between ourselves and the bed and the mattress in my room upstairs (or it would have found legs so sure as ever the Furnished bill was up) being presented by the gentlemen engraved "To Mrs. Lirriper a mark of grateful respect for her honorable conduct" gave me a turn which was too much for my feelings, till Mr. Betley which at that time had the parlors and loved his joke says "Cheer up Mrs. Lirriper, you should feel as if it was only your christening and they were your godfathers and godmothers which did promise for you." And it brought me round, and I don't mind confessing to you my dear that I then put a sandwich and a drop of sherry in a little basket and went down to Hatfield churchyard outside the coach and kissed my hand and laid it with a kind of proud and swelling love on my husband's grave, though bless you it had taken me so long to clear his name that my wedding-ring was worn quite fine and smooth when I laid it on the green waving grass.

I am an old woman now and my good looks are gone but that's me my dear over the plate-warmer and considered like in the times when you used to pay two guineas on ivory and took your chance pretty much how you came out, which made you very careful how you left it about afterwards because people were turned so red and uncomfortable by mostly guessing it was somebody else quite different, and there was once a certain person that had put his money in a hop business that came in one morning to pay his rent and his respects being the second floor that would have taken it down from its hook and put it in his breast-pocket — you understand my dear — for the L, he says of the original — only there was no mellowness in *his* voice and I wouldn't let him, but his opinion of it you may gather from his saying to it "Speak to me Emma!" which was far from a rational observation no doubt but still a tribute to its being a likeness, and I think myself it *was* like me when I was young and wore that sort of stays.

But it was about the Lodgings that I was intending to hold forth and certainly I ought to know something of the business having been in it so long, for it was early in the second year of my married life that I lost my poor Lirriper and I set up at Islington directly afterwards and afterwards came here, being two houses and eight-and-thirty years and some losses and a deal of experience.

Girls are your first trial after fixtures and they try you even worse than what I call the Wandering Christians, though why *they* should roam the earth looking for bills and then coming in and viewing the apartments and stickling about terms and never at all wanting them or dreaming of taking them being already provided, is a mystery I should be thankful to have explained if by any miracle it could be. It's wonderful they live so long and thrive so on it but I suppose the exercise makes it healthy, knocking so much and going from house to house and up and down stairs all day, and then their pretending to be so particular and punctual is a most astonishing thing, looking at their watches and saying "Could you give me the refusal of the rooms till twenty minutes past eleven the day after to-morrow in the forenoon, and supposing it to be considered essential by my friend from the country could there be a small iron bedstead put in the little room upon the stairs?" Why when I was new to it my dear I used to consider before I promised and to make my mind anxious with calculations and to get quite wearied out with disappointments, but now I says "Certainly by all means" well knowing it's a Wandering Christian and I shall hear no more about it, indeed by this time I know most of the Wandering Christians by sight as well as they know me, it being the habit of each individual revolving round London in that capacity to come back about twice a year, and it's very remarkable that it runs in families and the children grow up to it, but even were it otherwise I should no sooner hear of the friend from the country which is a certain sign than I should nod and say to myself You're a Wandering Christian, though whether they are (as I *have* heard) persons of small property with a taste for regular employment and frequent change of scene I cannot undertake to tell you.

Girls as I was beginning to remark are one of your first and your lasting troubles, being like your teeth which begin with convulsions and never cease tormenting you from the time you cut them till they cut you, and then you don't want to part with them which seems hard but we must all succumb or buy artificial, and even where you get a will nine times out of ten you'll get a dirty face with it and naturally lodgers do not like good society to be shown in with a smear of black across the nose or a smudgy eyebrow. Where they pick the black up is a mystery I cannot solve, as in the case of the willing-est girl that ever came into a house half-starved poor thing, a girl so willing that I called her Willing Sophy down upon her knees scrub-bing early and late and ever cheerful but always smiling with a black face. And I says to Sophy, "Now Sophy my good girl have a regular day for your stoves and keep the width of the Airy between yourself and the blacking and do not brush your hair with the bottoms of the saucepans and do not meddle with the snuffs of the candles and it stands to reason that it can no longer be" yet there it was and always on her nose, which turning up and being broad at the end seemed to boast of it and caused warning from a steady gentleman and excellent lodger with breakfast by the week but a little irritable and use of a sitting-room when required, his words being "Mrs. Lirriper I have arrived at the point of admitting that the Black is a man and a brother, but only in a natural form and when it can't be got off." Well consequently I put poor Sophy on to other work and forbid her answering the door or answering a bell on any account but she was so unfortunately willing that nothing would stop her flying up the kitchen-stairs whenever a bell was heard to tingle. I put it to her "O Sophy Sophy for goodness' goodness' sake where does it come from?" To which that poor unlucky willing mortal bursting out crying to see me so vexed replied "I took a deal of black into me ma'am when I was a small child being much neglected and I think it must be, that it works out," so it continuing to work out of that poor thing and not having another fault to find with her I says "Sophy what do you seriously think of my helping you away to New South Wales where it might not be noticed?" Nor did I ever repent the money which was well spent, for she married the ship's cook on the voyage (himself a Mulotter) and did well and lived happy, and so far as ever I heard it was *not* noticed in a new state of society to her dying day.

In what way Miss Wozenham lower down on the other side of the way reconciled it to her feelings as a lady (which she is not) to entice Mary Anne Perkinsop from my service is best known to herself, I do not know and I do not wish to know how opinions are formed at Wozenham's on any point. But Mary Anne Perkinsop although I behaved handsomely to her and she behaved unhandsomely to me was worth her weight in gold as overawing lodgers without driving them away, for lodgers would be far more sparing of their bells with

Mary Anne than I ever knew them to be with Maid or Mistress, which is a great triumph especially when accompanied with a cast in the eye and a bag of bones, but it was the steadiness of her way with them through her father's having failed in Pork. It was Mary Anne's looking so respectable in her person and being so strict in her spirits that conquered the tea-and-sugarest gentleman (for he weighed them both in a pair of scales every morning) that I have ever had to deal with and no lamb grew meeker, still it afterwards came round to me that Miss Wozenham happening to pass and seeing Mary Anne take in the milk of a milkman that made free in a rosy-faced way (I think no worse of him) with every girl in the street but was quite frozen up like the statue at Charing-cross by her, saw Mary Anne's value in the lodging business and went as high as one pound per quarter more, consequently Mary Anne with not a word betwixt us says "If *you* will provide yourself Mrs. Lirriper in a month from this day *I* have already done the same," which hurt me and I said so, and she then hurt me more by insinuating that her father having failed in Pork had laid her open to it.

My dear I do assure you it's a harassing thing to know what kind of girls to give the preference to, for if they are lively they get bell'd off their legs and if they are sluggish you suffer from it yourself in complaints and if they are sparkling-eyed they get made love to, and if they are smart in their persons they try on your Lodgers' bonnets and if they are musical I defy you to keep them away from bands and organs, and allowing for any difference you like in their heads their heads will be always out of window just the same. And then what the gentlemen like in girls the ladies don't, which is fruitful hot water for all parties, and then there's temper though such a temper as Caroline Maxey's I hope not often. A good-looking black-eyed girl was Caroline and a comely-made girl to your cost when she did break out and laid about her, as took place first and last through a new-married couple come to see London in the first floor and the lady very high and it *was* supposed not liking the good looks of Caroline having none of her own to spare, but anyhow she did try Caroline though that was no excuse. So one afternoon Caroline comes down into the kitchen flushed and flashing, and she says to me "Mrs. Lirriper that woman in the first has aggravated me past bearing," I says "Caroline keep your temper," Caroline says with a curdling laugh "Keep my temper? You're right Mrs. Lirriper, so I will. Capital D her!" bursts out Caroline (you might have struck me into the center of the earth with a feather when she said it) "I'll give her a touch of the temper that *I* keep!" Caroline downs with her hair my dear, screeches and rushes upstairs, I following as fast as my trembling legs could bear me, but before I got into the room the dinner-cloth and pink-and-white service all dragged off upon the floor with a crash and the new-married couple on their backs in the firegrate, him with the shovel and tongs and a dish of cucumber across him and a mercy it was summertime. "Caroline" I says "be calm," but she catches off my cap and tears it in her teeth as she passes me, then pounces on the new-married lady makes her a bundle of ribbons takes her by the two ears and knocks the back of her head upon the carpet Murder screaming all the time Policemen running down the street and Wozenham's windows (judge of my feelings when I came to know it) thrown up and Miss Wozenham calling out from the balcony with crocodile's tears "It's Mrs. Lirriper been overcharging somebody to madness — she'll be murdered — I always thought so — Pleeseman save her!" My dear four of them and Caroline behind the chiffoniere attacking with the poker and when disarmed prize-fighting with her double fists, and down and up and up and down and dreadful! But I couldn't bear to see the poor young creature roughly handled and her hair torn when they got the better of her, and I says "Gentlemen Policemen pray remember that her sex is the sex of your mothers and sisters and your sweethearts, and God bless them and you!" And there she was sitting down on the ground handcuffed, taking breath against the skirting-board and them cool with their coats in strips, and all she says was "Mrs. Lirriper I'm sorry as ever I touched *you,* for you're a kind motherly old thing," and it made me think that I had often wished I had been a mother indeed and how would my heart have felt if I had been the mother of that girl! Well you know it turned out at the Police-office that she had done it before, and she had her clothes away and was sent to prison, and when she was to come out I trotted off to the gate in the evening with just a morse of jelly in that little basket of mine to give her a mite of strength to face the world again, and there I met with a very decent mother waiting for her son through bad company and a stubborn one he was with his half-boots not laced. So out came Caroline and I says "Caroline come along with me and sit down under the wall where it's retired and eat a little trifle that I have brought with me to do you good," and she throws her arms round my neck and says sobbing "O why were you never a mother when there are such mothers as there are?" she says, and in half a minute more she begins to laugh and says "Did I really tear your cap to shreds?" and when I told her "You certainly did so Caroline" she laughed again and said while she patted my face "Then why do you wear such queer old caps you dear old thing? If you hadn't worn such queer old caps I don't think I should have done it even then." Fancy the girl! Nothing could get out of her what she was going to do except O she would do well enough, and we parted she being very thankful and kissing my hands, and I nevermore saw or heard of that girl, except that I shall always believe that a very genteel cap which was brought anonymous to me one Saturday night in an oilskin basket by a most impertinent young sparrow of a monkey whistling with dirty shoes on the clean steps and playing the harp on the Airy railings with a hoop-stick came from Caroline.

What you lay yourself open to my dear in the way of being the object of uncharitable suspicions when you go into the Lodging business I have not the words to tell you, but never was I so dishonorable as to have two keys nor would I willingly think it even of Miss Wozenham lower down on the other side of the way sincerely hoping that it may not be, though doubtless at the same time money cannot come from nowhere and it is not reason to suppose that Bradshaws put it in for love be it blotty as it may. It *is* a hardship hurting to the feelings that Lodgers open their minds so wide to the idea that you are trying to get the better of them and shut their minds so close to the idea that they are trying to get the better of you, but as Major Jackman says to me "I know the ways of this circular world Mrs. Lirriper, and that's one of 'em all round it" and many is the little ruffle in my mind that the Major has smoothed, for he is a clever man who has seen much. Dear dear, thirteen years have passed though it seems but yesterday since I was sitting with my glasses on at the open front parlor-window one evening in August (the parlors being then vacant) reading yesterday's paper my eyes for print being poor though still I am thankful to say a long sight at a distance, when I hear a gentleman come posting across the road and up the street in a dreadful rage talking to himself in a fury and d'ing and c'ing somebody. "By George!" says he out loud and clutching his walking-stick, "I'll go to Mrs. Lirriper's. Which is Mrs. Lirriper's?" Then looking round and seeing me he flourishes his hat right off his head as if I had been the queen and he says, "Excuse the intrusion madam, but pray madam can you tell me at what number in this street there resides a well-known and much-respected lady by the name of Lirriper?" A little flustered though I must say gratified I took off my glasses and courtesied and said "Sir, Mrs. Lirriper is your humble servant." "Astonishing!" says he. "A million pardons! Madam, may I ask you to have the kindness to direct one of your domestics to open the door to a gentleman in search of apartments, by the name of Jackman?" I had never heard the name but a politer gentleman I never hope to see, for says he "Madam I am shocked at your opening the door yourself to no worthier a fellow than Jemmy Jackman. After you madam. I never precede a lady." Then he comes into the parlors and he sniffs, and he says "Hah! These are parlors! Not musty cupboards" he says "but parlors, and no smell of coal-sacks." Now my dear it having been remarked by some inimical to the whole neighborhood that it always smells of coal-sacks which might prove a drawback to Lodgers if encouraged, I says to the Major gently though firmly that I think he is referring to Arundel or Surrey or Howard but not Norfolk. "Madam" says he "I refer to Wozenham's lower down over the way — madam you can form no notion what Wozenham's is — madam it is a vast coal-sack, and Miss Wozenham has the principles and manners of a female heaver — madam from the manner in which I have heard her mention you I know she has no appreciation of a lady, and from the manner in which she has conducted herself towards me I know she has no appreciation of a gentleman — madam my name is Jackman — should you require any other reference than what I have already said, I name the Bank of England — perhaps you know it!" Such was the beginning of the Major's occupying the parlors and from that hour to this the same and a most obliging Lodger and punctual in all respects except one irregular which I need not particularly specify, but made up for by his being a protection and at all times ready to fill in the papers of the Assessed Taxes and Juries and that, and once collared a young man with the drawing-room clock under his coat, and once on the parapets with his own hands and blankets put out the kitchen, chimney and afterwards attending the summons made a most eloquent speech against the Parish before the magistrates and saved the engine, and ever quite the gentleman though passionate. And certainly Miss Wozenham's detaining the

trunks and umbrella was not in a liberal spirit though it may have
been according to her rights in law or an act *I* would myself have
stooped to, the Major being so much the gentleman that though he
is far from tall he seems almost so when he has his shirt-frill out and
his frock-coat on and his hat with the curly brims, and in what service he was I cannot truly tell you my dear whether Militia or Foreign,
for I never heard him even name himself as Major but always simple
"Jemmy Jackman" and once soon after he came when I felt it my
duty to let him know that Miss Wozenham had put it about that he
was no Major and I took the liberty of adding "which you are Sir" his
words were "Madam at any rate I am not a Minor, and sufficient for
the day is the evil thereof" which cannot be denied to be the sacred
truth, nor yet his military ways of having his boots with only the dirt
brushed off taken to him in the front parlor every morning on a
clean plate and varnishing them himself with a little sponge and
a saucer and a whistle in a whisper so sure as ever his breakfast
is ended, and so neat his ways that it never soils his linen which is
scrupulous though more in quality than quantity, neither that nor
his mustachios which to the best of my belief are done at the same
time and which are as black and shining as his boots, his head of hair
being a lovely white.

It was the third year nearly up of the Major's being in the parlors
that early one morning in the month of February when Parliament
was coming on and you may therefore suppose a number of impostors
were about ready to take hold of anything they could get, a gentleman and a lady from the country came in to view the Second, and I
well remember that I had been looking out of window and had
watched them and the heavy sleet driving down the street together
looking for bills. I did not quite take to the face of the gentleman
though he was good-looking too but the lady was a very pretty young
thing and delicate, and it seemed too rough for her to be out at all
though she had only come from the Adelphi Hotel which would not
have been much above a quarter of a mile if the weather had been
less severe. Now it did so happen my dear that I had been forced to
put five shillings weekly additional on the Second in consequence of
a loss from running away full dressed as if going out to a dinner-
party, which was very artful and had made me rather suspicious taking it along with Parliament, so when the gentleman proposed three
months certain and the money in advance and leave them reserved to

renew on the same terms for six months more, I says I was not quite certain but that I might have engaged myself to another party but would step downstairs and look into it if they would take a seat. They took a seat and I went down to the handle of the Major's door that I had already began to consult finding it a great blessing, and I knew by his whistling in a whisper that he was varnishing his boots which was generally considered private, however he kindly calls out "If it's you, madam, come in," and I went in and told him.

"Well, madam," says the Major rubbing his nose — as I did fear at the moment with the black sponge but it was only his knuckle, he being always neat and dexterous with his fingers — "well, madam, I suppose you would be glad of the money?"

I was delicate of saying "Yes" too out, for a little extra color rose into the Major's cheeks and there was irregularity which I will not particularly specify in a quarter which I will not name.

"I am of opinion, madam," says the Major "that when money is ready for you — when it is ready for you, Mrs. Lirriper — you ought to take it. What is there against it, madam, in this case upstairs?"

"I really cannot say there is anything against it, Sir, still I thought I would consult you."

"You said a newly married couple, I think, madam?" says the Major.

I says "Ye-es. Evidently. And indeed the young lady mentioned to me in a casual way that she had not been married many months."

The Major rubbed his nose again and stirred the varnish round and round in its little saucer with his piece of sponge and took to his whistling in a whisper for a few moments. Then he says "You would call it a Good Let, madam?"

"O certainly a Good Let Sir."

"Say they renew for the additional six months. Would it put you about very much madam if — if the worst was to come to the worst?" said the Major.

"Well I hardly know," I says to the Major. "It depends upon circumstances. Would *you* object Sir for instance?"

"I?" says the Major. "Object? Jemmy Jackman? Mrs. Lirriper close with the proposal."

So I went upstairs and accepted, and they came in next day which was Saturday and the Major was so good as to draw up a Memorandum of an agreement in a beautiful round hand and expressions that sounded to me equally legal and military, and Mr. Edson signed it on the Monday morning and the Major called upon Mr. Edson on the Tuesday and Mr. Edson called upon the Major on the Wednesday and the Second and the parlors were as friendly as could be wished.

The three months paid for had run out and we had got without any fresh overtures as to payment into May my dear, when there came an obligation upon Mr. Edson to go a business expedition right across the Isle of Man, which fell quite unexpected upon that pretty little thing and is not a place that according to my views is particularly in the way to anywhere at any time but that may be a matter of opinion. So short a notice was it that he was to go next day, and dreadfully she cried poor pretty, and I am sure I cried too when I saw her on the cold pavement in the sharp east wind — it being a very backward spring that year — taking a last leave of him with her pretty hair blowing this way and that and her arms clinging round his neck and him saying "There there there. Now let me go Peggy." And by that time it was plain that what the Major had been so accommodating as to say he would not object to happening in the house, would happen in it, and I told her as much when he was gone while I comforted her with my arm up the staircase, for I says "You will soon have others to keep up for my pretty and you must think of that."

His letter never came when it ought to have come and what she went through morning after morning when the postman brought none for her the very postman himself compassionated when she ran down to the door, and yet we cannot wonder at its being calculated to blunt the feelings to have all the trouble of other people's letters and none of the pleasure and doing it oftener in the mud and mizzle than not and at a rate of wages more resembling Little Britain than Great. But at last one morning when she was too poorly to come running downstairs he says to me with a pleased look in his face that made me next to love the man in his uniform coat though he was dripping wet "I have taken you first in the street this morning Mrs. Lirriper, for here's the one for Mrs. Edson." I went up to her bedroom with it as fast as ever I could go, and she sat up in bed when she saw it and kissed it and tore it open and then a blank stare came upon her. "It's very short!" she says lifting her large eyes to my face. "O Mrs. Lirriper it's very short!" I says "My dear Mrs. Edson no doubt that's because your husband hadn't time to write more just at that time." "No doubt, no doubt," says she, and puts her two hands on her face and turns round in her bed.

I shut her softly in and I crept downstairs and I tapped at the Major's door, and when the Major having his thin slices of bacon in his own Dutch oven saw me he came out of his chair and put me down on the sofa. "Hush!" says he, "I see something's the matter. Don't speak — take time." I says "O Major I'm afraid there's cruel work upstairs." "Yes yes," says he "I had begun to be afraid of it — take time." And then in opposition to his own words he rages out frightfully, and says "I shall never forgive myself madam, that I, Jemmy Jackman, didn't see it all that morning — didn't go straight upstairs when my boot-sponge was in my hand — didn't force it down his throat — and choke him dead with it on the spot!"

The Major and me agreed when we came to ourselves that just at present we could do no more than take on to suspect nothing and use our best endeavors to keep that poor young creature quiet, and what I ever should have done without the Major when it got about among the organ-men that quiet was our object is unknown, for he made lion and tiger war upon them to that degree that without see-ing it I could not have believed it was in any gentleman to have such a power of bursting out with fire-irons walking-sticks water-jugs coals potatoes off his table the very hat off his head, and at the same time so furious in foreign languages that they would stand with their candles half-turned fixed like the Sleeping Ugly — for I cannot say Beauty.

Ever to see the postman come near the house now gave me such a fear that it was a reprieve when he went by, but in about another ten days or a fortnight he says again, "Here's one for Mrs. Edson. — Is she pretty well?" "She is pretty well postman, but not well enough to rise so early as she used" which was so far gospel-truth.

I carried the letter in to the Major at his breakfast and I says tot-ering "Major I have not the courage to take it up to her."

"It's an ill-looking villain of a letter," says the Major.

"I have not the courage Major" I says again in a tremble "to take it up to her."

After seeming lost in consideration for some moments the Major says, raising his head as if something new and useful had occurred to his mind "Mrs. Lirriper, I shall never forgive myself that I,

Jemmy Jackman, didn't go straight upstairs that morning when my boot-sponge was in my hand — and force it down his throat — and choke him dead with it."

"Major" I says a little hasty "you didn't do it which is a blessing, for it would have done no good and I think your sponge was better employed on your own honorable boots."

So we got to be rational, and planned that I should tap at her bedroom door and lay the letter on the mat outside and wait on the upper landing for what might happen, and never was gunpowder cannon-balls or shells or rockets more dreaded than that dreadful letter was by me as I took it to the second floor.

A terrible loud scream sounded through the house the minute after she had opened it, and I found her on the floor lying as if her life was gone. My dear I never looked at the face of the letter which was lying open by her, for there was no occasion.

Everything I needed to bring her round the Major brought up with his own hands, besides running out to the chemist's for what was not in the house and likewise having the fiercest of all his many skirmishes with a musical instrument representing a ball-room I do not know in what particular country and company waltzing in and out at folding-doors with rolling eyes. When after a long time I saw her coming to, I slipped on the landing till I heard her cry, and then I went in and says cheerily "Mrs. Edson you're not well my dear and it's not to be wondered at," as if I had not been in before. Whether she believed or disbelieved I cannot say and it would signify nothing if I could, but I stayed by her for hours and then she God ever blesses me! and says she will try to rest for her head is bad.

"Major," I whispers, looking in at the parlors, "I beg and pray of you don't go out."

The Major whispers, "Madam, trust me I will do no such a thing. How is she?"

I says "Major the good Lord above us only knows what burns and rages in her poor mind. I left her sitting at her window. I am going to sit at mine."

It came on afternoon and it came on evening. Norfolk is a delightful street to lodge in — provided you don't go lower down — but of a summer evening when the dust and waste paper lie in it and stray children play in it and a kind of a gritty calm and bake settles on it and a peal of churchbells is practicing in the neighborhood it is a trifle dull, and never have I seen it since at such a time and never shall I see it evermore at such a time without seeing the dull June evening when that forlorn young creature sat at her open corner window on the Second and me at my open corner window (the other corner) on the Third. Something merciful, something wiser and better far than my own self, had moved me while it was yet light to sit in my bonnet and shawl, and as the shadows fell and the tide rose I could sometimes — when I put out my head and looked at her window below — see that she leaned out a little looking down the street. It was just settling dark when I saw *her* in the street.

So fearful of losing sight of her that it almost stops my breath while I tell it, I went downstairs faster than I ever moved in all my life and only tapped with my hand at the Major's door in passing it and slipping out. She was gone already. I made the same speed down the street and when I came to the corner of Howard-street I saw that she had turned it and was there plain before me going towards the west. O with what a thankful heart I saw her going along! .

She was quite unacquainted with London and had very seldom been out for more than an airing in our own street where she knew two or three little children belonging to neighbors and had sometimes stood among them at the street looking at the water. She must be going at hazard I knew, still she kept the bye-streets quite correctly as long as they would serve her, and then turned up into the Strand. But at every corner I could see her head turned one way, and that way was always the river way.

It may have been only the darkness and quiet of the Adelphi that caused her to strike into it but she struck into it much as readily as if she had set out to go there, which perhaps was the case. She went straight down to the Terrace and along it and looked over the iron rail, and I often woke afterwards in my own bed with the horror of seeing her do it. The desertion of the wharf below and the flowing of the high water there seemed to settle her purpose. She looked about as if to make out the way down, and she struck out the right way or the wrong way — I don't know which, for I don't know the place before or since — and I followed her the way she went.

It was noticeable that all this time she never once looked back. But there was now a great change in the manner of her going, and instead of going at a steady quick walk with her arms folded before her — among the dark dismal arches she went in a wild way with her arms opened wide, as if they were wings and she was flying to her death.

We were on the wharf and she stopped. I stopped. I saw her hands at her bonnet-strings, and I rushed between her and the brink and took her round the waist with both my arms. She might have drowned me, I felt then, but she could never have got quit of me.

Down to that moment my mind had been all in a maze and not half an idea had I had in it what I should say to her, but the instant I touched her it came to me like magic and I had my natural voice and my senses and even almost my breath.

"Mrs. Edson!" I says "My dear! Take care. How ever did you lose your way and stumble on a dangerous place like this? Why you must have come here by the most perplexing streets in all London. No wonder you are lost, I'm sure. And this place too! Why I thought nobody ever got here, except me to order my coals and the Major in the parlors to smoke his cigar!" — for I saw that blessed man close by, pretending to it.

"Hah — Hah — Hum!" coughs the Major.

"And good gracious me" I says, "why here he is!"

"Halloa! who goes there?" says the Major in a military manner.

"Well!" I says, "if this don't beat everything! Don't you know us Major Jackman?"

"Halloa!" says the Major. "Who calls on Jemmy Jackman?" (and more out of breath he was, and did it less like life than I should have expected.)

"Why here's Mrs. Edson Major" I says, "strolling out to cool her poor head which has been very bad, has missed her way and got lost, and Goodness knows where she might have got to but for me coming here to drop an order into my coal merchant's letter-box and you coming here to smoke your cigar! — And you really are not well enough my dear" I says to her "to be half so far from home without me. — And your arm will be very acceptable I am sure Major" I says to him "and I know she may lean upon it as heavy as she likes." And now we had both got her — thanks be Above! — one on each side.

She was all in a cold shiver and she so continued till I laid her on her own bed, and up to the early morning she held me by the hand and moaned and moaned "O wicked, wicked, wicked!" But when at last I made believe to droop my head and be overpowered with a dead sleep, I heard that poor young creature give such touching and such humble thanks for being preserved from taking her own life in

MRS. EDSON ON THE BRINK

her madness that I thought I should have cried my eyes out on the counterpane and I knew she was safe.

Being well enough to do and able to afford it, me and the Major laid our little plans next day while she was asleep worn out, and so I says to her as soon as I could do it nicely: "Mrs. Edson my dear, when Mr. Edson paid me the rent for these farther six months — "

She gave a start and I felt her large eyes look at me, but I went on with it and with my needlework.

"— I can't say that I am quite sure I dated the receipt right. Could you let me look at it?"

She laid her frozen cold hand upon mine and she looked through me when I was forced to look up from my needlework, but I had taken the precaution of having on my spectacles.

"I have no receipt" says she.

"Ah! Then he has got it" I says in a careless way. "It's of no great consequence. A receipt's a receipt."

From that time she always had hold of my hand when I could spare it which was generally only when I read to her, for of course she and me had our bits of needlework to plod at and neither of us was very handy at those little things, though I am still rather proud of my share in them too considering. And though she took to all I read to her, I used to fancy that next to what was taught upon the Mount she took most of all to His gentle compassion for us poor women and to His young life and to how His mother was proud of Him and treasured His sayings in her heart. She had a grateful look in her eyes that never never never will be out of mine until they are closed in my last sleep, and when I chanced to look at her without thinking of it I would always meet that look, and she would often offer me her trembling lip to kiss, much more like a little affectionate half-brokenhearted child than ever I can imagine any grown person.

One time the trembling of this poor lip was so strong and her tears ran down so fast that I thought she was going to tell me all her woe, so I takes her two hands in mine and I says:

"No my dear not now, you had best not try to do it now. Wait for better times when you have got over this and are strong, and then you shall tell me whatever you will. Shall it be agreed?"

With our hands still joined she nodded her head many times, and she lifted my hands and put them to her lips and to her bosom.

"Only one word now my dear" I says. "Is there anyone?"

She looked inquiringly "Anyone?"

"That I can go to?"

She shook her head.

"No one that I can bring?"

She shook her head.

"No one is wanted by *me* my dear. Now that may be considered past and gone."

Not much more than a week afterwards — for this was far on in the time of our being so together — I was bending over at her bedside with my ear down to her lips, by turns listening for her breath and looking for a sign of life in her face. At last it came in a solemn way — not in a flash but like a kind of pale faint light brought very slow to the face.

She said something to me that had no sound in it, but I saw she asked me:

"Is this death?"

And I says:

"Poor dear poor dear, I think it is."

Knowing somehow that she wanted me to move her weak right hand, I took it and laid it on her breast and then folded her other hand upon it, and she prayed a good good prayer and I joined in it poor me though there were no words spoke. Then I brought the baby in its wrappers from where it lay, and I says:

"My dear this is sent to a childless old woman. This is for me to take care of."

The trembling lip was put up towards my face for the last time, and I dearly kissed it.

"Yes my dear," I says. "Please God! Me and the Major."

I don't know how to tell it right, but I saw her soul brighten and leap up, and get free and fly away in the grateful look.

*   *   *

So this is the why and wherefore of its coming to pass my dear that we called him Jemmy, being after the Major his own godfather with Lirriper for a surname being after myself, and never was a dear child such a brightening thing in a Lodgings or such a playmate to his grandmother as Jemmy to this house and me, and always good and minding what he was told (upon the whole) and soothing for the temper and making everything pleasanter except when he grew old enough to drop his cap down Wozenham's Airy and they wouldn't hand it up to him, and being worked into a state I put on my best bonnet and gloves and parasol with the child in my hand and I says "Miss Wozenham I little thought ever to have entered *your* house but unless my grandson's cap is instantly restored, the laws of this country regulating the property of the Subject shall at length decide betwixt yourself and me, cost what it may." With a sneer upon her face which did strike me I must say as being expressive of two keys but it may have been a mistake and if there is any doubt let Miss Wozenham have the full benefit of it as is but right, she rang the bell and she says "Jane, is there a street-child's old cap down our Airy?" I says "Miss Wozenham before your housemaid answers that question you must allow me to inform you to your face that my grandson is *not* a street-child and is *not* in the habit of wearing old caps. In fact" I says "Miss Wozenham I am far from sure that my grandson's cap may not be newer than your own" which was perfectly savage in me, her lace being the commonest machine-make washed and torn besides, but I had been put into a state to begin with fomented by impertinence. Miss Wozenham says red in the face "Jane you heard my question, is there any child's cap down our Airy?" "Yes ma'am" says Jane "I think I did see some such rubbish a-lying there." "Then" says Miss Wozenham "let these visitors out, and then throw up that worthless article out of my premises." But here the child who had been staring at Miss Wozenham with all his eyes and more, frowns down his little eyebrows purses up his little mouth puts his chubby legs far apart turns his little dimpled fists round and round slowly over one another like a little coffee-mill, and says to her "Oo impdent to mi Gran, me tut oor hi!" "O!" says Miss Wozenham looking down scornfully at the Mite "this is not a street-child is it not? Really!" I bursts out laughing and I says "Miss Wozenham if this ain't a pretty sight to you I don't envy your feelings and I wish you good-day. Jemmy come along with Gran." And I was still in the best of humors though his cap came flying up into the street as if it had been just turned on out of the water-plug, and I went home laughing all the way, all owing to that dear boy.

The miles and miles that me and the Major have travelled with Jemmy in the dusk between the lights are not to be calculated, Jemmy driving on the coach-box which is the Major's brass-bound writing desk on the table, me inside in the easy-chair and the Major

Guard up behind with a brown-paper horn doing it real wonderful. I do assure you my dear that sometimes when I have taken a few winks in my place inside the coach and have come half awake by the flashing light of the fire and have heard that precious pet driving and the Major blowing up behind to have the change of horses ready when we got to the Inn, I have half believed we were on the old North Road that my poor Lirriper knew so well. Then to see that child and the Major both wrapped up getting down to warm their feet and going stamping about and having glasses of ale out of the paper match-boxes on the chimney-piece is to see the Major enjoying it fully as much as the child I am very sure, and it's equal to any play when Coachee opens the coach-door to look in at me inside and say "Wery 'past that 'tage. — 'Prightened old lady?"

But what my inexpressible feelings were when we lost that child can only be compared to the Major's which were not a shade better, through his straying out at five years old and eleven o'clock in the forenoon and never heard of by word or sign or deed till half-past nine at night, when the Major had gone to the Editor of the *Times* newspaper to put in an advertisement, which came out next day four-and-twenty hours after he was found, and which I mean always carefully to keep in my lavender drawer as the first printed account of him. The more the day got on, the more I got distracted and the Major too and both of us made worse by the composed ways of the police though very civil and obliging and what I must call their obstinacy in not entertaining the idea that he was stolen. "We mostly find mum" says the sergeant who came round to comfort me, which he didn't at all and he had been one of the private constables in Caroline's time to which he referred in his opening words when he said "Don't give way to uneasiness in your mind mum, it'll all come as right as my nose did when I got the same barked by that young woman in your second floor" — says this sergeant "we mostly find mum as people ain't over-anxious to have what I may call second-hand children. *You*'ll get him back mum." "O but my dear good Sir" I says clasping my hands and wringing them and clasping them again "he is such an uncommon child!" "Yes mum" says the sergeant, "we mostly find that too mum. The question is what his clothes were worth." "His clothes" I says "were not worth much Sir for he had only got his playing-dress on, but the dear child! — " "All right mum" says the sergeant. "*You*'ll get him back mum. And even if he'd had his best clothes on, it wouldn't come to worse than his being found wrapped up in a cabbage-leaf, a shivering in a lane." His words pierced my heart like daggers and daggers, and me and the Major ran in and out like wild things all day long till the Major returning from his interview with the Editor of the *Times* at night rushes into my little room hysterical and squeezes my hand and wipes his eyes and says "Joy joy — officer in plain clothes came up on the steps as I was letting myself in — compose your feelings — Jemmy's found." Consequently I fainted away and when I came to, embraced the legs of the officer in plain clothes who seemed to be taking a kind of quiet inventory in his mind of the property in my little room with brown whiskers, and I says "Blessings on you Sir where is the Darling?" and he says "In Kennington Station House." I was dropping at his feet Stone at the image of that Innocence in cells with murderers when he adds "He followed the Monkey." I says deeming it slang language "O Sir explain for a loving grand-mother what Monkey!" He says "Him in the spangled cap with the strap under the chin, as won't keep on — him as sweeps the cross-ings on a round table and don't want to draw his sabre more than he can help." Then I understood it all and most thankfully thanked him, and me and the Major and him drove over to Kennington and there we found our boy lying quite comfortable before a blazing fire having sweetly played himself to sleep upon a small accordion nothing like so big as a flat-iron which they had been so kind to lend him for the purpose and which it appeared had been stopped upon a very young person.

My dear the system upon which the Major commenced and as I may say perfected Jemmy's learning when he was so small that if the dear was on the other side of the table you had to look under it instead of over it to see him with his mother's own bright hair in beautiful curls, is a thing that ought to be known to the Throne and Lords and Commons and then might obtain some promotion for the Major which he well deserves and would be none the worse for (speaking between friends) L. S. D.-ically. When the Major first undertook his learning he says to me:

"I'm going madam," he says "to make our child a Calculating Boy."

"Major," I says, "you terrify me and may do the pet a permanent injury you would never forgive yourself."

"Madam," says the Major, "next to my regret that when I had my boot-sponge in my hand, I didn't choke that scoundrel with it — on the spot — "

"There! For Gracious' sake," I interrupts, "let his conscience find him without sponges."

"— I say next to that regret, madam," says the Major "would be the regret with which my breast," which he tapped, "would be surcharged if this fine mind was not early cultivated. But mark me madam," says the Major holding up his forefinger "cultivated on a principle that will make it a delight."

"Major" I says "I will be candid with you and tell you openly that if ever I find the dear child fall off in his appetite I shall know it is his calculations and shall put a stop to them at two minutes' notice. Or if I find them mounting to his head" I says, "or striking anyways cold to his stomach or leading to anything approaching flabbiness in his legs, the result will be the same, but Major you are a clever man and have seen much and you love the child and are his own godfather, and if you feel a confidence in trying try."

"Spoken madam" says the Major "like Emma Lirriper. All I have to ask, madam, is that you will leave my godson and myself to make a week or two's preparations for surprising you, and that you will give me leave to have up and down any small articles not actually in use that I may require from the kitchen."

"From the kitchen Major?" I says half feeling as if he had a mind to cook the child.

"From the kitchen" says the Major, and smiles and swells, and at the same time looks taller.

So I passed my word and the Major and the dear boy were shut up together for half an hour at a time through a certain while, and never could I hear anything going on betwixt them but talking and laughing and Jemmy clapping his hands and screaming out numbers, so I says to myself "it has not harmed him yet" nor could I on examining the dear find any signs of it anywhere about him which was likewise a great relief. At last one day Jemmy brings me a card in joke in the Major's neat writing "The Messrs. Jemmy Jackman" for we had given him the Major's other name too "request the honor of Mrs. Lirriper's company at the Jackman Institution in the front parlor this evening at five, military time, to witness a few slight feats of elementary arithmetic." And if you'll believe me there in the front parlor at five punctual to the moment was the Major behind the Pembroke table with both leaves up and a lot of things from the kitchen tidily set out on old newspapers spread atop of it, and there was the Mite stood up on a chair with his rosy cheeks flushing and his eyes sparkling clusters of diamonds.

"Now Gran" says he, "oo tit down and don't oo touch ler poople" — for he saw with every one of those diamonds of his that I was going to give him a squeeze.

"Very well Sir" I says "I am obedient in this good company I am sure." And I sits down in the easy-chair that was put for me, shaking my sides.

But picture my admiration when the Major going on almost as quick as if he was conjuring sets out all the articles he names, and says "Three saucepans, an Italian iron, a hand-bell, a toasting-fork, a nutmeg-grater, four potlids, a spice-box, two egg-cups, and a chopping-board — how many?" and when that Mite instantly cries "Tifteen, tut down tive and carry ler 'toppin-board" and then claps his hands draws up his legs and dances on his chair.

My dear with the same astonishing ease and correctness him and the Major added up the tables chairs and sofy, the picters fenders and fire-irons their own selves me and the cat and the eyes in Miss Wozenham's head, and whenever the sum was done Young Roses and Diamonds claps his hands and draws up his legs and dances on his chair.

The pride of the Major! (*"Here's* a mind ma'am!" he says to me behind his hand.)

Then he says aloud, "We now come to the next elementary rule — which is called — "

"Umtraction!" cries Jemmy.

"Right," says the Major. "We have here a toasting-fork, a potato in its natural state, two potlids, one egg-cup, a wooden spoon, and two skewers, from which it is necessary for commercial purposes to subtract a sprat-gridiron, a small pickle-jar, two lemons, one pepper-castor, a blackbeetle-trap, and a knob of the dresser-drawer — what remains?"

"Toatin-fork!" cries Jemmy.

"In numbers how many?" says the Major.

"One!" cries Jemmy.

(*"Here's* a boy, ma'am!" says the Major to me behind his hand.)

Then the Major goes on:

"We now approach the next elementary rule — which is entitled — "

"Tickleication" cries Jemmy.

"Correct" says the Major.

But my dear to relate to you in detail the way in which they multiplied fourteen sticks of firewood by two bits of ginger and a larding-needle, or divided pretty well everything else there was on the table by the heater of the Italian iron and a chamber candlestick, and got a lemon over, would make my head spin round and round and round as it did at the time. So I says "if you'll excuse my addressing the chair Professor Jackman I think the period of the lecture has now arrived when it becomes necessary that I should take a good hug of this young scholar." Upon which Jemmy calls out from his station on the chair, "Gran oo open oor arms and me'll make a 'pring into 'em." So I opened my arms to him as I had opened my sorrowful heart when his poor young mother lay a dying, and he had his jump and we had a good long hug together and the Major prouder than any peacock says to me behind his hand, "You need not let him know it madam" (which I certainly need not for the Major was quite audible) "but he is a boy!"

In this way Jemmy grew and grew and went to day-school and continued under the Major too, and in summer we were as happy as the days were long, and in winter we were as happy as the days were short and there seemed to rest a Blessing on the Lodgings for they as good as Let themselves and would have done it if there had been twice the accommodation, when sore and hard against my will I one day says to the Major:

"Major you know what I am going to break to you. Our boy must go to boarding-school."

It was a sad sight to see the Major's countenance drop, and I pitied the good soul with all my heart.

"Yes Major" I says, "though he is as popular with the Lodgers as you are yourself and though he is to you and me what only you and me know, still it is in the course of things and Life is made of partings and we must part with our Pet."

Bold as I spoke, I saw two Majors and half-a-dozen fireplaces, and when the poor Major put one of his neat bright-varnished boots upon the fender and his elbow on his knee and his head upon his hand and rocked himself a little to and fro, I was dreadfully cut up.

"But" says I clearing my throat "you have so well prepared him Major — he has had such a Tutor in you — that he will have none of the first drudgery to go through. And he is so clever besides that he'll soon make his way to the front rank."

"He is a boy" says the Major — having sniffed — "that has not his like on the face of the earth."

"True as you say Major, and it is not for us merely for our own sakes to do anything to keep him back from being a credit and an ornament wherever he goes and perhaps even rising to be a great man, is it Major? He will have all my little savings when my work is done (being all the world to me) and we must try to make him a wise man and a good man, mustn't we Major?"

"Madam" says the Major rising "Jemmy Jackman is becoming an older file than I was aware of, and you put him to shame. You are thoroughly right madam. You are simply and undeniably right. — And if you'll excuse me, I'll take a walk."

So the Major being gone out and Jemmy being at home, I got the child into my little room here and I stood him by my chair and I took his mother's own curls in my hand and I spoke to him loving and serious. And when I had reminded the darling how that he was now in his tenth year and when I had said to him about his getting on in life pretty much what I had said to the Major I broke to him how that we must have this same parting, and there I was forced to stop for there I saw of a sudden the well-remembered lip with its tremble, and it so brought back that time! But with the spirit that was in him he controlled it soon and he says gravely nodding through his tears, "I understand Gran — I know it *must* be, Gran — go on Gran, don't be afraid of *me*." And when I had said all that ever I could think of, he turned his bright steady face to mine and he says just a little broken here and there "You shall see Gran that I can be a man and that I can do anything that is grateful and loving to you — and if I don't grow up to be what you would like to have me — I hope it will be — because I shall die." And with that he sat down by me and I went on to tell him of the school of which I had excellent recommendations and where it was and how many scholars and what games they played as I had heard and what length of holidays, to all of which he listened bright and clear. And so it came that at last he says "And now dear Gran let me kneel down here where I have been used to say my prayers and let me fold my face for just a minute in your gown and let me cry, for you have been more than father — more than mother — more than brothers sisters friends — to me!" And so he did cry and I too and we were both much the better for it.

From that time forth he was true to his word and ever blithe and ready, and even when me and the Major took him down into Lincolnshire he was far the gayest of the party though for sure and certain he might easily have been that, but he really was and put life into us only when it came to the last Good-bye, he says with a wistful look, "You wouldn't have me not really sorry would you Gran?" and when I says "No dear, Lord forbid!" he says "I am glad of that!" and ran in out of sight.

But now that the child was gone out of the Lodgings the Major fell into a regularly moping state. It was taken notice of by all the Lodgers that the Major moped. He hadn't even the same air of being rather tall that he used to have, and if he varnished his boots with a single gleam of interest it was as much as he did.

One evening the Major came into my little room to take a cup of tea and a morsel of buttered toast and to read Jemmy's newest letter which had arrived that afternoon (by the very same postman more than middle-aged upon the Beat now), and the letter raising him up a little I says to the Major:

"Major you mustn't get into a moping way."

The Major shook his head. "Jemmy Jackman madam," he says with a deep sigh, "is an older file than I thought him."

"Moping is not the way to grow younger Major."

"My dear madam," says the Major, "is there *any* way of growing younger?"

Feeling that the Major was getting rather the best of that point I made a diversion to another.

"Thirteen years! Thir-teen years! Many Lodgers have come and gone, in the thirteen years that you have lived in the parlors Major."

"Hah!" says the Major warming. "Many madam, many."

"And I should say you have been familiar with them all?"

"As a rule (with its exceptions like all rules) my dear madam" says the Major, "they have honored me with their acquaintance, and not unfrequently with their confidence."

Watching the Major as he drooped his white head and stroked his black mustachios and moped again, a thought which I think must have been going about looking for an owner somewhere dropped into my old noddle if you will excuse the expression.

"The walls of my Lodgings" I says in a casual way — for my dear it is of no use going straight at a man who mopes — "might have something to tell if they could tell it."

The Major neither moved nor said anything but I saw he was attending with his shoulders my dear — attending with his shoulders to what I said. In fact I saw that his shoulders were struck by it.

"The dear boy was always fond of story-books" I went on, like as if I was talking to myself. "I am sure this house — his own home — might write a story or two for his reading one day or another."

The Major's shoulders gave a dip and a curve and his head came up in his shirt-collar. The Major's head came up in his shirt-collar as I hadn't seen it come up since Jemmy went to school.

"It is unquestionable that in intervals of cribbage and a friendly rubber, my dear madam," says the Major, "and also over what used to be called in my young times — in the salad days of Jemmy Jackman — the social glass, I have exchanged many a reminiscence with your Lodgers."

My remark was — I confess I made it with the deepest and artfullest of intentions — "I wish our dear boy had heard them!"

"Are you serious madam?" asks the Major starting and turning full round.

"Why not Major?"

"Madam" says the Major, turning up one of his cuffs, "they shall be written for him."

"Ah! Now you speak" I says giving my hands a pleased clap. "Now you are in a way out of moping Major!"

"Between this and my holidays — I mean the dear boy's" says the Major turning up his other cuff, "a good deal may be done towards it."

"Major you are a clever man and you have seen much and not a doubt of it."

"I'll begin," says the Major looking as tall as ever he did, "tomorrow."

My dear the Major was another man in three days and he was

himself again in a week and he wrote and wrote and wrote with his pen scratching like rats behind the wainscot, and whether he had many grounds to go upon or whether he did at all romance I cannot tell you, but what he has written is in the left-hand glass closet of the little bookcase close behind you.

CHAPTER II

HOW THE PARLORS ADDED A FEW WORDS

I have the honor of presenting myself by the name of Jackman. I esteem it a proud privilege to go down to posterity through the instrumentality of the most remarkable boy that ever lived — by the name of JEMMY JACKMAN LIRRIPER — and of my worthy and most highly respected friend, Mrs. Emma Lirriper, of Eighty-one Norfolk Street, Strand, in the County of Middlesex, in the United Kingdom of Great Britain and Ireland.

It is not for me to express the rapture with which we received that dear and eminently remarkable boy, on the occurrence of his first Christmas holidays. Suffice it to observe that when he came flying into the house with two splendid prizes (Arithmetic, and Exemplary Conduct), Mrs. Lirriper and myself embraced with emotion and instantly took him to the Play, where we were all three admirably entertained.

Nor is it to render homage to the virtues of the best of her good and honored sex — whom, in deference to her unassuming worth, I will only here designate by the initials E. L. — that I add this record to the bundle of papers with which our, in a most distinguished degree, remarkable boy has expressed himself delighted, before reconsigning the same to the left-hand glass closet of Mrs. Lirriper's little bookcase.

Neither is it to obtrude the name of the old original superannuated obscure Jemmy Jackman, once (to his degradation) of Wozenham's, long (to his elevation) of Lirriper's. If I could be consciously guilty of that piece of bad taste, it would indeed be a work of supererogation, now that the name is borne by JEMMY JACKMAN LIRRIPER.

No, I take up my humble pen to register a little record of our strikingly remarkable boy, which my poor capacity regards as presenting a pleasant little picture of the dear boy's mind. The picture may be interesting to himself when he is a man.

Our first reunited Christmas-day was the most delightful one we have ever passed together. Jemmy was never silent for five minutes, except in church-time. He talked as we sat by the fire, he talked when we were out walking, he talked as we sat by the fire again, he talked incessantly at dinner, though he made a dinner almost as remarkable as himself. It was the spring of happiness in his fresh young heart flowing and flowing, and it fertilized (if I may be allowed so bold a figure) my much-esteemed friend, and J. J. the present writer.

There were only we three. We dined in my esteemed friend's little room, and our entertainment was perfect. But everything in the establishment is, in neatness, order, and comfort, always perfect. After dinner our boy slipped away to his old stool at my esteemed friend's knee, and there, with his hot chestnuts and his glass of brown sherry (really, a most excellent wine!) on a chair for a table, his face outshone the apples in the dish.

We talked of these jottings of mine, which Jemmy had read through and through by that time; and so it came about that my esteemed friend remarked, as she sat smoothing Jemmy's curls:

"And as you belong to the house, too, Jemmy — and so much more than the Lodgers, having been born in it — why, your story ought to be added to the rest, I think, one of these days."

Jemmy's eyes sparkled at this, and he said, "So *I* think, Gran."

Then he sat looking at the fire, and then he began to laugh in a sort of confidence with the fire, and then he said, folding his arms across my esteemed friend's lap, and raising his bright face to hers: "Would you like to hear a boy's story, Gran?"

"Of all things," replied my esteemed friend.

"Would you, godfather?"

"Of all things," I too replied.

"Well, then," said Jemmy, "I'll tell you one."

Here our indisputably remarkable boy gave himself a hug, and laughed again, musically, at the idea of his coming out in that new line. Then he once more took the fire into the same sort of confidence as before, and began:

"Once upon a time, When pigs drank wine, And monkeys chewed

tobaccer, 'Twas neither in your time nor mine, But that's no macker — "

"Bless the child!" cried my esteemed friend, "what's amiss with his brain?"

"It's poetry, Gran," returned Jemmy, shouting with laughter. "We always begin stories that way at school."

"Gave me quite a turn, Major," said my esteemed friend, fanning herself with a plate. "Thought he was light-headed!"

"In those remarkable times, Gran and godfather, there was once a boy — not me, you know."

"No, no," says my respected friend, "not you. Not him, Major, you understand?"

"No, no," says I.

"And he went to school in Rutlandshire — "

"Why not Lincolnshire?" says my respected friend.

"Why not, you dear old Gran? Because *I* go to school in Lincolnshire, don't I?"

"Ah, to be sure!" says my respected friend. "And it's not Jemmy, you understand, Major?"

"No, no," says I.

"Well!" our boy proceeded, hugging himself comfortably, and laughing merrily (again in confidence with the fire), before he again looked up in Mrs. Lirriper's face, "and so he was tremendously in love with his schoolmaster's daughter, and she was the most beautiful creature that ever was seen, and she had brown eyes, and she had brown hair all curling beautifully, and she had a delicious voice, and she was delicious altogether, and her name was Seraphina."

"What's the name of *your* schoolmaster's daughter, Jemmy?" asks my respected friend.

"Polly!" replied Jemmy, pointing his forefinger at her. "There now! Caught you! Ha, ha, ha!"

When he and my respected friend had had a laugh and a hug together, our admittedly remarkable boy resumed with a great relish:

"Well! And so he loved her. And so he thought about her, and dreamed about her, and made her presents of oranges and nuts, and would have made her presents of pearls and diamonds if he could have afforded it out of his pocket-money, but he couldn't. And so her father — O, he WAS a Tartar! Keeping the boys up to the mark, holding examinations once a month, lecturing upon all sorts of subjects at all sorts of times, and knowing everything in the world out of book. And so this boy — "

"Had he any name?" asks my respected friend.

"No, he hadn't, Gran. Ha, ha! There now! Caught you again!"

After this, they had another laugh and another hug, and then our boy went on.

"Well! And so this boy, he had a friend about as old as himself at the same school, and his name (for He *had* a name, as it happened) was — let me remember — was Bobbo."

"Not Bob," says my respected friend.

"Of course not," says Jemmy. "What made you think it was, Gran? Well! And so this friend was the cleverest and bravest and best-looking and most generous of all the friends that ever were, and so he was in love with Seraphina's sister, and so Seraphina's sister was in love with him, and so they all grew up."

"Bless us!" says my respected friend. "They were very sudden about it."

"So they all grew up," our boy repeated, laughing heartily, "and Bobbo and this boy went away together on horseback to seek their fortunes, and they partly got their horses by favor, and partly in a bargain; that is to say, they had saved up between them seven and fourpence, and the two horses, being Arabs, were worth more, only the man said he would take that, to favor them. Well! And so they made their fortunes and came prancing back to the school, with their pockets full of gold, enough to last forever. And so they rang at the parents' and visitors' bell (not the back gate), and when the bell was answered they proclaimed 'The same as if it was scarlet fever! Every boy goes home for an indefinite period!' And then there was great hurrahing, and then they kissed Seraphina and her sister — each his own love, and not the other's on any account — and then they ordered the Tartar into instant confinement."

"Poor man!" said my respected friend.

"Into instant confinement, Gran," repeated Jemmy, trying to look severe and roaring with laughter; "and he was to have nothing to eat but the boys' dinners, and was to drink half a cask of their beer every day. And so then the preparations were made for the two weddings, and there were hampers, and potted things, and sweet things, and nuts, and postage-stamps, and all manner of things. And so they were so jolly, that they let the Tartar out, and he was jolly too."

"I am glad they let him out," says my respected friend, "because he had only done his duty."

"O, but hadn't he overdone it, though!" cried Jemmy. "Well! And so then this boy mounted his horse, with his bride in his arms, and cantered away, and cantered on and on till he came to a certain place where he had a certain Gran and a certain godfather — not you two, you know."

"No, no," we both said.

"And there he was received with great rejoicings, and he filled the cupboard and the bookcase with gold, and he showered it out on his Gran and his godfather because they were the two kindest and dearest people that ever lived in this world. And so while they were sitting up to their knees in gold, a knocking was heard at the street door, and who should it be but Bobbo, also on horseback with his bride in his arms, and what had he come to say but that he would take (at double rent) all the Lodgings forever, that were not wanted by this boy and this Gran and this godfather, and that they would all live together, and all be happy! And so they were, and so it never ended!"

"And was there no quarrelling?" asked my respected friend, as Jemmy sat upon her lap and hugged her.

"No! Nobody ever quarrelled."

"And did the money never melt away?"

"No! Nobody could ever spend it all."

"And did none of them ever grow older?"

"No! Nobody ever grew older after that."

"And did none of them ever die?"

"O, no, no, no, Gran!" exclaimed our dear boy, laying his cheek upon her breast, and drawing her closer to him. "Nobody ever died."

"Ah, Major, Major!" says my respected friend, smiling benignly upon me, "this beats our stories. Let us end with the Boy's story, Major, for the Boy's story is the best that is ever told!"

In submission to which request on the part of the best of women, I have here noted it down as faithfully as my best abilities, coupled with my best intentions, would admit, subscribing it with my name,

J. JACKMAN

THE PARLORS
MRS. LIRRIPER'S LODGINGS

MRS.

LIRRIPER'S

LEGACY

*

IN TWO CHAPTERS

Mrs. Lirriper's Legacy

I. MRS. LIRRIPER RELATES HOW SHE WENT ON, AND WENT OVER

AH! IT'S PLEASANT to drop into my own easy-chair my dear though a little palpitating what with trotting upstairs and what with trotting down, and why kitchen stairs should all be corner stairs is for the builders to justify though I do not think they fully understand their trade and never did, else why the sameness and why not more conveniences and fewer draughts and likewise making a practice of laying the plaster on too thick I am well convinced which holds the damp, and as to chimney-pots putting them on by guesswork like hats at a party and no more knowing what their effect will be upon the smoke bless you than I do if so much, except that it will mostly be either to send it down your throat in a straight form or give it a twist before it goes there. And what I says speaking as I find of those new metal chimneys all manner of shapes (there's a row of 'em at Miss Wozenham's lodging-house lower down on the other side of the way) is that they only work your smoke into artificial patterns for you before you swallow it and that I'd quite as soon swallow mine plain, the flavor being the same, not to mention the conceit of putting up signs on the top of your house to show the forms in which you take your smoke into your inside.

Being here before your eyes my dear in my own easy-chair in my own quiet room in my own Lodging-House Number Eighty-one Norfolk Street Strand London situated midway between the city and St. James's — if anything is where it used to be with these hotels calling themselves Limited but called unlimited by Major Jackman

197

rising up everywhere and rising up into flagstaffs where they can't go any higher, but my mind of those monsters is give me a landlord's or landlady's wholesome face when I come off a journey and not a brass plate with an electrified number clicking out of it which it's not in nature can be glad to see me and to which I don't want to be hoisted like molasses at the Docks and left there telegraphing for help with the most ingenious instruments but quite in vain — being here my dear I have no call to mention that I am still in the Lodgings as a business hoping to die in the same and if agreeable to the clergy partly read over at Saint Clement's Danes and concluded in Hatfield churchyard when lying once again by my poor Lirriper ashes to ashes and dust to dust.

Neither should I tell you any news my dear in telling you that the Major is still a fixture in the Parlors quite as much so as the roof of the house, and that Jemmy is of boys the best and brightest and has ever had kept from him the cruel story of his poor pretty young mother Mrs. Edson being deserted in the second floor and dying in my arms, fully believing that I am his born Gran and him an orphan, though what with engineering since he took a taste for it and him and the Major making Locomotives out of parasols broken iron pots and cotton-reels and them absolutely a getting off the line and falling over the table and injuring the passengers almost equal to the originals it really is quite wonderful. And when I says to the Major, "Major can't you by *any* means give us a communication with the guard?" the Major says quite huffy, "No madam it's not to be done," and when I says "Why not?" the Major says, "That is between us who are in the Railway Interest madam and our friend the Right Honorable Vice-President of the Board of Trade" and if you'll believe me my dear the Major wrote to Jemmy at school to consult him on the answer I should have before I could get even that amount of unsatisfactoriness out of the man, the reason being that when we first began with the little model and the working signals beautiful and perfect (being in general as wrong as the real) and when I says laughing "What appointment am I to hold in this undertaking gentlemen?" Jemmy hugs me round the neck and tells me dancing, "You shall be the Public Gran" and consequently they put upon me just as much as ever they like and I sit a growling in my easy-chair.

My dear whether it is that a grown man as clever as the Major

cannot give half his heart and mind to anything — even a play-
thing — but must get into right down earnest with it, whether it is
so or whether it is not so I do not undertake to say, but Jemmy is
far outdone by the serious and believing ways of the Major in the
management of the United Grand Junction Lirriper and Jackman
Great Norfolk Parlor Line, "For" says my Jemmy with the sparkling eyes when it was christened, "we must have a whole mouthful of
name Gran or our dear old Public" and there the young rogue kissed
me, "won't stump up." So, the Public took the shares — ten at ninepence, and immediately when that was spent twelve Preference to
one-and-sixpence — and they were all signed by Jemmy and counter-
signed by the Major, and between ourselves much better worth the
money than some shares I have paid for in my time. In the same
holidays the line was made and worked and opened and ran excur-
sions and had collisions and burst its boilers and all sorts of accidents
and offenses all most regular correct and pretty. The sense of responsibility entertained by the Major as a military style of station-master
my dear starting the down train behind time and ringing one of
those little bells that you buy with the little coal-scuttles off the tray
round the man's neck in the street did him honor, but noticing the
Major of a night when he is writing out his monthly report to Jemmy
at school of the state of the Rolling Stock and the Permanent Way
and all the rest of it (the whole kept upon the Major's sideboard
and dusted with his own hands every morning before varnishing
his boots) I notice him as full of thought and care as full can be and
frowning in a fearful manner, but indeed the Major does nothing
by halves as witness his great delight in going out surveying with
Jemmy when he has Jemmy to go with, carrying a chain and a
measuring-tape and driving I don't know what improvements right
through Westminster Abbey and fully believed in the streets to be
knocking everything upside down by Act of Parliament. As please
Heaven will come to pass when Jemmy takes to that as a profession!

Mentioning my poor Lirriper brings into my head his own
youngest brother the Doctor though Doctor of what I am sure it
would be hard to say unless Liquor, for neither Physic nor Music
nor yet Law does Joshua Lirriper know a morsel of except continually being summoned to the County Court and having orders made
upon him which he runs away from, and once was taken in the
passage of this very house with an umbrella up and the Major's hat

on, giving his name with the door-mat round him as Sir Johnson Jones, K.C.B. in spectacles residing at the Horse Guards. On which occasion he had got into the house not a minute before, through the girl letting him on the mat when he sent in a piece of paper twisted more like one of those spills for lighting candles than a note, offering me the choice between thirty shillings in hand and his brains on the premises marked immediate and waiting for an answer. My dear it gave me such a dreadful turn to think of the brains of my poor dear Lirriper's own flesh and blood flying about the new oilcloth however unworthy to be so assisted, that I went out of my room here to ask him what he would take once for all not to do it for life when I found him in the custody of two gentlemen that I should have judged to be in the feather-bed trade if they had not announced the law, so fluffy were their personal appearance. "Bring your chains, Sir," says Joshua to the littlest of the two in the biggest hat, "rivet on my fetters!" Imagine my feelings when I pictered him clanking up Norfolk-street in irons and Miss Wozenham looking out of window! "Gentlemen," I says all of a tremble and ready to drop "please to bring him into Major Jackman's apartments." So they brought him into the Parlors, and when the Major spies his own curly-brimmed hat on him which Joshua Lirriper had whipped off its Peg in the passage for a military disguise he goes into such a tearing passion that he tips it off his head with his hand and kicks it up to the ceiling with his foot where it grazed long afterwards. "Major" I says "be cool and advise me what to do with Joshua my dead and gone Lirriper's own youngest brother." "Madam" says the Major "my advice is that you board and lodge him in a Powder Mill, with a handsome gratuity to the proprietor when exploded." "Major" I says "as a Christian you cannot mean your words." "Madam" says the Major "by the Lord I do!" and indeed the Major besides being with all his merits a very passionate man for his size had a bad opinion of Joshua on account of former troubles even unattended by liberties taken with his apparel. When Joshua Lirriper hears this conversation betwixt us he turns upon the littlest one with the biggest hat and says "Come Sir! Remove me to my vile dungeon. Where is my moldy straw?" My dear at the picter of him rising in my mind dressed almost entirely in padlocks like Baron Trenck in Jemmy's book I was so overcome that I burst into tears and I says to the Major, "Major take my keys and settle with these gentlemen or I shall never know a happy minute more," which was done several times both before and since, but still I must remember that Joshua Lirriper has his good feelings and shows them in being always so troubled in his mind when he cannot wear mourning for his brother. Many a long year have I left off my widow's mourning not being wishful to intrude, but the tender point in Joshua that I cannot help a little yielding to is when he writes "One single sovereign would enable me to wear a decent suit of mourning for my much-loved brother. I vowed at the time of his lamented death that I would ever wear sables in memory of him but Alas how short-sighted is man, How keep that vow when penniless!" It says a good deal for the strength of his feelings that he couldn't have been seven year old when my poor Lirriper died and to have kept to it ever since is highly creditable. But we know there's good in all of us — if we only knew where it was in some of us — and though it was far from delicate in Joshua to work upon the dear child's feelings when first sent to school and write down into Lincolnshire for his pocket-money by return of post and got it, still he is my poor Lirriper's own youngest brother and mightn't have meant not paying his bill at the Salisbury Arms when his affection took him down to stay a fortnight at Hatfield churchyard and might have meant to keep sober but for bad company. Consequently if the Major *had* played on him with the garden-engine which he got privately into his room without my knowing of it, I think that much as I should have regretted it there would have been words betwixt the Major and me. Therefore my dear though he played on Mr. Buffle by mistake being hot in his head, and though it might have been misrepresented down at Wozenham's into not being ready for Mr. Buffle in other respects he being the Assessed Taxes, still I do not so much regret it as perhaps I ought. And whether Joshua Lirriper will yet do well in life I cannot say, but I did hear of his coming out at a Private Theater in the character of a Bandit without receiving any offers afterwards from the regular managers.

Mentioning Mr. Buffle gives an instance of there being good in persons where good is not expected, for it cannot be denied that Mr. Buffle's manners when engaged in his business were not agreeable. To collect is one thing and to look about as if suspicious of the goods being gradually removing in the dead of the night by a back door is another, over-taxing you have no control but suspecting is voluntary. Allowances too must ever be made for a gentleman of the Major's warmth not relishing being spoke to with a pen in the mouth, and while I do not know that it is more irritable to my own feelings to have a low-crowned hat with a broad brim kept on in doors than any other hat still I can appreciate the Major's, besides which without bearing malice or vengeance the Major is a man that scores up arrears as his habit always was with Joshua Lirriper. So at last my dear the Major lay in wait for Mr. Buffle and it worried me a good deal. Mr. Buffle gives his rap of two sharp knocks one day and the Major bounces to the door. "Collector has called for two quarters' Assessed Taxes" says Mr. Buffle. "They are ready for him" says the Major and brings him in here. But on the way Mr. Buffle looks about him in his usual suspicious manner and the Major fires and asks him "Do you see a Ghost Sir?" "No Sir" says Mr. Buffle. "Because I have before noticed you" says the Major "apparently looking for a specter very hard beneath the roof of my respected friend. When you find that supernatural agent, be so good as point him out Sir." Mr. Buffle stares at the Major and then nods at me. "Mrs. Lirriper Sir" says the Major going off into a perfect steam and introducing me with his hand. "Pleasure of knowing her" says Mr. Buffle. "A — hum! — Jemmy Jackman Sir!" says the Major introducing himself. "Honor of knowing you by sight" says Mr. Buffle. "Jemmy Jackman Sir" says the Major wagging his head sideways in a sort of obstinate fury "presents to you his esteemed friend that lady Mrs. Emma Lirriper of Eighty-one Norfolk Street Strand London in the County of Middlesex in the United Kingdom of Great Britain and Ireland. Upon which occasion Sir," says the Major, "Jemmy Jackman takes your hat off." Mr. Buffle looks at his hat where the Major drops it on the floor, and he picks it up and puts it on again. "Sir" says the Major very red and looking him full in the face "there are two quarters of the Gallantry Taxes due and the Collector has called." Upon which if you can believe my words my dear the Major drops Mr. Buffle's hat off again. "This — " Mr. Buffle begins very angry with his pen in his mouth, when the Major steaming more and more says "Take your bit out Sir! Or by the whole infernal system of Taxation of this country and every individual figure in the National Debt, I'll get upon your back and ride you like a horse!" which it's my belief he would have done and even actually jerking his neat little legs ready for a spring as it was. "This," says Mr. Buffle without his pen "is an assault and I'll have the law of you." "Sir" replies the Major "if you

are a man of honor, your Collector of whatever may be due on the
Honorable Assessment by applying to Major Jackman at the Parlors
Mrs. Lirriper's Lodgings, may obtain what he wants in full at any
moment."

When the Major glared at Mr. Buffle with those meaning words
my dear I literally gasped for a teaspoonful of salvolatile in a wine-
glass of water, and I says "Pray let it go no farther gentlemen I beg
and beseech of you!" But the Major could be got to do nothing else
but snort long after Mr. Buffle was gone, and the effect it had upon
my whole mass of blood when on the next day of Mr. Buffle's rounds
the Major spruced himself up and went humming a tune up and
down the street with one eye almost obliterated by his hat there are
not expressions in Johnson's dictionary to state. But I safely put the
street door on the jar and got behind the Major's blinds with my
shawl on and my mind made up the moment I saw danger to rush
out screeching till my voice failed me and catch the Major round the
neck till my strength went and have all parties bound. I had not
been behind the blinds a quarter of an hour when I saw Mr. Buffle
approaching with his Collecting-books in his hand. The Major likewise saw him approaching and hummed louder and himself approached. They met before the Airy railings. The Major takes off his
hat at arm's length and says "Mr. Buffle I believe?" Mr. Buffle takes
off *his* hat at arm's length and says "That is my name Sir." Says the
Major "Have you any commands for me, Mr. Buffle?" Says Mr.
Buffle "Not any Sir." Then my dear both of 'em bowed very low and
haughty and parted, and whenever Mr. Buffle made his rounds in
future him and the Major always met and bowed before the Airy
railings, putting me much in mind of Hamlet and the other gentleman in mourning before killing one another, though I could have
wished the other gentleman had done it fairer and even if less polite
no poison.

Mr. Buffle's family were not liked in this neighborhood, for when
you are a householder my dear you'll find it does not come by nature to like the Assessed, and it was considered besides that a one-
horse pheayton ought not to have elevated Mrs. Buffle to that height
especially when purloined from the Taxes which I myself did consider uncharitable. But they were *not* liked and there was that domestic unhappiness in the family in consequence of their both being
very hard with Miss Buffle and one another on account of Miss

Buffle's favoring Mr. Buffle's articled young gentleman, that it *was* whispered that Miss Buffle would go either into a consumption or a convent she being so very thin and off her appetite and two close-shaved gentlemen with white bands round their necks peeping round the corner whenever she went out in waistcoats resembling black pinafores. So things stood towards Mr. Buffle when one night I was woke by a frightful noise and a smell of burning, and going to my bedroom window saw the whole street in a glow. Fortunately we had two sets empty just then and before I could hurry on some clothes I heard the Major hammering at the attics' doors and calling out "Dress yourselves! — Fire! Don't be frightened! — Fire! Collect your presence of mind! — Fire! All right — Fire!" most tremenjously. As I opened my bedroom door the Major came tumbling in over himself and me, and caught me in his arms. "Major" I says breathless "where is it?" "I don't know dearest madam" says the Major — "Fire! Jemmy Jackman will defend you to the last drop of his blood — Fire! If the dear boy was at home what a treat this would be for him — Fire!" and altogether very collected and bold except that he couldn't say a single sentence without shaking me to the very center with roaring Fire. We ran down to the drawing-room and put our heads out of window, and the Major calls to an unfeeling young monkey, scampering by be joyful and ready to split "Where is it? — Fire!" The monkey answers without stopping "O here's a lark! Old Buffle's been setting his house alight to prevent its being found out that he boned the Taxes. Hurrah! Fire!" And then the sparks came flying up and the smoke came pouring down and the crackling of flames and spatting of water and banging of engines and hacking of axes and breaking of glass and knocking at doors and the shouting and crying and hurrying and the heat and altogether gave me a dreadful palpitation. "Don't be frightened dearest madam," says the Major, " — Fire! There's nothing to be alarmed at — Fire! Don't open the street door till I come back — Fire! I'll go and see if I can be of any service — Fire! You're quite composed and comfortable ain't you? — Fire, Fire, Fire!" It was in vain for me to hold the man and tell him he'd be galloped to death by the engines — pumped to death by his over-exertions — wet-feeted to death by the slop and mess — flattened to death when the roofs fell in — his spirit was up and he went scampering off after the young monkey with all the breath he had and none to spare, and me and the girls huddled together at the parlor windows looking at the dreadful flames above the houses over the way, Mr. Buffle's being round the corner. Presently what should we see but some people running down the street straight to our door, and then the Major directing operations in the busiest way, and then some more people and then — carried in a chair similar to Guy Fawkes — Mr. Buffle in a blanket!

My dear the Major has Mr. Buffle brought up our steps and whisked into the parlor and carted out on the sofy, and then he and all the rest of them without so much as a word burst away again full speed, leaving the impression of a vision except for Mr. Buffle awful in his blanket with his eyes a rolling. In a twinkling they all burst back again with Mrs. Buffle in another blanket, which whisked in and carted out on the sofy they all burst off again and all burst back again with Miss Buffle in another blanket, which again whisked in and carted out they all burst off again and all burst back again with Mr. Buffle's articled young gentleman in another blanket — him a holding round the necks of two men carrying him by the legs, similar to the picter of the disgraceful creetur who has lost the fight (but where the chair I do not know) and his hair having the appearance of newly played upon. When all four of a row, the Major rubs his hands and whispers me with what little hoarseness he can get together, "If our dear remarkable boy was only at home what a delightful treat this would be for him!"

My dear we made them some hot tea and toast and some hot brandy-and-water with a little comfortable nutmeg in it, and at first they were scared and low in their spirits but being fully insured got sociable. And the first use Mr. Buffle made of his tongue was to call the Major his Preserver and his best of friends and to say "My forever dearest Sir let me make you known to Mrs. Buffle" which also addressed him as her Preserver and her best of friends and was fully as cordial as the blanket would admit of. Also Miss Buffle. The articled young gentleman's head was a little light and he sat a moaning "Robina is reduced to cinders, Robina is reduced to cinders!" Which went more to the heart on account of his having got wrapped in his blanket as if he was looking out of a violinceller case, until Mr. Buffle says "Robina speak to him!" Miss Buffle says "Dear George!" and but for the Major's pouring down brandy-and-water on the instant which caused a catching in his throat owing to the nutmeg and a violent fit of coughing it might have proved too much for his strength. When the articled young gentleman got the better of it Mr. Buffle leaned up against Mrs. Buffle being two bundles, a little while in confidence, and then says with tears in his eyes which the Major noticing wiped, "We have not been an united family, let us after this danger become so, take her George." The young gentleman could not put his arm out far to do it, but his spoken expressions were very beautiful though of a wandering class. And I do not know that I ever had a much pleasanter meal than the breakfast we took together after we had all dozed, when Miss Buffle made tea very sweetly in quite the Roman style as depicted formerly at Covent Garden Theatre and when the whole family was most agreeable, as they have ever proved since that night when the Major stood at the foot of the Fire-Escape and claimed them as they came down — the young gentleman head-foremost, which accounts. And though I do not say that we should be less liable to think ill of one another if strictly limited to blankets, still I do say that we might most of us come to a better understanding if we kept one another less at a distance.

Why there's Wozenham's lower down on the other side of the street. I had a feeling of much soreness several years respecting what I must still ever call Miss Wozenham's systematic underbidding and the likeness of the house in Bradshaw having far too many windows and a most umbrageous and outrageous Oak which never yet was seen in Norfolk-street nor yet a carriage and four at Wozenham's door, which it would have been far more to Bradshaw's credit to have drawn a cab. This frame of mind continued bitter down to the very afternoon in January last when one of my girls, Sally Rairyganoo which I still suspect of Irish extraction though family represented Cambridge, else why abscond with a bricklayer of the Limerick persuasion and be married in pattens not waiting till his black eye was decently got round with all the company fourteen in number and one horse fighting outside on the roof of the vehicle — I repeat my dear my ill-regulated state of mind towards Miss Wozenham continued down to the very afternoon of January last past when Sally Rairyganoo came banging (I can use no milder expression) into my room with a jump which may be Cambridge and may not, and said "Hurroo Missis! Miss Wozenham's sold up!" My dear when I had it thrown in my face and conscience that the girl Sally had reason to think I could be glad of the ruin of a fellow-creeter, I burst into tears and dropped back in my chair and I says "I am ashamed of myself!"

Well! I tried to settle to my tea but I could not do it what with thinking of Miss Wozenham and her distresses. It was a wretched night and I went up to a front window and looked over at Wozenham's and as well as I could make it out down the street in the fog it was the dismallest of the dismal and not a light to be seen. So at last I says to myself "This will not do," and I puts on my oldest bonnet and shawl not wishing Miss Wozenham to be reminded of my best at such a time, and lo and behold you I goes over to Wozenham's and knocks. "Miss Wozenham at home?" I says turning my head when I heard the door go. And then I saw it was Miss Wozenham herself who had opened it and sadly worn she was poor thing and her eyes all swelled and swelled with crying. "Miss Wozenham" I says "it is several years since there was a little unpleasantness betwixt us on the subject of my grandson's cap being down your Airy. I have overlooked it and I hope you have done the same." "Yes Mrs. Lirriper" she says in a surprise "I have." "Then my dear" I says "I should be glad to come in and speak a word to you." Upon my calling her my dear Miss Wozenham breaks out a crying most pitiful, and a not unfeeling elderly person that might have been better shaved in a nightcap with a hat over it offering a polite apology for the mumps having worked themselves into his constitution, and also for sending home to his wife on the bellows which was in his hand as a writing-desk, looks out of the back parlor and says "The lady wants a word of comfort" and goes in again. So I was able to say quite natural "Wants a word of comfort does she Sir? Then please the pigs she shall have it!" And Miss Wozenham and me we go into the front room with a wretched light that seemed to have been crying too and was sputtering out, and I says "Now my dear, tell me all," and she wrings her hands and says "O Mrs. Lirriper that man is in possession here, and I have not a friend in the world who is able to help me with a shilling."

It doesn't signify a bit what a talkative old body like me said to Miss Wozenham when she said that, and so I'll tell you instead my dear that I'd have given thirty shillings to have taken her over to tea, only I durstn't on account of the Major. Not you see but what I knew I could draw the Major out like thread and wind him round my finger on most subjects and perhaps even on that if I was to set myself to it, but him and me had so often belied Miss Wozenham to one another that I was shamefaced, and I knew she had offended his pride and never mine, and likewise I felt timid that that Rairy-ganoo girl might make things awkward. So I says "My dear if you could give me a cup of tea to clear my muddle of a head I should better understand your affairs." And we had the tea and the affairs too and after all it was but forty pound, and — There! she's as industrious and straight a creeter as ever lived and has paid back half of it already, and where's the use of saying more, particularly when it ain't the point? For the point is that when she was a kissing my hands and holding them in hers and kissing them again and blessing blessing blessing, I cheered up at last and I says "Why what a waddling old goose I have been my dear to take you for something so very different!" "Ah but I too" says she "how have *I* mistaken *you!*" "Come for goodness' sake tell me" I says "what you thought of me?" "O" says she "I thought you had no feeling for such a hard hand-to-mouth life as mine, and were rolling in affluence." I says shaking my sides (and very glad to do it for I had been a choking quite long enough) "Only look at my figure my dear and give me your opinion whether if I was in affluence I should be likely to roll in it?" That did it! We got as merry as grigs (whatever *they* are, if you happen to know my dear — *I* don't) and I went home to my blessed home as happy and as thankful as could be. But before I make an end of it, think even of my having misunderstood the Major! Yes! For next forenoon the Major came into my little room with his brushed hat in his hand and he begins "My dearest madam — " and then put his face in his hat as if he had just come into church. As I sat all in a maze he came out of his hat and began again. "My esteemed and beloved friend — " and then went into his hat again. "Major," I cries out frightened "has anything happened to our darling boy?" "No, no, no" says the Major "but Miss Wozenham has been here this morning to make her excuses to me, and by the Lord I can't get over what she told me." "Hoity toity, Major," I says "you don't know yet that I was afraid of you last night and didn't think half as well of you as I ought! So come out of church Major and forgive me like a dear old friend and I'll never do so any more." And I leave you to judge my dear whether I ever did or will. And how affecting to think of Miss Wozenham out of her small income and her losses doing so much for her poor old father, and keeping a brother that had had the misfortune to soften his brain against the hard mathematics as neat as a new pin in the three back represented to lodgers as a lumber-room and consuming a whole shoulder of mutton whenever provided!

And now my dear I really am a going to tell you about my Legacy if you're inclined to favor me with your attention, and I did fully intend to have come straight to it only one thing does so bring up another. It was the month of June and the day before Midsummer Day when my girl Winifred Madgers — she was what is termed a Plymouth Sister, and the Plymouth Brother that made away with her was quite right, for a tidier young woman for a wife never came into a house and afterwards called with the beautifullest Plymouth Twins — it was the day before Midsummer Day when Winifred Madgers comes and says to me "A gentleman from the Consul's wishes particular to speak to Mrs. Lirriper." If you'll believe me my dear the Consols at the bank where I have a little matter for Jemmy got into my head, and I says "Good gracious I hope he ain't had any dreadful fall!" Says Winifred "He don't look as if he had ma'am." And I says "Show him in."

The gentleman came in dark and with his hair cropped what I should consider too close, and he says very polite "Madame Lirrwiper!" "I says "Yes Sir. Take a chair." "I come," says he "frrwom the Frrwench Consul's." So I saw at once that it wasn't the Bank of England. "We have rrweceived," says the gentleman turning his r's very curious and skillful, "frrwom the Mairrwie at Sens, a communication which I will have the honor to rrwead. Madame Lirrwiper understands Frrwench?" "O dear no Sir!" says I. "Madame Lirriper don't understand anything of the sort." "It matters not," says the gentleman, "I will trrwanslate."

With that my dear the gentleman after reading something about a Department and a Marie (which Lord forgive me I supposed till the Major came home was Mary, and never was I more puzzled than to think how that young woman came to have so much to do with it) translated a lot with the most obliging pains, and it came to this — That in the town of Sens in France an unknown Englishman lay a dying. That he was speechless and without motion. That in his lodging there was a gold watch and a purse containing such and such money and a trunk containing such and such clothes, but no passport and no papers, except that on his table was a pack of cards and that he had written in pencil on the back of the ace of hearts: "To the authorities. When I am dead, pray send what is left, as a last Legacy, to Mrs. Lirriper Eighty-one Norfolk Street Strand London." When the gentleman had explained all this, which seemed to be drawn up much more methodical than I should have given the French credit for, not at that time knowing the nation, he put the document into my hand. And much the wiser I was for that you may be sure, except that it had the look of being made out upon grocery paper and was stamped all over with eagles.

"Does Madame Lirrwiper" says the gentleman, "believe she rrwe-cognizes her unfortunate compatrrwiot?"

You may imagine the flurry it put me into my dear to be talked to about my compatriots.

I says "Excuse me. Would you have the kindness Sir to make your language as simple as you can?"

"This Englishman unhappy, at the point of death. This compa-trrwiot afflicted," says the gentleman.

"Thank you, Sir," I says "I understand you now. No Sir I have not the least idea who this can be."

"Has Madame Lirrwiper no son, no nephew, no godson, no frrwiend, no acquaintance of any kind in Frrwance?"

"To my certain knowledge" says I "no relation or friend, and to the best of my belief no acquaintance."

"Pardon me. You take Locataires?" says the gentleman.

My dear fully believing he was offering me something with his obliging foreign manners — snuff for anything I knew — I gave a little bend of my head and I says if you'll credit it, "No I thank you. I have not contracted the habit."

The gentleman looks perplexed and says "Lodgers!"

"Oh!" says I laughing. "Bless the man! Why yes to be sure!"

"May it not be a former lodger?" says the gentleman. "Some lodger that you pardoned some rrwent? You have pardoned lodgers some rrwent?"

"Hem! It has happened Sir" says I, "but I assure you I can call to mind no gentleman of that description that this is at all likely to be."

In short my dear, we could make nothing of it, and the gentleman noted down what I said and went away. But he left me the paper of which he had two with him, and when the Major came in I says to the Major as I put it in his hand "Major here's Old Moore's Almanac with the hieroglyphic complete, for your opinion."

It took the Major a little longer to read than I should have thought, judging from the copious flow with which he seemed to be gifted when attacking the organ-men, but at last he got through it, and stood a gazing at me in amazement.

"Major" I says "you're paralyzed."

"Madam" says the Major, "Jemmy Jackman is doubled up."

Now it did so happen that the Major had been out to get a little information about railroads and steamboats, as our boy was coming home for his Midsummer holidays next day and we were going to take him somewhere for a treat and a change. So while the Major stood a gazing it came into my head to say to him "Major I wish you'd go and look at some of your books and maps, and see whereabouts this same town of Sens is in France."

The Major he roused himself and he went into the Parlors and he poked about a little, and he came back to me and he says, "Sens my dearest madam is seventy-odd miles south of Paris."

With what I may truly call a desperate effort "Major," I says "we'll go there with our blessed boy."

If ever the Major was beside himself it was at the thoughts of that journey. All day long he was like the wild man of the woods after meeting with an advertisement in the papers telling him something to his advantage, and early next morning hours before Jemmy could possibly come home he was outside in the street ready to call out to him that we was all a going to France. Young Rosycheeks you may believe was as wild as the Major, and they did carry on to that degree that I says "If you two children ain't more orderly I'll pack you both off to bed." And then they fell to cleaning up the Major's telescope to see France with, and went out and bought a leather bag with a snap to hang round Jemmy, and him to carry the money like a little Fortunatus with his purse.

If I hadn't passed my word and raised their hopes, I doubt if I could have gone through with the undertaking but it was too late to go back now. So on the second day after Midsummer Day we went off by the morning mail. And when we came to the sea which I had never seen but once in my life and that when my poor Lirriper was courting me, the freshness of it and the deepness and the airiness and to think that it had been rolling ever since and that it was always a rolling and so few of us minding, made me feel quite serious. But I felt happy too and so did Jemmy and the Major and not much motion on the whole, though me with a swimming in the head and a sinking but able to take notice that the foreign insides appear to be constructed hollower than the English, leading to much more tremenjous noises when bad sailors.

But my dear the blueness and the lightness and the colored look of everything and the very sentry-boxes striped and the shining rattling drums and the little soldiers with their waists and tidy gaiters, when we got across to the Continent — it made me feel as if I don't know what — as if the atmosphere had been lifted off me. And as to lunch why bless you if I kept a man-cook and two kitchen-maids I couldn't get it done for twice the money, and no injured young woman a glaring at you and grudging you and acknowledging your patronage by wishing that your food might choke you, but so civil and so hot and attentive and every way comfortable except Jemmy pouring wine down his throat by tumblers-full and me expecting to see him drop under the table.

And the way in which Jemmy spoke his French was a real charm. It was often wanted of him, for whenever anybody spoke a syllable to me I says "Non-comprenny, you're very kind, but it's no use — Now Jemmy!" and then Jemmy he fires away at 'em lovely, the only thing wanting in Jemmy's French being as it appeared to me that he hardly ever understood a word of what they said to him which made it scarcely of the use it might have been though in other respects a perfect Native, and regarding the Major's fluency I should have been of the opinion judging French by English that there might have been a greater choice of words in the language though still I must admit that if I hadn't known him when he asked a military gentleman in a grey cloak what o'clock it was I should have took him for a Frenchman born.

Before going on to look after my Legacy we were to make one regular day in Paris, and I leave you to judge my dear what a day *that* was with Jemmy and the Major and the telescope and me and the prowling young man at the inn door (but very civil too) that went along with us to show the sights. All along the railway to Paris Jemmy and the Major had been frightening me to death by stooping down on the platforms at stations to inspect the engines underneath

JEMMY AND GRAN IN PARIS

their mechanical stomachs, and by creeping in and out I don't know where all, to find improvements for the United Grand Junction Parlor, but when we got out into the brilliant streets on a bright morning they gave up all their London improvements as a bad job and gave their minds to Paris. Says the prowling young man to me "Will I speak Inglis No?" So I says "If you can young man I shall take it as a favor," but after half-an-hour of it when I fully believed the man had gone mad and me too I says "Be so good as fall back on your French Sir," knowing that then I shouldn't have the agonies of trying to understand him, which was a happy release. Not that I lost much more than the rest either, for I generally noticed that when he had described something very long indeed and I says to Jemmy "What does he say Jemmy?" Jemmy says looking with vengeance in his eye "He is so jolly indistinct!" and that when he had described it longer all over again and I says to Jemmy "Well Jemmy what's it all about?" Jemmy says "He says the building was repaired in seventeen hundred and four, Gran."

Wherever that prowling young man formed his prowling habits I cannot be expected to know, but the way in which he went round the corner while we had our breakfasts and was there again when we swallowed the last crumb was most marvelous, and just the same at dinner and at night, prowling equally at the theater and the inn gateway and the shop doors when we bought a trifle or two and everywhere else but troubled with a tendency to spit. And of Paris I can tell you no more my dear than that it's town and country both in one, and carved stone and long streets of high houses and gardens and fountains and statues and trees and gold, and immensely big soldiers and immensely little soldiers and the pleasantest nurses with the whitest caps a playing at skipping-rope with the bunchiest babies in the flattest caps, and clean table-cloths spread everywhere for dinner and people sitting out of doors smoking and sipping all day long and little plays being acted in the open air for little people and every shop a complete and elegant room, and everybody seeming to play at everything in this world. And as to the sparkling lights my dear after dark, glittering high up and low down and on before and on behind and all round, and the crowd of theaters and the crowd of people and the crowd of all sorts, it's pure enchantment. And pretty well the only thing that grated on me was that whether you pay your fare at the railway or whether you change your money at a money-dealer's or whether you take your ticket at the theater, the lady or gentleman is caged up (I suppose by government) behind the strongest iron bars having more of a Zoological appearance than a free country.

Well to be sure when I did after all get my precious bones to bed that night, and my Young Rogue came in to kiss me and asks "What do you think of this lovely lovely Paris, Gran?" I says "Jemmy I feel as if it was beautiful fireworks being let off in my head." And very cool and refreshing the pleasant country was next day when we went on to look after my Legacy, and rested me much and did me a deal of good.

So at length and at last my dear we come to Sens, a pretty little town with a great two-towered cathedral and the rooks flying in and out of the loopholes and another tower atop of one of the towers like a sort of a stone pulpit. In which pulpit with the birds skimming below him if you'll believe me, I saw a speck while I was resting at the inn before dinner which they made signs to me was Jemmy and which really was. I had been a fancying as I sat in the balcony of the hotel that an Angel might light there and call down to the people to be good, but I little thought what Jemmy all unknown to himself was a calling down from that high place to some one in the town.

The pleasantest-situated inn my dear! Right under the two towers, with their shadows a changing upon it all day like a kind of a sundial, and country people driving in and out of the courtyard in carts and hooded cabriolets and such like, and a market outside in front of the cathedral, and all so quaint and like a picter. The Major and me agreed that whatever came of my Legacy this was the place to stay in for our holiday, and we also agreed that our dear boy had best not be checked in his joy that night by the sight of the Englishman if he was still alive, but that we would go together and alone. For you are to understand that the Major not feeling himself quite equal in his wind to the height to which Jemmy had climbed, had come back to me and left him with the Guide.

So after dinner when Jemmy had set off to see the river, the Major went down to the Mairie, and presently came back with a military character in a sword and spurs and a cocked hat and a yellow shoulder-belt and long tags about him that he must have found inconvenient. And the Major says "The Englishman still lies in the same state dearest madam. This gentleman will conduct us to his lodging."

Upon which the military character pulled off his cocked hat to me, and I took notice that he had shaved his forehead in imitation of Napoleon Bonaparte but not like.

We went out at the courtyard gate and past the great doors of the cathedral and down a narrow High-street where the people were sitting chatting at their shop doors and the children were at play. The military character went in front and he stopped at a pork-shop with a little statue of a pig sitting up, in the window, and a private door that a donkey was looking out of.

When the donkey saw the military character he came slipping out on the pavement to turn round and then clattered along the passage into a back yard. So the coast being clear, the Major and me were conducted up the common stair and into the front room on the second, a bare room with a red tiled floor and the outside lattice blinds pulled close to darken it. As the military character opened the blinds I saw the tower where I had seen Jemmy, darkening as the sun got low, and I turned to the bed by the wall and saw the Englishman.

It was some kind of brain fever he had had, and his hair was all gone, and some wetted folded linen lay upon his head. I looked at him very attentive as he lay there all wasted away with his eyes closed, and I says to the Major:

"I never saw this face before."

The Major looked at him very attentive too, and he says:

"*I* never saw this face before."

When the Major explained our words to the military character, that gentleman shrugged his shoulders and showed the Major the card on which it was written about the Legacy for me. It had been written with a weak and trembling hand in bed, and I knew no more of the writing than of the face. Neither did the Major.

Though lying there alone, the poor creetur was as well taken care of as could be hoped, and would have been quite unconscious of any one's sitting by him then. I got the Major to say that we were not going away at present and that I would come back to-morrow and watch a bit by the bedside. But I got him to add — and I shook my head hard to make it stronger — "We agree that we never saw this face before."

Our boy was greatly surprised when we told him sitting out in the balcony in the starlight, and he ran over some of those stories of for-

mer Lodgers, of the Major's putting down, and asked wasn't it possible that it might be this lodger or that lodger. It was not possible,
and we went to bed.

In the morning just at breakfast-time the military character came
jingling round, and said that the doctor thought from the signs he
saw there might be some rally before the end. So I says to the Major
and Jemmy, "You two boys go and enjoy yourselves, and I'll take my
Prayer Book and go sit by the bed." So I went, and I sat there some
hours, reading a prayer for him poor soul now and then, and it was
quite on in the day when he moved his hand.

He had been so still, that the moment he moved I knew of it, and I
pulled off my spectacles and laid down my book and rose and
looked at him. From moving one hand he began to move both, and
then his action was the action of a person groping in the dark. Long
after his eyes had opened, there was a film over them and he still felt
for his way out into light. But by slow degrees his sight cleared and
his hands stopped. He saw the ceiling, he saw the wall, he saw me.
As his sight cleared, mine cleared too, and when at last we looked in
one another's faces, I started back and I cries passionately:

"O you wicked wicked man! Your sin has found you out!"

For I knew him, the moment life looked out of his eyes, to be Mr.
Edson, Jemmy's father who had so cruelly deserted Jemmy's young
unmarried mother who had died in my arms, poor tender creetur,
and left Jemmy to me.

"You cruel wicked man! You bad black traitor!"

With the little strength he had, he made an attempt to turn over
on his wretched face to hide it. His arm dropped out of the bed and
his head with it, and there he lay before me crushed in body and in
mind. Surely the miserablest sight under the summer sun!

"O blessed Heaven," I says a crying, "teach me what to say to this
broken mortal! I am a poor sinful creetur, and the Judgment is not
mine."

As I lifted my eyes up to the clear bright sky, I saw the high tower
where Jemmy had stood above the birds, seeing that very window;
and the last look of that poor pretty young mother when her soul
brightened and got free, seemed to shine down from it.

"O man, man, man!" I says, and I went on my knees beside the
bed; "if your heart is rent asunder and you are truly penitent for
what you did, Our Saviour will have mercy on you yet!"

As I leaned my face against the bed, his feeble hand could just move itself enough to touch me. I hope the touch was penitent. It tried to hold my dress and keep hold, but the fingers were too weak to close.

I lifted him back upon the pillows and I says to him:
"Can you hear me?"
He looked yes.
"Do you know me?"
He looked yes, even yet more plainly.
"I am not here alone. The Major is with me. You recollect the Major?"
Yes. That is to say he made out yes, in the same way as before.
"And even the Major and I are not alone. My grandson — his godson — is with us. Do you hear? My grandson."
The fingers made another trial to catch at my sleeve, but could only creep near it and fall.
"Do you know who my grandson is?"
Yes.
"I pitied and loved his lonely mother. When his mother lay a dying I said to her, 'My dear, this baby is sent to a childless old woman.' He has been my pride and joy ever since. I love him as dearly as if he had drunk from my breast. Do you ask to see my grandson before you die?"
Yes.
"Show me, when I leave off speaking, if you correctly understand what I say. He has been kept unacquainted with the story of his birth. He has no knowledge of it. No suspicion of it. If I bring him here to the side of this bed, he will suppose you to be a perfect stranger. It is more than I can do to keep from him the knowledge that there is such wrong and misery in the world; but that it was ever so near him in his innocent cradle I have kept from him, and I do keep from him, and I ever will keep from him, for his mother's sake, and for his own."
He showed me that he distinctly understood, and the tears fell from his eyes.
"Now rest, and you shall see him."
So I got him a little wine and some brandy, and I put things straight about his bed. But I began to be troubled in my mind lest Jemmy and the Major might be too long of coming back. What with

this occupation for my thoughts and hands, I didn't hear a foot upon the stairs, and was startled when I saw the Major stopped short in the middle of the room by the eyes of the man upon the bed, and knowing him then, as I had known him a little while ago.

There was anger in the Major's face, and there was horror and repugnance and I don't know what. So I went up to him and I led him to the bedside, and when I clasped my hands and lifted of them up, the Major did the like.

"O Lord" I says "Thou knowest what we two saw together of the sufferings and sorrows of that young creetur now with Thee. If this dying man is truly penitent, we two together humbly pray Thee to have mercy on him!"

The Major says "Amen!" and then after a little stop I whispers him, "Dear old friend fetch our beloved boy." And the Major, so clever as to have got to understand it all without being told a word, went away and brought him.

Never never never shall I forget the fair bright face of our boy when he stood at the foot of the bed, looking at his unknown father. And O so like his dear young mother then!

"Jemmy," I says, "I have found out all about this poor gentleman who is so ill, and he did lodge in the old house once. And as he wants to see all belonging to it, now that he is passing away, I sent for you."

"Ah poor man!" says Jemmy stepping forward and touching one of his hands with great gentleness. "My heart melts for him. Poor, poor man!"

The eyes that were so soon to close forever turned to me, and I was not that strong in the pride of my strength that I could resist them.

"My darling boy, there is a reason in the secret history of this fellow-creetur lying as the best and worst of us must all lie one day, which I think would ease his spirit in his last hour if you would lay your cheek against his forehead and say, 'May God forgive you!' "

"O Gran," says Jemmy with a full heart "I am not worthy!" But he leaned down and did it. Then the faltering fingers made out to catch hold of my sleeve at last, and I believe he was a-trying to kiss me when he died.

*   *   *

There my dear! There you have the story of my Legacy in full, and it's worth ten times the trouble I have spent upon it if you are pleased to like it.

You might suppose that it set us against the little French town of Sens, but no we didn't find that. I found myself that I never looked up at the high tower atop of the other tower, but the days came back again when that fair young creetur with her pretty bright hair trusted in me like a mother, and the recollection made the place so peaceful to me as I can't express. And every soul about the hotel down to the pigeons in the courtyard made friends with Jemmy and the Major, and went lumbering away with them on all sorts of expeditions in all sorts of vehicles drawn by rampagious cart-horses — with heads and without — mud for paint and ropes for harness — and every new friend dressed in blue like a butcher, and every new horse standing on his hind legs wanting to devour and consume every other horse, and every man that had a whip to crack crack-crack-crack-crack-cracking it as if it was a schoolboy with his first. As to the Major my dear that man lived the greater part of his time with a little tumbler in one hand and a bottle of small wine in the other, and whenever he saw anybody else with a little tumbler, no matter who it was — the military character with the tags, or the inn-servants at their supper in the courtyard, or townspeople a chatting on a bench, or country people a starting home after Market — down rushes the Major to clink his glass against their glasses and cry — Hola! Vive Somebody! or Vive Something! as if he was beside himself. And though I could not quite approve of the Major's doing it, still the ways of the world are the ways of the world varying according to the different parts of it, and dancing at all in the open Square with a lady that kept a barber's shop my opinion is that the Major was right to dance his best and to lead off with a power that I did not think was in him, though I was a little uneasy at the Barricading sound of the cries that were set up by the other dancers and the rest of the company, until when I says "What are they ever calling out Jemmy?" Jemmy says, "They're calling out Gran, Bravo the Military English! Bravo the Military English!" which was very gratifying to my feelings as a Briton and became the name the Major was known by.

But every evening at a regular time we all three sat out in the balcony of the hotel at the end of the courtyard, looking up at the golden and rosy light as it changed on the great towers, and looking at the shadows of the towers as they changed on all about us ourselves included, and what do you think we did there? My dear, if Jemmy hadn't brought some other of those stories of the Major's taking down from the telling of former lodgers at Eighty-one Norfolk-street, and if he didn't bring 'em out with this speech:

"Here you are Gran! Here you are godfather! More of 'em! *I*'ll read. And though you wrote 'em for me, godfather, I know you won't disapprove of my making 'em over to Gran; will you?"

"No, my dear boy," says the Major. "Everything we have is hers, and we are hers."

"Hers ever affectionately and devotedly J. Jackman, and J. Jackman Lirriper," cries the Young Rogue giving me a close hug. "Very well then godfather. Look here. As Gran is in the Legacy way just now, I shall make these stories a part of Gran's Legacy. I'll leave 'em to her. What do you say godfather?"

"Hip hip Hurrah!" says the Major.

"Very well then," cries Jemmy all in a bustle. "Vive the Military English! Vive the Lady Lirriper! Vive the Jemmy Jackman Ditto! Vive the Legacy! Now, you look out, Gran. And you look out, godfather. *I*'ll read! and I'll tell you what I'll do besides. On the last night of our holiday here when we are all packed and going away, I'll top up with something of my own."

"Mind you do Sir" says I.

CHAPTER II

MRS. LIRRIPER RELATES HOW JEMMY
TOPPED UP

Well my dear and so the evening readings of those jottings of the Major's brought us round at last to the evening when we were all packed and going away next day, and I do assure you that by that time though it was deliciously comfortable to look forward to the dear old house in Norfolk-street again, I had formed quite a high opinion of the French nation and had noticed them to be much more homely and domestic in their families and far more simple and amiable in their lives than I had ever been led to expect, and it did strike me between ourselves that in one particular they might be imitated to advantage by another nation which I will not mention, and that is in the courage with which they take their little enjoyments on little means and with little things and don't let solemn big-wigs stare them out of countenance or speechify them dull, of which said solemn big-wigs I have ever had the one opinion that I wish they were all made comfortable separately in coppers with the lids on and never let out any more.

"Now young man," I says to Jemmy when we brought our chairs into the balcony that last evening, "you please to remember who was to 'top up.' "

"All right Gran" says Jemmy. "I am the illustrious personage."

But he looked so serious after he had made me that light answer, that the Major raised his eyebrows at me and I raised mine at the Major.

"Gran and godfather," says Jemmy, "you can hardly think how much my mind has run on Mr. Edson's death."

It gave me a little check. "Ah! it was a sad scene my love" I says, "and sad remembrances come back stronger than merry. But this" I says after a little silence, to rouse myself and the Major and Jemmy all together, "is not topping up. Tell us your story my dear."

"I will" says Jemmy.

"What is the date Sir?" says I. "Once upon a time when pigs drank wine?"

"No Gran," says Jemmy, still serious; "once upon a time when the French drank wine."

Again I glanced at the Major, and the Major glanced at me.

"In short, Gran and godfather," says Jemmy, looking up, "the date is this time, and I'm going to tell you Mr. Edson's story."

The flutter that it threw me into. The change of color on the part of the Major!

"That is to say, you understand," our bright-eyed boy says, "I am going to give you my version of it. I shall not ask whether it's right or not, firstly because you said you knew very little about it, Gran, and secondly because what little you did know was a secret."

I folded my hands in my lap and I never took my eyes off Jemmy as he went running on.

"The unfortunate gentleman" Jemmy commences, "who is the subject of our present narrative was the son of Somebody, and was born Somewhere, and chose a profession Somehow. It is not with those parts of his career that we have to deal; but with his early attachment to a young and beautiful lady."

I thought I should have dropped. I durstn't look at the Major; but I knew what his state was, without looking at him.

"The father of our ill-starred hero" says Jemmy, copying as it seemed to me the style of some of his story-books, "was a worldly man who entertained ambitious views for his only son and who firmly set his face against the contemplated alliance with a virtuous but penniless orphan. Indeed he went so far as roundly to assure our hero that unless he weaned his thoughts from the object of his devoted affection, he would disinherit him. At the same time, he proposed as a suitable match the daughter of a neighboring gentleman of a good estate, who was neither ill-favored nor unamiable, and whose eligibility in a pecuniary point of view could not be disputed. But young Mr. Edson, true to the first and only love that had inflamed his breast, rejected all considerations of self-advancement, and, deprecating his father's anger in a respectful letter, ran away with her."

My dear I had begun to take a turn for the better, but when it come to running away I began to take another turn for the worse.

"The lovers" says Jemmy "fled to London and were united at the altar of Saint Clement's Danes. And it is at this period of their simple but touching story that we find them inmates of the dwelling of a highly respected and beloved lady of the name of Gran, residing within a hundred miles of Norfolk-street."

I felt that we were almost safe now, I felt that the dear boy had no suspicion of the bitter truth, and I looked at the Major for the first time and drew a long breath. The Major gave me a nod.

"Our hero's father" Jemmy goes on "proving implacable and carrying his threat into unrelenting execution, the struggles of the young couple in London were severe, and would have been far more so, but for their good angel's having conducted them to the abode of Mrs. Gran; who, divining their poverty (in spite of their endeavors to conceal it from her), by a thousand delicate arts smoothed their rough way, and alleviated the sharpness of their first distress."

Here Jemmy took one of my hands in one of his, and began a marking the turns of his history by making me give a beat from time to time upon his other hand.

"After a while, they left the house of Mrs. Gran, and pursued their fortunes through a variety of successes and failures elsewhere. But in all reverses, whether for good or evil, the words of Mr. Edson to the fair young partner of his life were, 'Unchanging Love and Truth will carry us through all!' "

My hand trembled in the dear boy's, those words so wofully unlike the fact.

"Unchanging Love and Truth" says Jemmy over again, as if he had a proud kind of a noble pleasure in it, "will carry us through all! Those were his words. And so they fought their way, poor but gallant and happy, until Mrs. Edson gave birth to a child."

"A daughter," I says.

"No," says Jemmy, "a son. And the father was so proud of it that he could hardly bear it out of his sight. But a dark cloud overspread the scene. Mrs. Edson sickened, drooped, and died."

"Ah! Sickened, drooped, and died!" I says.

"And so Mr. Edson's only comfort, only hope on earth, and only stimulus to action, was his darling boy. As the child grew older, he grew so like his mother that he was her living picture. It used to make him wonder why his father cried when he kissed him. But unhappily he was like his mother in constitution as well as in face, and he died too before he had grown out of childhood. Then Mr. Edson, who had good abilities, in his forlornness and despair, threw them all to the winds. He became apathetic, reckless, lost. Little by little he sank down, down, down, down, until at last he almost lived (I think) by gaming. And so sickness overtook him in the town of Sens in France, and he lay down to die. But now that he laid him down when all was done, and looked back upon the green Past beyond the time when he had covered it with ashes, he thought gratefully of the good Mrs. Gran long lost sight of, who had been so kind to him and his young wife in the early days of their marriage, and he left the little that he had as a last Legacy to her. And she, being brought to see him, at first no more knew him than she would know from seeing the ruin of a Greek or Roman Temple, what it used to be before it fell; but at length she remembered him. And then he told her, with tears, of his regret for the misspent part of his life, and besought her to think as mildly of it as she could, because it was the poor fallen Angel of his unchanging Love and Constancy after all. And because she had her grandson with her, and he fancied that his own boy, if he had lived, might have grown to be something like him, he asked her to let him touch his forehead with his cheek and say certain parting words."

Jemmy's voice sank low when it got to that and tears filled my eyes, and filled the Major's.

"You little Conjurer" I says, "how did you ever make it all out? Go in and write it every word down, for it's a wonder."

Which Jemmy did, and I have repeated it to you my dear from his writing.

Then the Major took my hand and kissed it, and said, "Dearest madam all has prospered with us."

"Ah Major" I says drying my eyes, "we needn't have been afraid. We might have known it. Treachery don't come natural to beaming youth; but trust and pity, love and constancy — they do, thank God!"

DOCTOR

MARIGOLD

IN THREE CHAPTERS

Dr. Marigold

I. TO BE TAKEN IMMEDIATELY

I AM A Cheap Jack, and my own father's name was Willum Marigold. It was in his lifetime supposed by some that his name was William, but my own father always consistently said, No, it was Willum. On which point I content myself with looking at the argument this way: If a man is not allowed to know his own name in a free country, how much is he allowed to know in a land of slavery? As to looking at the argument through the medium of the Register, Willum Marigold come into the world before Registers come up much — and went out of it too. They wouldn't have been greatly in his line neither, if they had chanced to come up before him.

I was born on the Queen's highway, but it was the King's at that time. A doctor was fetched to my own mother by my own father, when it took place on a common; and in consequence of his being a very kind gentleman, and accepting no fee but a tea-tray, I was named Doctor, out of gratitude and compliment to him. There you have me. Doctor Marigold.

I am at present a middle-aged man of a broadish build, in cords, leggings, and a sleeved waistcoat the strings of which is always gone behind. Repair them how you will, they go like fiddle-strings. You have been to the theater, and you have seen one of the wiolin-players screw up his wiolin, after listening to it as if it had been whispering the secret to him that it feared it was out of order, and then you have heard it snap. That's as exactly similar to my waistcoat as a waistcoat and a wiolin can be like one another.

I am partial to a white hat, and I like a shawl round my neck wore

227

loose and easy. Sitting down is my favorite posture. If I have a taste in point of personal jewelry, it is mother-of-pearl buttons. There you have me again, as large as life.

The doctor having accepted a tea-tray, you'll guess that my father was a Cheap Jack before me. You are right. He was. It was a pretty tray. It represented a large lady going along a serpentining up-hill gravel-walk, to attend a little church. Two swans had likewise come astray with the same intentions. When I call her a large lady, I don't mean in point of breadth, for there she fell below my views, but she more than made it up in heighth; her heighth and slimness was — in short THE heighth of both.

I often saw that tray, after I was the innocently smiling cause (or more like screeching one) of the doctor's standing it up on a table against the wall in his consulting-room. Whenever my own father and mother were in that part of the country, I used to put my head (I have heard my own mother say it was flaxen curls at that time, though you wouldn't know an old hearth-broom from it now till you come to the handle, and found it wasn't me) in at the doctor's door, and the doctor was always glad to see me, and said, "Aha, my brother practitioner! Come in, little M.D. How are your inclinations as to sixpence?"

You can't go on forever, you'll find, nor yet could my father nor yet my mother. If you don't go off as a whole when you are about due, you're liable to go off in part, and two to one your head's the part. Gradually my father went off his, and my mother went off hers. It was in a harmless way, but it put out the family where I boarded them. The old couple, though retired, got to be wholly and solely devoted to the Cheap Jack business, and were always selling the family off. Whenever the cloth was laid for dinner, my father began rattling the plates and dishes, as we do in our line when we put up crockery for a bid, only he had lost the trick of it, and mostly let 'em drop and broke 'em. As the old lady had been used to sit in the cart, and hand the articles out one by one to the old gentleman on the footboard to sell, just in the same way she handed him every item of the family's property, and they disposed of it in their own imaginations from morning to night. At last the old gentleman, lying bed-ridden in the same room with the old lady, cries out in the old patter, fluent, after having been silent for two days and nights: "Now here, my jolly companions every one — which the Nightingale club in a village was held, At the sign of the Cabbage and Shears, Where the singers no doubt would have greatly excelled, But for want of taste, voices, and ears — now, here, my jolly companions, every one, is a working model of a used-up old Cheap Jack, without a tooth in his head, and with a pain in every bone: so like life that it would be just as good if it wasn't better, just as bad if it wasn't worse, and just as new if it wasn't worn out. Bid for the working model of the old Cheap Jack, who has drunk more gunpowder tea with the ladies in his time than would blow the lid off a washerwoman's copper, and carry it as many thousands of miles higher than the moon as naught nix naught, divided by the national debt, carry nothing to the poor-rates, three under, and two over. Now, my hearts of oak and men of straw, what do you say for the lot? Two shillings, a shilling, tenpence, eightpence, sixpence, fourpence. Twopence? Who said twopence? The gentleman in the scarecrow's hat? I am ashamed of the gentleman in the scarecrow's hat. I really am ashamed of him for his want of public spirit. Now I'll tell you what I'll do with you. Come! I'll throw you in a working model of a old woman that was married to the old Cheap Jack so long ago that upon my word and honor it took place in Noah's Ark, before the Unicorn could get in to forbid the banns by blowing a tune upon his horn. There now! Come! What do you say for both? I'll tell you what I'll do with you. I don't bear you malice for being so backward. Here! If you make me a bid that'll only reflect a little credit on your town, I'll throw you in a warming-pan for nothing, and lend you a toasting-fork for life. Now come; what do you say after that splendid offer? Say two pound, say thirty shillings, say a pound, say ten shillings, say five, say two and six? You don't say even two and six? You say two and three? No. You shan't have the lot for two and three. I'd sooner give it to you, if you was good-looking enough. Here! Missis! Chuck the old man and woman into the cart, put the horse to, and drive 'em away and bury 'em!" Such were the last words of Willum Marigold, my own father, and they were carried out, by him and by his wife, my own mother, on one and the same day, as I ought to know, having followed as mourner.

My father had been a lovely one in his time at the Cheap Jack work, as his dying observations went to prove. But I top him. I don't say it because it's myself, but because it has been universally acknowledged by all that has had the means of comparison. I have worked at it. I have measured myself against other public speakers — Members of Parliament, Platforms, Pulpits, Counsel learned in the law — and where I have found 'em good, I have took a bit of imagination from 'em, and where I have found 'em bad, I have let 'em alone. Now I'll tell you what. I mean to go down into my grave declaring that of all the callings ill used in Great Britain, the Cheap Jack calling is the worst used. Why ain't we a profession? Why ain't we endowed with privileges? Why are we forced to take out a hawkers's license, when no such thing is expected of the political hawkers? Where's the difference betwixt us? Except that we are Cheap Jacks, and they are Dear Jacks, *I* don't see any difference but what's in our favor.

For look here! Say it's election time. I am on the footboard of my cart in the market-place, on a Saturday night. I put up a general miscellaneous lot. I say: "Now here, my free and independent woters, I'm a going to give you such a chance as you never had in all your born days, nor yet the days preceding. Now I'll show you what I am a going to do with you. Here's a pair of razors that'll shave you closer than the Board of Guardians; here's a flat-iron worth its weight in gold; here's a frying-pan artificially flavored with essence of beefsteaks to that degree that you've only got for the rest of your lives to fry bread and dripping in it and there you are replete with animal food; here's a genuine chronometer watch in such a solid silver case that you may knock at the door with it when you come home late from a social meeting, and rouse your wife and family, and save up your knocker for the postman; and here's half-a-dozen dinner plates that you may play the cymbals with to charm the baby when it's fractious. Stop! I'll throw you in another article, and I'll give you that, and it's a rolling-pin; and if the baby can only get it well into its mouth when its teeth is coming and rub the gums once with it, they'll come through double, in a fit of laughter equal to being tickled. Stop again! I'll throw you in another article, because I don't like the looks of you, for you haven't the appearance of buyers unless I lose by you, and because I'd rather lose than not take money to-night, and that's a looking-glass in which you may see how ugly you look when you don't bid. What do you say now? Come! Do you say a pound? Not you, for you haven't got it. Do you say ten shillings? Not you, for you owe more to the tallyman. Well then, I'll tell you what I'll do with you. I'll heap 'em all on the footboard of the cart — there they are! razors, flat-iron, frying-pan, chronometer watch, dinner plates, rolling-pin, and looking-glass — take 'em all away for four shillings, and I'll give you sixpence for your trouble!" This is me, the Cheap Jack. But on the Monday morning, in the same market-place, comes the Dear Jack on the hustings — *his* cart — and what does *he* say? "Now my free and independent woters, I am a going to give you such a chance" (he begins just like me) "as you never had in all your born days, and that's the chance of sending Myself to Parliament. Now I'll tell you what I am a going to do for you. Here's the interests of this magnificent town promoted above all the rest of the civilized and uncivilized earth. Here's your railways carried, and your neighbors' railways jockeyed. Here's all your sons in the Post-office. Here's Britannia smiling on you. Here's the eyes of Europe on you. Here's uniwersal prosperity for you, repletion of animal food, golden cornfields, gladsome homesteads, and rounds of applause from your own hearts, all in one lot, and that's myself. Will you take me as I stand? You won't? Well, then, I'll tell you what I'll do with you. Come now! I'll throw you in anything you ask for. There! Church-rates, abolition of church-rates, more malt tax, no malt tax, uniwersal education to the highest mark, or uniwersal ignorance to the lowest, total abolition of flogging in the army or a dozen for every private once a month all round. Wrongs of Men or Rights of Women — only say which it shall be, take 'em or leave 'em, and I'm of your opinion altogether, and the lot's your own on your own terms. There! You won't take it yet! Well, then, I'll tell you what I'll do with you. Come! You *are* such free and independent woters, and I *am* so proud of you — you *are* such a noble and enlightened constituency, and I *am* so ambitious of the honor and dignity of being your member, which is by far the highest level to which the wings of the human mind can soar — that I'll tell you what I'll do with you. I'll throw you in all the public-houses in your magnificent town for nothing. Will that content you? It won't? You won't take the lot yet? Well, then, before I put the horse in and drive away, and make the offer to the next most magnificent town that can be discovered, I'll tell you what I'll do. Take the lot, and I'll drop two thousand pound in the streets of your magnificent town for them to pick up that can. Not enough? Now look here. This is the very furthest that I'm a going to. I'll make it two thousand five hundred. And still you won't? Here, missis! Put the horse — no, stop half a moment, I shouldn't like to turn my back upon you neither for a trifle, I'll make it two thousand seven hundred and fifty pound. There! Take the lot on your own terms, and I'll count out two thousand seven hundred and fifty pound on the footboard of the cart, to be dropped in the streets of your magnificent town for them to pick up that can. What do you say? Come now! You won't do better, and you may do worse. You take it? Hooray! Sold again, and got the seat!"

These Dear Jacks soap the people shameful, but we Cheap Jacks don't. We tell 'em the truth about themselves to their faces, and scorn to court 'em. As to wenturesomeness in the way of puffing up the lots, the Dear Jacks beats us hollow. It is considered in the Cheap Jack calling, that better patter can be made out of a gun than any article we put up from the cart, except a pair of spectacles. I often hold forth about a gun for a quarter of an hour, and feel as if I need never leave off. But when I tell 'em what the gun can do, and what the gun has brought down, I never go half so far as the Dear Jacks do when they make speeches in praise of *their* guns — their great guns that set 'em on to do it. Besides, I'm in business for myself: I ain't sent down into the market-place to order, as they are. Besides, again, my guns don't know what I say in their laudation, and their guns do, and the whole concern of 'em have reason to be sick and ashamed all round. These are some of my arguments for declaring that the Cheap Jack calling is treated ill in Great Britain, and for turning warm when I think of the other Jacks in question setting themselves up to pretend to look down upon it.

I courted my wife from the footboard of the cart. I did indeed. She was a Suffolk young woman, and it was in Ipswich market-place right opposite the corn-chandler's shop. I had noticed her up at a window last Saturday that was, appreciating highly. I had took to her, and I had said to myself, "If not already disposed of, I'll have that lot." Next Saturday that come, I pitched the cart on the same pitch, and I was in very high feather indeed, keeping 'em laughing the whole of the time, and getting off the goods briskly. At last I took out of my waistcoat-pocket a small lot wrapped in soft paper, and I put it this way (looking up at the window where she was). "Now here, my blooming English maidens, is an article, the last article of the present evening's sale, which I offer to only you, the ovely Suffolk Dumplings biling over with beauty, and I won't take a bid of a thousand pounds for from any man alive. Now what is it? Why, I'll tell you what it is. It's made of fine gold, and it's not broke, hough there's a hole in the middle of it, and it's stronger than any etter that ever was forged, though it's smaller than any finger in my et of ten. Why ten? Because, when my parents made over my prop-rty to me, I tell you true, there was twelve sheets, twelve towels, welve table-cloths, twelve knives, twelve forks, twelve tablespoons, und twelve teaspoons, but my set of fingers was two short of a dozen, und could never since be matched. Now what else is it? Come, I'll ell you. It's a hoop of solid gold, wrapped in a silver curl-paper, that I myself took off the shining locks of the ever-beautiful old lady in Threadneedle-street, London city; I wouldn't tell you so if I hadn't he paper to show, or you mightn't believe it even of me. Now what else is it? It's a man-trap and a handcuff, the parish stocks and a leg-ock, all in gold and all in one. Now what else is it? It's a wedding-ring. Now I'll tell you what I'm a going to do with it. I'm not a going to offer this lot for money; but I mean to give it to the next of you beauties that laughs, and I'll pay her a visit to-morrow morning at exactly half after nine o'clock as the chimes go, and I'll take her out for a walk to put up the banns." *She* laughed, and got the ring handed up to her. When I called in the morning, she says, "O dear! It's never you, and you never mean it?" "It's ever me," says I, "and I am ever yours, and I ever mean it." So we got married, after being out up three times — which, by the bye, is quite in the Cheap Jack way again, and shows once more how the Cheap Jack customs per-vade society.

She wasn't a bad wife, but she had a temper. If she could have parted with that one article at a sacrifice, I wouldn't have swopped her away in exchange for any other woman in England. Not that I ever did swop her away, for we lived together till she died, and that was thirteen year. Now, my lords and ladies and gentlefolks all, I'll let you into a secret, though you won't believe it. Thirteen year of temper in a Palace would try the worst of you, but thirteen year of temper in a Cart would try the best of you. You are kept so very close to it in a cart, you see. There's thousands of couples among you getting on like sweet ile upon a whetstone in houses five and six pairs of stairs high, that would go to the Divorce Court in a cart.

Whether the jolting makes it worse, I don't undertake to decide; but in a cart it does come home to you, and stick to you. Wiolence in a cart is *so* wiolent, and aggrawation in a cart is *so* aggrawating.

We might have had such a pleasant life! A roomy cart, with the large goods hung outside, and the bed slung underneath it when on the road, an iron pot and a kettle, a fireplace for the cold weather, a chimney for the smoke, a hanging-shelf and a cupboard, a dog and a horse. What more do you want? You draw off upon a bit of turf in a green lane or by the roadside, you hobble your old horse and turn him grazing, you light your fire upon the ashes of the last visitors, you cook your stew, and you wouldn't call the Emperor of France your father. But have a temper in the cart, flinging language and the hardest goods in stock at you, and where are you then? Put a name to your feelings.

My dog knew as well when she was on the turn as I did. Before she broke out, he would give a howl, and bolt. How he knew it, was a mystery to me; but the sure and certain knowledge of it would wake him up out of his soundest sleep, and he would give a howl, and bolt. At such times I wished I was him.

The worst of it was, we had a daughter born to us, and I love children with all my heart. When she was in her furies she beat the child. This got to be so shocking, as the child got to be four or five year old, that I have many a time gone on with my whip over my shoulder, at the old horse's head, sobbing and crying worse than ever little Sophy did. For how could I prevent it? Such a thing is not to be tried with such a temper — in a cart — without coming to a fight. It's in the natural size and formation of a cart to bring it to a fight. And then the poor child got worse terrified than before, as well as worse hurt generally, and her mother made complaints to the next people we lighted on, and the word went round, "Here's a wretch of a Cheap Jack been a beating his wife."

Little Sophy was such a brave child! She grew to be quite devoted to her poor father, though he could do so little to help her. She had a wonderful quantity of shining dark hair, all curling natural about her. It is quite astonishing to me now, that I didn't go tearing mad when I used to see her run from her mother before the cart, and her mother catch her by this hair, and pull her down by it, and beat her.

Such a brave child I said she was! Ah! with reason.

"Don't you mind next time, father dear," she would whisper to me, with her little face still flushed, and her bright eyes still wet; "if I don't cry out, you may know I am not much hurt. And even if I do cry out, it will only be to get mother to let go and leave off." What I have seen the little spirit bear — for me — without crying out!

Yet in other respects her mother took great care of her. Her clothes were always clean and neat, and her mother was never tired of working at 'em. Such is the inconsistency in things. Our being down in the marsh country in unhealthy weather, I consider the cause of Sophy's taking bad low fever; but however she took it, once she got it she turned away from her mother for evermore, and nothing would persuade her to be touched by her mother's hand. She would shiver and say, "No, no, no," when it was offered at, and would hide her face on my shoulder, and hold me tighter round the neck.

The Cheap Jack business had been worse than ever I had known it, what with one thing and what with another (and not least with railroads, which will cut it all to pieces, I expect, at last), and I was run dry of money. For which reason, one night at that period of little Sophy's being so bad, either we must have come to a dead-lock for victuals and drink, or I must have pitched the cart as I did.

I couldn't get the dear child to lie down or leave go of me, and indeed I hadn't the heart to try, so I stepped out on the footboard with her holding round my neck. They all set up a laugh when they see us, and one chuckle-headed Joskin (that I hated for it) made the bidding, "Tuppence for her!"

"Now, you country boobies," says I, feeling as if my heart was a heavy weight at the end of a broken sashline, "I give you notice that I am a going to charm the money out of your pockets, and to give you so much more than your money's worth that you'll only persuade yourselves to draw your Saturday night's wages ever again arterwards by the hopes of meeting me to lay 'em out with, which you never will, and why not? Because I've made my fortune by selling my goods on a large scale for seventy-five per cent less than I give for 'em, and I am consequently to be elevated to the House of Peers next week, by the title of the Duke of Cheap and Markis Jackaloorul. Now let's know what you want to-night, and you shall have it. But first of all, shall I tell you why I have got this little girl round my neck? You don't want to know? Then you shall. She belongs to the Fairies. She's a fortune-teller. She can tell me all about you in a whisper, and can put me up to whether you're going to buy a lot or leave it. Now do you want a saw? No, she says you don't, because you're too clumsy to use one. Else here's a saw which would be a lifelong blessing to a handy man, at four shillings, at three and six, at three, at two and six, at two, at eighteen-pence. But none of you shall have it at any price, on account of your well-known awkwardness, which would make it manslaughter. The same objection applies to this set of three planes which I won't let you have neither, so don't bid for 'em. Now I am a going to ask her what you do want." (Then I whispered, "Your head burns so, that I am afraid it hurts you bad, my pet," and she answered, without opening her heavy eyes, "Just a little, father.") "O! This little fortune-teller says it's a memorandum-book you want. Then why didn't you mention it? Here it is. Look at it. Two hundred super-fine hot-pressed wire-wove pages — if you don't believe me, count 'em — ready ruled for your expenses, an everlastingly pointed pencil to put 'em down with, a double-bladed pen-knife to scratch 'em out with, a book of printed tables to calculate your income with, and a camp-stool to sit down upon while you give your mind to it! Stop! And an umbrella to keep the moon off when you give your mind to it on a pitch-dark night. Now I won't ask you how much for the lot, but how little? How little are you thinking of? Don't be ashamed to mention it, because my fortune-teller knows already." (Then making believe to whisper, I kissed her, and she kissed me.) "Why, she says you are thinking of as little as three and threepence! I couldn't have believed it, even of you, unless she told me. Three and threepence! And a set of printed tables in the lot that'll calculate your income up to forty thousand a year! With an income of forty thousand a year, you grudge three and sixpence. Well then, I'll tell you my opinion. I so despise the threepence, that I'd sooner take three shillings. There. For three shillings, three shillings, three shillings! Gone. Hand 'em over to the lucky man."

As there had been no bid at all, everybody looked about and grinned at everybody, while I touched little Sophy's face and asked her if she felt faint, or giddy. "Not very, father. It will soon be over." Then turning from the pretty patient eyes, which were opened now, and seeing nothing but grins across my lighted grease-pot, I went on again in my Cheap Jack style. "Where's the butcher?" (My sorrowful eye had just caught sight of a fat young butcher on the outside of

LITTLE SOPHY SHRINKS FROM HER FATE

the crowd.) "She says the good luck is the butcher's. Where is he?" Everybody handed on the blushing butcher to the front, and there was a roar, and the butcher felt himself obliged to put his hand in his pocket, and take the lot. The party so picked out, in general, does feel obliged to take the lot — good four times out of six. Then we had another lot, the counterpart of that one, and sold it sixpence cheaper, which is always wery much enjoyed. Then we had the spectacles. It ain't a special profitable lot, but I put 'em on, and I see what the Chancellor of the Exchequer is going to take off the taxes, and I see what the sweetheart of the young woman in the shawl is doing at home, and I see what the Bishops has got for dinner, and a deal more that seldom fails to fetch 'em up in their spirits; and the better their spirits, the better their bids. Then we had the ladies' lot — the teapot, tea-caddy, glass sugar-basin, half-a-dozen spoons, and caudle-cup — and all the time I was making similar excuses to give a look or two and say a word or two to my poor child. It was while the second ladies' lot was holding 'em enchained that I felt her lift herself a little on my shoulder, to look across the dark street. "What troubles you, darling?" "Nothing troubles me, father. I am not at all troubled. But don't I see a pretty churchyard over there?" "Yes, my dear." "Kiss me twice, dear father, and lay me down to rest upon that churchyard grass so soft and green." I staggered back into the cart with her head dropped on my shoulder, and I says to her mother, "Quick. Shut the door! Don't let those laughing people see!" "What's the matter?" she cries. "O woman, woman," I tells her, "you'll never catch my little Sophy by her hair again, for she has flown away from you!"

Maybe those were harder words than I meant 'em; but from that time forth my wife took to brooding, and would sit in the cart or walk beside it, hours at a stretch, with her arms crossed, and her eyes looking on the ground. When her furies took her (which was rather seldomer than before) they took her in a new way, and she banged herself about to that extent that I was forced to hold her. She got none the better for a little drink now and then, and through some years I used to wonder, as I plodded along at the old horse's head, whether there was many carts upon the road that held so much dreariness as mine, for all my being looked up to as the King of the Cheap Jacks. So sad our lives went on till one summer evening, when, as we were coming into Exeter, out of the farther West of England, we saw a woman beating a child in a cruel manner, who screamed, "Don't beat me! O mother, mother, mother!" Then my wife stopped her ears, and ran away like a wild thing, and next day she was found in the river.

Me and my dog were all the company left in the cart now; and the dog learned to give a short bark when they wouldn't bid, and to give another and a nod of his head when I asked him, "Who said half a crown? Are you the gentleman, Sir, that offered half a crown?" He attained to an immense height of popularity, and I shall always believe taught himself entirely out of his own head to growl at any person in the crowd that bid as low as sixpence. But he got to be well on in years, and one night when I was conwulsing York with the spectacles, he took a conwulsion on his own account upon the very footboard by me, and it finished him.

Being naturally of a tender turn, I had dreadful lonely feelings on me arter this. I conquered 'em at selling times, having a reputation to keep (not to mention keeping myself), but they got me down in private, and rolled upon me. That's often the way with us public characters. See us on the footboard, and you'd give pretty well anything you possess to be us. See us off the footboard, and you'd add a trifle to be off your bargain. It was under those circumstances that I come acquainted with a giant. I might have been too high to fall into conversation with him, had it not been for my lonely feelings. For the general rule is, going round the country, to draw the line at dressing up. When a man can't trust his getting a living to his undisguised abilities, you consider him below your sort. And this giant when on view figured as a Roman.

He was a languid young man, which I attribute to the distance betwixt his extremities. He had a little head and less in it, he had weak eyes and weak knees, and altogether you couldn't look at him without feeling that there was greatly too much of him both for his joints and his mind. But he was an amiable though timid young man (his mother let him out, and spent the money), and we come acquainted when he was walking to ease the horse betwixt two fairs. He was called Rinaldo di Velasco, his name being Pickleson.

This giant, otherwise Pickleson, mentioned to me under the seal of confidence that, beyond his being a burden to himself, his life was made a burden to him by the cruelty of his master towards a step-daughter who was deaf and dumb. Her mother was dead, and she had no living soul to take her part, and was used most hard. She travelled with his master's caravan only because there was nowhere to leave her, and this giant, otherwise Pickleson, did go so far as to believe that his master often tried to lose her. He was such a very languid young man, that I don't know how long it didn't take him to get this story out, but it passed through his defective circulation to his top extremity in course of time.

When I heard this account from the giant, otherwise Pickleson, and likewise that the poor girl had beautiful long dark hair, and was often pulled down by it and beaten, I couldn't see the giant through what stood in my eyes. Having wiped 'em, I give him six-pence (for he was kept as short as he was long), and he laid it out in two three-penn'orths of gin-and-water, which so brisked him up, that he sang the Favorite Comic of Shivery Shakey, ain't it cold? — a popular effect which his master had tried every other means to get out of him as a Roman wholly in vain.

His master's name was Mim, a wery hoarse man, and I knew him to speak to. I went to that Fair as a mere civilian, leaving the cart outside the town, and I looked about the back of the Vans while the performing was going on, and at last, sitting dozing against a muddy cart-wheel, I came upon the poor girl who was deaf and dumb. At the first look I might almost have judged that she had escaped from the Wild Beast Show; but at the second I thought better of her, and thought that if she was more cared for and more kindly used she would be like my child. She was just the same age that my own daughter would have been, if her pretty head had not fell down upon my shoulder that unfortunate night.

To cut it short, I spoke confidential to Mim while he was beating the gong outside betwixt two lots of Pickleson's publics, and I put it to him. "She lies heavy on your own hands; what'll you take for her?" Mim was a most ferocious swearer. Suppressing that part of his reply which was much the longest part, his reply was, "A pair of braces." "Now I'll tell you," says I, "what I'm a going to do with you. I'm a going to fetch you half-a-dozen pair of the primest braces in the cart, and then to take her away with me." Says Mim (again ferocious), "I'll believe it when I've got the goods, and no sooner." I made all the haste I could, lest he should think twice of it, and the bargain was completed, which Pickleson he was thereby so relieved in his mind that he come out at his little back door, longways like a serpent, and give us Shivery Shakey in a whisper among the wheels at parting.

It was happy days for both of us when Sophy and me began to travel in the cart. I at once give her the name of Sophy, to put her ever towards me in the attitude of my own daughter. We soon made out to begin to understand one another, through the goodness of the Heavens, when she knowed that I meant true and kind by her. In a very little time she was wonderful fond of me. You have no idea what it is to have anybody wonderful fond of you, unless you have been got down and rolled upon by the lonely feelings that I have mentioned as having once got the better of me.

You'd have laughed — or the reverse — it's according to your disposition — if you could have seen me trying to teach Sophy. At first I was helped — you'd never guess by what — milestones. I got some large alphabets in a box, all the letters separate on bits of bone, and saying we was going to WINDSOR, I give her those letters in that order, and then at every milestone I showed her those same letters in that same order again, and pointed towards the abode of royalty. Another time I give her CART, and then chalked the same upon the cart. Another time I give her DOCTOR MARIGOLD, and hung a corresponding inscription outside my waistcoat. People that met us might stare a bit and laugh, but what did I care, if she caught the idea? She caught it after long patience and trouble, and then we did begin to get on swimmingly, I believe you! At first she was a little given to consider me the cart, and the cart the abode of royalty, but that soon wore off.

We had our signs, too, and they was hundreds in number. Sometimes she would sit looking at me and considering hard how to communicate with me about something fresh — how to ask me what she wanted explained — and then she was (or I thought she was; what does it signify?) so like my child with those years added to her, that I half-believed it was herself, trying to tell me where she had been to up in the skies, and what she had seen since that unhappy night when she flied away. She had a pretty face, and now that there was no one to drag at her dark hair, and it was all in order, there was a something touching in her looks that made the cart most peaceful and most quiet, though not at all melancholy. [N.B. In the Cheap Jack patter, we generally sound it lemonjolly, and it gets a laugh.]

The way she learnt to understand any look of mine was truly

surprising. When I sold of a night, she would sit in the cart unseen by them outside, and would give a eager look into my eyes when I looked in, and would hand me straight the precise article or articles I wanted. And then she would clap her hands, and laugh for joy. And as for me, seeing her so bright, and remembering what she was when I first lighted on her, starved and beaten and ragged, leaning asleep against the muddy cart-wheel, it gave me such heart that I gained a greater height of reputation than ever, and I put Pickleson down (by the name of Mim's Travelling Giant otherwise Pickleson) for a fypunnote in my will.

This happiness went on in the cart till she was sixteen years old. By which time I began to feel not satisfied that I had done my whole duty by her, and to consider that she ought to have better teaching than I could give her. It drew a many tears on both sides when I commenced explaining my views to her; but what's right is right, and you can't neither by tears nor laughter do away with its character.

So I took her hand in mine, and I went with her one day to the Deaf and Dumb establishment in London, and when the gentleman come to speak to us, I says to him: "Now I'll tell you what I'll do with you, Sir. I am nothing but a Cheap Jack, but of late years I have laid by for a rainy day notwithstanding. This is my only daughter (adopted), and you can't produce a deafer nor a dumber. Teach her the most that can be taught her in the shortest separation that can be named — state the figure for it — and I am game to put the money down. I won't bate you a single farthing, Sir, but I'll put down the money here and now, and I'll thankfully throw you in a pound to take it. There!" The gentleman smiled, and then, "Well, well," says he, "I must first know what she has learned already. How do you communicate with her?" Then I showed him, and she wrote in printed writing many names of things and so forth; and we held some sprightly conversation, Sophy and me, about a little story in a book which the gentleman showed her, and which she was able to read. "This is most extraordinary," says the gentleman; "is it possible that you have been her only teacher?" "I have been her only teacher, Sir," I says, "besides herself." "Then," says the gentleman, and more acceptable words was never spoken to me, "you're a clever fellow, and a good fellow." This he makes known to Sophy, who kisses his hands, clasps her own, and laughs and cries upon it.

We saw the gentleman four times in all, and when he took down my name and asked how in the world it ever chanced to be Doctor, it come out that he was own nephew by the sister's side, if you'll believe me, to the very Doctor that I was called after. This made our footing still easier, and he says to me:

"Now, Marigold, tell me what more do you want your adopted daughter to know?"

"I want her, Sir, to be cut off from the world as little as can be, considering her deprivations, and therefore to be able to read whatever is wrote with perfect ease and pleasure."

"My good fellow," urges the gentleman, opening his eyes wide, "why *I* can't do that myself!"

I took his joke, and gave him a laugh (knowing by experience how flat you fall without it), and I mended my words accordingly.

"What do you mean to do with her afterwards?" asks the gentleman, with a sort of a doubtful eye. "To take her about the country?"

"In the cart, Sir, but only in the cart. She will live a private life, you understand, in the cart. I should never think of bringing her infirmities before the public. I wouldn't make a show of her for any money."

The gentleman nodded, and seemed to approve.

"Well," says he, "can you part with her for two years?"

"To do her that good—yes, Sir."

"There's another question," says the gentleman, looking towards her — "can she part with you for two years?"

I don't know that it was a harder matter of itself (for the other was hard enough to me), but it was harder to get over. However, she was pacified to it at last, and the separation betwixt us was settled. How it cut up both of us when it took place, and when I left her at the door in the dark of an evening, I don't tell. But I know this; remembering that night, I shall never pass that same establishment without a heartache and a swelling in the throat; and I couldn't put you up the best of lots in sight of it with my usual spirit — no, not even the gun, nor the pair of spectacles — for five hundred pound reward from the Secretary of State for the Home Department, and throw in the honor of putting my legs under his mahogany arterwards.

Still, the loneliness that followed in the cart was not the old loneliness, because there was a term put to it, however long to look forward to; and because I could think, when I was anyways down, that she belonged to me and I belonged to her. Always planning for her coming back, I bought in a few months' time another cart, and what do you think I planned to do with it? I'll tell you. I planned to fit it up with shelves and books for her reading, and to have a seat in it where I could sit and see her read, and think that I had been her first teacher. Not hurrying over the job, I had the fittings knocked together in contriving ways under my own inspection, and here was her bed in a berth with curtains, and there was her reading-table, and here was her writing-desk, and elsewhere was her books in rows upon rows, picters and no picters, bindings and no bindings, gilt-edged and plain, just as I could pick 'em up for her in lots up and down the country, North and South and West and East, Winds liked best and winds liked least, Here and there and gone astray, Over the hills and far away. And when I had got together pretty well as many books as the cart would neatly hold, a new scheme come into my head, which, as it turned out, kept my time and attention a good deal employed, and helped me over the two years' stile.

Without being of an awaricious temper, I like to be the owner of things. I shouldn't wish, for instance, to go partners with yourself in the Cheap Jack cart. It's not that I mistrust you, but that I'd rather know it was mine. Similarly, very likely you'd rather know it was yours. Well! A kind of a jealousy began to creep into my mind when I reflected that all those books would have been read by other people long before they was read by her. It seemed to take away from her being the owner of 'em like. In this way, the question got into my head: Couldn't I have a book new-made express for her, which she should be the first to read?

It pleased me, that thought did; and as I never was a man to let a thought sleep (you must wake up all the whole family of thoughts you've got and burn their nightcaps, or you won't do in the Cheap Jack line), I set to work at it. Considering that I was in the habit of changing so much about the country, and that I should have to find out a literary character here to make a deal with, and another literary character there to make a deal with, as opportunities presented, I hit on the plan that this same book should be a general miscellaneous lot — like the razors, flat-iron, chronometer watch, dinner plates, rolling-pin, and looking-glass — and shouldn't be offered as a single individual article, like the spectacles or the gun. When I had come to that conclusion, I come to another, which shall likewise be yours.

Often had I regretted that she never had heard me on the footboard, and that she never could hear me. It ain't that *I* am vain, but that *you* don't like to put your own light under a bushel. What's the worth of your reputation, if you can't convey the reason for it to the person you most wish to value it? Now I'll put it to you. Is it worth sixpence, fippence, fourpence, threepence, twopence, a penny, a halfpenny, a farthing? No, it ain't. Not worth a farthing. Very well, then. My conclusion was that I would begin her book with some account of myself. So that, through reading a specimen or two of me on the footboard, she might form an idea of my merits there. I was aware that I couldn't do myself justice. A man can't write his eye (at least *I* don't know how to), nor yet can a man write his voice, nor the rate of his talk, nor the quickness of his action, nor his general spicy way. But he can write his turns of speech, when he is a public speaker — and indeed I have heard that he very often does, before he speaks 'em.

Well! Having formed that resolution, then come the question of a name. How did I hammer that hot iron into shape? This way. The most difficult explanation I had ever had with her was, how I come to be called Doctor, and yet was no Doctor. After all, I felt that I had failed of getting it correctly into her mind, with my utmost pains. But trusting to her improvement in the two years, I thought that I might trust to her understanding it when she should come to read it as put down by my own hand. Then I thought I would try a joke with her and watch how it took, by which of itself I might fully judge of her understanding it. We had first discovered the mistake we had dropped into, through her having asked me to prescribe for her when she had supposed me to be a Doctor in the medical point of view; so thinks I, "Now, if I give this book the name of my Prescriptions, and if she catches the idea that my only Prescriptions are for her amusement and interest — to make her laugh in a pleasant way, or to make her cry in a pleasant way — it will be a delightful proof to both of us that we have got over our difficulty." It fell out to absolute perfection. For when she saw the book, as I had it got up — the printed and pressed book — lying on her desk in her cart, and saw the title, DOCTOR MARIGOLD'S PRESCRIPTIONS, she looked at me for a moment with astonishment, then fluttered the leaves, then broke out a laughing in the charmingest way, then felt her pulse and shook her head, then turned the pages pretending to read them most attentive, then kissed the book to me, and put it to her bosom with both her hands. I never was better pleased in all my life!

But let me not anticipate. (I take that expression out of a lot of romances I bought for her. I never opened a single one of 'em — and I have opened many — but I found the romancer saying "let me not anticipate." Which being so, I wonder why he did anticipate, or who asked him to it.) Let me not, I say, anticipate. This same book took up all my spare time. It was no play to get the other articles together in the general miscellaneous lot, but when it come to my own article! There! I couldn't have believed the blotting, nor yet the buckling to at it, nor the patience over it. Which again is like the footboard. The public have no idea.

At last it was done, and the two years' time was gone after all the other time before it, and where it's all gone to, who knows? The new cart was finished — yellow outside, relieved with wermilion and brass fittings — the old horse was put in it, a new 'un and a boy being laid on for the Cheap Jack cart, and I cleaned myself up to go and fetch her. Bright cold weather it was, cart-chimneys smoking, carts pitched private on a piece of waste ground over at Wandsworth, where you may see 'em from the Sou'western Railway when not upon the road. (Look out of the right-hand window going down.)

"Marigold," says the gentleman, giving his hand hearty, "I am very glad to see you."

"Yet I have my doubts, Sir," says I, "if you can be half as glad to see me as I am to see you."

"The time has appeared so long — has it, Marigold?"

"I won't say that, Sir, considering its real length; but —"

"What a start, my good fellow!"

Ah! I should think it was! Grown such a woman, so pretty, so intelligent, so expressive! I knew then that she must be really like my child, or I could never have known her, standing quiet by the door.

"You are affected," says the gentleman in a kindly manner.

"I feel, Sir," says I, "that I am but a rough chap in a sleeved waistcoat."

"I feel," says the gentleman, "that it was you who raised her from misery and degradation, and brought her into communication with her kind. But why do we converse alone together, when we can converse so well with her? Address her in your own way."

"I am such a rough chap in a sleeved waistcoat, Sir," says I, "and she is such a graceful woman, and she stands so quiet at the door!"

"Try if she moves at the old sign," says the gentleman.

They had got it up together o'purpose to please me! For when I give her the old sign, she rushed to my feet, and dropped upon her knees, holding up her hands to me with pouring tears of love and joy; and when I took her hands and lifted her, she clasped me round the neck, and lay there; and I don't know what a fool I didn't make of myself, until we all three settled down into talking without sound, as if there was a something soft and pleasant spread over the whole world for us.

[A portion is here omitted from the text, having reference to the sketches contributed by other writers; but the reader will be pleased to have what follows retained in a note:

"Now I'll tell you what I am a-going to do with you. I am a-going to offer you the general miscellaneous lot, her own book, never read by anybody else but me, added to and completed by me after her first reading of it, eight-and-forty printed pages, six-and-ninety columns, Whiting's own work, Beaufort House to wit, thrown off by the steam-ingine, best of paper, beautiful green wrapper, folded like clean linen come home from the clear-starcher's, and so exquisitely stitched that, regarded as a piece of needlework alone, it's better than the sampler of a seamstress undergoing a Competitive examination for Starvation before the Civil Service Commissioners — and I offer the lot for what? For eight pound? Not so much. For six pound? Less. For four pound. Why, I hardly expect you to believe me, but that's the sum. Four pound! The stitching alone cost half as much again. Here's forty-eight original pages, ninety-six original columns, for four pound. You want more for the money? Take it. Three whole pages of advertisements of thrilling interest thrown in for nothing. Read 'em and believe 'em. More? My best of wishes for your merry Christmases and your happy New Years, your long lives and your true prosperities. Worth twenty pound good if they are delivered as I send them. Remember! Here's a final prescription added, "To be taken for life," which will tell you how the cart broke down, and where the journey ended. You think Four Pound too much? And still you think so? Come! I'll tell you what then. Say Four Pence, and keep the secret."]

CHAPTER II

TO BE TAKEN WITH A
GRAIN OF SALT

I have always noticed a prevalent want of courage, even among persons of superior intelligence and culture, as to imparting their own psychological experiences when those have been of a strange sort. Almost all men are afraid that what they could relate in such wise would find no parallel or response in a listener's internal life, and might be suspected or laughed at. A truthful traveller, who should have seen some extraordinary creature in the likeness of a sea-serpent, would have no fear of mentioning it; but the same traveller, having had some singular presentiment, impulse, vagary of thought, vision (so called), dream, or other remarkable mental impression, would hesitate considerably before he would own to it. To this reticence I attribute much of the obscurity in which such subjects are involved. We do not habitually communicate our experiences of these subjective things as we do our experiences of objective creation. The consequence is, that the general stock of experience in this regard appears exceptional, and really is so, in respect of being miserably imperfect.

In what I am going to relate, I have no intention of setting up, opposing, or supporting, any theory whatever. I know the history of the Bookseller of Berlin, I have studied the case of the wife of a late Astronomer Royal as related by Sir David Brewster, and I have followed the minutest details of a much more remarkable case of Spectral Illusion occurring within my private circle of friends. It may be necessary to state as to this last, that the sufferer (a lady) was in no degree, however distant, related to me. A mistaken assumption on that head might suggest an explanation of a part of my own case — but only a part — which would be wholly without foundation. It cannot be referred to my inheritance of any developed peculiarity, nor had I ever before any at all similar experience, nor have I ever had any at all similar experience since.

It does not signify how many years ago, or how few, a certain

murder was committed in England, which attracted great attention.
We hear more than enough of murderers as they rise in succession
to their atrocious eminence, and I would bury the memory of this
particular brute, if I could, as his body was buried, in Newgate Jail.
I purposely abstain from giving any direct clew to the criminal's
individuality.

When the murder was first discovered, no suspicion fell — or I
ought rather to say, for I cannot be too precise in my facts, it was
nowhere publicly hinted that any suspicion fell — on the man who
was afterwards brought to trial. As no reference was at that time
made to him in the newspapers, it is obviously impossible that any
description of him can at that time have been given in the newspapers. It is essential that this fact be remembered.

Unfolding at breakfast my morning paper, containing the account
of that first discovery, I found it to be deeply interesting, and I read
it with close attention. I read it twice, if not three times. The discovery had been made in a bedroom, and, when I laid down the
paper, I was aware of a flash — rush — flow — I do not know what to
call it — no word I can find is satisfactorily descriptive — in which
I seemed to see that bedroom passing through my room, like a picture impossibly painted on a running river. Though almost instan-
taneous in its passing, it was perfectly clear; so clear that I distinctly,
and with a sense of relief, observed the absence of the dead body
from the bed.

It was in no romantic place that I had this curious sensation, but
in chambers in Piccadilly, very near to the corner of St. James's-
street. It was entirely new to me. I was in my easy-chair at the moment, and the sensation was accompanied with a peculiar shiver
which started the chair from its position. (But it is to be noted that
the chair ran easily on castors.) I went to one of the windows (there
are two in the room, and the room is on the second floor) to refresh
my eyes with the moving objects in Piccadilly. It was a bright autumn
morning, and the street was sparkling and cheerful. The wind was
high. As I looked out, it brought down from the Park a quantity of
fallen leaves, which a gust took, and whirled into a spiral pillar. As
the pillar fell and the leaves dispersed, I saw two men on the opposite
side of the way, going from West to East. They were one behind the
other. The foremost man often looked back over his shoulder. The
second man followed him, at a distance of some thirty paces, with his

right hand menacingly raised. First, the singularity and steadiness of this threatening gesture in so public a thoroughfare attracted my attention; and next, the more remarkable circumstance that nobody heeded it. Both men threaded their way among the other passengers with a smoothness hardly consistent even with the action of walking on a pavement; and no single creature, that I could see, gave them place, touched them, or looked after them. In passing before my windows, they both stared up at me. I saw their two faces very distinctly, and I knew that I could recognize them anywhere. Not that I had consciously noticed anything very remarkable in either face, except that the man who went first had an unusually lowering appearance, and that the face of the man who followed him was of the color of impure wax.

I am a bachelor, and my valet and his wife constitute my whole establishment. My occupation is in a certain Branch Bank, and I wish that my duties as head of a Department were as light as they are popularly supposed to be. They kept me in town that autumn, when I stood in need of change. I was not ill, but I was not well. My reader is to make the most that can be reasonably made of my feeling jaded, having a depressing sense upon me of a monotonous life, and being "slightly dyspeptic." I am assured by my renowned doctor that my real state of health at that time justifies no stronger description, and I quote his own from his written answer to my request for it.

As the circumstances of the murder, gradually unravelling, took stronger and stronger possession of the public mind, I kept them away from mine by knowing as little about them as was possible in the midst of the universal excitement. But I knew that a verdict of Wilful Murder had been found against the suspected murderer, and that he had been committed to Newgate for trial. I also knew that his trial had been postponed over one Sessions of the Central Criminal Court, on the ground of general prejudice and want of time for the preparation of the defence. I may further have known, but I believe I did not, when, or about when, the Sessions to which his trial stood postponed would come on.

My sitting-room, bedroom, and dressing-room, are all on one floor. With the last there is no communication but through the bedroom. True, there is a door in it, once communicating with the staircase; but a part of the fitting of my bath has been — and had then been for some years — fixed across it. At the same period, and as a part of the same arrangement, the door had been nailed up and canvased over.

I was standing in my bedroom late one night, giving some directions to my servant before he went to bed. My face was towards the only available door of communication with the dressing-room, and it was closed. My servant's back was towards that door. While I was speaking to him, I saw it open, and a man look in, who very earnestly and mysteriously beckoned to me. That man was the man who had gone second of the two along Piccadilly, and whose face was the color of impure wax.

The figure, having beckoned, drew back, and closed the door. With no longer pause than was made by my crossing the bedroom, I opened the dressing-room door, and looked in. I had a lighted candle already in my hand. I felt no inward expectation of seeing the figure in the dressing-room, and I did not see it there.

Conscious that my servant stood amazed, I turned round to him, and said: "Derrick, could you believe that in my cool senses I fancied I saw a——" As I there laid my hand upon his breast, with a sudden start he trembled violently, and said, "O Lord, yes, Sir! A dead man beckoning!"

Now I do not believe that this John Derrick, my trusty and attached servant for more than twenty years, had any impression whatever of having seen any such figure, until I touched him. The change in him was so startling, when I touched him, that I fully believe he derived his impression in some occult manner from me at that instant.

I bade John Derrick bring some brandy, and I gave him a dram, and was glad to take one myself. Of what had preceded that night's phenomenon, I told him not a single word. Reflecting on it, I was absolutely certain that I had never seen that face before, except on the one occasion in Piccadilly. Comparing its expression when beckoning at the door with its expression when it had stared up at me as I stood at my window, I came to the conclusion that on the first occasion it had sought to fasten itself upon my memory, and that on the second occasion it had made sure of being immediately remembered.

I was not very comfortable that night, though I felt a certainty, difficult to explain, that the figure would not return. At daylight I fell into a heavy sleep, from which I was awakened by John Derrick's coming to my bedside with a paper in his hand.

This paper, it appeared, had been the subject of an altercation at the door between its bearer and my servant. It was a summons to me to serve upon a Jury at the forthcoming Sessions of the Central Criminal Court at the Old Bailey. I had never before been summoned on such a Jury, as John Derrick well knew. He believed — I am not certain at this hour whether with reason or otherwise — that that class of Jurors were customarily chosen on a lower qualification than mine, and he had at first refused to accept the summons. The man who served it had taken the matter very coolly. He had said that my attendance or non-attendance was nothing to him; there the summons was; and I should deal with it at my own peril, and not at his.

For a day or two I was undecided whether to respond to this call, or take no notice of it. I was not conscious of the slightest mysterious bias, influence, or attraction, one way or other. Of that I am as strictly sure as of every other statement that I make here. Ultimately I decided, as a break in the monotony of my life, that I would go.

The appointed morning was a raw morning in the month of November. There was a dense brown fog in Piccadilly, and it became positively black and in the last degree oppressive East of Temple Bar. I found the passages and staircases of the Court-House flaringly lighted with gas, and the Court itself similarly illuminated. I *think* that, until I was conducted by officers into the Old Court and saw its crowded state, I did not know that the Murderer was to be tried that day. I *think* that, until I was so helped into the Old Court with considerable difficulty, I did not know into which of the two Courts sitting my summons would take me. But this must not be received as a positive assertion, for I am not completely satisfied in my mind on either point.

I took my seat in the place appropriated to Jurors in waiting, and I looked about the Court as well as I could through the cloud of fog and breath that was heavy in it. I noticed the black vapor hanging like a murky curtain outside the great windows, and I noticed the stifled sound of wheels on the straw or tan that was littered in the street; also, the hum of the people gathered there, which a shrill whistle, or a louder song or hail than the rest, occasionally pierced. Soon afterwards the Judges, two in number, entered, and took their seats. The buzz in the Court was awfully hushed. The direction was given to put the Murderer to the bar. He appeared there. And in that same instant I recognized in him the first of the two men who had gone down Piccadilly.

If my name had been called then, I doubt if I could have answered to it audibly. But it was called about sixth or eighth in the panel, and I was by that time able to say "Here!" Now, observe. As I stepped into the box, the prisoner, who had been looking on attentively, but with no sign of concern, became violently agitated, and beckoned to his attorney. The prisoner's wish to challenge me was so manifest, that it occasioned a pause, during which the attorney, with his hand upon the dock, whispered with his client, and shook his head. I afterwards had it from that gentleman, that the prisoner's first affrighted words to him were, *"At all hazards, challenge that man!"* But that, as he would give no reason for it, and admitted that he had not even known my name until he heard it called and I appeared, it was not done.

Both on the ground already explained, that I wish to avoid reviving the unwholesome memory of that Murderer, and also because a detailed account of his long trial is by no means indispensable to my narrative, I shall confine myself closely to such incidents in the ten days and nights during which we, the Jury, were kept together, as directly bear on my own curious personal experience. It is in that, and not in the Murderer, that I seek to interest my reader. It is to that, and not to a page of the Newgate Calendar, that I beg attention.

I was chosen Foreman of the Jury. On the second morning of the trial, after evidence had been taken for two hours (I heard the church clocks strike), happening to cast my eyes over my brother jurymen, I found an inexplicable difficulty in counting them. I counted them several times, yet always with the same difficulty. In short, I made them one too many.

I touched the brother juryman whose place was next me, and I whispered to him, "Oblige me by counting us." He looked surprised by the request, but turned his head and counted. "Why," says he, suddenly, "we are Thirt — ; but no, it's not possible. No. We are twelve."

According to my counting that day, we were always right in detail, but in the gross we were always one too many. There was no appearance — no figure — to account for it; but I had now an inward foreshadowing of the figure that was surely coming.

The Jury were housed at the London Tavern. We all slept in one large room on separate tables, and we were constantly in the charge and under the eye of the officer sworn to hold us in safe-keeping. I see no reason for suppressing the real name of that officer. He was intelligent, highly polite, and obliging, and (I was glad to hear) much respected in the City. He had an agreeable presence, good eyes, enviable black whiskers, and a fine sonorous voice. His name was Mr. Harker.

When we turned into our twelve beds at night, Mr. Harker's bed was drawn across the door. On the night of the second day, not being disposed to lie down, and seeing Mr. Harker sitting on his bed, I went and sat beside him, and offered him a pinch of snuff. As Mr. Harker's hand touched mine in taking it from my box, a peculiar shiver crossed him, and he said, "Who is this?"

Following Mr. Harker's eyes, and looking along the room, I saw again the figure I expected — the second of the two men who had gone down Piccadilly. I rose, and advanced a few steps; then stopped, and looked round at Mr. Harker. He was quite unconcerned, laughed, and said in a pleasant way, "I thought for a moment we had a thirteenth juryman, without a bed. But I see it is the moonlight."

Making no revelation to Mr. Harker, but inviting him to take a walk with me to the end of the room, I watched what the figure did. It stood for a few moments by the bedside of each of my eleven brother jurymen, close to the pillow. It always went to the right-hand side of the bed, and always passed out crossing the foot of the next bed. It seemed, from the action of the head, merely to look down pensively at each recumbent figure. It took no notice of me, or of my bed, which was that nearest to Mr. Harker's. It seemed to go out where the moonlight came in, through a high window, as by an aërial flight of stairs.

Next morning at breakfast, it appeared that everybody present had dreamed of the murdered man last night, except myself and Mr. Harker.

I now felt as convinced that the second man who had gone down Piccadilly was the murdered man (so to speak), as if it had been borne into my comprehension by his immediate testimony. But even this took place, and in a manner for which I was not at all prepared.

On the fifth day of the trial, when the case for the prosecution was drawing to a close, a miniature of the murdered man, missing from his bedroom upon the discovery of the deed, and afterwards found in a hiding-place where the Murderer had been seen digging, was put in evidence. Having been identified by the witness under examination, it was handed up to the Bench, and thence handed down to be inspected by the Jury. As an officer in a black gown was making his way with it across to me, the figure of the second man who had gone down Piccadilly impetuously started from the crowd, caught the miniature from the officer, and gave it to me with his own hands, at the same time saying, in a low and hollow tone — before I saw the miniature, which was in a locket — *"I was younger then, and my face was not then drained of blood."* It also came between me and the brother juryman to whom I would have given the miniature, and between him and the brother juryman to whom he would have given it, and so passed it on through the whole of our number, and back into my possession. Not one of them, however, detected this.

At table, and generally when we were shut up together in Mr. Harker's custody, we had from the first naturally discussed the day's proceedings a good deal. On that fifth day, the case for the prosecution being closed, and we having that side of the question in a completed shape before us, our discussion was more animated and serious. Among our number was a vestryman — the densest idiot I have ever seen at large — who met the plainest evidence with the most preposterous objections, and who was sided with by two flabby parochial parasites; all the three impanelled from a district so delivered over to Fever that they ought to have been upon their own trial for five hundred Murders. When these mischievous blockheads were at their loudest, which was towards midnight, while some of us were already preparing for bed, I again saw the murdered man. He stood grimly behind them, beckoning to me. On my going towards them, and striking into the conversation, he immediately retired. This was the beginning of a separate series of appearances, confined to that long room in which *we* were confined. Whenever a knot of my brother jurymen laid their heads together, I saw the head of the murdered man among theirs. Whenever their comparison of notes was going against him, he would solemnly and irresistibly beckon to me.

It will be borne in mind that down to the production of the miniature, on the fifth day of the trial, I had never seen the Appearance in Court. Three changes occurred now that we entered on the case for the defence. Two of them I will mention together, first. The figure was now in Court continually, and it never there addressed itself to me, but always to the person who was speaking at the time. For instance: the throat of the murdered man had been cut straight across. In the opening speech for the defence, it was suggested that the deceased might have cut his own throat. At that very moment, the figure, with its throat in the dreadful condition referred to (this it had concealed before), stood at the speaker's elbow, motioning across and across its windpipe, now with the right hand, now with the left, vigorously suggesting to the speaker himself the impossibility of such a wound having been self-inflicted by either hand. For another instance: a witness to character, a woman, deposed to the prisoner's being the most amiable of mankind. The figure at that instant stood on the floor before her, looking her full in the face, and pointing out the prisoner's evil countenance with an extended arm and an outstretched finger.

The third change now to be added impressed me strongly as the most marked and striking of all. I do not theorize upon it; I accurately state it, and there leave it. Although the Appearance was not itself perceived by those whom it addressed, its coming close to such persons was invariably attended by some trepidation or disturbance on their part. It seemed to me as if it were prevented, by laws to which I was not amenable, from fully revealing itself to others, and yet as if it could invisibly, dumbly, and darkly overshadow their minds. When the leading counsel for the defence suggested that hypothesis of suicide, and the figure stood at the learned gentleman's elbow, frightfully sawing at its severed throat, it is undeniable that the counsel faltered in his speech, lost for a few seconds the thread of his ingenious discourse, wiped his forehead with his handkerchief, and turned extremely pale. When the witness to character was confronted by the Appearance, her eyes most certainly did follow the direction of its pointed finger, and rest in great hesitation and trouble upon the prisoner's face. Two additional illustrations will suffice. On the eighth day of the trial, after the pause which was every day made early in the afternoon for a few minutes' rest and refreshment, I came back into Court with the rest of the Jury some little time before the return of the Judges. Standing up in the box and looking about me, I thought the figure was not there, until, chancing to raise my eyes to the gallery, I saw it bending forward, and leaning over a very decent woman, as if to assure itself whether the Judges had resumed their seats or not. Immediately afterwards that woman screamed, fainted, and was carried out. So with the venerable, sagacious, and patient Judge who conducted the trial. When the case was over, and he settled himself and his papers to sum up, the murdered man, entering by the Judges' door, advanced to his Lordship's desk, and looked eagerly over his shoulder at the pages of his notes which he was turning. A change came over his Lordship's face; his hand stopped; the peculiar shiver, that I knew so well, passed over him; he faltered, "Excuse me, gentlemen, for a few moments. I am somewhat oppressed by the vitiated air"; and did not recover until he had drunk a glass of water.

Through all the monotony of six of those interminable ten days — the same Judges and others on the bench, the same Murderer in the dock, the same lawyers at the table, the same tones of question and answer rising to the roof of the Court, the same scratching of the Judge's pen, the same ushers going in and out, the same lights kindled at the same hour when there had been any natural light of day, the same foggy curtain outside the great windows when it was foggy, the same rain pattering and dripping when it was rainy, the same footmarks of turnkeys and prisoner day after day on the same sawdust, the same keys locking and unlocking the same heavy doors — through all the wearisome monotony which made me feel as if I had been Foreman of the Jury for a vast period of time, and Piccadilly had flourished coevally with Babylon, the murdered man never lost one trace of his distinctness in my eyes, nor was he at any moment less distinct than anybody else. I must not omit, as a matter of fact, that I never once saw the Appearance which I call by the name of the murdered man look at the Murderer. Again and again I wondered, "Why does he not?" But he never did.

Nor did he look at me, after the production of the miniature, until the last closing minutes of the trial arrived. We retired to consider, at seven minutes before ten at night. The idiotic vestryman and his two parochial parasites gave us so much trouble that we twice returned into Court to beg to have certain extracts from the Judge's notes re-read. Nine of us had not the smallest doubt about those passages, neither, I believe, had any one in the Court; the dunderheaded triumvirate, however, having no idea but obstruction,

A NEW SOPHY, A NEW CART

disputed them for that very reason. At length we prevailed, and finally the Jury returned into Court at ten minutes past twelve.

The murdered man at that time stood directly opposite the Jury-box, on the other side of the Court. As I took my place, his eyes rested on me with great attention; he seemed satisfied, and slowly shook a great grey veil, which he carried on his arm for the first time, over his head and whole form. As I gave in our verdict, "Guilty," the veil collapsed, all was gone, and his place was empty.

The Murderer, being asked by the Judge, according to usage, whether he had anything to say before sentence of Death should be passed upon him, indistinctly muttered something which was described in the leading newspapers of the following day as "a few rambling, incoherent, and half-audible words, in which he was understood to complain that he had not had a fair trial, because the Foreman of the Jury was prepossessed against him." The remarkable declaration that he really made was this: *"My Lord, I knew I was a doomed man, when the Foreman of my Jury came into the box. My Lord, I knew he would never let me off, because, before I was taken, he somehow got to my bedside in the night, woke me, and put a rope round my neck."*

CHAPTER III

TO BE TAKEN FOR LIFE

So every item of my plan was crowned with success. Our reunited life was more than all that we had looked forward to. Content and joy went with us as the wheels of the two carts went round, and the same stopped with us when the two carts stopped. I was as pleased and as proud as a Pug-Dog with his muzzle black-leaded for a evening party, and his tail extra curled by machinery.

But I had left something out of my calculations. Now, what had I left out? To help you to guess I'll say, a figure. Come. Make a guess and guess right. Nought? No. Nine? No. Eight? No. Seven? No. Six? No. Five? No. Four? No. Three? No. Two? No. One? No. Now I'll tell you what I'll do with you. I'll say it's another sort of figure altogether. There. Why then, says you, it's a mortal figure. No, nor yet a mortal figure. By such means you get yourself penned into a corner, and you can't help guessing a *imm*ortal figure. That's about it. Why didn't you say so sooner?

Yes. It was a immortal figure that I had altogether left out of my calculations. Neither man's, nor woman's, but a child's. Girl's or boy's? Boy's. "I, says the sparrow, with my bow and arrow." Now you have got it.

We were down at Lancaster, and I had done two nights more than fair average business (though I cannot in honor recommend them as a quick audience) in the open square there, near the end of the street where Mr. Sly's King's Arms and Royal Hotel stands. Mim's travelling giant, otherwise Pickleson, happened at the self-same time to be trying it on in the town. The genteel lay was adopted with him. No hint of a van. Green baize alcove leading up to Pickleson in a Auction Room. Printed poster, "Free list suspended, with the exception of that proud boast of an enlightened country, a free press. Schools admitted by private arrangement. Nothing to raise a blush in the cheek of youth or shock the most fastidious." Mim swearing most horrible and terrific, in a pink calico pay-place, at the slackness of the public. Serious handbill in the shops, importing that it was all but impossible to come to a right understanding of the history of David without seeing Pickleson.

I went to the Auction Room in question, and I found it entirely empty of everything but echoes and mouldiness, with the single exception of Pickleson on a piece of red drugget. This suited my purpose, as I wanted a private and confidential word with him, which was: "Pickleson. Owing much happiness to you, I put you in my will for a fypunnote; but, to save trouble, here's fourpunten down, which may equally suit your views, and let us so conclude the transaction." Pickleson, who up to that remark had had the dejected appearance of a long Roman rushlight that couldn't anyhow get lighted, brightened up at his top extremity, and made his acknowledgments in a way which (for him) was parliamentary eloquence. He likewise did add, that, having ceased to draw as a Roman, Mim had made proposals for his going in as a conwerted Indian Giant worked upon by The Dairyman's Daughter. This, Pickleson, having no acquaintance with the tract named after that young woman, and not being willing to couple gag with his serious views, had declined to do, thereby leading to words and the total stoppage of the unfortunate young man's beer. All of which, during the whole of the interview, was confirmed by the ferocious growling of Mim down below in the pay-place, which shook the giant like a leaf.

But what was to the present point in the remarks of the travelling giant, otherwise Pickleson, was this: "Doctor Marigold" — I give his words without a hope of conweying their feebleness — "who is the strange young man that hangs about your carts?" — "The strange young *man?*" I gives him back, thinking that he meant her, and his languid circulation had dropped a syllable. "Doctor," he returns, with a pathos calculated to draw a tear from even a manly eye, "I am weak, but not so weak yet as that I don't know my words. I repeat them, Doctor. The strange young man." It then appeared that Pickleson, being forced to stretch his legs (not that they wanted it) only at times when he couldn't be seen for nothing, to wit in the dead of the night and towards daybreak, had twice seen hanging about my carts, in that same town of Lancaster where I had been only two nights, this same unknown young man.

It put me rather out of sorts. What it meant as to particulars I no more foreboded then than you forebode now, but it put me rather out of sorts. Howsoever, I made light of it to Pickleson, and I took leave of Pickleson, advising him to spend his legacy in getting up his stamina, and to continue to stand by his religion. Towards morning I kept a look out for the strange young man, and — what was more — I saw the strange young man. He was well dressed and well looking. He loitered very nigh my carts, watching them like as if he was taking care of them, and soon after daybreak turned and went away. I sent a hail after him, but he never started or looked round, or took the smallest notice.

We left Lancaster within an hour or two, on our way towards Carlisle. Next morning, at daybreak, I looked out again for the strange young man. I did not see him. But next morning I looked out again, and there he was once more. I sent another hail after him, but as before he gave not the slightest sign of being anyways disturbed. This put a thought into my head. Acting on it I watched him in different manners and at different times not necessary to enter into, till I found that this strange young man was deaf and dumb.

The discovery turned me over, because I knew that a part of that establishment where she had been was allotted to young men (some of them well off), and I thought to myself, "If she favors him, where am I? and where is all that I have worked and planned for?" Hoping

— I must confess to the selfishness — that she might *not* favor him, I set myself to find out. At last I was by accident present at a meeting between them in the open air, looking on leaning behind a fir-tree without their knowing of it. It was a moving meeting for all the three parties concerned. I knew every syllable that passed between them as well as they did. I listened with my eyes, which had come to be as quick and true with deaf and dumb conversation as my ears with the talk of people that can speak. He was a-going out to China as clerk in a merchant's house, which his father had been before him. He was in circumstances to keep a wife, and he wanted her to marry him and go along with him. She persisted, no. He asked if she didn't love him. Yes, she loved him dearly, dearly; but she could never disappoint her beloved, good, noble, generous, and I-don't-know-what-all father (meaning me, the Cheap Jack in the sleeved waistcoat), and she would stay with him, Heaven bless him! though it was to break her heart. Then she cried most bitterly, and that made up my mind.

While my mind had been in an unsettled state about her favoring this young man, I had felt that unreasonable towards Pickleson, that it was well for him he had got his legacy down. For I often thought, "If it hadn't been for this same weak-minded giant, I might never have come to trouble my head and wex my soul about the young man." But, once that I knew she loved him — once that I had seen her weep for him — it was a different thing. I made it right in my mind with Pickleson on the spot, and I shook myself together to do what was right by all.

She had left the young man by that time (for it took a few minutes to get me thoroughly well shook together), and the young man was leaning against another of the fir-trees — of which there was a cluster — with his face upon his arm. I touched him on the back. Looking up and seeing me, he says, in our deaf-and-dumb talk, "Do not be angry."

"I am not angry, good boy. I am your friend. Come with me."

I left him at the foot of the steps of the Library Cart, and I went up alone. She was drying her eyes.

"You have been crying, my dear."

"Yes, father."

"Why?"

"A headache."

"Not a heartache?"

"I said a headache, father."

"Doctor Marigold must prescribe for that headache."

She took up the book of my Prescriptions, and held it up with a forced smile; but seeing me keep still and look earnest, she softly laid it down again, and her eyes were very attentive.

"The Prescription is not there, Sophy."

"Where is it?"

"Here, my dear."

I brought her young husband in, and I put her hand in his, and my only farther words to both of them were these: "Doctor Marigold's last Prescription. To be taken for life." After which I bolted.

When the wedding came off, I mounted a coat (blue, and bright buttons), for the first and last time in all my days, and I give Sophy away with my own hand. There were only us three and the gentleman who had had charge of her for those two years. I give the wedding dinner of four in the Library Cart. Pigeon-pie, a leg of pickled pork, a pair of fowls, and suitable garden stuff. The best of drinks. I give them a speech, and the gentleman give us a speech, and all our jokes told, and the whole went off like a sky-rocket. In the course of the entertainment I explained to Sophy that I should keep the Library Cart as my living-cart when not upon the road, and that I should keep all her books for her just as they stood, till she come back to claim them. So she went to China with her young husband, and it was a parting sorrowful and heavy, and I got the boy I had another service; and so as of old, when my child and wife were gone, I went plodding along alone, with my whip over my shoulder, at the old horse's head.

Sophy wrote me many letters, and I wrote her many letters. About the end of the first year she sent me one in an unsteady hand: "Dearest father, not a week ago I had a darling little daughter, but I am so well that they let me write these words to you. Dearest and best father, I hope my child may not be deaf and dumb, but I do not yet know." When I wrote back, I hinted the question; but as Sophy never answered that question, I felt it to be a sad one, and I never repeated it. For a long time our letters were regular, but then they got irregular, through Sophy's husband being moved to another station, and through my being always on the move. But we were in one another's thoughts, I was equally sure, letters or no letters.

Five years, odd months, had gone since Sophy went away. I was still the King of the Cheap Jacks, and at a greater height of popularity than ever. I had had a first-rate autumn of it, and on the twenty-third of December, one thousand eight hundred and sixty four, I found myself at Uxbridge, Middlesex, clean sold out. So I jogged up to London with the old horse, light and easy, to have my Christmas-eve and Christmas-day alone by the fire in the Library Cart, and then to buy a regular new stock of goods all round, to sell 'em again and get the money.

I am a neat hand at cookery, and I'll tell you what I knocked up for my Christmas-eve dinner in the Library Cart. I knocked up a beefsteak-pudding for one, with two kidneys, a dozen oysters, and a couple of mushrooms thrown in. It's a pudding to put a man in good humor with everything, except the two bottom buttons of his waist-coat. Having relished that pudding and cleared away, I turned the lamp low, and sat down by the light of the fire, watching it as it shone upon the backs of Sophy's books.

Sophy's books so brought up Sophy's self, that I saw her touching face quite plainly, before I dropped off dozing by the fire. This may be a reason why Sophy, with her deaf-and-dumb child in her arms, seemed to stand silent by me all through my nap. I was on the road, off the road, in all sorts of places, North and South and West and East, Winds liked best and winds liked least, Here and there and gone astray, Over the hills and far away, and still she stood silent by me, with her silent child in her arms. Even when I woke with a start, she seemed to vanish, as if she had stood by me in that very place only a single instant before.

I had started at a real sound, and the sound was on the steps of the cart. It was the light hurried tread of a child, coming clambering up That tread of a child had once been so familiar to me, that for half a moment I believed I was a-going to see a little ghost.

But the touch of a real child was laid upon the outer handle of the door, and the handle turned, and the door opened a little way, and a real child peeped in. A bright little comely girl with large dark eyes.

Looking full at me, the tiny creature took off her mite of a straw hat, and a quantity of dark curls fell all about her face. Then she opened her lips, and said in a pretty voice,

"Grandfather!"

"Ah, my God!" I cries out. "She can speak!"

"Yes, dear grandfather. And I am to ask you whether there was ever any one that I remind you of?"

In a moment Sophy was round my neck, as well as the child, and her husband was a-wringing my hand with his face hid, and we all had to shake ourselves together before we could get over it. And when we did begin to get over it, and I saw the pretty child a-talking, pleased and quick and eager and busy, to her mother, in the signs that I had first taught her mother, the happy and yet pitying tears fell rolling down my face.

MUGBY

JUNCTION

IN FOUR CHAPTERS

Mugby Junction

I. BARBOX BROTHERS

"Guard! What place is this?"

"Mugby Junction, Sir."

"A windy place!"

"Yes, it mostly is, Sir."

"And looks comfortless indeed!"

"Yes, it generally does, Sir."

"Is it a rainy night still?"

"Pours, Sir."

"Open the door. I'll get out."

"You'll have, Sir," said the guard, glistening with drops of wet, and looking at the tearful face of his watch by the light of his lantern as the traveller descended, "three minutes here."

"More, I think. — For I am not going on."

"Thought you had a through ticket, Sir?"

"So I have, but I shall sacrifice the rest of it. I want my luggage."

"Please to come to the van and point it out, Sir. Be good enough to look very sharp, Sir. Not a moment to spare."

The guard hurried to the luggage van, and the traveller hurried after him. The guard got into it, and the traveller looked into it.

"Those two large black portmanteaus in the corner where your light shines. Those are mine."

"Name upon 'em, Sir?"

"Barbox Brothers."

"Stand clear, Sir, if you please. One. Two. Right!" Lamp waved. Signal lights ahead already changing. Shriek from engine. Train gone.

"Mugby Junction!" said the traveller, pulling up the woollen

267

muffler round his throat with both hands. "At past three o'clock of a tempestuous morning! So!"

He spoke to himself. There was no one else to speak to. Perhaps, though there had been anyone else to speak to, he would have preferred to speak to himself. Speaking to himself he spoke to a man within five years of fifty either way, who had turned grey too soon, like a neglected fire; a man of pondering habit, brooding carriage of the head, and suppressed internal voice; a man with many indications on him of having been much alone.

He stood unnoticed on the dreary platform, except by the rain and by the wind. Those two vigilant assailants made a rush at him. "Very well," said he, yielding. "It signifies nothing to me to what quarter I turn my face."

Thus, at Mugby Junction, at past three o'clock of a tempestuous morning, the traveller went where the weather drove him.

Not but what he could make a stand when he was so minded, for, coming to the end of the roofed shelter (it is of considerable extent at Mugby Junction), and looking out upon the dark night, with a yet darker spirit-wing of storm beating its wild way through it, he faced about, and held his own as ruggedly in the difficult direction as he had held it in the easier one. Thus, with a steady step, the traveller went up and down, up and down, up and down, seeking nothing and finding it.

A place replete with shadowy shapes, this Mugby Junction in the black hours of the four-and-twenty. Mysterious goods trains, covered with palls and gliding on like vast weird funerals, conveying themselves guiltily away from the presence of the few lighted lamps, as if their freight had come to a secret and unlawful end. Half-miles of coal pursuing in a Detective manner, following when they lead, stopping when they stop, backing when they back. Red-hot embers showering out upon the ground, down this dark avenue, and down the other, as if torturing fires were being raked clear; concurrently, shrieks and groans and grinds invading the ear, as if the tortured were at the height of their suffering. Iron-barred cages full of cattle jangling by midway, the drooping beasts with horns entangled, eyes frozen with terror, and mouths too: at least they have long icicles (or what seem so) hanging from their lips. Unknown languages in the air, conspiring in red, green, and white characters. An earthquake, accompanied with thunder and lightning, going up express to London. Now, all quiet, all rusty, wind and rain in possession, lamps extinguished, Mugby Junction dead and indistinct, with its robe drawn over its head, like Cæsar.

Now, too, as the belated traveller plodded up and down, a shadowy train went by him in the gloom which was no other than the train of a life. From whatsoever intangible deep cutting or dark tunnel it emerged, here it came, unsummoned and unannounced, stealing upon him, and passing away into obscurity. Here mournfully went by a child who had never had a childhood or known a parent, inseparable from a youth with a bitter sense of his namelessness, coupled to a man the enforced business of whose best years had been distasteful and oppressive, linked to an ungrateful friend, dragging after him a woman once beloved. Attendant, with many a clank and wrench, were lumbering cares, dark meditations, huge dim disappointments, monotonous years, a long jarring line of the discords of a solitary and unhappy existence.

" — Yours, Sir?"

The traveller recalled his eyes from the waste into which they had been staring, and fell back a step or so under the abruptness, and perhaps the chance appropriateness, of the question.

"Oh! My thoughts were not here for the moment. Yes. Yes. Those two portmanteaus are mine. Are you a Porter?"

"On Porter's wages, Sir. But I am Lamps."

The traveller looked a little confused.

"Who did you say you are?"

"Lamps, Sir," showing an oily cloth in his hand, as further explanation.

"Surely, surely. Is there any hotel or tavern here?"

"Not exactly here, Sir. There IS a Refreshment Room here, but — " Lamps, with a mighty serious look, gave his head a warning roll that plainly added — "but it's a blessed circumstance for you that it's not open."

"You couldn't recommend it, I see, if it was available?"

"Ask your pardon, Sir. If it was — ?"

"Open?"

"It ain't my place, as a paid servant of the company, to give my opinion on any of the company's toepics" — he pronounced it more like toothpicks — "beyond lamp-ile and cottons," returned Lamps in a confidential tone; "but, speaking as a man, I wouldn't recommend my father (if he was to come to life again) to go and try how he'd be treated at the Refreshment Room. Not speaking as a man, no, I would *not*."

The traveller nodded conviction. "I suppose I can put up in the town? There is a town here?" For the traveller (though a stay-at-home compared with most travellers) had been, like many others, carried on the steam winds and the iron tides through that Junction before, without having ever, as one might say, gone ashore there.

"Oh yes, there's a town, Sir! Anyways, there's town enough to put up in. But," following the glance of the other at his luggage, "this is a very dead time of the night with us, Sir. The deadest time. I might a'most call it our deadest and buriedest time."

"No porters about?"

"Well, Sir, you see," returned Lamps, confidential again, "they in general goes off with the gas. That's how it is. And they seem to have overlooked you, through your walking to the furder end of the platform. But, in about twelve minutes or so, she may be up."

"Who may be up?"

"The three forty-two, Sir. She goes off in a sidin' till the Up X passes, and then she" — here an air of hopeful vagueness pervaded Lamps — "does all as lays in her power."

"I doubt if I comprehend the arrangement."

"I doubt if anybody do, Sir. She's a Parliamentary, Sir. And, you see, a Parliamentary, or a Skirmishun — "

"Do you mean an Excursion?"

"That's it, Sir. — A Parliamentary or a Skirmishun, she mostly *doos* go off into a sidin'. But, when she *can* get a chance, she's whistled out of it and she's whistled up into doing' all as" — Lamps again wore the air of a highly sanguine man who hoped for the best — "all as lays in her power."

He then explained that porters on duty, being required to be in attendance on the Parliamentary matron in question, would doubtless turn up with the gas. In the meantime, if the gentleman would not very much object to the smell of lamp-oil, and would accept the warmth of his little room — The gentleman, being by this time very cold, instantly closed with the proposal.

A greasy little cabin it was, suggestive, to the sense of smell, of a cabin in a Whaler. But there was a bright fire burning in its rusty grate, and on the floor there stood a wooden stand of newly trimmed and lighted lamps, ready for carriage service. They made a bright show, and their light, and the warmth, accounted for the popularity of the room, as borne witness to by many impressions of velveteen trousers on a form by the fire, and many rounded smears and smudges of stooping velveteen shoulders on the adjacent wall. Various untidy shelves accommodated a quantity of lamps and oil-cans, and also a fragrant collection of what looked like the pocket-handkerchiefs of the whole lamp family.

As Barbox Brothers (so to call the traveller on the warranty of his luggage) took his seat upon the form, and warmed his now ungloved hands at the fire, he glanced aside at a little deal desk, much blotched with ink, which his elbow touched. Upon it were some scraps of coarse paper, and a superannuated steel pen in very reduced and gritty circumstances.

From glancing at the scraps of paper, he turned involuntarily to his host, and said, with some roughness:

"Why, you are never a poet, man?"

Lamps had certainly not the conventional appearance of one, as he stood modestly rubbing his squab nose with a handkerchief so exceedingly oily, that he might have been in the act of mistaking himself for one of his charges. He was a spare man of about the Barbox Brothers' time of life, with his features whimsically drawn upward as if they were attracted by the roots of his hair. He had a peculiarly shining transparent complexion, probably occasioned by constant oleaginous application; and his attractive hair, being cut short, and being grizzled, and standing straight up on end as if it in its turn were attracted by some invisible magnet above it, the top of his head was not very unlike a lamp-wick.

"But, to be sure, it's no business of mine," said Barbox Brothers. "That was an impertinent observation on my part. Be what you like."

"Some people, Sir," remarked Lamps in a tone of apology, "are sometimes what they don't like."

"Nobody knows that better than I do," sighed the other. "I have been what I don't like, all my life."

"When I first took, Sir," resumed Lamps, "to composing little Comic-Songs-like — "

Barbox Brothers eyed him with great disfavor.

" — To composing little Comic-Songs-like — and what was more hard — to singing 'em afterwards," said Lamps, "it went against the grain at that time, it did indeed."

Something that was not all oil here shining in Lamps's eye, Barbox Brothers withdrew his own a little disconcerted, looked at the fire, and put a foot on the top bar. "Why did you do it, then?" he asked after a short pause; abruptly enough, but in a softer tone. "If you didn't want to do it, why did you do it? Where did you sing them? Public-house?"

To which Mr. Lamps returned the curious reply: "Bedside."

At this moment, while the traveller looked at him for elucidation, Mugby Junction started suddenly, trembled violently, and opened its gas eyes. "She's got up!" Lamps announced, excited. "What lays in her power is sometimes more, and sometimes less; but it's laid in her power to get up to-night, by George!"

The legend "Barbox Brothers," in large white letters on two black surfaces, was very soon afterwards trundling on a truck through a silent street, and, when the owner of the legend had shivered on the pavement half an hour, what time the porter's knocks at the Inn Door knocked up the whole town first, and the Inn last, he groped his way into the close air of a shut-up house, and so groped between the sheets of a shut-up bed that seemed to have been expressly refrigerated for him when last made.

II

"You remember me, Young Jackson?"

"What do I remember if not you? You are my first remembrance. It was you who told me that was my name. It was you who told me that on every twentieth of December my life had a penitential anniversary in it called a birthday. I suppose the last communication was truer than the first!"

"What am I like, Young Jackson?"

"You are like a blight all through the year to me. You are like a hard-lined, thin-lipped, repressive, changeless woman with a wax mask on. You are like the Devil to me; most of all when you teach me religious things, for you make me abhor them."

"You remember me, Mr. Young Jackson?" In another voice from another quarter.

"Most gratefully, Sir. You were the ray of hope and prospering ambition in my life. When I attended your course, I believed that I should come to be a great healer, and I felt almost happy — even though I was still the one boarder in the house with that horrible mask, and ate and drank in silence and constraint with the mask before me, every day. As I had done every, every, every day, through my school-time and from my earliest recollection."

"What am I like, Mr. Young Jackson?"

"You are like a Superior Being to me. You are like Nature beginning to reveal herself to me. I hear you again, as one of the hushed crowd of young men kindling under the power of your presence and knowledge, and you bring into my eyes the only exultant tears that ever stood in them."

"You remember Me, Mr. Young Jackson?" In a grating voice from quite another quarter.

"Too well. You made your ghostly appearance in my life one day, and announced that its course was to be suddenly and wholly changed. You showed me which was my wearisome seat in the Galley of Barbox Brothers. (When *they* were, if they ever were, is unknown to me; there was nothing of them but the name when I bent to the oar.) You told me what I was to do, and what to be paid; you told me afterwards, at intervals of years, when I was to sign for the Firm, when I became a partner, when I became the Firm. I know no more of it, or of myself."

"What am I like, Mr. Young Jackson?"

"You are like my father, I sometimes think. You are hard enough and cold enough so to have brought up an acknowledged son. I see your scanty figure, your close brown suit, and your tight brown wig; but you, too, wear a wax mask to your death. You never by a chance remove it — it never by a chance falls off — and I know no more of you."

Throughout this dialogue, the traveller spoke to himself at his window in the morning, as he had spoken to himself at the Junction overnight. And as he had then looked in the darkness, a man who had turned grey too soon, like a neglected fire: so he now looked in the sunlight, an ashier grey, like a fire which the brightness of the sun put out.

The firm of Barbox Brothers had been some offshoot or irregular branch of the Public Notary and bill-broking tree. It had gained for itself a griping reputation before the days of Young Jackson, and the reputation had stuck to it and to him. As he had imperceptibly come into possession of the dim den up in the corner of a court off Lombard Street, on whose grimy windows the inscription Barbox Brothers had for many long years daily interposed itself between him and the sky, so he had insensibly found himself a personage held in chronic distrust, whom it was essential to screw tight to every transaction in which he engaged, whose word was never to be taken without his attested bond, whom all dealers with openly set up guards and wards against. This character had come upon him through no act of his own. It was as if the original Barbox had stretched himself down upon the office floor, and had thither caused to be conveyed Young Jackson in his sleep, and had there effected a metempsychosis and exchange of persons with him. The discovery — aided in its turn by the deceit of the only woman he had ever loved, and the deceit of the only friend he had ever made; who eloped from him to be married together — the discovery, so followed up, completed what his earliest rearing had begun. He shrank, abashed, within the form of Barbox, and lifted up his head and heart no more.

But he did at last effect one great release in his condition. He broke the oar he had plied so long, and he scuttled and sank the galley. He prevented the gradual retirement of an old conventional business from him, by taking the initiative and retiring from it. With enough to live on (though, after all, with not too much), he obliterated the firm of Barbox Brothers from the pages of the Post-Office Directory and the face of the earth, leaving nothing of it but its name on two portmanteaus.

"For one must have some name in going about, for people to pick up," he explained to Mugby High Street, through the Inn window, "and that name at least was real once. Whereas, Young Jackson! — Not to mention its being a sadly satirical misnomer for Old Jackson."

He took up his hat and walked out, just in time to see, passing along on the opposite side of the way, a velveteen man, carrying his day's dinner in a small bundle that might have been larger without suspicion of gluttony, and pelting away towards the Junction at a great pace.

"There's Lamps!" said Barbox Brothers. "And by-the-bye — "

Ridiculous, surely, that a man so serious, so self-contained, and not yet three days emancipated from a routine of drudgery, should stand rubbing his chin in the street, in a brown study about Comic Songs.

"Bedside?" said Barbox Brothers testily. "Sings them at the bedside? Why at the bedside, unless he goes to bed drunk? Does, I shouldn't wonder. But it's no business of mine. Let me see. Mugby Junction, Mugby Junction. Where shall I go next? As it came into my head last night when I woke from an uneasy sleep in the carriage and found myself here, I can go anywhere from here. Where shall I go? I'll go and look at the Junction by daylight. There's no hurry, and I may like the look of one Line better than another."

But there were so many Lines. Gazing down upon them from a bridge at the Junction, it was as if the concentrating Companies formed a great Industrial Exhibition of the works of extraordinary ground spiders that spun iron. And then so many of the Lines went such wonderful ways, so crossing and curving among one another, that the eye lost them. And then some of them appeared to start with the fixed intention of going five hundred miles, and all of a sudden gave it up at an insignificant barrier, or turned off into a workshop. And then others, like intoxicated men, went a little way very straight, and surprisingly slued round and came back again. And then others were so chock-full of trucks of coal, others were so blocked with trucks of casks, others were so gorged with trucks of ballast, others were so set apart for wheeled objects like immense iron cotton-reels: while others were so bright and clear, and others were so delivered over to rust and ashes and idle wheelbarrows out of work, with their legs in the air (looking much like their masters on strike), that there was no beginning, middle, or end to the bewilderment.

Barbox Brothers stood puzzled on the bridge, passing his right hand across the lines on his forehead, which multiplied while he looked down, as if the railway Lines were getting themselves photographed on that sensitive plate. Then was heard a distant ringing of bells and blowing of whistles. Then, puppet-looking heads of men popped out of boxes in perspective, and popped in again. Then, prodigious wooden razors, set up on end, began shaving the atmosphere. Then, several locomotive engines in several directions began to scream and be agitated. Then, along one avenue a train came in.

Then, along another two trains appeared that didn't come in, but stopped without. Then, bits of trains broke off. Then, a struggling horse became involved with them. Then, the locomotives shared the bits of trains, and ran away with the whole.

"I have not made my next move much clearer by this. No hurry. No need to make up my mind to-day, or to-morrow, nor yet the day after. I'll take a walk."

It fell out somehow (perhaps he meant it should) that the walk tended to the platform at which he had alighted, and to Lamps's room. But Lamps was not in his room. A pair of velveteen shoulders were adapting themselves to one of the impressions on the wall by Lamps's fireplace, but otherwise the room was void. In passing back to get out of the station again, he learned the cause of this vacancy, by catching sight of Lamps on the opposite line of railway, skipping along the top of a train, from carriage to carriage, and catching lighted namesakes thrown up to him by a coadjutor.

"He is busy. He has not much time for composing or singing Comic Songs this morning, I take it."

The direction he pursued now was into the country, keeping very near to the side of one great Line of railway, and within easy view of others. "I have half a mind," he said, glancing around, "to settle the question from this point, by saying, 'I'll take this set of rails, or that, or t'other, and stick to it.' They separate themselves from the confusion, out here, and go their ways."

Ascending a gentle hill of some extent, he came to a few cottages. There, looking about him as a very reserved man might who had never looked about him in his life before, he saw some six or eight young children come merrily trooping and whooping from one of the cottages, and disperse. But not until they had all turned at the little garden-gate, and kissed their hands to a face at the upper window: a low window enough, although the upper, for the cottage had but a story of one room above the ground.

Now, that the children should do this was nothing; but that they should do this to a face lying on the sill of the open window, turned towards them in a horizontal position, and apparently only a face, was something noticeable. He looked up at the window again. Could only see a very fragile, though a very bright face, lying on one cheek on the window-sill. The delicate smiling face of a girl or woman.

Framed in long bright brown hair, round which was tied a light blue band or fillet, passing under the chin.

He walked on, turned back, passed the window again, shyly glanced up again. No change. He struck off by a winding branch road at the top of the hill — which he must otherwise have descended — kept the cottages in view, worked his way round at a distance so as to come out once more into the main road, and be obliged to pass the cottages again. The face still lay on the window-sill, but not so much inclined towards him. And now there were a pair of delicate hands too. They had the action of performing on some musical instrument, and yet it produced no sound that reached his ears.

"Mugby Junction must be the maddest place in England," said Barbox Brothers, pursuing his way down the hill. "The first thing I find here is a Railway Porter who composes comic songs to sing at his bedside. The second thing I find here is a face, and a pair of hands playing a musical instrument that *don't* play!"

The day was a fine bright day in the early beginning of November, the air was clear and inspiriting, and the landscape was rich in beautiful colors. The prevailing colors in the court off Lombard Street, London city, had been few and somber. Sometimes, when the weather elsewhere was very bright indeed, the dwellers in those tents enjoyed a pepper-and-salt-colored day or two, but their atmosphere's usual wear was slate or snuff-colored.

He relished his walk so well that he repeated it next day. He was a little earlier at the cottage than on the day before, and he could hear the children upstairs singing to a regular measure, and clapping out the time with their hands.

"Still, there is no sound of any musical instrument," he said, listening at the corner, "and yet I saw the performing hands again as I came by. What are the children singing? Why, good Lord, they can never be singing the multiplication table?"

They were, though, and with infinite enjoyment. The mysterious face had a voice attached to it, which occasionally led or set the children right. Its musical cheerfulness was delightful. The measure at length stopped, and was succeeded by a murmuring of young voices, and then by a short song which he made out to be about the current month of the year, and about what work it yielded to the laborers in the fields and farmyards. Then there was a stir of little feet, and the children came trooping and whooping out, as on the previous day. And again, as on the previous day, they all turned at the garden-gate, and kissed their hands — evidently to the face on the window-sill, though Barbox Brothers from his retired post of disadvantage at the corner could not see it.

But, as the children dispersed, he cut off one small straggler — a brown-faced boy with flaxen hair — and said to him:

"Come here, little one. Tell me, whose house is that?"

The child, with one swarthy arm held up across his eyes, half in shyness, and half ready for defence said from behind the inside of his elbow:

"Phœbe's."

"And who," said Barbox Brothers, quite as much embarrassed by his part in the dialogue as the child could possibly be by his, "is Phœbe?"

To which the child made answer: "Why, Phœbe, of course."

The small but sharp observer had eyed his questioner closely, and had taken his moral measure. He lowered his guard, and rather assumed a tone with him: as having discovered him to be an unaccustomed person in the art of polite conversation.

"Phœbe," said the child, "can't be anybobby else but Phœbe. Can she?"

"No, I suppose not."

"Well," returned the child, "then why did you ask me?"

Deeming it prudent to shift his ground, Barbox Brothers took up a new position.

"What do you do there? Up there in that room where the open window is. What do you do there?"

"Cool," said the child.

"Eh?"

"Co-o-ol," the child repeated in a louder voice, lengthening out the word with a fixed look and great emphasis, as much as to say: "What's the use of your having grown up, if you're such a donkey as not to understand me?"

"Ah! School, school," said Barbox Brothers. "Yes, yes, yes. And Phœbe teaches you?"

The child nodded.

"Good boy."

"Tound it out, have you?" said the child.

"Yes, I have found it out. What would you do with twopence, if I gave it you?"

"Pend it."

The knock-down promptitude of this reply leaving him not a leg to stand upon, Barbox Brothers produced the twopence with great lameness, and withdrew in a state of humiliation.

But, seeing the face on the window-sill as he passed the cottage, he acknowledged its presence there with a gesture, which was not a nod, not a bow, not a removal of his hat from his head, but was a diffident compromise between or struggle with all three. The eyes in the face seemed amused, or cheered, or both, and the lips modestly said: "Good day to you, Sir."

"I find I must stick for a time to Mugby Junction," said Barbox Brothers with much gravity, after once more stopping on his return road to look at the Lines where they went their several ways so quietly. "I can't make up my mind yet which iron road to take. In fact, I must get a little accustomed to the Junction before I can decide."

So, he announced at the Inn that he was "going to stay on for the present," and improved his acquaintance with the Junction that night, and again next morning, and again next night and morning: going down to the station, mingling with the people there, looking about him down all the avenues of railway, and beginning to take an interest in the incomings and outgoings of the trains. At first, he often put his head into Lamps's little room, but he never found Lamps there. A pair or two of velveteen shoulders he usually found there, stooping over the fire, sometimes in connection with a clasped knife and a piece of bread and meat; but the answer to his inquiry, "Where's Lamps?" was, either that he was "t'other side the line," or, that it was his off-time, or (in the latter case) his own personal introduction to another Lamps who was not his lamps. However, he was not so desperately set upon seeing Lamps now, but he bore the disappointment. Nor did he so wholly devote himself to his severe application to the study of Mugby Junction as to neglect exercise. On the contrary, he took a walk every day, and always the same walk. But the weather turned cold and wet again, and the window was never open.

III

At length, after a lapse of some days, there came another streak of fine bright hardy autumn weather. It was a Saturday. The window was open, and the children were gone. Not surprising, this, for he had patiently watched and waited at the corner until they *were* gone.

"Good day," he said to the face; absolutely getting his hat clear off his head this time.

"Good day to you, Sir."

"I am glad you have a fine sky again to look at."

"Thank you, Sir. It is kind of you."

"You are an invalid, I fear?"

"No, Sir. I have very good health."

"But are you not always lying down?"

"Oh yes, I am always lying down, because I cannot sit up! But I am not an invalid."

The laughing eyes seemed highly to enjoy his great mistake.

"Would you mind taking the trouble to come in, Sir? There is a beautiful view from this window. And you would see that I am not at all ill — being so good as to care."

It was said to help him, as he stood irresolute, but evidently desiring to enter, with his diffident hand on the latch of the garden-gate. It did help him, and he went in.

The room upstairs was a very clean white room with a low roof. Its only inmate lay on a couch that brought her face to a level with the window. The couch was white too; and her simple dress or wrapper being light blue, like the band around her hair, she had an ethereal look, and a fanciful appearance of lying among clouds. He felt that she instinctively perceived him to be by habit a downcast taciturn man; it was another help to him to have established that understanding so easily, and got it over.

There was an awkward constraint upon him, nevertheless, as he touched her hand, and took a chair at the side of her couch.

"I see now," he began, not at all fluently, "how you occupy your hand. Only seeing you from the path outside, I thought you were playing upon something."

She was engaged in very nimbly and dexterously making lace. A lace-pillow lay upon her breast; and the quick movements and changes of her hands upon it, as she worked, had given them the action he had misinterpreted.

"That is curious," she answered with a bright smile. "For I often fancy, myself, that I play tunes while I am at work."

"Have you any musical knowledge?"

She shook her head.

"I think I could pick out tunes, if I had any instrument, which could be made as handy to me as my lace-pillow. But I dare say I deceive myself. At all events, I shall never know."

"You have a musical voice. Excuse me; I have heard you sing."

"With the children?" she answered, slightly coloring. "Oh yes. I sing with the dear children, if it can be called singing."

Barbox Brothers glanced at the two small forms in the room, and hazarded the speculation that she was fond of children, and that she was learned in new systems of teaching them?

"Very fond of them," she said, shaking her head again; "but I know nothing of teaching, beyond the interest I have in it, and the pleasure it gives me when they learn. Perhaps your overhearing my little scholars sing some of their lessons has led you so far astray as to think me a grand teacher? Ah! I thought so! No, I have only read and been told about that system. It seemed so pretty and pleasant, and to treat them so like the merry Robins they are, that I took up with it in my little way. You don't need to be told what a very little way mine is, Sir," she added with a glance at the small forms and round the room.

All this time her hands were busy at her lace-pillow. As they still continued so, and as there was a kind of substitute for conversation in the click and play of its pegs, Barbox Brothers took the opportunity of observing her. He guessed her to be thirty. The charm of her transparent face and large bright brown eyes was, not that they were passively resigned, but that they were actively and thoroughly cheerful. Even her busy hands, which of their own thinness alone might have besought compassion, plied their task with a gay courage that made mere compassion an unjustifiable assumption of superiority, and an impertinence.

He saw her eyes in the act of rising towards his, and he directed his towards the prospect, saying: "Beautiful, indeed!"

"Most beautiful, Sir. I have sometimes had a fancy that I would like to sit up, for once, only to try how it looks to an erect head. But what a foolish fancy that would be to encourage! It cannot look more lovely to anyone than it does to me."

Her eyes were turned to it, as she spoke, with most delighted admiration and enjoyment. There was not a trace in it of any sense of deprivation.

"And those threads of railway, with their puffs of smoke and steam changing places so fast, make it so lively for me," she went on. "I think of the number of people who *can* go where they wish, on their business, or their pleasure; I remember that the puffs make signs to me that they are actually going while I look; and that enlivens the prospect with abundance of company, if I want company. There is the great Junction, too. I don't see it under the foot of the hill, but I can very often hear it, and I always know it is there. It seems to join me, in a way, to I don't know how many places and things that *I* shall never see."

With an abashed kind of idea that it might have already joined himself to something he had never seen, he said constrainedly: "Just so."

"And so you see, Sir," pursued Phœbe, "I am not the invalid you thought me, and I am very well off indeed."

"You have a happy disposition," said Barbox Brothers: perhaps with a slight excusatory touch for his own disposition.

"Ah! But you should know my father," she replied. "His is the happy disposition! — Don't mind, Sir!" For his reserve took the alarm at a step upon the stairs, and he distrusted that he would be set down for a troublesome intruder. "This is my father coming."

The door opened, and the father paused there.

"Why, Lamps!" exclaimed Barbox Brothers, starting from his chair. "How do you DO, Lamps?"

To which Lamps responded: "The gentleman for Nowhere! How do you DO, Sir?"

And they shook hands, to the greatest admiration and surprise of Lamps's daughter.

"I have looked you up half-a-dozen times since that night," said Barbox Brothers, "but have never found you."

"So I've heerd on, Sir, so I've heerd on," returned Lamps. "It's your being noticed so often down at the Junction, without taking any train, that has begun to get you the name among us of the gentleman for Nowhere. No offense in my having called you by it when took by surprise, I hope, Sir?"

"None at all. It's as good a name for me as any other you could call me by. But may I ask you a question in the corner here?"

Lamps suffered himself to be led aside from his daughter's couch by one of the buttons of his velveteen jacket.

"Is this the bedside where you sing your songs?"

Lamps nodded.

The gentleman for Nowhere clapped him on the shoulder, and they faced about again.

"Upon my word, my dear," said Lamps then to his daughter, looking from her to her visitor, "it is such an amaze to me, to find you brought acquainted with this gentleman, that I must (if this gentleman will excuse me) take a rounder."

Mr. Lamps demonstrated in action what this meant, by pulling out his oily handkerchief rolled up in the form of a ball, and giving himself an elaborate smear, from behind the right ear, up the cheek, across the forehead, and down the other cheek to behind his left ear. After this operation he shone exceedingly.

"It's according to my custom when particular warmed up by any agitation, Sir," he offered by way of apology. "And really, I am throwed into that state of amaze by finding you brought acquainted with Phœbe, that I — that I think I will, if you'll excuse me, take another rounder." Which he did, seeming to be greatly restored by it.

They were now both standing by the side of her couch, and she was working at her lace-pillow. "Your daughter tells me," said Barbox Brothers, still in a half-reluctant shamefaced way, "that she never sits up."

"No, Sir, nor never has done. You see, her mother (who died when she was a year and two months old) was subject to very bad fits, and as she had never mentioned to me that she *was* subject to fits, they couldn't be guarded against. Consequently, she dropped the baby when took, and this happened."

"It was very wrong of her," said Barbox Brothers with a knitted brow, "to marry you, making a secret of her infirmity."

"Well, Sir!" pleaded Lamps in behalf of the long-deceased. "You see, Phœbe and me, we have talked that over too. And Lord bless us! Such a number on us has our infirmities, what with fits, and what with misfits, of one sort and another, that if we confessed to 'em all before we got married, most of us might never get married."

"Might not that be for the better?"

"Not in this case, Sir," said Phœbe, giving her hand to her father.

"No, not in this case, Sir," said her father, patting it between his own.

"You correct me," returned Barbox Brothers with a blush; "and I must look so like a Brute, that at all events it would be super-fluous in me to confess to *that* infirmity. I wish you would tell me a little more about yourselves. I hardly know how to ask it of you, for I am conscious that I have a bad stiff manner, a dull discouraging way with me, but I wish you would."

"With all our hearts, Sir," returned Lamps gaily for both. "And first of all, that you may know my name — "

"Stay!" interposed the visitor with a slight flush. "What signifies your name? Lamps is name enough for me. I like it. It is bright and expressive. What do I want more?"

"Why, to be sure, Sir," returned Lamps. "I have in general no other name down at the Junction; but I thought, on account of your being here as a first-class single, in a private character, that you might — "

The visitor waved the thought away with his hand, and Lamps acknowledged the mark of confidence by taking another rounder.

"You are hard-worked, I take for granted?" said Barbox Brothers, when the subject of the rounder came out of it much dirtier than he went into it.

Lamps was beginning, "Not particular so" — when his daughter took him up.

"Oh yes, Sir, he is very hard-worked. Fourteen, fifteen, eighteen hours a day. Sometimes twenty-four hours at a time."

"And you," said Barbox Brothers, "what with your school, Phœbe, and what with your lace-making — "

"But my school is a pleasure to me," she interrupted, opening her brown eyes wider, as if surprised to find him so obtuse. "I began it when I was but a child, because it brought me and other children into company, don't you see? *That* was not work. I carry it on still, because it keeps children about me. *That* is not work. I do it as love, not as work. Then my lace-pillow"; her busy hands had stopped, as if her argument required all her cheerful earnestness, but now went on again at the name; "it goes with my thoughts when I think, and it goes with my tunes when I hum any, and *that's* not work. Why, you yourself thought it was music, you know, Sir. And so it is to me."

"Everything is!" cried Lamps radiantly. "Everything is music to her, Sir."

"My father is, at any rate," said Phœbe, exultingly pointing her thin forefinger at him. "There is more music in my father than there is in a brass band."

"I say! My dear! It's very fillyillially done, you know; but you are flattering your father," he protested, sparkling.

"No, I am not, Sir, I assure you. No, I am not. If you could hear my father sing, you would know I am not. But you never will hear him sing, because he never sings to any one but me. However tired he is, he always sings to me when he comes home. When I lay here long ago, quite a poor little broken doll, he used to sing to me. More than that, he used to make songs, bringing in whatever little jokes we had between us. More than that, he often does so to this day. Oh! I'll tell of you, father, as the gentleman has asked about you. He is a poet, Sir."

"I shouldn't wish the gentleman, my dear," observed Lamps, for the moment turning grave, "to carry away that opinion of your father, because it might look as if I was given to asking the stars in a molloncolly manner what they was up to. Which I wouldn't at once waste the time, and take the liberty, my dear."

"My father," resumed Phœbe, amending her text, "is always on the bright side, and the good side. You told me, just now, I had a happy disposition. How can I help it?"

"Well; but, my dear," returned Lamps argumentatively, "how can *I* help it? Put it to yourself, Sir. Look at her. Always as you see her now. Always working — and after all, Sir, for but a very few shillings a week — always contented, always lively, always interested in others, of all sorts. I said, this moment, she was always as you see her now. So she is, with a difference that comes to much the same. For, when it is my Sunday off and the morning bells have done ringing, I hear the prayers and thanks read in the touchingest way, and I have the hymns sung to me — so soft, Sir, that you couldn't hear 'em out of this room — in notes that seem to me, I am sure, to come from Heaven and go back to it."

It might have been merely through the association of these words with their sacredly quiet time, or it might have been through the larger association of the words with the Redeemer's presence beside the bedridden; but here her dexterous fingers came to a stop on the lace-pillow, and clasped themselves around his neck as he bent down. There was great natural sensibility in both father and daughter, the visitor could easily see; but each made it, for the other's sake, retiring, not demonstrative; and perfect cheerfulness, intuitive or acquired, was either the first or second nature of both. In a very few moments Lamps was taking another rounder with his comical features beaming, while Phœbe's laughing eyes (just a glistening speck or so upon their lashes) were again directed by turns to him, and to her work, and to Barbox Brothers.

"When my father, Sir," she said brightly, "tells you about my being interested in other people, even though they know nothing about me — which, by-the-bye, I told you myself — you ought to know how that comes about. That's my father's doing."

"No, it isn't!" he protested.

"Don't you believe him, Sir; yes, it is. He tells me of everything he sees down at his work. You would be surprised what a quantity he gets together for me every day. He looks into the carriages, and tells me how the ladies are dressed — so that I know all the fashions! He looks into the carriages, and tells me what pairs of lovers he sees, and what new-married couples on their wedding trip — so that I know all about that! He collects chance newspapers and books — so that I have plenty to read! He tells me about the sick people who are travelling to try to get better — so that I know all about them! In short, as I began by saying, he tells me everything he sees and makes out down at his work, and you can't think what a quantity he does see and make out."

"As to collecting newspapers and books, my dear," said Lamps, "it's clear I can have no merit in that, because they're not my perquisites. You see, Sir, it's this way: A Guard, he'll say to me, 'Hallo, here you are, Lamps. I've saved this paper for your daughter. How is she a-going on?' A Head Porter, he'll say to me, 'Here! Catch hold, Lamps. Here's a couple of wollumes for your daughter. Is she pretty much where she were?' And that's what makes it double welcome, you see. If she had a thousand pound in a box, they wouldn't trouble themselves about her; but being what she is — that is, you understand," Lamps added, somewhat hurriedly, "not having a thousand pound in a box — they take thought for her. And as concerning the young pairs, married and unmarried, it's only natural I should bring home what little I can about *them,* seeing that there's not a Couple of either sort in the neighborhood that don't come of their own accord to confide in Phœbe."

She raised her eyes triumphantly to Barbox Brothers as she said:

"Indeed, Sir, that is true. If I could have got up and gone to church, I don't know how often I should have been a bridesmaid. But, if I could have done that, some girls in love might have been jealous of me, and, as it is, no girl is jealous of me. And my pillow would not have been half as ready to put the piece of cake under, as I always find it," she added, turning her face on it with a light sigh, and a smile at her father.

The arrival of a little girl, the biggest of the scholars, now led to an understanding on the part of Barbox Brothers, that she was the domestic of the cottage, and had come to take active measures in it, attended by a pail that might have extinguished her, and a broom three times her height. He therefore rose to take his leave, and took it; saying that, if Phœbe had no objection, he would come again.

He had muttered that he would come "in the course of his walks." The course of his walks must have been highly favorable to his return, for he returned after an interval of a single day.

"You thought you would never see me any more, I suppose?" he said to Phœbe as he touched her hand, and sat down by her couch.

"Why should I think so?" was her surprised rejoinder.

"I took it for granted you would mistrust me."

"For granted, Sir? Have you been so much mistrusted?"

"I think I am justified in answering yes. But I may have mistrusted, too, on my part. No matter just now. We were speaking of the Junction last time. I have passed hours there since the day before yesterday."

"Are you now the gentleman for Somewhere?" she asked with a smile.

"Certainly for Somewhere; but I don't yet know Where. You would never guess what I am travelling from. Shall I tell you? I am travelling from my birthday."

Her hands stopped in her work, and she looked at him with incredulous astonishment.

"Yes," said Barbox Brothers, not quite easy in his chair, "from my birthday. I am, to myself, an unintelligible book with the earlier chapters all torn out, and thrown away. My childhood had no grace of childhood, my youth had no charm of youth, and what can be expected from such a lost beginning?" His eyes meeting hers as they were addressed intently to him, something seemed to stir within his breast, whispering: "Was this bed a place for the graces of childhood and the charms of youth to take to kindly? Oh, shame, shame!"

"It is a disease with me," said Barbox Brothers, checking himself, and making as though he had a difficulty in swallowing something, "to go wrong about that. I don't know how I came to speak of that. I hope it is because of an old misplaced confidence in one of your sex involving an old bitter treachery. I don't know. I am all wrong together."

Her hands quietly and slowly resumed their work. Glancing at her, he saw that her eyes were thoughtfully following them.

"I am travelling from my birthday," he resumed, "because it has always been a dreary day to me. My first free birthday coming round some five or six weeks hence, I am travelling to put its predecessors far behind me, and to try to crush the day — or, at all events, put it out of my sight — by heaping new objects on it."

As he paused, she looked at him; but only shook her head as being quite at a loss.

"This is unintelligible to your happy disposition," he pursued, abiding by his former phrase as if there were some lingering virtue of self-defense in it. "I knew it would be, and am glad it is. However, on this travel of mine (in which I mean to pass the rest of my days, having abandoned all thought of a fixed home), I stopped, as you have heard from your father, at the Junction here. The extent of its ramifications quite confused me as to whither I should go, *from* here. I have not yet settled, being still perplexed among so many roads. What do you think I mean to do? How many of the branching roads can you see from your window?"

Looking out, full of interest, she answered, "Seven."

"Seven," said Barbox Brothers, watching her with a grave smile. "Well! I propose to myself at once to reduce the gross number to those very seven, and gradually to fine them down to one — the most promising for me — and to take that."

"But how will you know, Sir, which *is* the most promising?" she asked, with her brightened eyes roving over the view.

"Ah!" said Barbox Brothers with another grave smile, and considerably improving in his ease of speech. "To be sure. In this way. Where your father can pick up so much every day for a good purpose, I may once and again pick up a little for an indifferent purpose. The gentleman for Nowhere must become still better known at the Junction. He shall continue to explore it, until he attaches something that he has seen, heard, or found out, at the head of each of the seven roads, to the road itself. And so his choice of a road shall be determined by his choice among his discoveries."

Her hands still busy, she again glanced at the prospect, as if it comprehended something that had not been in it before, and laughed as if it yielded her new pleasure.

"But I must not forget," said Barbox Brothers, "(having got so far) to ask a favor. I want your help in this expedient of mine. I want to bring you what I pick up at the heads of the seven roads that you lie here looking out at, and to compare notes with you about it. May I? They say two heads are better than one. I should say myself that probably depends upon the heads concerned. But I am quite sure, though we are so newly acquainted, that your head and your father's have found out better things, Phœbe, than ever mine of itself discovered."

She gave him her sympathetic right hand, in perfect rapture with his proposal, and eagerly and gratefully thanked him.

"That's well!" said Barbox Brothers. "Again I must not forget (having got so far) to ask a favor. Will you shut your eyes?"

Laughing playfully at the strange nature of the request, she did so.

"Keep them shut," said Barbox Brothers, going softly to the door, and coming back. "You are on your honor, mind, not to open your eyes until I tell you that you may?"

"Yes! On my honor."

"Good. May I take your lace-pillow from you for a minute?"

Still laughing and wondering, she removed her hands from it, and he put it aside.

"Tell me. Did you see the puffs of smoke and steam made by the morning fast-train yesterday on road number seven from here?"

"Behind the elm-trees and the spire?"

"That's the road," said Barbox Brothers, directing his eyes towards it.

"Yes. I watched them melt away."

"Anything unusual in what they expressed?"

"No!" she answered merrily.

"Not complimentary to me, for I was in that train. I went — don't open your eyes — to fetch you this, from the great ingenious town. It is not half so large as your lace-pillow, and lies easily and lightly in its place. These little keys are like the keys of a miniature piano, and you supply the air required with your left hand. May you pick out delightful music from it, my dear! For the present — you can open your eyes now — good-bye!"

In his embarrassed way, he closed the door upon himself, and only saw, in doing so, that she ecstatically took the present to her bosom and caressed it. The glimpse gladdened his heart, and yet saddened it; for so might she, if her youth had flourished in its natural course, have taken to her breast that day the slumbering music of her own child's voice.

CHAPTER II

BARBOX BROTHERS AND CO.

With good-will and earnest purpose, the gentleman for Nowhere began, on the very next day, his researches at the heads of the seven roads. The results of his researches, as he and Phœbe afterwards set them down in fair writing, hold their due places in this veracious chronicle. But they occupied a much longer time in the getting together than they ever will in the perusal. And this is probably the case with most reading matter, except when it is of that highly beneficial kind (for Posterity) which is "thrown off in a few moments of leisure" by the superior poetic geniuses who scorn to take prose pains.

It must be admitted, however, that Barbox by no means hurried himself. His heart being in his work of good-nature, he revelled in it. There was the joy, too (it was a true joy to him), of sometimes sitting by, listening to Phœbe as she picked out more and more discourse from her musical instrument, and as her natural taste and ear refined daily upon her first discoveries. Besides being a pleasure, this was an occupation, and in the course of weeks it consumed hours. It resulted that his dreaded birthday was close upon him before he had troubled himself any more about it.

The matter was made more pressing by the unforeseen circumstance that the councils held (at which Mr. Lamps, beaming most brilliantly, on a few rare occasions assisted) respecting the road to be selected were, after all, in nowise assisted by his investigations. For, he had connected this interest with this road, or that interest with the other, but could deduce no reason from it for giving any road the preference. Consequently, when the last council was holden, that part of the business stood, in the end, exactly where it had stood in the beginning.

"But, Sir," remarked Phœbe, "we have only six roads after all. Is the seventh road dumb?"

"The seventh road? Oh!" said Barbox Brothers, rubbing his chin. "That is the road I took, you know, when I went to get your little present. That is *its* story, Phœbe."

"Would you mind taking that road again, Sir?" she asked with hesitation.

"Not in the least; it is a great high-road after all."

"I should like you to take it," returned Phœbe with a persuasive smile, "for the love of that little present which must ever be so dear to me. I should like you to take it, because that road can never be again like any other road to me. I should like you to take it, in remembrance of your having done me so much good: of your having made me so much happier! If you leave me by the road you travelled when you went to do me this great kindness," sounding a faint chord as she spoke, "I shall feel, lying here watching at my window, as if it must conduct you to a prosperous end, and bring you back some day."

"It shall be done, my dear; it shall be done."

So at last the gentleman for Nowhere took a ticket for Somewhere, and his destination was the great ingenious town.

He had loitered so long about the Junction that it was the eighteenth of December when he left it. "High time," he reflected, as he seated himself in the train, "that I started in earnest! Only one clear day remains between me and the day I am running away from. I'll push onward for the hill-country to-morrow. I'll go to Wales."

It was with some pains that he placed before himself the undeniable advantages to be gained in the way of novel occupation for his senses from misty mountains, swollen streams, rain, cold, a wild seashore, and rugged roads. And yet he scarcely made them out as distinctly as he could have wished. Whether the poor girl, in spite of her new resource, her music, would have any feeling of loneliness upon her now — just at first — that she had not had before; whether she saw those very puffs of steam and smoke that he saw, as he sat in the train thinking of her; whether her face would have any pensive shadow on it as they died out of the distant view from her window; whether, in telling him he had done her so much good, she had not unconsciously corrected his old moody bemoaning of his station in life, by setting him thinking that a man might be a great healer, if he would, and yet not be a great doctor; these and other similar meditations got between him and his Welsh picture. There was within him, too, that dull sense of vacuity which follows separation from an object of interest, and cessation of a pleasant pursuit; and this sense, being quite new to him, made him restless. Further, in losing Mugby Junction, he had found himself again; and he was not the more enamored of himself for having lately passed his time in better company.

But surely here, not far ahead, must be the great ingenious town. This crashing and clashing that the train was undergoing, and this coupling on to it of a multitude of new echoes, could mean nothing less than approach to the great station. It did mean nothing less. After some stormy flashes of town lightning, in the way of swift revelations of red brick blocks of houses, high red brick chimney-shafts, vistas of red brick railway-arches, tongues of fire, blocks of smoke, valleys of canal, and hills of coal, there came the thundering in at the journey's end.

Having seen his portmanteaus safely housed in the hotel he chose, and having appointed his dinner hour, Barbox Brothers went out for a walk in the busy streets. And now it began to be suspected by him that Mugby Junction was a Junction of many branches, invisible as well as visible, and had joined him to an endless number of by-ways. For, whereas he would, but a little while ago, have walked these streets blindly brooding, he now had eyes and thoughts for a new external world. How the many toiling people lived, and loved, and died; how wonderful it was to consider the various trainings of eye and hand, the nice distinctions of sight and touch, that separated them into classes of workers, and even into classes of workers at subdivisions of one complete whole which combined their many intelligences and forces, though of itself but some cheap object of use or ornament in common life; how good it was to know that such assembling in a multitude on their part, and such contribution of their several dexterities towards a civilizing end, did not deteriorate them as it was the fashion of the supercilious May-flies of humanity to pretend, but engendered among them a self-respect, and yet a modest desire to be much wiser than they were (the first evinced in their well-balanced bearing and manner of speech when he stopped to ask a question; the second, in the announcements of their popular studies and amusements on the public walls); these considerations, and a host of such, made his walk a memorable one. "I too am but a little part of a great whole," he began to think; "and to be serviceable to myself and others, or to be happy, I must cast my interest into, and draw it out of, the common stock."

Although he had arrived at his journey's end for the day by noon, he had since insensibly walked about the town so far and so long that the lamp-lighters were now at their work in the streets, and the shops were sparkling up brilliantly. Thus reminded to turn towards his quarters, he was in the act of doing so, when a very little hand crept into his, and a very little voice said:

"Oh! if you please, I am lost!"

He looked down, and saw a very little fair-haired girl.

"Yes," she said, confirming her words with a serious nod. "I am indeed. I am lost!"

Greatly perplexed, he stopped, looked about him for help, descried none, and said, bending low:

"Where do you live, my child?"

"I don't know where I live," she returned. "I am lost."

"What is your name?"

"Polly."

"What is your other name?"

The reply was prompt, but unintelligible.

Imitating the sound as he caught it, he hazarded the guess, "Trivits."

"Oh no!" said the child, shaking her head. "Nothing like that."

"Say it again, little one."

An unpromising business. For this time it had quite a different sound.

He made the venture, "Paddens?"

"Oh no!" said the child. "Nothing like that."

"Once more. Let us try it again, dear."

A most hopeless business. This time it swelled into four syllables. "It can't be Tappitarver?" said Barbox Brothers, rubbing his head with his hat in discomfiture.

"No! It ain't," the child quietly assented.

On her trying this unfortunate name once more, with extraordinary efforts at distinctness, it swelled into eight syllables at least.

"Ah! I think," said Barbox Brothers with a desperate air of resignation, "that we had better give it up."

"But I am lost," said the child, nestling her little hand more closely in his, "and you'll take care of me, won't you?"

If ever a man were disconcerted by division between compassion on the one hand, and the very imbecility of irresolution on the other, here the man was. "Lost!" he repeated, looking down at the child. "I am sure *I* am. What is to be done?"

"Where do *you* live?" asked the child, looking up at him wistfully.

"Over there," he answered, pointing vaguely in the direction of his hotel.

"Hadn't we better go there?" said the child.

"Really," he replied, "I don't know but what we had."

So they set off, hand-in-hand. He, through comparison of himself against his little companion, with a clumsy feeling on him as if he had just developed into a foolish giant. She, clearly elevated in her own tiny opinion by having got him so neatly out of his embarrassment.

"We are going to have dinner when we get there, I suppose?" said Polly.

"Well," he rejoined, "I — Yes, I suppose we are."

"Do you like your dinner?" asked the child.

"Why, on the whole," said Barbox Brothers, "yes, I think I do."

"I do mine," said Polly. "Have you any brothers and sisters?"

"No. Have you?"

"Mine are dead."

"Oh!" said Barbox Brothers. With that absurd sense of unwieldiness of mind and body weighing him down, he would have not known how to pursue the conversation beyond this curt rejoinder, but that the child was always ready for him.

POLLY RESCUED BY BARBOX BROTHERS

"What," she asked, turning her soft hand coaxingly in his, "are you going to do to amuse me after dinner?"

"Upon my soul, Polly," exclaimed Barbox Brothers, very much at a loss, "I have not the slightest idea!"

"Then I tell you what," said Polly. "Have you got any cards at your house?"

"Plenty," said Barbox Brothers in a boastful vein.

"Very well. Then I'll build houses, and you shall look at me. You mustn't blow, you know."

"Oh no," said Barbox Brothers. "No, no, no. No blowing. Blowing's not fair."

He flattered himself that he had said this pretty well for an idiotic monster; but the child, instantly perceiving the awkwardness of his attempt to adapt himself to her level, utterly destroyed his hopeful opinion of himself by saying compassionately: "What a funny man you are!"

Feeling, after this melancholy failure, as if he every minute grew bigger and heavier in person, and weaker in mind, Barbox gave himself up for a bad job. No giant ever submitted more meekly to be led in triumph by all-conquering Jack than he to be bound in slavery to Polly.

"Do you know any stories?" she asked him.

He was reduced to the humiliating confession: "No."

"What a dunce you must be, mustn't you?" said Polly.

He was reduced to the humiliating confession: "Yes."

"Would you like me to teach you a story? But you must remember it, you know, and be able to tell it right to somebody else afterwards."

He professed that it would afford him the highest mental gratification to be taught a story, and that he would humbly endeavor to retain it in his mind. Whereupon Polly, giving her hand a new little turn in his, expressive of settling down for enjoyment, commenced a long romance, of which every relishing clause began with the words: "So this," or "And so this." As, "So this boy"; or, "So this fairy"; or, "And so this pie was four yards round, and two yards and a quarter deep." The interest of the romance was derived from the intervention of this fairy to punish this boy for having a greedy appetite. To achieve which purpose, this fairy made this pie, and this boy ate and ate and ate, and his cheeks swelled and swelled and swelled. There were many tributary circumstances, but the forcible interest culminated in the total consumption of this pie, and the bursting of this boy. Truly he was a fine sight, Barbox Brothers, with serious attentive face, and ear bent down, much jostled on the pavements of the busy town, but afraid of losing a single incident of the epic, lest he should be examined in it by-and-by, and found deficient.

Thus they arrived at the hotel. And there he had to say at the bar, and said awkwardly enough: "I have found a little girl!"

The whole establishment turned out to look at the little girl. Nobody knew her; nobody could make out her name, as she set it forth — except one chambermaid, who said it was Constantinople — which it wasn't.

"I will dine with my young friend in a private room," said Barbox Brothers to the hotel authorities, "and perhaps you will be so good as to let the police know that the pretty baby is here. I suppose she is sure to be inquired for soon, if she has not been already. Come along, Polly."

Perfectly at ease and peace, Polly came along, but, finding the stairs rather stiff work, was carried up by Barbox Brothers. The dinner was a most transcendent success, and the Barbox sheepishness, under Polly's directions how to mince her meat for her, and how to diffuse gravy over the plate with a liberal and equal hand, was another fine sight.

"And now," said Polly, "while we are at dinner, you be good, and tell me that story I taught you."

With the tremors of a Civil Service examination upon him, and very uncertain indeed, not only as to the epoch at which the pie appeared in history, but also as to the measurements of that indispensable fact, Barbox Brothers made a shaky beginning, but under encouragement did very fairly. There was a want of breadth observable in his rendering of the cheeks, as well as the appetite, of the boy; and there was a certain tameness in his fairy, referable to an under-current of desire to account for her. Still, as the first lumbering performance of a good-humored monster, it passed muster.

"I told you to be good," said Polly, "and you are good, ain't you?"

"I hope so," replied Barbox Brothers.

Such was his deference that Polly, elevated on a platform of sofa cushions in a chair at his right hand, encouraged him with a pat or two on the face from the greasy bowl of her spoon, and even with a gracious kiss. In getting on her feet upon her chair, however, to give him this last reward, she toppled forward among the dishes, and caused him to exclaim, as he effected her rescue: "Gracious Angels! Whew! I thought we were in the fire, Polly!"

"What a coward you are, ain't you?" said Polly when replaced.

"Yes, I am rather nervous," he replied. "Whew! Don't, Polly! Don't flourish your spoon, or you'll go over sideways. Don't tilt up your legs when you laugh, Polly, or you'll go over backwards. Whew! Polly, Polly, Polly," said Barbox Brothers, nearly succumbing to despair, "we are environed with dangers!"

Indeed, he could descry no security from the pitfalls that were yawning for Polly, but in proposing to her, after dinner, to sit upon a low stool. "I will, if you will," said Polly. So, as peace of mind should go before all, he begged the waiter to wheel aside the table, bring a pack of cards, a couple of footstools, and a screen, and close in Polly and himself before the fire, as it were in a snug room within the room. Then, finest sight of all, was Barbox Brothers on his footstool, with a pint decanter on the rug, contemplating Polly as she built successfully, and growing blue in the face with holding his breath, lest he should blow the house down.

"How you stare, don't you?" said Polly in a houseless pause.

Detected in the ignoble fact, he felt obliged to admit, apologetically: "I am afraid I was looking rather hard at you, Polly."

"Why do you stare?" asked Polly.

"I cannot," he murmured to himself, "recall why. — I don't know, Polly."

"You must be a simpleton to do things and not know why, mustn't you?" said Polly.

In spite of which reproof, he looked at the child again intently, as she bent her head over her card structure, her rich curls shading her face. "It is impossible," he thought, "that I can ever have seen this pretty baby before. Can I have dreamed of her? In some sorrowful dream?"

He could make nothing of it. So he went into the building trade as a journeyman under Polly, and they built three stories high, four stories high; even five.

"I say! Who do you think is coming?" asked Polly, rubbing her eyes after tea.

He guessed: "The waiter?"

"No," said Polly, "the dustman. I am getting sleepy."

A new embarrassment for Barbox Brothers!

"I don't think I am going to be fetched to-night," said Polly. "What do you think?"

He thought not, either. After another quarter of an hour, the dustman not merely impending, but actually arriving, recourse was had to the Constantinopolitan chambermaid: who cheerily undertook that the child should sleep in a comfortable and wholesome room, which she herself would share.

"And I know you will be careful, won't you," said Barbox Brothers, as a new fear dawned upon him, "that she don't fall out of bed?"

Polly found this so highly entertaining that she was under the necessity of clutching him round the neck with both arms as he sat on his footstool picking up the cards, and rocking him to and fro, with her dimpled chin on his shoulder.

"Oh, what a coward you are, ain't you?" said Polly. "Do *you* fall out of bed?"

"N — not generally, Polly."

"No more do I."

With that, Polly gave him a reassuring hug or two to keep him going, and then giving that confiding mite of a hand of hers to be swallowed up in the hand of the Constantinopolitan chambermaid, trotted off, chattering, without a vestige of anxiety.

He looked after her, had the screen removed and the table and chairs replaced, and still looked after her. He paced the room for half an hour. "A most engaging little creature, but it's not that. A most winning little voice, but it's not that. That has much to do with it, but there is something more. How can it be that I seem to know this child? What was it she imperfectly recalled to me when I felt her touch in the street, and, looking down at her, saw her looking up at me?"

"Mr. Jackson!"

With a start he turned towards the sound of the subdued voice, and saw his answer standing at the door.

"Oh, Mr. Jackson, do not be severe with me! Speak a word of encouragement to me, I beseech you."

"You are Polly's mother."

"Yes."

Yes. Polly herself might come to this, one day. As you see what the rose was in its faded leaves; as you see what the summer growth of the woods was in their wintry branches; so Polly might be traced, one day, in a careworn woman like this, with her hair turned grey. Before him were the ashes of a dead fire that had once burned bright. This was the woman he had loved. This was the woman he had lost. Such had been the constancy of his imagination to her, so had Time spared her under its withholding, that now, seeing how roughly the inexorable hand had struck her, his soul was filled with pity and amazement.

He led her to a chair, and stood leaning on a corner of the chimneypiece, with his head resting on his hand, and his face half averted.

"Did you see me in the street, and show me to your child?" he asked.

"Yes."

"Is the little creature, then, a party to deceit?"

"I hope there is no deceit. I said to her, 'We have lost our way, and I must try to find mine by myself. Go to that gentleman, and tell him you are lost. You shall be fetched by-and-by.' Perhaps you have not thought how very young she is?"

"She is very self-reliant."

"Perhaps because she is so young."

He asked, after a short pause, "Why did you do this?"

"Oh, Mr. Jackson, do you ask me? In the hope that you might see something in my innocent child to soften your heart towards me. Not only towards me, but towards my husband."

He suddenly turned about, and walked to the opposite end of the room. He came back again with a slower step, and resumed his former attitude, saying:

"I thought you had emigrated to America?"

"We did. But life went ill with us there, and we came back."

"Do you live in this town?"

"Yes. I am a daily teacher of music here. My husband is a bookkeeper."

"Are you — forgive my asking — poor?"

"We earn enough for our wants. That is not our distress. My husband is very, very ill of a lingering disorder. He will never recover — "

"You check yourself. If it is for want of the encouraging word you spoke of, take it from me. I cannot forget the old time, Beatrice."

"God bless you!" she replied with a burst of tears, and gave him her trembling hand.

"Compose yourself. I cannot be composed if you are not, for to see you weep distresses me beyond expression. Speak freely to me. Trust me."

She shaded her face with her veil, and after a little while spoke calmly. Her voice had the ring of Polly's.

"It is not that my husband's mind is at all impaired by his bodily suffering, for I assure you that is not the case. But in his weakness, and in his knowledge that he is incurably ill, he cannot overcome the ascendancy of one idea. It preys upon him, embitters every moment of his painful life, and will shorten it."

She stopping, he said again: "Speak freely to me. Trust me."

"We have had five children before this darling, and they all lie in their little graves. He believes that they have withered away under a curse, and that it will blight this child like the rest."

"Under what curse?"

"Both I and he have it on our conscience that we tried you very heavily, and I do not know but that, if I were as ill as he, I might suffer in my mind as he does. This is the constant burden: 'I believe, Beatrice, I was the only friend that Mr. Jackson ever cared to make, though I was so much his junior. The more influence he acquired in the business, the higher he advanced me, and I was alone in his private confidence. I came between him and you, and I took you from him. We were both secret, and the blow fell when he was wholly unprepared. The anguish it caused a man so compressed must have been terrible; the wrath it awakened inappeasable. So, a curse came to be invoked on our poor pretty little flowers, and they fall.' "

"And you, Beatrice," he asked, when she had ceased to speak, and there had been a silence afterwards, "how say you?"

"Until within these few weeks I was afraid of you, and I believed that you would never, never forgive."

"Until within these few weeks," he repeated. "Have you changed your opinion of me within these few weeks?"

"Yes."

"For what reason?"

"I was getting some pieces of music in a shop in this town, when, to my terror, you came in. As I veiled my face and stood in the dark end of the shop, I heard you explain that you wanted a musical instrument for a bedridden girl. Your voice and manner were so softened, you showed such interest in its selection, you took it away yourself with so much tenderness of care and pleasure, that I knew you were a man with a most gentle heart. Oh, Mr. Jackson, Mr. Jackson, if you could have felt the refreshing rain of tears that followed for me!"

Was Phœbe playing at that moment on her distant couch? He seemed to hear her.

"I inquired in the shop where you lived, but could get no information. As I had heard you say that you were going back by the next train (but you did not say where), I resolved to visit the station at about that time of day, as often as I could, between my lessons, on the chance of seeing you again. I have been there very often, but saw you no more until to-day. You were meditating as you walked the street, but the calm expression of your face emboldened me to send my child to you. And when I saw you bend your head to speak tenderly to her, I prayed to GOD to forgive me for having ever brought a sorrow on it. I now pray to you to forgive me, and to forgive my husband. I was very young, he was young too, and, in the ignorant hardihood of such a time of life, we don't know what we do to those who have undergone more discipline. You generous man! You good man! So to raise me up and make nothing of my crime against you!" — for he would not see her on her knees, and soothed her as a kind father might have soothed an erring daughter — "thank you, bless you, thank you!"

When he next spoke, it was after having drawn aside the window curtain and looked out awhile. Then he only said:

"Is Polly asleep?"

"Yes. As I came in, I met her going away upstairs, and put her to bed myself."

"Leave her with me for to-morrow, Beatrice, and write me your address on this leaf of my pocket-book. In the evening I will bring her home to you — and to her father."

*   *   *

"Hallo!" cried Polly, putting her saucy sunny face in at the door next morning when breakfast was ready: "I thought I was fetched last night?"

"So you were, Polly, but I asked leave to keep you here for the day, and to take you home in the evening."

"Upon my word!" said Polly. "You are very cool, ain't you?"

However, Polly seemed to think it a good idea, and added:

"I suppose I must give you a kiss, though you *are* cool."

The kiss given and taken, they sat down to breakfast in a highly conversational tone.

"Of course, you are going to amuse me?" said Polly.

"Oh, of course!" said Barbox Brothers.

In the pleasurable height of her anticipations, Polly found it indispensable to put down her piece of toast, cross one of her little fat knees over the other, and bring her little fat right hand down into her left hand with a business-like slap. After this gathering of herself together, Polly, by that time a mere heap of dimples, asked in a wheedling manner:

"What are we going to do, you dear old thing?"

"Why, I was thinking," said Barbox Brothers, " — but are you fond of horses, Polly?"

"Ponies, I am," said Polly, "especially when their tails are long. But horses — n — no — too big, you know."

"Well," pursued Barbox Brothers, in a spirit of grave mysterious confidence adapted to the importance of the consultation, "I did see yesterday, Polly, on the walls, pictures of two long-tailed ponies, speckled all over — "

"No, no, NO!" cried Polly, in an ecstatic desire to linger on the charming details. "Not speckled all over!"

"Speckled all over. Which ponies jump through hoops — "

"No, no, NO!" cried Polly as before. "They never jump through hoops!"

"Yes, they do. Oh, I assure you they do! And eat pie in pinafores — "

"Ponies eating pie in pinafores!" said Polly. "What a story-teller you are, ain't you?"

"Upon my honor. — And fire off guns."

(Polly hardly seemed to see the force of the ponies resorting to fire-arms.)

"And I was thinking," pursued the exemplary Barbox, "that if you and I were to go to the Circus where these ponies are, it would do our constitutions good."

"Does that mean amuse us?" inquired Polly. "What long words you do use, don't you?"

Apologetic for having wandered out of his depth, he replied:

"That means amuse us. That is exactly what it means. There are many other wonders besides the ponies, and we shall see them all. Ladies and gentlemen in spangled dresses, and elephants and lions and tigers."

Polly became observant of the teapot, with a curled-up nose indicating some uneasiness of mind.

"They never get out, of course," she remarked as a mere truism.

"The elephants and lions and tigers? Oh, dear no!"

"Oh, dear no!" said Polly. "And of course nobody's afraid of the ponies shooting anybody."

"Not the least in the world."

"No, no, not the least in the world," said Polly.

"I was also thinking," proceeded Barbox, "that if we were to look in at the toy-shop, to choose a doll — "

"Not dressed!" cried Polly with a clap of her hands. "No, no, NO, not dressed!"

"Full-dressed. Together with a house, and all things necessary for house-keeping — "

Polly gave a little scream, and seemed in danger of falling into a swoon of bliss.

"What a darling you are!" she languidly exclaimed, leaning back in her chair. "Come and be hugged, or I must come and hug you."

This resplendent programme was carried into execution with the utmost rigor of the law. It being essential to make the purchase of the doll its first feature — or that lady would have lost the ponies — the toy-shop expedition took precedence. Polly in the magic warehouse, with a doll as large as herself under each arm, and a neat assortment of some twenty more on view upon the counter, did indeed present a spectacle of indecision not quite compatible with unalloyed happiness, but the light cloud passed. The lovely specimen oftenest chosen, oftenest rejected, and finally abided by, was of Circassian descent, possessing as much boldness of beauty as was reconcilable with extreme feebleness of mouth, and combining a sky-blue silk pelisse with rose-colored satin trousers, and a black velvet hat: which this fair stranger to our northern shores would seem to have founded on the portraits of the late Duchess of Kent.

The name this distinguished foreigner brought with her from beneath the glowing skies of a sunny clime was (on Polly's authority) Miss Melluka, and the costly nature of her outfit as a housekeeper, from the Barbox coffers, may be inferred from the two facts that her silver tea-spoons were as large as her kitchen poker, and that the proportions of her watch exceeded those of her frying-pan. Miss Melluka was graciously pleased to express her entire approbation of the Circus, and so was Polly; for the ponies *were* speckled, and brought down nobody when they fired, and the savagery of the wild beasts appeared to be mere smoke — which article, in fact, they did produce in large quantities from their insides. The Barbox absorption in the general subject throughout the realization of these delights was again a sight to see, nor was it less worthy to behold at dinner, when he drank to Miss Melluka, tied stiff in a chair opposite to Polly (the fair Circassian possessing an unbendable spine), and even induced the waiter to assist in carrying out with due decorum the prevailing glorious idea. To wind up, there came the agreeable fever of getting Miss Melluka and all her wardrobe and rich possessions into a fly with Polly, to be taken home. But, by that time, Polly had become unable to look upon such accumulated joys with waking eyes, and had withdrawn her consciousness into the wonderful Paradise of a child's sleep. "Sleep, Polly, sleep," said Barbox Brothers, as her head dropped on his shoulder; "you shall not fall out of this bed easily, at any rate!"

What rustling piece of paper he took from his pocket, and carefully folded into the bosom of Polly's frock, shall not be mentioned. He said nothing about it, and nothing shall be said about it. They drove to a modest suburb of the great ingenious town, and stopped at the fore-court of a small house.

"Do not wake the child," said Barbox Brothers softly to the driver; "I will carry her in as she is."

Greeting the light at the opened door which was held by Polly's mother, Polly's bearer passed on with mother and child into a ground-floor room. There, stretched on a sofa, lay a sick man, sorely wasted, who covered his eyes with his emaciated hands.

"Tresham," said Barbox in a kindly voice, "I have brought you back your Polly, fast asleep. Give me your hand, and tell me you are better."

The sick man reached forth his right hand, and bowed his head over the hand into which it was taken, and kissed it. "Thank you, thank you! I may say that I am well and happy."

"That's brave," said Barbox. "Tresham, I have a fancy — Can you make room for me beside you here?"

He sat down on the sofa as he said the words, cherishing the plump peachy cheek that lay uppermost on his shoulder.

"I have a fancy, Tresham (I am getting quite an old fellow now, you know, and old fellows may take fancies into their heads sometimes), to give up Polly, having found her, to no one but you. Will you take her from me?"

As the father held out his arms for the child, each of the two men looked steadily at the other.

"She is very dear to you, Tresham?"

"Unutterably dear."

"God bless her! It is not much, Polly," he continued, turning his eyes upon her peaceful face as he apostrophized her, "it is not much, Polly, for a blind and sinful man to invoke a blessing on something so far better than himself as a little child is; but it would be much — much upon his cruel head, and much upon his guilty soul — if he could be so wicked as to invoke a curse. He had better have a millstone round his neck, and be cast into the deepest sea. Live and thrive, my pretty baby!" Here he kissed her. "Live and prosper, and become in time the mother of other little children, like the Angels who behold The Father's face!"

He kissed her again, gave her up gently to both her parents, and went out.

But he went not to Wales. No, he never went to Wales. He went straightway for another stroll about the town, and he looked in upon the people at their work, and at their play, here, there, everywhere, and where not. For he was Barbox Brothers and Co. now, and had taken thousands of partners into the solitary firm.

He had at length got back to his hotel room, and was standing before his fire refreshing himself with a glass of hot drink which he had stood upon the chimneypiece, when he heard the town clocks striking, and, referring to his watch, found the evening to have so slipped away, that they were striking twelve. As he put up his watch again, his eyes met those of his reflection in the chimney-glass.

"Why, it's your birthday already," he said, smiling. "You are looking very well. I wish you many happy returns of the day."

He had never before bestowed that wish upon himself. "By Jupiter!" he discovered, "it alters the whole case of running away from one's birthday! It's a thing to explain to Phœbe. Besides, here is quite a long story to tell her, that has sprung out of the road with no story. I'll go back, instead of going on. I'll go back by my friend Lamps's Up X presently."

He went back to Mugby Junction, and, in point of fact, he established himself at Mugby Junction. It was the convenient place to live in, for brightening Phœbe's life. It was the convenient place to live in, for having her taught music by Beatrice. It was the convenient place to live in, for occasionally borrowing Polly. It was the convenient place to live in, for being joined at will to all sorts of agreeable places and persons. So, he became settled there, and, his house standing in an elevated situation, it is noteworthy of him in conclusion, as Polly herself might (not irreverently) have put it:

"There was an Old Barbox who lived on a hill,
And if he ain't gone, he lives there still."

HERE FOLLOWS THE SUBSTANCE OF WHAT WAS SEEN, HEARD, OR OTHERWISE PICKED UP, BY THE GENTLEMAN FOR NOWHERE, IN HIS CAREFUL STUDY OF THE JUNCTION.

CHAPTER III

MAIN LINE: THE BOY AT MUGBY

I am the boy at Mugby. That's about what *I* am.

You don't know what I mean? What a pity! But I think you do. I think you must. Look here. I am the boy at what is called The Refreshment Room at Mugby Junction, and what's proudest boast is, that it never yet refreshed a mortal being.

Up in a corner of the Down Refreshment Room at Mugby Junction, in the height of twenty-seven cross draughts (I've often counted 'em while they brush the First-Class hair twenty-seven ways), behind the bottles, among the glasses, bounded on the nor'west by the beer, stood pretty far to the right of a metallic object that's at times the

THE BOY AT MUGBY JUNCTION

tea-urn and at times the soup-tureen, according to the nature of the last twang imparted to its contents which are the same groundwork, fended off from the traveller by a barrier of stale sponge-cakes erected atop of the counter, and lastly exposed sideways to the glare of Our Missis's eye — you ask a Boy so sitiwated, next time you stop in a hurry at Mugby, for anything to drink; you take particular notice that he'll try to seem not to hear you, that he'll appear in a absent manner to survey the Line through a transparent medium composed of your head and body, and that he won't serve you as long as you can possibly bear it. That's me.

What a lark it is! We are the Model Establishment, we are, at Mugby. Other Refreshment Rooms send their imperfect young ladies up to be finished off by Our Missis. For some of the young ladies, when they're new to the business, come into it mild! Ah! Our Missis, she soon takes that out of 'em. Why, I originally come into the business meek myself. But Our Missis, she soon took that out of *me*.

What a delightful lark it is! I look upon us Refreshmenters as ockipying the only proudly independent footing on the Line. There's Papers, for instance — my honorable friend, if he will allow me to call him so — him as belongs to Smith's bookstall. Why, he no more dares to be up to our Refreshmenting games than he dares to jump atop of a locomotive with her steam at full pressure, and cut away upon her alone, driving himself, at limited-mail speed. Papers, he'd get his head punched at every compartment, first, second, and third, the whole length of a train, if he was to ventur to imitate my demeanor. It's the same with the porters, the same with the guards, the same with the ticket clerks, the same the whole way up to the secretary, traffic-manager, or very chairman. There ain't a one among 'em on the nobly independent footing we are. Did you ever catch one of *them*, when you wanted anything of him, making a system of surveying the Line through a transparent medium composed of your head and body? I should hope not.

You should see our Bandolining Room at Mugby Junction. It's led to by the door behind the counter, which you'll notice usually stands ajar, and it's the room where Our Missis and our young ladies Bandolines their hair. You should see 'em at it, betwixt trains, Bandolining away, as if they was anointing themselves for the combat. When you're telegraphed, you should see their noses all a-going up with scorn, as if it was a part of the working of the same Cooke and Wheatstone electrical machinery. You should hear Our Missis give the word, "Here comes the Beast to be Fed!" and then you should see 'em indignantly skipping across the Line, from the Up to the Down, or Wicer Warsaw, and begin to pitch the stale pastry into the plates, and chuck the sawdust sangwiches under the glass covers, and get out the — ha, ha, ha! — the sherry — O my eye, my eye! — for your Refreshment.

It's only in the Isle of the Brave and Land of the Free (by which, of course, I mean to say Britannia) that Refreshmenting is so effective, so 'olesome, so constitutional a check upon the public. There was a Foreigner, which having politely, with his hat off, beseeched our young ladies and Our Missis for "a leetel gloss hoff prarndee," and having had the Line surveyed through him by all and no other acknowledgment, was a-proceeding at last to help himself, as seems to be the custom in his own country, when Our Missis, with her hair almost a-coming un-Bandolined with rage, and her eyes omitting sparks, flew at him, cotched the decanter out of his hand, and said, "Put it down! I won't allow that!" The foreigner turned pale, stepped back with his arms stretched out in front of him, his hands clasped, and his shoulders riz, and exclaimed, "Ah! Is it possible, this! That these disdaineous females and this ferocious old woman are placed here by the administration, not only to empoison the voyagers, but to affront them! Great Heaven! How arrives it? The English people. Or is he then a slave? Or idiot?" Another time, a merry, wideawake American gent had tried the sawdust and spit it out, and had tried the Sherry and spit that out, and had tried in vain to sustain exhausted natur upon Butter-Scotch, and had been rather extra Bandolined and Line-surveyed through, when, as the bell was ringing and he paid Our Missis, he says, very loud and good-tempered: "I tell Yew what 'tis, ma'arm. I la'af. Theer! I la'af. I Dew. I oughter ha' seen most things, for I hail from the Onlimited side of the Atlantic Ocean, and I haive travelled right slick over the Limited, head on through Jeerusalemm and the East, and likeways France and Italy, Europe Old World, and am now upon the track to the Chief Europian Village; but such an Institution as Yew, and Yewer young ladies, and Yewer fixin's solid and liquid, afore the glorious Tarnal I never did see yet! And if I hain't found the eighth wonder of monarchical Creation, in finding Yew, and Yewer young ladies, and Yewer fixin's solid and liquid, all as aforesaid, established in a country where the people air not absolute Loo-naticks, I am Extra Double Darned with a Nip and Frizzle to the innermostest grit! Wheerfur — Theer! — I la'af! I Dew, ma'arm. I la'af!" And so he went, stamping and shaking his sides, along the platform all the way to his own compartment.

I think it was her standing up agin the Foreigner as giv' Our Missis the idea of going over to France, and droring a comparison betwixt Refreshmenting as followed among the frog-eaters, and Refreshmenting as triumphant in the Isle of the Brave and Land of the Free (by which, of course, I mean to say agin, Britannia). Our young ladies, Miss Whiff, Miss Piff, and Mrs. Sniff, was unanimous opposed to her going; for, as they says to Our Missis one and all, it is well beknown to the hends of the herth as no other nation except Britain has a idea of anythink, but above all of business. Why then should you tire yourself to prove what is already proved? Our Missis, however (being a teazer at all pints) stood out grim obstinate, and got a return pass by South-eastern Tidal, to go right through, if such should be her dispositions, to Marseilles.

Sniff is husband to Mrs. Sniff, and is a regular insignificant cove. He looks arter the sawdust department in a back room, and is sometimes, when we are very hard put to it, let behind the counter with a corkscrew; but never when it can be helped, his demeanor towards the public being disgusting servile. How Mrs. Sniff ever come so far to lower herself as to marry him, I don't know; but I suppose *he* does, and I should think he wished he didn't, for he leads a awful life. Mrs. Sniff couldn't be much harder with him if he was public. Similarly, Miss Whiff and Miss Piff, taking the tone of Mrs. Sniff, they shoulder Sniff about when he *is* let in with a corkscrew, and they whisk things out of his hands when in his servility he is a-going to let the public have 'em, and they snap him up when in the crawling baseness of his spirit he is a-going to answer a public question, and they drore more tears into his eyes than ever the mustard does which he all day long lays on to the sawdust. (But it ain't strong.) Once, when Sniff had the repulsiveness to reach across to get the milk-pot to hand over for a baby, I see Our Missis in her rage catch him by both his shoulders, and spin him out into the Bandolining Room.

But Mrs. Sniff — how different! She's the one! She's the one as you'll notice to be always looking another way from you, when you look at her. She's the one with the small waist buckled in tight in front, and with the lace cuffs at her wrists, which she puts on the edge of the counter before her, and stands a-smoothing while the public foams. This smoothing the cuffs and looking another way while the public foams is the last accomplishment taught to the young ladies as come to Mugby to be finished by Our Missis; and it's always taught by Mrs. Sniff.

When Our Missis went away upon her journey, Mrs. Sniff was left in charge. She did hold the public in check most beautiful! In all my time, I never see half so many cups of tea given without milk to people as wanted it with, nor half so many cups of tea with milk given to people as wanted it without. When foaming ensued, Mrs. Sniff would say: "Then you'd better settle it among yourselves, and change with one another." It was a most highly delicious lark. I enjoyed the Refreshmenting business more than ever, and was so glad I had took to it when young.

Our Missis returned. It got circulated among the young ladies, and it as it might be penetrated to me through the crevices of the Bando-lining Room, that she had Orrors to reveal, if revelations so contemptible could be dignified with the name. Agitation become awakened. Excitement was up in the stirrups. Expectation stood a-tip-toe. At length it was put forth that on our slacked evening in the week, and at our slackest time of that evening betwixt trains, Our Missis would give her views of foreign Refreshmenting, in the Bandolining Room.

It was arranged tasteful for the purpose. The Bandolining table and glass was hid in a corner, a armchair was elevated on a packing-case for Our Missis's ockypation, a table and a tumbler of water (no sherry in it, thankee) was placed beside it. Two of the pupils, the season being autumn, and hollyhocks and dahlias being in, ornamented the wall with three devices in those flowers. On one might be read, "MAY ALBION NEVER LEARN"; on another, "KEEP THE PUBLIC DOWN"; on another, "OUR REFRESHMENTING CHARTER." The whole had a beautiful appearance, with which the beauty of the sentiments corresponded.

On Our Missis's brow was wrote Severity, as she ascended the fatal platform. (Not that that was anythink new.) Miss Whiff and Miss Piff sat at her feet. Three chairs from the Waiting Room might have been perceived by a average eye, in front of her, on which the pupils was accommodated. Behind them a very close observer might have discerned a Boy. Myself.

"Where," said Our Missis, glancing gloomily around, "is Sniff?"

"I thought it better," answered Mrs. Sniff, "that he should not be let to come in. He is such an Ass."

"No doubt," assented Our Missis. "But for that reason is it not desirable to improve his mind?"

"Oh, nothing will ever improve *him*," said Mrs. Sniff.

"However," pursued Our Missis, "call him in, Ezekiel."

I called him in. The appearance of the low-minded cove was hailed with disapprobation from all sides, on account of his having brought his corkscrew with him. He pleaded "the force of habit."

"The force!" said Mrs. Sniff. "Don't let us have you talking about force, for Gracious' sake. There! Do stand still where you are, with your back against the wall."

He is a smiling piece of vacancy, and he smiled in the mean way in which he will even smile at the public if he gets a chance (language can say no meaner of him), and he stood upright near the door with the back of his head agin the wall, as if he was a-waiting for somebody to come and measure his heighth for the Army.

"I should not enter, ladies," says Our Missis, "on the revolting disclosures I am about to make, if it was not in the hope that they will cause you to be yet more implacable in the exercise of the power you wield in a constitutional country, and yet more devoted to the constitutional motto which I see before me" — it was behind her, but the words sounded better so — " 'May Albion never learn!' "

Here the pupils as had made the motto admired it, and cried, "Hear! Hear! Hear!" Sniff, showing an inclination to join in chorus, got himself frowned down by every brow.

"The baseness of the French," pursued Our Missis, "as displayed in the fawning nature of their Refreshmenting, equals, if not surpasses, anythink as was ever heard of the baseness of the celebrated Bonaparte."

Miss Whiff, Miss Piff, and me, we drored a heavy breath, equal to saying, "We thought as much!" Miss Whiff and Miss Piff seeming to object to my droring mine along with theirs, I drored another to aggravate 'em.

"Shall I be believed," says Our Missis, with flashing eyes, "when

I tell you that no sooner had I set my foot upon that treacherous shore — "

Here Sniff, either bursting out mad, or thinking aloud, says, in a low voice:

"Feet. Plural, you know."

The cowering that come upon him when he was spurned by all eyes, added to his being beneath contempt, was sufficient punishment for a cove so grovelling. In the midst of a silence rendered more impressive by the turned-up female noses with which it was pervaded, Our Missis went on:

"Shall I be believed when I tell you, that no sooner had I landed," this word with a killing look at Sniff, "on that treacherous shore, than I was ushered into a Refreshment Room where there were — I do not exaggerate — actually eatable things to eat?"

A groan burst from the ladies. I not only did myself the honor of jining, but also of lengthening it out.

"Where there were," Our Missis added, "not only eatable things to eat, but also drinkable things to drink?"

A murmur, swelling almost into a scream, ariz. Miss Piff, trembling with indignation, called out, "Name!"

"I *will* name," said Our Missis. "There was roast fowls, hot and cold; there was smoking roast veal surrounded with browned potatoes; there was hot soup with (again I ask shall I be credited?) nothing bitter in it, and no flour to choke off the consumer; there was a variety of cold dishes set off with jelly; there was salad; there was — mark me! *fresh* pastry, and that of a light construction; there was a luscious show of fruit; there was bottles and decanters of sound small wine, of every size, and adapted to every pocket; the same odious statement will apply to brandy; and these were set out upon the counter so that all could help themselves."

Our Missis's lips so quivered, that Mrs. Sniff, though scarcely less convulsed than she were, got up and held the tumbler to them.

"This," proceeds Our Missis, "was my first unconstitutional experience. Well would it have been if it had been my last and worst. But no. As I proceeded farther into that enslaved and ignorant land, its aspect became more hideous. I need not explain to this assembly the ingredients and formation of the British Refreshment sangwich?"

Universal laughter — except from Sniff, who, as sangwich-cutter, shook his head in a state of the utmost dejection as he stood with it agin the wall.

"Well!" said Our Missis, with dilated nostrils. "Take a fresh crisp, long, crusty penny loaf made of the whitest and best flour. Cut it longwise through the middle. Insert a fair and nicely fitting slice of ham. Tie a smart piece of ribbon round the middle of the whole to bind it together. Add at one end a neat wrapper of clean white paper by which to hold it. And the universal French Refreshment sangwich busts on your disgusted vision."

A cry of "Shame!" from all — except Sniff, which rubbed his stomach with a soothing hand.

"I need not," said Our Missis, "explain to this assembly the usual formation and fitting of the British Refreshment Room?"

No, no, and laughter. Sniff agin shaking his head in low spirits agin the wall.

"Well," said Our Missis, "what would you say to a general decoration of everythink, to hangings (sometimes elegant), to easy velvet furniture, to abundance of little tables, to abundance of little seats, to brisk bright waiters, to great convenience, to a pervading cleanliness and tastefulness positively addressing the public, and making the Beast thinking itself worth the pains?"

Contemptuous fury on the part of all the ladies. Mrs. Sniff looking as if she wanted somebody to hold her, and everybody else looking as if they'd rayther not.

"Three times," said Our Missis, working herself into a truly terrimenjious state — "three times did I see these shameful things, only between the coast and Paris, and not counting either: at Hazebroucke, at Arras, at Amiens. But worse remains. Tell me, what would you call a person who should propose in England that there should be kept, say at our own model Mugby Junction, pretty baskets, each holding an assorted cold lunch and dessert for one, each at a certain fixed price, and each within a passenger's power to take away, to empty in the carriage at perfect leisure, and to return at another station fifty or a hundred miles farther on?"

There was disagreement what such a person should be called. Whether revolutionist, atheist, Bright (I said him), or Un-English. Miss Piff screeched her shrill opinion last, in the words: "A malignant maniac!"

"I adopt," says Our Missis, "the brand set upon such a person by the righteous indignation of my friend Miss Piff. A malignant maniac. Know, then, that that malignant maniac has sprung from the congenial soil of France, and that his malignant madness was in unchecked action on this same part of my journey."

I noticed that Sniff was a-rubbing his hands, and that Mrs. Sniff had got her eye upon him. But I did not take more particular notice, owing to the excited state in which the young ladies was, and to feeling myself called upon to keep it up with a howl.

"On my experience south of Paris," said Our Missis, in a deep tone, "I will not expatiate. Too loathsome were the task! But fancy this. Fancy a guard coming round, with the train at full speed, to inquire how many for dinner. Fancy his telegraphing forward the number of dinners. Fancy every one expected, and the table elegantly laid for the complete party. Fancy a charming dinner, in a charming room, and the head-cook, concerned for the honor of every dish, superintending in his clean white jacket and cap. Fancy the Beast travelling six hundred miles on end, very fast, and with great punctuality, yet being taught to expect all this to be done for it!"

A spirited chorus of "The Beast!"

I noticed that Sniff was agin a-rubbing his stomach with a soothing hand, and that he had drored up one leg. But agin I didn't take particular notice, looking on myself as called upon to stimulate public feeling. It being a lark besides.

"Putting everything together," said Our Missis, "French Refreshmenting comes to this, and oh, it comes to a nice total! First: eatable things to eat, and drinkable things to drink."

A groan from the young ladies, kep' up by me.

"Second: convenience, and even elegance."

Another groan from the young ladies, kep' up by me.

"Third: moderate charges."

This time a groan from me, kep' up by the young ladies.

"Fourth: and here," says Our Missis, "I claim your angriest sympathy — attention, common civility, nay, even politeness!"

Me and the young ladies regularly raging mad all together.

"And I cannot in conclusion," says Our Missis, with her spitefullest sneer, "give you a completer pictur of that despicable nation (after what I have related), than assuring you that they wouldn't bear our constitutional ways and noble independence at Mugby Junction, for a single month, and that they would turn us to the right-about and put another system in our places, as soon as look at us; perhaps sooner, for I do not believe they have the good taste to care to look at us twice."

The swelling tumult was arrested in its rise. Sniff, bore away by his servile disposition, had drored up his leg with a higher and a higher relish, and was now discovered to be waving his corkscrew over his head. It was at this moment that Mrs. Sniff, who had kep' her eye upon him like the fabled obelisk, descended on her victim. Our Missis followed them both out, and cries was heard in the sawdust department.

You come into the Down Refreshment Room, at the Junction, making believe you don't know me, and I'll pint you out with my right thumb over my shoulder which is Our Missis, and which is Miss Whiff, and which is Miss Piff, and which is Mrs. Sniff. But you won't get a chance to see Sniff, because he disappeared that night. Whether he perished, tore to pieces, I cannot say; but his corkscrew alone remains, to bear witness to the servility of his disposition.

CHAPTER IV

NO. I BRANCH LINE: THE SIGNAL-MAN

"Halloa! Below there!"

When he heard a voice thus calling to him, he was standing at the door of his box, with a flag in his hand, furled round its short pole. One would have thought, considering the nature of the ground, that he could not have doubted from what quarter the voice came; but instead of looking up to where I stood on the top of the steep cutting nearly over his head, he turned himself about, and looked down the Line. There was something remarkable in his manner of doing so, though I could not have said for my life what. But I know it was re-markable enough to attract my notice, even though his figure was foreshortened and shadowed, down in the deep trench, and mine was high above him, so steeped in the glow of an angry sunset, that I had shaded my eyes with my hand before I saw him at all.

"Halloa! Below!"

From looking down the Line, he turned himself about again, and, raising his eyes, saw my figure high above him.

"Is there any path by which I can come down and speak to you?"

He looked up at me without replying, and I looked down at him without pressing him too soon with a repetition of my idle question. Just then there came a vague vibration in the earth and air, quickly changing into a violent pulsation, and an oncoming rush that caused me to start back, as though it had force to draw me down. When such vapor as rose to my height from this rapid train had passed me, and was skimming away over the landscape, I looked down again, and saw him refurling the flag he had shown while the train went by.

I repeated my inquiry. After a pause, during which he seemed to regard me with fixed attention, he motioned with his rolled-up flag towards a point on my level, some two or three hundred yards distant. I called down to him, "All right!" and made for that point. There, by dint of looking closely about me, I found a rough zigzag descending path notched out, which I followed.

The cutting was extremely deep, and unusually precipitate. It was made through a clammy stone, that became oozier and wetter as I went down. For these reasons, I found the way long enough to give me time to recall a singular air of reluctance or compulsion with which he had pointed out the path.

When I came down low enough upon the zigzag descent to see him again, I saw that he was standing between the rails on the way by which the train had lately passed, in an attitude as if he were waiting for me to appear. He had his left hand at his chin, and that left elbow rested on his right hand, crossed over his breast. His attitude was one of such expectation and watchfulness that I stopped a moment, wondering at it.

I resumed my downward way, and stepping out upon the level of the railroad, and drawing nearer to him, saw that he was a dark sallow man, with a dark beard and rather heavy eyebrows. His post was in as solitary and dismal a place as ever I saw. On either side, a dripping-wet wall of jagged stone, excluding all view but a strip of sky; the perspective one way only a crooked prolongation of this great dungeon; the shorter perspective in the other direction terminating in a gloomy red light, and the gloomier entrance to a black tunnel, in whose massive architecture there was a barbarous, depressing, and forbidding air. So little sunlight ever found its way to this spot, that it had an earthy, deadly smell; and so much cold wind rushed through it, that it struck chill to me, as if I had left the natural world.

Before he stirred, I was near enough to him to have touched him. Not even then removing his eyes from mine, he stepped back one step, and lifted his hand.

This was a lonesome post to occupy (I said), and it had riveted my attention when I looked down from up yonder. A visitor was a rarity, I should suppose; not an unwelcome rarity, I hoped? In me, he merely saw a man who had been shut up within narrow limits all his life, and who, being at last set free, had a newly awakened interest in these great works. To such purpose I spoke to him; but I am far from sure of the terms I used; for, besides that I am not happy in opening any conversation, there was something in the man that daunted me.

He directed a most curious look towards the red light near the tunnel's mouth, and looked all about it, as if something were missing from it, and then looked at me.

That light was part of his charge? Was it not?

He answered in a low voice — "Don't you know it is?"

The monstrous thought came into my mind, as I perused the fixed eyes and the saturnine face, that this was a spirit, not a man. I have speculated since, whether there may have been infection in his mind.

In my turn, I stepped back. But in making the action, I detected in his eyes some latent fear of me. This put the monstrous thought to flight. "You look at me," I said, forcing a smile, "as if you had a dread of me."

"I was doubtful," he returned, "whether I had seen you before."

"Where?"

He pointed to the red light he had looked at.

"There?" I said.

Intently watchful of me, he replied (but without sound), "Yes."

"My good fellow, what should I do there? However, be that as it may, I never was there, you may swear."

"I think I may," he rejoined. "Yes; I am sure I may."

His manner cleared, like my own. He replied to my remarks with readiness, and in well-chosen words. Had he much to do there? Yes;

that was to say, he had enough responsibility to bear; but exactness and watchfulness were what was required of him, and of actual work — manual labor — he had next to none. To change that signal, to trim those lights, and to turn this iron handle now and then, was all he had to do under that head. Regarding those many long and lonely hours of which I seemed to make so much, he could only say that the routine of his life had shaped itself into that form, and he had grown used to it. He had taught himself a language down here — if only to know it by sight, and to have formed his own crude ideas of its pronunciation, could be called learning it. He had also worked at fractions and decimals, and tried a little algebra; but he was, and had been as a boy, a poor hand at figures. Was it necessary for him when on duty always to remain in that channel of damp air, and could he never rise into the sunshine from between those high stone walls? Why, that depended upon times and circumstances. Under some conditions there would be less upon the Line than under others, and the same held good as to certain hours of the day and night. In bright weather, he did choose occasions for getting a little above these lower shadows; but, being at all times liable to be called by his electric bell, and at such times listening for it with redoubled anxiety, the relief was less than I would suppose.

He took me into his box, where there was a fire, a desk for an official book in which he had to make certain entries, a telegraphic instrument with its dial, face, and needles, and the little bell of which he had spoken. On my trusting that he would excuse the remark that he had been well educated, and (I hoped I might say without offense), perhaps educated above that station, he observed that instances of slight incongruity in such wise would rarely be found wanting among large bodies of men; that he had heard it was so in workhouses, in the police force, even in that last desperate resource, the army; and that he knew it was so, more or less, in any great railway staff. He had been, when young (if I could believe it, sitting in that hut — he scarcely could), a student of natural philosophy, and had attended lectures; but he had run wild, misused his opportunities, gone down, and never risen again. He had no complaint to offer about that. He had made his bed, and he lay upon it. It was far too late to make another.

All that I have here condensed he said in a quiet manner, with his grave dark regards divided between me and the fire. He threw in the word, "Sir," from time to time, and especially when he referred to his youth — as though to request me to understand that he claimed to be nothing but what I found him. He was several times interrupted by the little bell, and had to read off messages, and send replies. Once he had to stand without the door, and display a flag as a train passed, and make some verbal communication to the driver. In the discharge of his duties, I observed him to be remarkably exact and vigilant, breaking off his discourse at a syllable and remaining silent until what he had to do was done.

In a word, I should have set this man down as one of the safest of men to be employed in that capacity, but for the circumstance that while he was speaking to me he twice broke off with a fallen color, turned his face towards the little bell when it did NOT ring, opened the door of the hut (which was kept shut to exclude the unhealthy damp), and looked out towards the red light near the mouth of the tunnel. On both of those occasions, he came back to the fire with the inexplicable air upon him which I had remarked, without being able to define, when we were so far asunder.

Said I, when I rose to leave him, "You almost make me think that I have met with a contented man."

(I am afraid I must acknowledge that I said it to lead him on.)

"I believe I used to be so," he rejoined, in the low voice in which he had first spoken; "but I am troubled, Sir, I am troubled."

He would have recalled the words if he could. He had said them, however, and I took them up quickly.

"With what? What is your trouble?"

"It is very difficult to impart, Sir. It is very, very difficult to speak of. If ever you make me another visit, I will try to tell you."

"But I expressly intend to make you another visit. Say, when shall it be?"

"I go off early in the morning, and I shall be on again at ten to-morrow night, Sir."

"I will come at eleven."

He thanked me, and went out at the door with me. "I'll show my white light, Sir," he said, in his peculiar low voice, "till you have found the way up. When you have found it, don't call out! And when you are at the top, don't call out!"

His manner seemed to make the place strike colder to me, but I said no more than, "Very well."

"And when you come down to-morrow night, don't call out! Let me ask you a parting question. What made you cry, 'Halloa! Below there!' to-night?"

"Heaven knows," said I. "I cried something to that effect — "

"Not to that effect, Sir. Those were the very words. I know them well."

"Admit those were the very words. I said them, no doubt, because I saw you below."

"For no other reason?"

"What other reason could I possibly have?"

"You had no feeling that they were conveyed to you in any supernatural way?"

"No."

He wished me good night, and held up his light. I walked by the side of the down Line of rails (with a very disagreeable sensation of a train coming behind me) until I found the path. It was easier to mount than to descend, and I got back to my inn without any adventure.

Punctual to my appointment, I placed my foot on the first notch of the zigzag next night, as the distant clocks were striking eleven. He was waiting for me at the bottom, with his white light on. "I have not called out," I said, when we came close together; "may I speak now?" "By all means, Sir." "Good night, then, and here's my hand." "Good night, Sir, and here's mine." With that we walked side by side to his box, entered it, closed the door, and sat down by the fire.

"I have made up my mind, Sir," he began, bending forward as soon as we were seated, and speaking in a tone but a little above a whisper, "that you shall not have to ask me twice what troubles me. I took you for some one else yesterday evening. That troubles me."

"That mistake?"

"No. That some one else."

"Who is it?"

"I don't know."

"Like me?"

"I don't know. I never saw the face. The left arm is across the face, and the right arm is waved — violently waved. This way."

I followed his action with my eyes, and it was the action of an arm gesticulating, with the utmost passion and vehemence, "For God's sake, clear the way!"

"One moonlight night," said the man, "I was sitting here, when I heard a voice cry, 'Halloa! Below there!' I started up, looked from that door, and saw this Some one else standing by the red light near the tunnel, waving as I just now showed you. The voice seemed hoarse with shouting, and it cried, 'Look out! Look out!' And then again, 'Halloa! Below there! Look out!' I caught up my lamp, turned it on red, and ran towards the figure, calling, 'What's wrong? What has happened? Where?' It stood just outside the blackness of the tunnel. I advanced so close upon it that I wondered at its keeping the sleeve across its eyes. I ran right up at it, and had my hand stretched out to pull the sleeve away, when it was gone."

"Into the tunnel?" said I.

"No. I ran on into the tunnel, five hundred yards. I stopped, and held my lamp above my head, and saw the figures of the measured distance, and saw the wet stains stealing down the walls and trickling through the arch. I ran out again faster than I had run in (for I had a mortal abhorrence of the place upon me), and I looked all round the red light with my own red light, and I went up the iron ladder to the gallery atop of it, and I came down again, and ran back here. I telegraphed both ways. 'An alarm has been given. Is anything wrong?' The answer came back, both ways, 'All well.'"

Resisting the slow touch of a frozen finger tracing out my spine, I showed him how that this figure must be a deception of his sense of sight; and how that figures, originating in disease of the delicate nerves that minister to the functions of the eye, were known to have often troubled patients, some of whom had become conscious of the nature of their affliction, and had even proved it by experiments upon themselves. "As to an imaginary cry," said I, "do but listen for a moment to the wind in this unnatural valley while we speak so low, and to the wild harp it makes of the telegraph wires."

That was all very well, he returned, after we had sat listening for a while, and he ought to know something of the wind and the wires — he who so often passed long winter nights there, alone and watching. But he would beg to remark that he had not finished.

I asked his pardon, and he slowly added these words, touching my arm —

"Within six hours after the Appearance, the memorable accident on this Line happened, and within ten hours the dead and wounded were brought along through the tunnel over the spot where the figure had stood."

A disagreeable shudder crept over me, but I did my best against it. It was not to be denied, I rejoined, that this was a remarkable coincidence, calculated deeply to impress his mind. But it was unquestionable that remarkable coincidences did continually occur, and they must be taken into account in dealing with such a subject. Though to be sure I must admit, I added (for I thought I saw that he was going to bring the objection to bear upon me), men of common sense did not allow much for coincidences in making the ordinary calculations of life.

He again begged to remark that he had not finished.

I again begged his pardon for being betrayed into interruptions.

"This," he said, again laying his hand upon my arm, and glancing over his shoulder with hollow eyes, "was just a year ago. Six or seven months passed, and I had recovered from the surprise and shock, when one morning, as the day was breaking, I, standing at the door, looked towards the red light, and saw the spectre again." He stopped, with a fixed look at me.

"Did it cry out?"

"No. It was silent."

"Did it wave its arm?"

"No. It leaned against the shaft of the light, with both hands before the face. Like this."

Once more I followed his action with my eyes. It was an action of mourning. I have seen such an attitude in stone figures on tombs.

"Did you go up to it?"

"I came in and sat down, partly to collect my thoughts, partly because it had turned me faint. When I went to the door again, daylight was above me, and the ghost was gone."

"But nothing followed? Nothing came of this?"

He touched me on the arm with his forefinger twice or thrice, giving a ghastly nod each time:

"That very day, as a train came out of the tunnel, I noticed, at a carriage window on my side, what looked like a confusion of hands and heads, and something waved. I saw it just in time to signal the driver, Stop! He shut off, and put his brake on, but the train drifted past here a hundred and fifty yards or more. I ran after it, and, as I went along, heard terrible screams and cries. A beautiful young lady had died instantaneously in one of the compartments, and was brought in here, and laid down on this floor between us."

Involuntarily I pushed my chair back, as I looked from the boards at which he pointed to himself.

"True, Sir. True. Precisely as it happened, so I tell it you."

I could think of nothing to say, to any purpose, and my mouth was very dry. The wind and the wires took up the story with a long lamenting wail.

He resumed. "Now, Sir, mark this, and judge how my mind is troubled. The spectre came back a week ago. Ever since, it has been there, now and again, by fits and starts."

"At the light?"

"At the Danger-light."

"What does it seem to do?"

He repeated, if possible with increased passion and vehemence, that former gesticulation of, "For God's sake, clear the way!"

Then he went on. "I have no peace or rest for it. It calls to me, for many minutes together, in an agonized manner, 'Below there! Look out! Look out!' It stands waving to me. It rings my little bell — "

I caught at that. "Did it ring your bell yesterday evening when I was here, and you went to the door?"

"Twice."

"Why, see," said I, "how your imagination misleads you. My eyes were on the bell, and my ears were open to the bell, and if I am a living man, it did NOT ring at those times. No, nor at any other time, except when it was rung in the natural course of physical things by the station communicating with you."

He shook his head. "I have never made a mistake as to that yet, Sir. I have never confused the spectre's ring with the man's. The ghost's ring is a strange vibration in the bell that it derives from nothing else, and I have not asserted that the bell stirs to the eye. I don't wonder that you failed to hear it. But I heard it."

"And did the spectre seem to be there, when you looked out?"

"It WAS there."

"Both times?"

He repeated firmly: "Both times."

"Will you come to the door with me, and look for it now?"

He bit his under lip as though he were somewhat unwilling, but arose. I opened the door, and stood on the step, while he stood in the doorway. There was the Danger-light. There was the dismal mouth of the tunnel. There were the high, wet stone walls of the cutting. There were the stars above them.

"Do you see it?" I asked him, taking particular note of his face. His eyes were prominent and strained, but not very much more so, perhaps, than my own had been when I had directed them earnestly towards the same spot.

"No," he answered. "It is not there."

"Agreed," said I.

We went in again, shut the door, and resumed our seats. I was thinking how best to improve this advantage, if it might be called one, when he took up the conversation in such a matter-of-course way, so assuming that there could be no serious question of fact between us, that I felt myself placed in the weakest of positions.

"By this time you will fully understand, Sir," he said, "that what troubles me so dreadfully is the question, What does the spectre mean?"

I was not sure, I told him, that I did fully understand.

"What is its warning against?" he said, ruminating, with his eyes on the fire, and only by times turning them on me. "What is the danger? Where is the danger? There is danger overhanging somewhere on the Line. Some dreadful calamity will happen. It is not to be doubted this third time, after what has gone before. But surely this is a cruel haunting of *me*. What can *I* do?"

He pulled out his handkerchief, and wiped the drops from his heated forehead.

"If I telegraph Danger, on either side of me, or on both, I can give no reason for it," he went on, wiping the palms of his hands. "I should get into trouble, and do no good. They would think I was mad. This is the way it would work — Message: 'Danger! Take care!' Answer: 'What Danger? Where?' Message: 'Don't know. But, for God's sake, take care!' They would displace me. What else could they do?"

His pain of mind was most pitiable to see. It was the mental torture of a conscientious man, oppressed beyond endurance by an unintelligible responsibility involving life.

"When it first stood under the Danger-light," he went on, putting his dark hair back from his head, and drawing his hands outward across and across his temples in an extremity of feverish distress, "why not tell me where that accident was to happen — if it must happen? Why not tell me how it could be averted — if it could have been averted? When on its second coming it hid its face, why not tell me, instead, 'She is going to die. Let them keep her at home'? If it came, on those two occasions, only to show me that its warnings were true, and so to prepare me for the third, why not warn me plainly now? And I, Lord help me! A mere poor signal-man on this solitary station! Why not go to somebody with credit to be believed, and power to act?"

When I saw him in this state, I saw that for the poor man's sake, as well as for the public safety, what I had to do for the time was to compose his mind. Therefore, setting aside all question of reality or unreality between us, I represented to him that whoever thoroughly discharged his duty must do well, and that at least it was his comfort that he understood his duty, though he did not understand these confounding Appearances. In this effort I succeeded far better than in the attempt to reason him out of his conviction. He became calm; the occupations incidental to his post as the night advanced began to make larger demands on his attention: and I left him at two in the morning. I had offered to stay through the night, but he would not hear of it.

That I more than once looked back at the red light as I ascended the pathway, that I did not like the red light, and that I should have slept but poorly if my bed had been under it, I see no reason to conceal. Nor did I like the two sequences of the accident and the dead girl. I see no reason to conceal that either.

But what ran most in my thoughts was the consideration how ought I to act, having become the recipient of this disclosure? I had proved the man to be intelligent, vigilant, painstaking, and exact; but how long might he remain so, in his state of mind? Though in a subordinate position, still he held a most important trust, and would I (for instance) like to stake my own life on the chances of his continuing to execute it with precision?

Unable to overcome a feeling that there would be something treacherous in my communicating what he had told me to his superiors in the Company, without first being plain with himself and proposing a middle course to him, I ultimately resolved to offer to accompany him (otherwise keeping his secret for the present) to the wisest medical practitioner we could hear of in those parts, and to take his opinion. A change in his time of duty would come round next night, he had apprised me, and he would be off an hour or two after sunrise, and on again soon after sunset. I had appointed to return accordingly.

Next evening was a lovely evening, and I walked out early to enjoy it. The sun was not yet quite down when I traversed the field-path near the top of the deep cutting. I would extend my walk for an hour, I said to myself, half an hour on and half an hour back, and it would then be time to go to my signal-man's box.

Before pursuing my stroll, I stepped to the brink, and mechanically looked down, from the point from which I had first seen him. I cannot describe the thrill that seized upon me, when, close at the mouth of the tunnel, I saw the appearance of a man, with his left sleeve across his eyes, passionately waving his right arm.

The nameless horror that oppressed me passed in a moment, for in a moment I saw that this appearance of a man was a man indeed, and that there was a little group of other men, standing at a short distance, to whom he seemed to be rehearsing the gesture he made. The Danger-light was not yet lighted. Against its shaft, a little low hut, entirely new to me, had been made of some wooden supports and tarpaulin. It looked no bigger than a bed.

With an irresistible sense that something was wrong — with a flashing self-reproachful fear that fatal mischief had come of my leaving the man there, and causing no one to be sent to overlook or correct what he did — I descended the notched path with all the speed I could make.

"What is the matter?" I asked the men.

"Signal-man killed this morning, Sir."

"Not the man belonging to that box?"

"Yes, Sir."

"Not the man I know?"

"You will recognize him, Sir, if you knew him," said the man who spoke for the others, solemnly uncovering his own head, and raising an end of the tarpaulin, "for his face is quite composed."

"O, how did this happen, how did this happen?" I asked, turning from one to another as the hut closed in again.

"He was cut down by an engine, Sir. No man in England knew his work better. But somehow he was not clear of the outer rail. It was just at broad day. He had struck the light, and had the lamp in his hand. As the engine came out of the tunnel, his back was towards her, and she cut him down. That man drove her, and was showing how it happened. Show the gentleman, Tom."

The man, who wore a rough dark dress, stepped back to his former place at the mouth of the tunnel.

"Coming round the curve in the tunnel, Sir," he said, "I saw him at the end, like as if I saw him down a perspective-glass. There was no time to check speed, and I knew him to be very careful. As he didn't seem to take heed of the whistle, I shut it off when we were running down upon him, and called to him as loud as I could call."

"What did you say?"

"I said, 'Below there! Look out! Look out! For God's sake, clear the way!'"

I started.

"Ah! it was a dreadful time, Sir. I never left off calling to him. I put this arm before my eyes not to see, and I waved this arm to the last; but it was no use."

Without prolonging the narrative to dwell on any one of its curious circumstances more than on any other, I may, in closing it, point out the coincidence that the warning of the Engine-Driver included, not only the words which the unfortunate Signal-man had repeated to me as haunting him, but also the words which I myself — not he — had attached, and that only in my own mind, to the gesticulation he had imitated.

"BIRTHS.

MRS. MEEK,

OF A SON"

"Births. Mrs. Meek, of a Son"

MY NAME is Meek. I am, in fact, Mr. Meek. That son is mine and Mrs. Meek's. When I saw the announcement in the *Times,* I dropped the paper. I had put it in, myself, and paid for it, but it looked so noble that it overpowered me.

As soon as I could compose my feelings, I took the paper up to Mrs. Meek's bedside. "Maria Jane," said I (I allude to Mrs. Meek), "you are now a public character." We read the review of our child, several times, with feelings of the strongest emotion; and I sent the boy who cleans the boots and shoes to the office for fifteen copies. No reduction was made on taking that quantity.

It is scarcely necessary for me to say, that our child had been expected. In fact, it had been expected, with comparative confidence, for some months. Mrs. Meek's mother, who resides with us — of the name of Bigby — had made every preparation for its admission to our circle.

I hope and believe I am a quiet man. I will go farther. I *know* I am a quiet man. My constitution is tremulous, my voice was never loud, and, in point of stature, I have been from infancy, small. I have the greatest respect for Maria Jane's Mama. She is a most remarkable woman. I honor Maria Jane's Mama. In my opinion she would storm a town, single-handed, with a hearth-broom, and carry it. I have never known her to yield any point whatever to mortal man. She is calculated to terrify the stoutest heart.

Still — but I will not anticipate.

The first intimation I had of any preparations being in progress, on the part of Maria Jane's Mama, was one afternoon, several months ago. I came home earlier than usual from the office, and, proceeding into the dining-room, found an obstruction behind the door, which prevented it from opening freely. It was an obstruction of a soft nature. On looking in, I found it to be a female.

The female in question stood in the corner behind the door, consuming Sherry Wine. From the nutty smell of that beverage pervading the apartment, I have no doubt she was consuming a second glassful. She wore a black bonnet of large dimensions, and was copious in figure. The expression of her countenance was severe and discontented. The words to which she gave utterance on seeing me were these, "Oh git along with you, Sir, if *you* please; me and Mrs. Bigby don't want no male parties here!"

That female was Mrs. Prodgit.

I immediately withdrew, of course. I was rather hurt, but I made no remark. Whether it was that I showed a lowness of spirits after dinner, in consequence of feeling that I seemed to intrude, I cannot say. But Maria Jane's Mama said to me on her retiring for the night: in a low distinct voice, and with a look of reproach that completely subdued me: "George Meek, Mrs. Prodgit is your wife's nurse!"

I bear no ill-will towards Mrs. Prodgit. Is it likely that I, writing this with tears in my eyes, should be capable of deliberate animosity towards a female, so essential to the welfare of Maria Jane? I am willing to admit that Fate may have been to blame, and not Mrs. Prodgit; but it is undeniably true, that the latter female brought desolation and devastation into my lowly dwelling.

We were happy after her first appearance; we were sometimes exceedingly so. But whenever the parlor door was opened, and "Mrs. Prodgit!" announced (and she was very often announced), misery ensued. I could not bear Mrs. Prodgit's look. I felt that I was far from wanted, and had no business to exist in Mrs. Prodgit's presence. Between Maria Jane's Mama and Mrs. Prodgit, there was a dreadful, secret, understanding — a dark mystery and conspiracy, pointing me out as a being to be shunned. I appeared to have done something that was evil. Whenever Mrs. Prodgit called after dinner, I retired to my dressing-room — where the temperature is very low, indeed, in the wintry time of the year — and sat looking at my frosty breath as it rose before me, and at my rack of boots; a serviceable article of furniture, but never, in my opinion, an exhilarating object. The length of the councils that were held with Mrs. Prodgit, under these circumstances, I will not attempt to describe. I will merely remark, that Mrs. Prodgit always consumed Sherry Wine while the deliberations were in progress; that they always ended in Maria Jane's being in wretched spirits on the sofa; and that Maria Jane's Mama always received me, when I was recalled, with a look of desolate triumph that too plainly said, "*Now*, George Meek! You see my child, Maria Jane, a ruin, and I hope you are satisfied!"

I pass, generally, over the period that intervened between the day when Mrs. Prodgit entered her protest against male parties, and the ever-memorable midnight when I brought her to my unobtrusive home in a cab, with an extremely large box on the roof, and a bundle, a bandbox, and a basket, between the driver's legs. I have no objection to Mrs. Prodgit (aided and abetted by Mrs. Bigby, who I never can forget is the parent of Maria Jane) taking entire possession of my unassuming establishment. In the recesses of my own breast, the thought may linger that a man in possession cannot be so dreadful as a woman, and that woman Mrs. Prodgit; but I ought to bear a good deal, and I hope I can, and do. Huffing and snubbing prey upon my feelings; but I can bear them without complaint. They may tell in the long run; I may be hustled about, from post to pillar, beyond my strength; nevertheless, I wish to avoid giving rise to words in the family.

The voice of Nature, however, cries aloud in behalf of Augustus George, my infant son. It is for him that I wish to utter a few plaintive household words. I am not at all angry; I am mild — but miserable.

I wish to know why, when my child, Augustus George, was expected in our circle, a provision of pins was made, as if the little stranger were a criminal who was to be put to the torture immediately on his arrival, instead of a holy babe? I wish to know why haste was made to stick those pins all over his innocent form, in every direction? I wish to be informed why light and air are excluded from Augustus George, like poisons? Why, I ask, is my unoffending infant so hedged into a basket-bedstead, with dimity and calico, with miniature sheets and blankets, that I can only hear him snuffle (and no wonder!) deep down under the pink hood of a little bathing-machine, and can never peruse even so much of his lineaments as his nose.

Was I expected to be the father of a French Roll, that the brushes of All Nations were laid in, to rasp Augustus George? Am I to be told that his sensitive skin was ever intended by Nature to have rashes brought out upon it, by the premature and incessant use of those formidable little instruments?

Is my son a Nutmeg, that he is to be grated on the stiff edges of sharp frills? Am I the parent of a Muslin boy, that his yielding surface is to be crimped and small plaited? Or is my child composed of Paper or of Linen, that impressions of the finer getting-up art, practiced by the laundress, are to be printed off, all over his soft arms and legs, as I constantly observe them? The starch enters his soul; who can wonder that he cries?

Was Augustus George intended to have limbs, or to be born a Torso? I presume that limbs were the intention, as they are the usual practice. Then, why are my poor child's limbs fettered and tied up? Am I to be told that there is any analogy between Augustus George Meek and Jack Sheppard?

Analyze Castor Oil at any Institution of Chemistry that may be agreed upon, and inform me what resemblance, in taste, it bears to that natural provision which it is at once the pride and duty of Maria Jane to administer to Augustus George! Yet, I charge Mrs. Prodgit (aided and abetted by Mrs. Bigby) with systematically forcing Castor Oil on my innocent son, from the first hour of his birth. When that medicine, in its efficient action, causes internal disturbance to Augustus George, I charge Mrs. Prodgit (aided and abetted by Mrs. Bigby) with insanely and inconsistently administering opium to allay the storm she has raised! What is the meaning of this?

If the days of Egyptian Mummies are past, how dare Mrs. Prodgit require, for the use of my son, an amount of flannel and linen that would carpet my humble roof? Do I wonder that she requires it? No! This morning, within an hour, I beheld this agonizing sight. I beheld my son — Augustus George — in Mrs. Prodgit's hands, and on Mrs. Prodgit's knee, being dressed. He was at the moment, comparatively speaking, in a state of nature; having nothing on but an extremely short shirt, remarkably disproportionate to the length of his usual outer garments. Trailing from Mrs. Prodgit's lap, on the floor, was a long narrow roller or bandage — I should say of several yards in extent. In this, I saw Mrs. Prodgit tightly roll the body of my unoffending infant, turning him over and over, now presenting his unconscious face upwards, now the back of his bald head, until the unnatural feat was accomplished, and the bandage secured by a pin, which I have every reason to believe entered the body of my only child. In this tourniquet, he passes the present phase of his existence. Can I know it, and smile!

I fear I have been betrayed into expressing myself warmly, but I feel deeply. Not for myself; for Augustus George. I dare not interfere. Will any one? Will any publication? Any doctor? Any parent? Anybody? I do not complain that Mrs. Prodgit (aided and abetted by Mrs. Bigby) entirely alienates Maria Jane's affections from me, and interposes an impassable barrier between us. I do not complain of being made of no account. I do not want to be of any account. But Augustus George is a production of Nature (I cannot think otherwise), and I claim that he should be treated with some remote reference to Nature. In my opinion, Mrs. Prodgit is, from first to last, a convention and a superstition. Are all the faculty afraid of Mrs. Prodgit? If not, why don't they take her in hand and improve her?

P.S. Maria Jane's Mama boasts of her own knowledge of the subject, and says she brought up seven children besides Maria Jane. But how do *I* know that she might not have brought them up much better? Maria Jane herself is far from strong, and is subject to headaches, and nervous indigestion. Besides which, I learn from the statistical tables that one child in five dies within the first year of its life; and one child in three, within the fifth. That don't look as if we could never improve in these particulars, I think!

P.P.S. Augustus George is in convulsions.

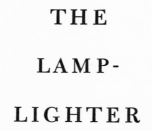

THE

LAMP-

LIGHTER

The

Lamplighter

"IF YOU talk of Murphy and Francis Moore, gentlemen," said the lamplighter who was in the chair, "I mean to say that neither of 'em ever had any more to do with the stars than Tom Grig had."

"And what had *he* to do with 'em?" asked the lamplighter who officiated as vice.

"Nothing at all," replied the other; "just exactly nothing at all."

"Do you mean to say you don't believe in Murphy, then?" demanded the lamplighter who had opened the discussion.

"I mean to say I believe in Tom Grig," replied the chairman. "Whether I believe in Murphy, or not, is a matter between me and my conscience; and whether Murphy believes in himself, or not, is a matter between him and his conscience. Gentlemen, I drink your healths."

The lamplighter who did the company this honor, was seated in the chimney-corner of a certain tavern, which has been, time out of mind, the Lamplighters' House of Call. He sat in the midst of a circle of lamplighters, and was the cacique, or chief of the tribe.

If any of our readers have had the good fortune to behold a lamplighter's funeral, they will not be surprised to learn that lamplighters are a strange and primitive people; that they rigidly adhere to old ceremonies and customs which have been handed down among them from father to son since the first public lamp was lighted out of doors; that they intermarry, and betroth their children in infancy; that they enter into no plots or conspiracies (for who ever heard of a traitorous

339

lamplighter?); that they commit no crimes against the laws of their country (there being no instance of a murderous or burglarious lamplighter); that they are, in short, notwithstanding their apparently volatile and restless character, a highly moral and reflective people: having among themselves as many traditional observances as the Jews, and being, as a body, if not as old as the hills, at least as old as the streets. It is an article of their creed that the first faint glimmering of true civilization shone in the first street-light maintained at the public expense. They trace their existence and high position in the public esteem, in a direct line to the heathen mythology; and hold that the history of Prometheus himself is but a pleasant fable, whereof the true hero is a lamplighter.

"Gentlemen," said the lamplighter in the chair, "I drink your healths."

"And, perhaps, Sir," said the vice, holding up his glass, and rising a little way off his seat and sitting down again, in token that he recognized and returned the compliment, "perhaps you will add to that condescension by telling us who Tom Grig was, and how he came to be connected in your mind with Francis Moore, Physician."

"Hear, hear, hear!" cried the lamplighters generally.

"Tom Grig, gentlemen," said the chairman, "was one of us; and it happened to him, as it don't often happen to a public character in our line, that he had his what-you-may-call-it cast."

"His head?" said the vice.

"No," replied the chairman, "not his head."

"His face, perhaps?" said the vice. "No, not his face." "His legs?" "No, not his legs." Nor yet his arms, nor his hands, nor his feet, nor his chest, all of which were severally suggested.

"His nativity, perhaps?"

"That's it," said the chairman, awakening from his thoughtful attitude at the suggestion. "His nativity. That's what Tom had cast, gentlemen."

"In plaister?" asked the vice.

"I don't rightly know how it's done," returned the chairman. "But I suppose it was."

And there he stopped as if that were all he had to say; whereupon there arose a murmur among the company, which at length resolved itself into a request, conveyed through the vice, that he would go on. This being exactly what the chairman wanted, he mused for a little time, performed that agreeable ceremony which is popularly termed wetting one's whistle, and went on thus:

"Tom Grig, gentlemen, was, as I have said, one of us; and I may go further, and say he was an ornament to us, and such a one as only the good old times of oil and cotton could have produced. Tom's family, gentlemen, were all lamplighters."

"Not the ladies, I hope?" asked the vice.

"They had talent enough for it, Sir," rejoined the chairman, "and would have been, but for the prejudices of society. Let women have their rights, Sir, and the females of Tom's family would have been every one of 'em in office. But that emancipation hasn't come yet, and hadn't then, and consequently they confined themselves to the bosoms of their families, cooked the dinners, mended the clothes, minded the children, comforted their husbands, and attended to the house-keeping generally. It's a hard thing upon the women, gentlemen, that they are limited to such a sphere of action as this; very hard.

"I happen to know all about Tom, gentlemen, from the circumstance of his uncle by his mother's side having been my particular friend. His (that's Tom's uncle's) fate was a melancholy one. Gas was the death of him. When it was first talked of, he laughed. He wasn't angry; he laughed at the credulity of human nature. 'They might as well talk,' he says, 'of laying on an everlasting succession of glowworms'; and then he laughed again, partly at his joke, and partly at poor humanity.

"In course of time, however, the thing got ground, the experiment was made, and they lighted up Pall Mall. Tom's uncle went to see it. I've heard that he fell off his ladder fourteen times that night, from weakness, and that he would certainly have gone on falling till he killed himself, if his last tumble hadn't been into a wheelbarrow which was going his way, and humanely took him home. 'I foresee in this,' says Tom's uncle faintly, and taking to his bed as he spoke — 'I foresee in this,' he says, 'the breaking up of our profession. There's no more going the rounds to trim by daylight, no more dribbling down of the oil on the hats and bonnets of ladies and gentlemen when one feels in spirits. Any low fellow can light a gas-lamp. And it's all up.' In this state of mind, he petitioned the government for — I want a word again, gentlemen — what do you call that which they give to people when it's found out, at last, that they've never been of any use, and have been paid too much for doing nothing?"

"Compensation?" suggested the vice.

"That's it," said the chairman. "Compensation. They didn't give it him, though, and then he got very fond of his country all at once, and went about saying that gas was a death-blow to his native land, and that it was a plot of the radicals to ruin the country and destroy the oil and cotton trade forever, and that the whales would go and kill themselves privately, out of sheer spite and vexation at not being caught. At last he got right-down cracked; called his tobacco-pipe a gas-pipe; thought his tears were lamp-oil; and went on with all manner of nonsense of that sort, till one night he hung himself on a lamp-iron in Saint Martin's Lane, and there was an end of *him*.

"Tom loved him, gentlemen, but he survived it. He shed a tear over his grave, got very drunk, spoke a funeral oration that night in the watch-house, and was fined five shillings for it, in the morning. Some men are none the worse for this sort of thing. Tom was one of 'em. He went that very afternoon on a new beat: as clear in his head, and as free from fever as Father Mathew himself.

"Tom's new beat, gentlemen, was — I can't exactly say where, for that he'd never tell; but I know it was in a quiet part of town, where there were some queer old houses. I have always had it in my head that it must have been somewhere near Canonbury Tower in Islington, but that's a matter of opinion. Wherever it was, he went upon it, with a bran-new ladder, a white hat, a brown holland jacket and trousers, a blue neckerchief, and a sprig of full-blown double wall-flower in his buttonhole. Tom was always genteel in his appearance, and I have heard from the best judges, that if he had left his ladder at home that afternoon, you might have took him for a lord.

"He was always merry, was Tom, and such a singer, that if there was any encouragement for native talent, he'd have been at the opera. He was on his ladder, lighting his first lamp, and singing to himself in a manner more easily to be conceived than described, when he hears the clock strike five, and suddenly sees an old gentleman with a telescope in his hand, throw up a window and look at him very hard.

"Tom didn't know what could be passing in this old gentleman's mind. He thought it likely enough that he might be saying within himself, 'Here's a new lamplighter — a good-looking young fellow — shall I stand something to drink?' Thinking this possible, he keeps quite still, pretending to be very particular about the wick, and looks at the old gentleman sideways, seeming to take no notice of him.

"Gentlemen, he was one of the strangest and most mysterious-looking files that ever Tom clapped his eyes on. He was dressed all slovenly and untidy, in a great gown of a kind of bed-furniture pattern, with a cap of the same on his head; and a long old flapped waistcoat; with no braces, no strings, very few buttons — in short, with hardly any of those artificial contrivances that hold society together. Tom knew by these signs, and by his not being shaved, and by his not being over-clean, and by a sort of wisdom not quite awake, in his face, that he was a scientific old gentleman. He often told me that if he could have conceived the possibility of the whole Royal Society being boiled down into one man, he should have said the old gentleman's body was that Body.

"The old gentleman claps the telescope to his eye, looks all round, sees nobody else in sight, stares at Tom again, and cries out very loud:

" 'Hal-loa!'

" 'Halloa, Sir,' says Tom from the ladder; 'and halloa again, if you come to that.'

" 'Here's an extraordinary fulfilment,' says the old gentleman, 'of a prediction of the planets.'

" 'Is there?' says Tom. 'I'm very glad to hear it.'

" 'Young man,' says the old gentleman, 'you don't know me.'

" 'Sir,' says Tom, 'I have not that honor; but I shall be happy to drink your health, notwithstanding.'

" 'I read,' cries the old gentleman, without taking any notice of this politeness on Tom's part — 'I read what's going to happen, in the stars.'

"Tom thanked him for the information, and begged to know if anything particular was going to happen in the stars, in the course of a week or so; but the old gentleman, correcting him, explained that he read in the stars what was going to happen on dry land, and that he was acquainted with all the celestial bodies.

" 'I hope they're all well, Sir,' says Tom — 'everybody.'

" 'Hush!' cries the old gentleman. 'I have consulted the book of Fate with rare and wonderful success. I am versed in the great sciences of astrology and astronomy. In my house here, I have every description of apparatus for observing the course and motion of the planets. Six months ago, I derived from this source, the knowledge that precisely as the clock struck five this afternoon a stranger would present himself — the destined husband of my young and lovely niece — in reality of illustrious and high descent, but whose birth would be enveloped in uncertainty and mystery. Don't tell me yours isn't,' says the old gentleman, who was in such a hurry to speak that he couldn't get the words out fast enough, 'for I know better.'

"Gentlemen, Tom was so astonished when he heard him say this, that he could hardly keep his footing on the ladder, and found it necessary to hold on by the lamp-post. There *was* a mystery about his birth. His mother had always admitted it. Tom had never known who was his father, and some people had gone so far as to say that even *she* was in doubt.

"While he was in this state of amazement, the old gentleman leaves the window, bursts out of the house-door, shakes the ladder, and Tom, like a ripe pumpkin, comes sliding down into his arms.

" 'Let me embrace you,' he says, folding his arms about him, and nearly lighting up his old bed-furniture gown at Tom's link. 'You're a man of noble aspect. Everything combines to prove the accuracy of my observations. You have had mysterious promptings within you,' he says; 'I know you have had whisperings of greatness, eh?' he says.

" 'I think I have,' says Tom — Tom was one of those who can persuade themselves to anything they like — 'I've often thought I wasn't the small beer I was taken for.'

" 'You were right,' cries the old gentleman, hugging him again. 'Come in. My niece awaits us.'

" 'Is the young lady tolerable good-looking, Sir?' says Tom, hanging fire rather, as he thought of her playing the piano, and knowing French, and being up to all manner of accomplishments.

" 'She's beautiful!' cries the old gentleman, who was in such a terrible bustle that he was all in a perspiration. 'She has a graceful carriage, an exquisite shape, a sweet voice, a countenance beaming with animation and expression; and the eye,' he says, rubbing his hands, 'of a startled fawn.'

"Tom supposed this might mean, what was called among his circle of acquaintance, 'a game eye'; and, with a view to this defect, inquired whether the young lady had any cash.

" 'She has five thousand pounds,' cries the old gentleman. 'But what of that? what of that? A word in your ear. I'm in search of the philosopher's stone. I have very nearly found it — not quite. It turns everything to gold; that's its property.'

"Tom naturally thought it must have a deal of property; and said that when the old gentleman did get it, he hoped he'd be careful to keep it in the family.

" 'Certainly,' he says, 'of course. Five thousand pounds! What's five thousand pounds to us? What's five million?' he says. 'What's five thousand million? Money will be nothing to us. We shall never be able to spend it fast enough.'

" 'We'll try what we can do, Sir,' says Tom.

" 'We will,' says the old gentleman. 'Your name?'

" 'Grig,' says Tom.

"The old gentleman embraced him again, very tight; and without speaking another word, dragged him into the house in such an excited manner, that it was as much as Tom could do to take his link and ladder with him, and put them down in the passage.

"Gentlemen, if Tom hadn't been always remarkable for his love of truth, I think you would still have believed him when he said that all this was like a dream. There is no better way for a man to find out whether he is really asleep or awake, than calling for something to eat. If he's in a dream, gentlemen, he'll find something wanting in the flavor, depend upon it.

"Tom explained his doubts to the old gentleman, and said that if there was any cold meat in the house, it would ease his mind very much to test himself at once. The old gentleman ordered up a venison pie, a small ham, and a bottle of very old Madeira. At the first mouthful of pie and the first glass of wine, Tom smacks his lips and cries out, 'I'm awake — wide awake'; and to prove that he was so, gentlemen, he made an end of 'em both.

"When Tom had finished his meal (which he never spoke of afterwards without tears in his eyes), the old gentleman hugs him again, and says, 'Noble stranger! let us visit my young and lovely niece.' Tom, who was a little elevated with the wine, replies, 'The noble stranger is agreeable!' At which words the old gentleman took him by the hand, and led him to the parlor; crying as he opened the door, 'Here is Mr. Grig, the favorite of the planets!'

"I will not attempt a description of female beauty, gentlemen, for every one of us has a model of his own that suits his own taste best.

In this parlor that I'm speaking of, there were two young ladies; and if every gentleman present, will imagine two models of his own in their places, and will be kind enough to polish 'em up to the very highest pitch of perfection, he will then have a faint conception of their uncommon radiance.

"Besides these two young ladies, there was their waiting-woman, that under any other circumstances Tom would have looked upon as a Venus; and besides her, there was a tall, thin, dismal-faced young gentleman, half man and half boy, dressed in a childish suit of clothes very much too short in the legs and arms; and looking, according to Tom's comparison, like one of the wax juveniles from a tailor's door, grown up and run to seed. Now, this youngster stamped his foot upon the ground and looked very fierce at Tom, and Tom looked fierce at him — for to tell the truth, gentlemen, Tom more than half suspected that when they entered the room he was kissing one of the young ladies; and for anything Tom knew, you observe, it might be *his* young lady — which was not pleasant.

" 'Sir,' says Tom, 'before we proceed any further, will you have the goodness to inform me who this young Salamander' — Tom called him that for aggravation, you perceive, gentlemen — 'who this young Salamander may be?'

" 'That, Mr. Grig,' says the old gentleman, 'is my little boy. He was christened Galileo Isaac Newton Flamstead. Don't mind him. He's a mere child.'

" 'And a very fine child too,' says Tom — still aggravating, you'll observe — 'of his age, and as good as fine, I have no doubt. How do you do, my man?' with which kind and patronizing expressions, Tom reached up to pat him on the head, and quoted two lines about little boys, from Doctor Watts's Hymns, which he had learnt at a Sunday School.

"It was very easy to see, gentlemen, by this youngster's frowning and by the waiting-maid's tossing her head and turning up her nose, and by the young ladies turning their backs and talking together at the other end of the room, that nobody but the old gentleman took very kindly to the noble stranger. Indeed, Tom plainly heard the waiting-woman say of her master, that so far from being able to read the stars as he pretended, she didn't believe he knew his letters in 'em, or at best that he had got further than words in one syllable; but Tom, not minding this (for he was in spirits after the Madeira),

TOM GRIG COURTS DESTINY

looks with an agreeable air towards the young ladies, and kissing his hand to both, says to the old gentleman, 'Which is which?'

" 'This,' says the old gentleman, leading out the handsomest, if one of 'em could possibly be said to be handsomer than the other — 'this is my niece, Miss Fanny Barker.'

" 'If you'll permit me, Miss,' says Tom, 'being a noble stranger and a favorite of the planets, I will conduct myself as such.' With these words, he kisses the young lady in a very affable way, turns to the old gentleman, slaps him on the back, and says, 'When's it to come off, my buck?'

"The young lady colored so deep, and her lip trembled so much, gentlemen, that Tom really thought she was going to cry. But she kept her feelings down, and turning to the old gentleman, says, 'Dear uncle, though you have the absolute disposal of my hand and fortune, and though you mean well in disposing of 'em thus, I ask you whether you don't think this is a mistake? Don't you think, dear uncle,' she says, 'that the stars must be in error? Is it not possible that the comet may have put 'em out?'

" 'The stars,' says the old gentleman, 'couldn't make a mistake if they tried. Emma,' he says to the other young lady.

" 'Yes, papa,' says she.

" 'The same day that makes your cousin Mrs. Grig will unite you to the gifted Mooney. No remonstrance — no tears. Now, Mr. Grig, let me conduct you to that hallowed ground, that philosophical retreat, where my friend and partner, the gifted Mooney of whom I have just now spoken, is even now pursuing those discoveries which shall enrich us with the precious metal, and make us masters of the world. Come, Mr. Grig,' he says.

" 'With all my heart, Sir,' replies Tom; 'and luck to the gifted Mooney, say I — not so much on his account as for our worthy selves!' With this sentiment, Tom kissed his hand to the ladies again, and followed him out; having the gratification to perceive, as he looked back, that they were all hanging on by the arms and legs of Galileo Isaac Newton Flamstead, to prevent him from following the noble stranger, and tearing him to pieces.

"Gentlemen, Tom's father-in-law that was to be, took him by the hand, and having lighted a little lamp, led him across a paved courtyard at the back of the house, into a very large, dark, gloomy room: filled with all manner of bottles, globes, books, telescopes, crocodiles, alligators, and other scientific instruments of every kind. In the center of this room was a stove or furnace, with what Tom called a pot, but which in my opinion was a crucible, in full boil. In one corner was a sort of ladder leading through the roof; and up this ladder the old gentleman pointed, as he said in a whisper:

" 'The observatory. Mr. Mooney is even now watching for the precise time at which we are to come into all the riches of the earth. It will be necessary for he and I, alone in that silent place, to cast your nativity before the hour arrives. Put the day and minute of your birth on this piece of paper, and leave the rest to me.'

" 'You don't mean to say,' says Tom, doing as he was told and giving him back the paper, 'that I'm to wait here long, do you? It's a precious dismal place.'

" 'Hush!' says the old gentleman. 'It's hallowed ground. Farewell!'

" 'Stop a minute,' says Tom. 'What a hurry you're in! What's in that large bottle yonder?'

" 'It's a child with three heads,' says the old gentleman; 'and everything else in proportion.'

" 'Why don't you throw him away?' says Tom. 'What do you keep such unpleasant things here for?'

" 'Throw him away?' cries the old gentleman. 'We use him constantly in astrology. He's a charm.'

" 'I shouldn't have thought it,' says Tom, 'from his appearance. *Must* you go, I say?'

"The old gentleman makes him no answer, but climbs up the ladder in a greater bustle than ever. Tom looked after his legs till there was nothing of him left, and then sat down to wait; feeling (so he used to say) as comfortable as if he was going to be made a freemason, and they were heating the pokers.

"Tom waited so long, gentlemen, that he began to think it must be getting on for midnight at least, and felt more dismal and lonely than ever he had done in all his life. He tried every means of whiling away the time, but it never had seemed to move so slow. First, he took a nearer view of the child with three heads, and thought what a comfort it must have been to his parents. Then he looked up a long telescope which was pointed out of the window, but saw nothing particular, in consequence of the stopper being on at the other end. Then he came to a skeleton in a glass case, labelled, 'Skeleton of a Gentleman — prepared by Mr. Mooney' — which made him hope that Mr. Mooney might not be in the habit of preparing gentlemen that way without their own consent. A hundred times, at least, he looked into the pot where they were boiling the philosopher's stone down to the proper consistency, and wondered whether it was nearly done. 'When it is,' thinks Tom, 'I'll send out for sixpenn'orth of sprats, and turn 'em into gold fish for a first experiment.' Besides which, he made up his mind, gentlemen, to have a country-house and a park; and to plant a bit of it with a double row of gas-lamps a mile long, and go out every night with a French-polished mahogany ladder, and two servants in livery behind him, to light 'em for his own pleasure.

"At length and at last, the old gentleman's legs appeared upon the steps leading through the roof, and he came slowly down: bringing along with him, the gifted Mooney. This Mooney, gentlemen, was even more scientific in appearance than his friend; and had, as Tom often declared upon his word and honor, the dirtiest face we can possibly know of, in this imperfect state of existence.

"Gentlemen, you are all aware that if a scientific man isn't absent in his mind, he's of no good at all. Mr. Mooney was so absent, that when the old gentleman said to him, 'Shake hands with Mr. Grig,' he put out his leg. 'Here's a mind, Mr. Grig!' cries the old gentleman in a rapture. 'Here's philosophy! Here's rumination! Don't disturb him,' he says, 'for this is amazing!'

"Tom had no wish to disturb him, having nothing particular to say; but he was so uncommonly amazing, that the old gentleman got impatient, and determined to give him an electric shock to bring him to — 'for you must know, Mr. Grig,' he says, 'that we always keep a strongly charged battery, ready for that purpose.' These means being resorted to, gentlemen, the gifted Mooney revived with a loud roar, and he no sooner came to himself than both he and the old gentleman looked at Tom with compassion, and shed tears abundantly.

" 'My dear friend,' says the old gentleman to the Gifted, 'prepare him.'

" 'I say,' cries Tom, falling back, 'none of that, you know. No preparing by Mr. Mooney if you please.'

" 'Alas!' replies the old gentleman, 'you don't understand us. My friend, inform him of his fate. — I can't.'

"The Gifted mustered up his voice, after many efforts, and informed Tom that his nativity had been carefully cast, and he would expire at exactly thirty-five minutes, twenty-seven seconds, and five-sixths of a second past nine o'clock, a.m., on that day two months.

"Gentlemen, I leave you to judge what were Tom's feelings at this announcement, on the eve of matrimony and endless riches. 'I think,' he says in a trembling voice, 'there must be a mistake in the working of that sum. Will you do me the favor to cast it up again?' — 'There is no mistake,' replies the old gentleman, 'it is confirmed by Francis Moore, Physician. Here is the prediction for to-morrow two months.' And he showed him the page, where sure enough were these words — 'The decease of a great person may be looked for, about this time.'

" 'Which,' says the old gentleman, 'is clearly you, Mr. Grig.'

" 'Too clearly,' cries Tom, sinking into a chair, and giving one hand to the old gentleman, and one to the Gifted. 'The orb of day has set on Thomas Grig forever!'

"At this affecting remark, the Gifted shed tears again, and the other two mingled their tears with his, in a kind — if I may use the expression — of Mooney and Co.'s entire. But the old gentleman recovering first, observed that this was only a reason for hastening the marriage, in order that Tom's distinguished race might be transmitted to posterity; and requesting the Gifted to console Mr. Grig during his temporary absence, he withdrew to settle the preliminaries with his niece immediately.

"And now, gentlemen, a very extraordinary and remarkable occurrence took place; for as Tom sat in a melancholy way in one chair, and the Gifted sat in a melancholy way in another, a couple of doors were thrown violently open, the two young ladies rushed in, and one knelt down in a loving attitude at Tom's feet, and the other at the Gifted's. So far, perhaps, as Tom was concerned — as he used to say — you will say there was nothing strange in this: but you will be of a different opinion when you understand that Tom's young lady was kneeling to the Gifted, and the Gifted's young lady was kneeling to Tom.

" 'Halloa! stop a minute!' cries Tom; 'here's a mistake. I need condoling with by sympathizing woman, under my afflicting circumstances; but we're out in the figure. Change partners, Mooney.'

" 'Monster!' cries Tom's young lady, clinging to the Gifted.

" 'Miss!' says Tom. 'Is *that* your manners?'

" 'I abjure thee!' cries Tom's young lady. 'I renounce thee. I never will be thine. Thou,' she says to the Gifted, 'art the object of my first and all-engrossing passion. Wrapt in thy sublime visions, thou hast not perceived my love; but, driven to despair, I now shake off the woman and avow it. Oh, cruel, cruel man!' With which reproach she laid her head upon the Gifted's breast, and put her arms about him in the tenderest manner possible, gentlemen.

" 'And I,' says the other young lady, in a sort of ecstasy, that made Tom start — 'I hereby abjure my chosen husband too. Hear me, Goblin!' — this was to the Gifted — 'Hear me! I hold thee in the deepest detestation. The maddening interview of this one night has filled my soul with love — but not for thee. It is for thee, for thee, young man,' she cries to Tom. 'As Monk Lewis finely observes, Thomas, Thomas, I am thine, Thomas, Thomas, thou art mine: thine forever, mine forever!' with which words, she became very tender likewise.

"Tom and the Gifted, gentlemen, as you may believe, looked at each other in a very awkward manner, and with thoughts not at all complimentary to the two young ladies. As to the Gifted, I have heard Tom say often, that he was certain he was in a fit, and had it inwardly.

" 'Speak to me! Oh, speak to me!' cries Tom's young lady to the Gifted.

" 'I don't want to speak to anybody,' he says, finding his voice at last, and trying to push her away. 'I think I had better go. I'm — I'm frightened,' he says, looking about as if he had lost something.

" 'Not one look of love!' she cries. 'Hear me while I declare — '

" 'I don't know how to look a look of love,' he says, all in a maze. 'Don't declare anything. I don't want to hear anybody.'

" 'That's right!' cries the old gentleman (who it seems had been listening). 'That's right! Don't hear her. Emma shall marry you to-morrow, my friend, whether she likes it or not, and *she* shall marry Mr. Grig.'

"Gentlemen, these words were no sooner out of his mouth than Galileo Isaac Newton Flamstead (who it seems had been listening too) darts in, and spinning round and round, like a young giant's top, cries, 'Let her. Let her. I'm fierce; I'm furious. I give her leave. I'll never marry anybody after this — never. It isn't safe. She is the falsest of the false,' he cries, tearing his hair and gnashing his teeth; 'and I'll live and die a bachelor!'

" 'The little boy,' observed the Gifted gravely, 'albeit of tender years, has spoken wisdom. I have been led to the contemplation of woman-kind, and will not adventure on the troubled waters of matrimony.'

" 'What!' says the old gentleman, 'not marry my daughter! Won't you, Mooney? Not if I make her? Won't you? Won't you?'

" 'No,' says Mooney, 'I won't. And if anybody asks me any more, I'll run away, and never come back again.'

" 'Mr. Grig,' says the old gentleman, 'the stars must be obeyed. You have not changed your mind because of a little girlish folly — eh, Mr. Grig?'

"Tom, gentlemen, had had his eyes about him, and was pretty sure that all this was a device and trick of the waiting-maid, to put him off his inclination. He had seen her hiding and skipping about the two doors, and had observed that a very little whispering from her pacified the Salamander directly. 'So,' thinks Tom, 'this is a plot — but it won't fit.'

" 'Eh, Mr. Grig?' says the old gentleman.

" 'Why, Sir,' says Tom, pointing to the crucible, 'if the soup's nearly ready — '

" 'Another hour beholds the consummation of our labors,' returned the old gentleman.

" 'Very good,' says Tom, with a mournful air. 'It's only for two months, but I may as well be the richest man in the world even for that time. I'm not particular, I'll take her, Sir. I'll take her.'

"The old gentleman was in a rapture to find Tom still in the same mind, and drawing the young lady towards him by little and little, was joining their hands by main force, when all of a sudden, gentlemen, the crucible blows up, with a great crash; everybody screams; the room is filled with smoke; and Tom, not knowing what may happen next, throws himself into a Fancy attitude, and says, 'Come on, if you're a man!' without addressing himself to anybody in particular.

" 'The labors of fifteen years,' says the old gentleman, clasping his hands and looking down upon the Gifted, who was saving the pieces, 'are destroyed in an instant!' — And I am told, gentlemen, by-the-bye, that this same philosopher's stone would have been discovered a hundred times at least, to speak within bounds, if it wasn't for the one unfortunate circumstance that the apparatus always blows up, when it's on the very point of succeeding.

"Tom turns pale when he hears the old gentleman expressing himself to this unpleasant effect, and stammers out that if it's quite agreeable to all parties, he would like to know exactly what has happened, and what change has really taken place in the prospects of that company.

" 'We have failed for the present, Mr. Grig,' says the old gentleman, wiping his forehead. 'And I regret it the more, because I have in fact invested my niece's five thousand pounds in this glorious speculation. But don't be cast down,' he says, anxiously — 'in another fifteen years, Mr. Grig — '

" 'Oh!' cries Tom, letting the young lady's hand fall. 'Were the stars very positive about this union, Sir?'

" 'They were,' says the old gentleman.

" 'I'm sorry to hear it,' Tom makes answer, 'for it's no go, Sir.'

" 'No what!' cries the old gentleman.

" 'Go, Sir,' says Tom fiercely. 'I forbid the banns.' And with these words — which are the very words he used — he sat himself down in a chair, and, laying his head upon the table, thought with a secret grief of what was to come to pass on that day two months.

"Tom always said, gentlemen, that that waiting-maid was the artfullest minx he had ever seen; and he left it in writing in this country when he went to colonize abroad, that he was certain in his own mind she and the Salamander had blown up the philosopher's stone on purpose, and to cut him out of his property. I believe Tom was in the right, gentlemen; but whether or no, she comes forward at this point, and says, 'May I speak, Sir?' and the old gentleman answering, 'Yes, you may,' she goes on to say that 'the stars are no doubt quite right in every respect, but Tom is not the man.' And she says, 'Don't you remember, Sir, that when the clock struck five this afternoon, you gave Master Galileo a rap on the head with your telescope, and told him to get out of the way?' 'Yes, I do,' says the old gentleman. 'Then,' says the waiting-maid, 'I say he's the man, and the prophecy is fulfilled.' The old gentleman staggers at this, as if somebody had hit him a blow on the chest, and cries, 'He! why he's a boy!' Upon that, gentlemen, the Salamander cries out that he'll be twenty-one next Lady-day; and complains that his father has always been so busy with the sun round which the earth revolves, that he has never taken any notice of the son that revolves round him; and that he hasn't had a new suit of clothes since he was fourteen; and that he wasn't even taken out of nankeen frocks and trousers till he was quite unpleasant in 'em; and touches on a good many more family matters to the same purpose. To make short of a long story, gentlemen, they all talk together, and cry together, and remind the old gentleman that as to the noble family, his own grandfather would have been lord mayor if he hadn't died at a dinner the year before; and they show him by all kinds of arguments that if the cousins are married, the prediction comes true every way. At last, the old gentleman being quite convinced, gives in; and joins their hands; and leaves his daughter to marry anybody she likes; and they are all well pleased; and the Gifted as well as any of them.

"In the middle of this little family party, gentlemen, sits Tom all the while, as miserable as you like. But, when everything else is arranged, the old gentleman's daughter says, that their strange conduct was a little device of the waiting-maid's to disgust the lovers he had chosen for 'em, and will he forgive her? and if he will, perhaps he might even find her a husband — and when she says that, she looks uncommon hard at Tom. Then the waiting-maid says that, oh dear! she couldn't abear Mr. Grig should think she wanted him to marry her; and that she had even gone so far as to refuse the last lamplighter, who was now a literary character (having set up as a billsticker); and that she hoped Mr. Grig would not suppose she was on her last legs by any means, for the baker was very strong in his attentions at that moment, and as to the butcher, he was frantic. And I don't know how much more she might have said, gentlemen (for, as you know, this kind of young women are rare ones to talk), if the old gentleman hadn't cut in suddenly, and asked Tom if he'd have her, with ten pounds to recompense him for his loss of time and disappointment, and as a kind of bribe to keep the story secret.

" 'It don't much matter, Sir,' says Tom, 'I ain't long for this world. Eight weeks of marriage, especially with this young woman, might reconcile me to my fate. I think,' he says, 'I could go off easy after that.' With which he embraces her with a very dismal face, and groans in a way that might move a heart of stone — even of philosopher's stone.

" 'Egad,' says the old gentleman, 'that reminds me — this bustle put it out of my head — there was a figure wrong. He'll live to a green old age — eighty-seven at least!'

" 'How much, Sir?' cries Tom.

" 'Eighty-seven!' says the old gentleman.

"Without another word, Tom flings himself on the old gentle-man's neck; throws up his hat; cuts a caper; defies the waiting-maid; and refers her to the butcher.

" 'You won't marry her!' says the old gentleman, angrily.

" 'And live after it!' says Tom. 'I'd sooner marry a mermaid with a small-tooth comb and looking-glass.'

" 'Then take the consequences,' says the other.

"With those words — I beg your kind attention here, gentlemen, for it's worth your notice — the old gentleman wetted the forefinger of his right hand in some of the liquor from the crucible that was spilled on the floor, and drew a small triangle on Tom's forehead. The room swam before his eyes, and he found himself in the watch-house."

"Found himself *where?*" cried the vice, on behalf of the company generally.

"In the watch-house," said the chairman. "It was late at night, and he found himself in the very watch-house from which he had been let out that morning."

"Did he go home?" asked the vice.

"The watch-house people rather objected to that," said the chair-man; "so he stopped there that night, and went before the magistrate in the morning. 'Why, you're here again, are you?' says the magis-trate, adding insult to injury; 'we'll trouble you for five shillings more, if you can conveniently spare the money.' Tom told him he had been enchanted, but it was of no use. He told the contractors the same, but they wouldn't believe him. It was very hard upon him, gentlemen, as he often said, for was it likely he'd go and invent such a tale? They shook their heads and told him he'd say anything but his prayers — as indeed he would; there's no doubt about that. It was the only imputation on his moral character that ever *I* heard of."

TO BE READ

AT DUSK

To Be Read

at Dusk

ONE, two, three, four, five. There were five of them.

Five couriers, sitting on a bench outside the convent on the summit of the Great St. Bernard in Switzerland, looking at the remote heights, stained by the setting sun, as if a mighty quantity of red wine had been broached upon the mountain top, and had not yet had time to sink into the snow.

This is not my simile. It was made for the occasion by the stoutest courier, who was a German. None of the others took any more notice of it than they took of me, sitting on another bench on the other side of the convent door, smoking my cigar, like them, and — also like them — looking at the reddened snow, and at the lonely shed hard by, where the bodies of belated travellers, dug out of it, slowly wither away, knowing no corruption in that cold region.

The wine upon the mountain top soaked in as we looked; the mountain became white; the sky, a very dark blue; the wind rose; and the air turned piercing cold. The five couriers buttoned their rough coats. There being no safer man to imitate in all such proceedings than a courier, I buttoned mine.

The mountain in the sunset had stopped the five couriers in a conversation. It is a sublime sight, likely to stop conversation. The mountain being now out of the sunset, they resumed. Not that I had heard any part of their previous discourse; for indeed, I had not then broken away from the American gentleman, in the travellers' parlor of the convent, who, sitting with his face to the fire, had undertaken to realize to me the whole progress of events which had led to the

359

accumulation by the Honorable Ananias Dodger of one of the largest acquisitions of dollars ever made in our country.

"My God!" said the Swiss courier, speaking in French, which I do not hold (as some authors appear to do) to be such an all-sufficient excuse for a naughty word, that I have only to write it in that language to make it innocent; "if you talk of ghosts — "

"But I *don't* talk of ghosts," said the German.

"Of what then?" asked the Swiss.

"If I knew of what then," said the German, "I should probably know a great deal more."

It was a good answer, I thought, and it made me curious. So I moved my position to that corner of my bench which was nearest to them, and leaning my back against the convent wall, heard perfectly, without appearing to attend.

"Thunder and lightning!" said the German, warming, "when a certain man is coming to see you, unexpectedly; and, without his own knowledge, sends some invisible messenger, to put the idea of him into your head all day, what do you call that? When you walk along a crowded street — at Frankfort, Milan, London, Paris — and think that a passing stranger is like your friend Heinrich, and then that another passing stranger is like your friend Heinrich, and so begin to have a strange foreknowledge that presently you'll meet your friend Heinrich — which you do, though you believed him at Trieste — what do you call *that?*"

"It's not uncommon, either," murmured the Swiss and the other three.

"Uncommon!" said the German. "It's as common as cherries in the Black Forest. It's as common as macaroni at Naples. And Naples reminds me! When the old Marchesa Senzanima shrieks at a card-party on the Chiaja — as I heard and saw her, for it happened in a Bavarian family of mine, and I was overlooking the service that evening — I say, when the old Marchesa starts up at the card-table, white through her rouge, and cries, 'My sister in Spain is dead! I felt her cold touch on my back!' — and when that sister *is* dead at the moment — what do you call that?"

"Or when the blood of San Gennaro liquefies at the request of the clergy — as all the world knows that it does regularly once a year, in my native city," said the Neapolitan courier after a pause, with a comical look, "what do you call that?"

"That!" cried the German. "Well, I think I know a name for that."

"Miracle?" said the Neapolitan, with the same sly face.

The German merely smoked and laughed; and they all smoked and laughed.

"Bah!" said the German, presently. "I speak of things that really do happen. When I want to see the conjurer, I pay to see a professed one, and have my money's worth. Very strange things do happen without ghosts. Ghosts! Giovanni Baptista, tell your story of the English bride. There's no ghost in that, but something full as strange. Will any man tell me what?"

As there was a silence among them, I glanced around. He whom I took to be Baptista was lighting a fresh cigar. He presently went on to speak. He was a Genoese, as I judged.

"The story of the English bride?" said he. "Basta! one ought not to call so slight a thing a story. Well, it's all one. But it's true. Observe me well, gentlemen, it's true. That which glitters is not always gold: but what I am going to tell, is true."

He repeated this more than once.

Ten years ago, I took my credentials to an English gentleman at Long's Hotel, in Bond Street, London, who was about to travel — it might be for one year, it might be for two. He approved of them; likewise of me. He was pleased to make inquiry. The testimony that he received was favorable. He engaged me by the six months, and my entertainment was generous.

He was young, handsome, very happy. He was enamored of a fair young English lady, with a sufficient fortune, and they were going to be married. It was the wedding-trip, in short, that we were going to take. For three months' rest in the hot weather (it was early summer then) he had hired an old place on the Riviera, at an easy distance from my city, Genoa, on the road to Nice. Did I know that place? Yes; I told him I knew it well. It was an old palace with great gardens. It was a little bare, and it was a little dark and gloomy, being close surrounded by trees; but it was spacious, ancient, grand, and on the seashore. He said it had been so described to him exactly, and he was well pleased that I knew it. For its being a little bare of furniture, all such places were. For its being a little gloomy, he had hired it principally for the gardens, and he and my mistress would pass the summer weather in their shade.

"So all goes well, Baptista?" said he.

"Indubitably, signore; very well."

We had a travelling chariot for our journey, newly built for us, and in all respects complete. All we had was complete; we wanted for nothing. The marriage took place. They were happy. *I* was happy, seeing all so bright, being so well situated, going to my own city, teaching my language in the rumble to the maid, la bella Carolina, whose heart was gay with laughter: who was young and rosy.

The time flew. But I observed — listen to this, I pray! (and here the courier dropped his voice) — I observed my mistress sometimes brooding in a manner very strange; in a frightened manner; in an unhappy manner; with a cloudy, uncertain alarm upon her. I think that I began to notice this when I was walking up hills by the carriage side, and master had gone on in front. At any rate, I remember that it impressed itself upon my mind one evening in the South of France, when she called to me to call master back; and when he came back, and walked for a long way, talking encouragingly and affectionately to her, with his hand upon the open window, and hers in it. Now and then, he laughed in a merry way, as if he were bantering her out of something. By-and-by, she laughed, and then all went well again.

It was curious. I asked la bella Carolina, the pretty little one, Was mistress unwell? — No. — Out of spirits? — No. — Fearful of bad roads, or brigands? — No. And what made it more mysterious was, the pretty little one would not look at me in giving answer, but *would* look at the view.

But one day she told me the secret.

"If you must know," said Carolina, "I find, from what I have overheard, that mistress is haunted."

"How haunted?"

"By a dream."

"What dream?"

"By a dream of a face. For three nights before her marriage, she saw a face in a dream — always the same face, and only One."

"A terrible face?"

"No. The face of a dark, remarkable-looking man, in black, with black hair and a grey moustache — a handsome man except for a reserved and secret air. Not a face she ever saw, or at all like a face she ever saw. Doing nothing in the dream but looking at her fixedly, out of darkness."

"Does the dream come back?"

"Never. The recollection of it, is all her trouble."

"And why does it trouble her?"

Carolina shook her head.

"That's master's question," said la bella. "She don't know. She wonders why, herself. But I heard her tell him, only last night, that if she was to find a picture of that face in our Italian house (which she is afraid she will) she did not know how she could ever bear it."

Upon my word, I was fearful after this (said the Genoese courier) of our coming to the old palazzo, lest some such ill-starred picture should happen to be there. I knew there were many there; and, as we got nearer and nearer to the place, I wished the whole gallery in the crater of Vesuvius. To mend the matter, it was a stormy dismal evening when we, at last, approached that part of the Riviera. It thundered; and the thunder of my city and its environs, rolling among the high hills, is very loud. The lizards ran in and out of the chinks in the broken stone wall of the garden, as if they were frightened; the frogs bubbled and croaked their loudest; the sea-wind moaned, and the wet trees dripped; and the lightning — body of San Lorenzo, how it lightened!

We all know what an old palace in or near Genoa is — how time and the sea air have blotted it — how the drapery painted on the outer walls has peeled off in great flakes of plaster — how the lower windows are darkened with rusty bars of iron — how the courtyard is overgrown with grass — how the outer buildings are dilapidated — how the whole pile seems devoted to ruin. Our palazzo was one of the true kind. It had been shut up close for months. Months? — years! — it had an earthy smell, like a tomb. The scent of the orange trees on the broad back terrace, and of the lemons ripening on the wall, and of some shrubs that grew around a broken fountain, had got into the house somehow, and had never been able to get out again. There was, in every room, an aged smell, grown faint with confinement. It pined in all the cupboards and drawers. In the little rooms of communication between great rooms, it was stifling. If you turned a picture — to come back to the pictures — there it still was, clinging to the wall behind the frame, like a sort of bat.

The lattice-blinds were close shut, all over the house. There were two ugly grey old women in the house, to take care of it; one of them with a spindle, who stood winding and mumbling in the doorway, and who would as soon have let in the devil as the air. Master, mistress, la bella Carolina, and I, went all through the palazzo. I went first, though I have named myself last, opening the windows and the lattice-blinds, and shaking down on myself splashes of rain, and scraps of mortar, and now and then a dozing mosquito, or a monstrous, fat, blotchy, Genoese spider.

When I had let the evening light into a room, master, mistress, and la bella Carolina, entered. Then we looked round at all the pictures, and I went forward again into another room. Mistress secretly had great fear of meeting with the likeness of that face — we all had; but there was no such thing. The Madonna and Bambino, San Francisco, San Sebastiano, Venus, Santa Caterina, Angels, Brigands, Friars, Temples at Sunset, Battles, White Horses, Forests, Apostles, Doges, all my old acquaintances many times repeated? — yes. Dark handsome man in black, reserved and secret, with black hair and grey moustache, looking fixedly at mistress out of darkness? — no.

At last we got through all the rooms and all the pictures, and came out into the gardens. They were pretty well kept, being rented by a gardener, and were large and shady. In one place there was a rustic theatre, open to the sky; the stage a green slope; the coulisses, three entrances upon a side, sweet-smelling leafy screens. Mistress moved her bright eyes, even there, as if she looked to see the face come in upon the scene; but all was well.

"Now, Clara," master said, in a low voice, "you see that it is nothing? You are happy."

Mistress was much encouraged. She soon accustomed herself to that grim palazzo, and would sing, and play the harp, and copy the old pictures, and stroll with master under the green trees and vines all day. She was beautiful. He was happy. He would laugh and say to me, mounting his horse for his morning ride before the heat:

"All goes well, Baptista!"

"Yes, signore, thank God, very well."

We kept no company. I took la bella to the Duomo and Annunciata, to the Café, to the Opera, to the village Festa, to the Public Garden, to the Day Theatre, to the Marionetti. The pretty little one was charmed with all she saw. She learnt Italian — heavens! miraculously! Was mistress quite forgetful of that dream? I asked Carolina sometimes. Nearly, said la bella — almost. It was wearing out.

One day master received a letter, and called me.

"Baptista!"

"Signore!"

"A gentleman who is presented to me will dine here to-day. He is called the Signor Dellombra. Let me dine like a prince."

It was an odd name. I did not know that name. But there had been many noblemen and gentlemen pursued by Austria on political suspicions, lately, and some names had changed. Perhaps this was one. Altro! Dellombra was as good a name to me as another.

When the Signor Dellombra came to dinner (said the Genoese courier in the low voice, into which he had subsided once before), I showed him into the reception-room, the great sala of the old palazzo. Master received him with cordiality, and presented him to mistress. As she rose, her face changed, she gave a cry, and fell upon the marble floor.

Then I turned my head to the Signor Dellombra, and saw that he was dressed in black, and had a reserved and secret air, and was a dark remarkable-looking man, with black hair and a grey moustache.

Master raised mistress in his arms, and carried her to her own room, where I sent la bella Carolina straight. La bella told me afterwards that mistress was nearly terrified to death, and that she wandered in her mind about her dream, all night.

Master was vexed and anxious — almost angry, and yet full of solicitude. The Signor Dellombra was a courtly gentleman, and spoke with great respect and sympathy of mistress's being so ill. The African wind had been blowing for some days (they had told him at his hotel of the Maltese Cross), and he knew that it was often hurtful. He hoped the beautiful lady would recover soon. He begged permission to retire, and to renew his visit when he should have the happiness of hearing that she was better. Master would not allow of this, and they dined alone.

He withdrew early. Next day he called at the gate, on horseback, to inquire for mistress. He did so two or three times in that week.

What I observed myself, and what la bella Carolina told me, united to explain to me that master had now set his mind on curing mistress of her fanciful terror. He was all kindness, but he was sensible and firm. He reasoned with her, that to encourage such fancies was to invite melancholy, if not madness. That it rested with herself to be herself. That if she once resisted her strange weakness, so successfully as to receive the Signor Dellombra as an English lady would receive any other guest, it was forever conquered. To make an end, the signore came again, and mistress received him without marked distress (though with constraint and apprehension still), and the evening passed serenely. Master was so delighted with this change, and so anxious to confirm it, that the Signor Dellombra became a constant guest. He was accomplished in pictures, books, and music; and his society, in any grim palazzo, would have been welcome.

I used to notice, many times, that mistress was not quite recovered. She would cast down her eyes and droop her head, before the Signor Dellombra, or would look at him with a terrified and fascinated glance, as if his presence had some evil influence or power upon her. Turning from her to him, I used to see him in the shaded gardens, or the large half-lighted sala, looking, as I might say, "fixedly upon her out of darkness." But, truly, I had not forgotten la bella Carolina's words describing the face in the dream.

After his second visit I heard master say:

"Now, see, my dear Clara, it's over! Dellombra has come and gone, and your apprehension is broken like glass."

"Will he — will he ever come again?" asked mistress.

"Again? Why, surely, over and over again! Are you cold?" (she shivered).

"No, dear — but — he terrifies me: are you sure that he need come again?"

"The surer for the question, Clara!" replied master, cheerfully.

But he was very hopeful of her complete recovery now, and grew more and more so every day. She was beautiful. He was happy.

"All goes well, Baptista?" he would say to me again.

"Yes, signore, thank God; very well."

We were all (said the Genoese courier, constraining himself to speak a little louder), we were all at Rome for the Carnival. I had been out, all day, with a Sicilian, a friend of mine, and a courier, who was there with an English family. As I returned at night to our hotel, I met the little Carolina, who never stirred from home alone, running distractedly along the Corso.

"Carolina! What's the matter?"

"O Baptista! O, for the Lord's sake! where is my mistress?"

"Mistress, Carolina?"

"Gone since morning — told me, when master went out on his day's journey, not to call her, for she was tired with not resting in the night (having been in pain), and would lie in bed until the evening; then get up refreshed. She is gone! — she is gone! Master has come back, broken down the door, and she is gone! My beautiful, my good, my innocent mistress!"

The pretty little one so cried, and raved, and tore herself that I could not have held her, but for her swooning on my arm as if she had been shot. Master came up — in manner, face, or voice, no more the master that I knew, than I was he. He took me (I laid the little one upon her bed in the hotel, and left her with the chamber-women), in a carriage, furiously through the darkness, across the desolate Campagna. When it was day, and we stopped at a miserable post-house, all the horses had been hired twelve hours ago, and sent away in different directions. Mark me! by the Signor Dellombra, who had passed there in a carriage, with a frightened English lady crouching in one corner.

I never heard (said the Genoese courier, drawing a long breath) that she was ever traced beyond that spot. All I know is, that she vanished into infamous oblivion, with the dreaded face beside her that she had seen in her dream.

"What do you call *that?*" said the German courier, triumphantly. "Ghosts! There are no ghosts *there!* What do you call this, that I am going to tell you? Ghosts! There are no ghosts *here!*"

I took an engagement once (pursued the German courier) with an English gentleman, elderly and a bachelor, to travel through my country, my Fatherland. He was a merchant who traded with my country and knew the language, but who had never been there since he was a boy — as I judge, some sixty years before.

His name was James, and he had a twin-brother John, also a bachelor. Between these brothers there was a great affection. They were in business together, at Goodman's Fields, but they did not live together. Mr. James dwelt in Poland Street, turning out of Oxford Street, London; Mr. John resided by Epping Forest.

Mr. James and I were to start for Germany in about a week. The exact day depended on business. Mr. John came to Poland Street (where I was staying in the house), to pass that week with Mr. James. But he said to his brother on the second day, "I don't feel very well, James. There's not much the matter with me; but I think I am a little gouty. I'll go home and put myself under the care of my old housekeeper, who understands my ways. If I get quite better, I'll come back and see you before you go. If I don't feel well enough to resume my visit where I leave it off, why *you* will come and see *me* before you go." Mr. James, of course, said he would, and they shook hands — both hands, as they always did — and Mr. John ordered out his old-fashioned chariot and rumbled home.

It was on the second night after that — that is to say, the fourth in the week — when I was awoke out of my sound sleep by Mr. James coming into my bedroom in his flannel-gown, with a lighted candle. He sat upon the side of my bed, and looking at me, said:

"Wilhelm, I have reason to think I have got some strange illness upon me."

I then perceived that there was a very unusual expression in his face.

"Wilhelm," said he, "I am not afraid or ashamed to tell you what I might be afraid or ashamed to tell another man. You come from a sensible country, where mysterious things are inquired into and are not settled to have been weighed and measured — or to have been unweighable and unmeasurable — or in either case to have been completely disposed of, for all time — ever so many years ago. I have just now seen the phantom of my brother."

I confess (said the German courier) that it gave me a little tingling of the blood to hear it.

"I have just now seen," Mr. James repeated, looking full at me, that I might see how collected he was, "the phantom of my brother John. I was sitting up in bed, unable to sleep, when it came into my room, in a white dress, and regarding me earnestly, passed up to the end of the room, glanced at some papers on my writing-desk, turned, and, still looking earnestly at me as it passed the bed, went out at the door. Now, I am not in the least mad, and am not in the least disposed to invest that phantom with any external existence out of myself. I think it is a warning to me that I am ill; and I think I had better be bled."

I got out of bed directly (said the German courier) and began to get on my clothes, begging him not to be alarmed, and telling him that I would go myself to the doctor. I was just ready, when we heard a loud knocking and ringing at the street door. My room being an attic at the back, and Mr. James's being the second-floor room in the front, we went down to his room, and put up the window, to see what was the matter.

"Is that Mr. James?" said a man below, falling back to the opposite side of the way to look up.

"It is," said Mr. James, "and you are my brother's man, Robert."

"Yes, Sir. I am sorry to say, Sir, that Mr. John is ill. He is very bad, Sir. It is even feared that he may be lying at the point of death. He wants to see you, Sir. I have a chaise here. Pray come to him. Pray lose no time."

Mr. James and I looked at one another. "Wilhelm," said he, "this is strange. I wish you to come with me!" I helped him to dress, partly there and partly in the chaise; and no grass grew under the horses' iron shoes between Poland Street and the Forest.

Now, mind! (said the German courier) I went with Mr. James into his brother's room, and I saw and heard myself what follows.

His brother lay upon his bed, at the upper end of a long bed-chamber. His old housekeeper was there, and others were there: I think three others were there, if not four, and they had been with him since early in the afternoon. He was in white, like the figure — necessarily so, because he had his night-dress on. He looked like the figure — necessarily so, because he looked earnestly at his brother when he saw him come into the room.

But, when his brother reached the bed-side, he slowly raised himself in bed, and looking full upon him, said these words:

"JAMES, YOU HAVE SEEN ME BEFORE, TO-NIGHT — AND YOU KNOW IT!"

And so died!

I waited, when the German courier ceased, to hear something said of this strange story. The silence was unbroken. I looked round, and the five couriers were gone: so noiselessly that the ghostly mountain might have absorbed them into its eternal snows. By this time, I was by no means in a mood to sit alone in that awful scene, with the chill air coming solemnly upon me — or, if I may tell the truth, to sit alone anywhere. So I went back into the convent-parlor, and, finding the American gentleman still disposed to relate the biography of the Honorable Ananias Dodger, heard it all out.

HUNTED

DOWN

IN FIVE CHAPTERS

Hunted Down

CHAPTER I

MOST OF US see some romances in life. In my capacity as Chief Manager of a Life Assurance Office, I think I have within the last thirty years seen more romances than the generality of men, however unpromising the opportunity may, at first sight, seem.

As I have retired, and live at my ease, I possess the means that I used to want, of considering what I have seen, at leisure. My experiences have a more remarkable aspect, so reviewed, than they had when they were in progress. I have come home from the Play now, and can recall the scenes of the Drama upon which the curtain has fallen, free from the glare, bewilderment, and bustle of the Theater.

Let me recall one of these Romances of the real world.

There is nothing truer than physiognomy, taken in connection with manner. The art of reading that book of which Eternal Wisdom obliges every human creature to present his or her own page with the individual character written on it, is a difficult one, perhaps, and is little studied. It may require some natural aptitude, and it must require (for everything does) some patience and some pains. That these are not usually given to it — that numbers of people accept a few stock commonplace expressions of the face as the whole list of characteristics, and neither seek nor know the refinements that are truest — that You, for instance, give a great deal of time and attention to the reading of music, Greek, Latin, French, Italian, Hebrew, if you please, and do not qualify yourself to read the face of the master or mistress looking over your shoulder teaching it to you — I assume to be five hundred times more probable than improbable.

Perhaps a little self-sufficiency may be at the bottom of this; facial expression requires no study from you, you think; it comes by nature to you to know enough about it, and you are not to be taken in.

I confess, for my part, that I *have* been taken in, over and over again. I have been taken in by acquaintances, and I have been taken in (of course) by friends; far oftener by friends than by any other class of persons. How came I to be so deceived? Had I quite misread their faces?

No. Believe me, my first impression of those people, founded on face and manner alone, was invariably true. My mistake was in suffering them to come nearer to me and explain themselves away.

CHAPTER II

The partition which separated my own office from our general outer office in the City was of thick plate-glass. I could see through it what passed in the outer office, without hearing a word. I had it put up in place of a wall that had been there for years — ever since the house was built. It is no matter whether I did or did not make the change in order that I might derive my first impression of strangers, who came to us on business, from their faces alone, without being influenced by anything they said. Enough to mention that I turned my glass partition to that account, and that a Life Assurance Office is at all times exposed to be practiced upon by the most crafty and cruel of the human race.

It was through my glass partition that I first saw the gentleman whose story I am going to tell.

He had come in without my observng it, and had put his hat and umbrella on the broad counter, and was bending over it to take some papers from one of the clerks. He was about forty or so, dark, exceedingly well dressed in black — being in mourning — and the hand he extended with a polite air, had a particularly well-fitting black kid glove upon it. His hair, which was elaborately brushed and oiled, was parted straight up the middle; and he presented this parting to the clerk, exactly (to my thinking) as if he had said, in so many words: "You must take me, if you please, my friend, just as I show myself. Come straight up here, follow the gravel path, keep off the grass, I allow no trespassing."

I conceived a very great aversion to that man the moment I thus saw him.

He had asked for some of our printed forms, and the clerk was giving them to him and explaining them. An obliged and agreeable smile was on his face, and his eyes met those of the clerk with a sprightly look. (I have known a vast quantity of nonsense talked about bad men not looking you in the face. Don't trust that conventional idea. Dishonesty will stare honesty out of countenance, any day in the week, if there is anything to be got by it.)

I saw, in the corner of his eyelash, that he became aware of my looking at him. Immediately he turned the parting in his hair toward the glass partition, as if he said to me with a sweet smile, "Straight up here, if you please. Off the grass!"

In a few moments he had put on his hat and taken up his umbrella, and was gone.

I beckoned the clerk into my room, and asked, "Who was that?"

He had the gentleman's card in his hand. "Mr. Julius Slinkton, Middle Temple."

"A barrister, Mr. Adams?"

"I think not, Sir."

"I should have thought him a clergyman, but for his having no Reverend here," said I.

"Probably, from his appearance," Mr. Adams replied, "he is reading for orders."

I should mention that he wore a dainty white cravat, and dainty linen altogether.

"What did he want, Mr. Adams?"

"Merely a form of proposal, Sir, and form of reference."

"Recommended here? Did he say?"

"Yes, he said he was recommended here by a friend of yours. He noticed you, but said that as he had not the pleasure of your personal acquaintance he would not trouble you."

"Did he know my name?"

"O yes, Sir! He said, 'There *is* Mr. Sampson, I see!' "

"A well-spoken gentleman, apparently?"

"Remarkably so, Sir."

"Insinuating manners, apparently?"

"Very much so, indeed, Sir."

"Hah!" said I. "I want nothing at present, Mr. Adams."

Within a fortnight of that day I went to dine with a friend of mine, a merchant, a man of taste, why buys pictures and books, and the first man I saw among the company was Mr. Julius Slinkton. There he was, standing before the fire, with good large eyes and an open expression of face; but still (I thought) requiring everybody to come at him by the prepared way he offered, and by no other.

I noticed him ask my friend to introduce him to Mr. Sampson, and my friend did so. Mr. Slinkton was very happy to see me. Not too happy; there was no over-doing of the matter; happy in a thoroughly well-bred, perfectly unmeaning way.

"I thought you had met," our host observed.

"No," said Mr. Slinkton. "I did look in at Mr. Sampson's office, on your recommendation; but I really did not feel justified in troubling Mr. Sampson himself, on a point in the everyday routine of an ordinary clerk."

I said I should have been glad to show him any attention on our friend's introduction.

"I am sure of that," said he, "and am much obliged. At another time, perhaps, I may be less delicate. Only, however, if I have real business; for I know, Mr. Sampson, how precious business time is, and what a vast number of impertinent people there are in the world."

I acknowledged his consideration with a slight bow. "You were thinking," said I, "of effecting a policy on your life."

"O dear no! I am afraid I am not so prudent as you pay me the compliment of supposing me to be, Mr. Sampson. I merely inquired for a friend. But you know what friends are in such matters. Nothing may ever come of it. I have the greatest reluctance to trouble men of business with inquiries for friends, knowing the probabilities to be a thousand to one that the friends will never follow them up. People are so fickle, so selfish, so inconsiderate. Don't you, in your business, find them so every day, Mr. Sampson?"

I was going to give a qualified answer; but he turned his smooth, white parting on me with its "Straight up here, if you please!" and I answered "Yes."

"I hear, Mr. Sampson," he resumed presently, for our friend had a new cook, and dinner was not so punctual as usual, "that your profession has recently suffered a great loss."

"In money?" said I.

He laughed at my ready association of loss with money, and replied, "No, in talent and vigor."

Not at once following out his allusion, I considered for a moment. "*Has* it sustained a loss of that kind?" said I. "I was not aware of it."

"Understand me, Mr. Sampson. I don't imagine that you have retired. It is not so bad as that. But Mr. Meltham —"

"O, to be sure!" said I. "Yes! Mr. Meltham, the young actuary of the 'Inestimable.' "

"Just so," he returned in a consoling way.

"He is a great loss. He was at once the most profound, the most original, and the most energetic man I have ever known connected with Life Assurance."

I spoke strongly; for I had a high esteem and admiration for Meltham; and my gentleman had indefinitely conveyed to me some suspicion that he wanted to sneer at him. He recalled me to my guard by presenting that trim pathway up his head, with its infernal "Not on the grass, if you please — the gravel."

"You knew him, Mr. Slinkton."

"Only by reputation. To have known him as an acquaintance or as a friend, is an honor I should have sought if he had remained in society, though I might never have had the good fortune to attain it, being a man of far inferior mark. He was scarcely above thirty, I suppose?"

"About thirty."

"Ah!" he sighed in his former consoling way. "What creatures we are! To break up, Mr. Sampson, and become incapable of business at that time of life! — Any reason assigned for the melancholy fact?"

("Humph!" thought I, as I looked at him. "But I won't go up the track, and I will go on the grass.")

"What reason have you heard assigned, Mr. Slinkton?" I asked, point-blank.

"Most likely a false one. You know what Rumor is, Mr. Sampson. I never repeat what I hear; it is the only way of paring the nails and shaving the head of Rumor. But when *you* ask me what reason I have heard assigned for Mr. Meltham's passing away from among men, it is another thing. I am not gratifying idle gossip then. I was told, Mr. Sampson, that Mr. Meltham had relinquished all his avocations and all his prospects, because he was, in fact, broken-hearted. A disappointed attachment I heard — though it hardly seems probable, in the case of a man so distinguished and so attractive."

"Attractions and distinctions are no armor against death," said I.

"O, she died? Pray pardon me. I did not hear that. That, indeed, makes it very, very sad. Poor Mr. Meltham! She died? Ah, dear me! Lamentable, lamentable!"

I still thought his pity was not quite genuine, and I still suspected an unaccountable sneer under all this, until he said, as we were parted, like the other knots of talkers, by the announcement of dinner:

"Mr. Sampson, you are surprised to see me so moved on behalf of a man whom I have never known. I am not so disinterested as you may suppose. I have suffered, and recently too, from death myself. I have lost one of two charming nieces, who were my constant companions. She died young — barely three-and-twenty; and even her remaining sister is far from strong. The world is a grave!"

He said this with deep feeling, and I felt reproached for the coldness of my manner. Coldness and distrust had been engendered in me, I knew, by my bad experiences; they were not natural to me; and I often thought how much I had lost in life, losing trustfulness, and how little I had gained, gaining hard caution. This state of mind being habitual to me, I troubled myself more about this conversation than I might have troubled myself about a greater matter. I listened to his talk at dinner, and observed how readily other men responded to it, and with what a graceful instinct he adapted his subjects to the knowledge and habits of those he talked with. As, in talking with me, he had easily started the subject I might be supposed to understand best, and to be the most interested in, so, in talking with others, he guided himself by the same rule. The company was of a varied character; but he was not at fault, that I could discover, with any member of it. He knew just as much of each man's pursuit as made him agreeable to that man in reference to it, and just as little as made it natural in him to seek modestly for information when the theme was broached.

As he talked and talked — but really not too much, for the rest of us seemed to force it upon him — I became quite angry with myself. I took his face to pieces in my mind, like a watch, and examined it in detail. I could not say much against any of his features separately; I could say even less against them when they were put together.

"Then is it not monstrous," I asked myself, "that because a man happens to part his hair straight up the middle of his head, I should permit myself to suspect, and even to detest him?"

(I may stop to remark that this was no proof of my sense. An observer of men who finds himself steadily repelled by some apparently trifling thing in a stranger is right to give it great weight. It may be the clue to the whole mystery. A hair or two will show where a lion is hidden. A very little key will open a very heavy door.)

I took my part in the conversation with him after a time, and we got on remarkably well. In the drawing-room I asked the host how long he had known Mr. Slinkton. He answered, not many months; he had met him at the house of a celebrated painter then present, who had known him well when he was travelling with his nieces in Italy for their health. His plans in life being broken by the death of one of them, he was reading with the intention of going back to college as a matter of form, taking his degree, and going into orders. I could not but argue with myself that here was the true explanation of his interest in poor Meltham, and that I had been almost brutal in my distrust on that simple head.

CHAPTER III

On the very next day but one I was sitting behind my glass partition, as before, when he came into the outer office, as before. The moment I saw him again without hearing him, I hated him worse than ever.

It was only for a moment that I had this opportunity; for he waved his tight-fitting black glove the instant I looked at him, and came straight in.

"Mr. Sampson, good-day! I presume, you see, upon your kind permission to intrude upon you. I don't keep my word in being justified by business, for my business here — if I may so abuse the word — is of the slightest nature."

I asked, was it anything I could assist him in?

"I thank you, no. I merely called to inquire outside whether my dilatory friend had been so false to himself as to be practical and sensible. But, of course, he has done nothing. I gave him your papers with my own hand, and he was hot upon the intention, but of course he has done nothing. Apart from the general human disinclination to do anything that ought to be done, I dare say there is a specialty about assuring one's life. You find it like will-making. People are so superstitious, and take it for granted they will die soon afterwards."

"Up here, if you please; straight up here, Mr. Sampson. Neither to the right nor to the left." I almost fancied I could hear him breathe the words as he sat smiling at me, with that intolerable parting exactly opposite the bridge of my nose.

"There is such a feeling sometimes, no doubt," I replied; "but I don't think it obtains to any great extent."

"Well," said he, with a shrug and a smile, "I wish some good angel would influence my friend in the right direction. I rashly promised his mother and sister in Norfolk to see it done, and he promised them that he would do it. But I suppose he never will."

He spoke for a minute or two on indifferent topics, and went away.

I had scarcely unlocked the drawers of my writing-table next morning, when he reappeared. I noticed that he came straight to the door in the glass partition, and did not pause a single moment outside.

"Can you spare me two minutes, my dear Mr. Sampson?"

"By all means."

"Much obliged," laying his hat and umbrella on the table; "I came early, not to interrupt you. The fact is, I am taken by surprise in reference to this proposal my friend has made."

"Has he made one?" said I.

"Ye-es," he answered, deliberately looking at me; and then a bright idea seemed to strike him — "or he only tells me he has. Perhaps that may be a new way of evading the matter. By Jupiter, I never thought of that!"

Mr. Adams was opening the morning's letters in the outer office. "What is the name, Mr. Slinkton?" I asked.

"Beckwith."

I looked out at the door and requested Mr. Adams, if there were a proposal in that name, to bring it in. He had already laid it out of his hand on the counter. It was easily selected from the rest, and he gave it me. Alfred Beckwith. Proposal to effect a policy with us for two thousand pounds. Dated yesterday.

"From the Middle Temple, I see, Mr. Slinkton."

"Yes. He lives on the same staircase with me; his door is opposite. I never thought he would make me his reference though."

"It seems natural enough that he should."

"Quite so, Mr. Sampson; but I never thought of it. Let me see." He took the printed paper from his pocket. "How am I to answer all these questions?"

"According to the truth, of course," said I.

"O, of course!" he answered, looking up from the paper with a smile; "I meant they were so many. But you do right to be particular. It stands to reason that you must be particular. Will you allow me to use your pen and ink?"

"Certainly."

"And your desk?"

"Certainly."

He had been hovering about between his hat and his umbrella for a place to write on. He now sat down in my chair, at my blotting-paper and inkstand, with the long walk up his head in accurate perspective before me, as I stood with my back to the fire.

Before answering each question he ran over it aloud, and discussed it. How long had he known Mr. Alfred Beckwith? That he had to calculate by years upon his fingers. What were his habits? No difficulty about them; temperate in the last degree, and took a little too much exercise, if anything. All the answers were satisfactory. When he had written them all, he looked them over, and finally signed them in a very pretty hand. He supposed he had now done with the business. I told him he was not likely to be troubled any farther. Should he leave the papers there? If he pleased. Much obliged. Good morning.

I had had one other visitor before him; not at the office, but at my own house. That visitor had come to my bedside when it was not yet daylight, and had been seen by no one else but by my faithful confidential servant.

A second reference paper (for we required always two) was sent down into Norfolk, and was duly received back by post. This, likewise, was satisfactorily answered in every respect. Our forms were all complied with; we accepted the proposal, and the premium for one year was paid.

CHAPTER IV

For six or seven months I saw no more of Mr. Slinkton. He called once at my house, but I was not at home; and he once asked me to dine with him in the Temple, but I was engaged. His friend's assurance was effected in March. Late in September or early in October I was down at Scarborough for a breath of sea-air, where I met him on the beach. It was a hot evening; he came toward me with his hat in his hand; and there was the walk I had felt so strongly disinclined to take in perfect order again, exactly in front of the bridge of my nose.

He was not alone, but had a young lady on his arm.

She was dressed in mourning, and I looked at her with great interest. She had the appearance of being extremely delicate, and her face was remarkably pale and melancholy; but she was very pretty. He introduced her as his niece, Miss Niner.

"Are you strolling, Mr. Sampson? Is it possible you can be idle?"

It *was* possible, and I *was* strolling.

"Shall we stroll together?"

"With pleasure."

The young lady walked between us, and we walked on the cool sea sand, in the direction of Filey.

"There have been wheels here," said Mr. Slinkton. "And now I look again, the wheels of a hand-carriage! Margaret, my love, your shadow without doubt!"

"Miss Niner's shadow?" I repeated, looking down at it on the sand.

"Not that one," Mr. Slinkton returned, laughing. "Margaret, my dear, tell Mr. Sampson."

"Indeed," said the young lady, turning to me, "there is nothing to tell — except that I constantly see the same invalid old gentleman at all times, wherever I go. I have mentioned it to my uncle, and he calls the gentleman my shadow."

"Does he live in Scarborough?" I asked.

"He is staying here."

"Do you live in Scarborough?"

"No, I am staying here. My uncle has placed me with a family here, for my health."

"And your shadow?" said I, smiling.

"My shadow," she answered, smiling too, "is — like myself — not very robust, I fear; for I lose my shadow sometimes, as my shadow loses me at other times. We both seem liable to confinement to the house. I have not seen my shadow for days and days; but it does oddly happen, occasionally, that wherever I go, for many days together, this gentleman goes. We have come together in the most unfrequented nooks on this shore."

"Is this he?" said I, pointing before us.

The wheels had swept down to the water's edge, and described a great loop on the sand in turning. Bringing the loop back towards us, and spinning it out as it came, was a hand-carriage, drawn by a man.

"Yes," said Miss Niner, "this really is my shadow, uncle."

As the carriage approached us and we approached the carriage, I saw within it an old man, whose head was sunk on his breast, and who was enveloped in a variety of wrappers. He was drawn by a very quiet but very keen-looking man, with iron-grey hair, who was slightly lame. They had passed us, when the carriage stopped, and the old gentleman within, putting out his arm, called to me by my name. I went back, and was absent from Mr. Slinkton and his niece for about five minutes.

When I rejoined them, Mr. Slinkton was the first to speak. Indeed, he said to me in a raised voice before I came up with him:

"It is well you have not been longer, or my niece might have died of curiosity to know who her shadow is, Mr. Sampson."

"An old East India Director," said I. "An intimate friend of our friend's, at whose house I first had the pleasure of meeting you. A certain Major Banks. You have heard of him?"

"Never."

"Very rich, Miss Niner; but very old, and very crippled. An amiable man, sensible — much interested in you. He has just been expatiating on the affection that he has observed to exist between you and your uncle."

Mr. Slinkton was holding his hat again, and he passed his hand up the straight walk, as if he himself went up it serenely, after me.

"Mr. Sampson," he said, tenderly pressing his niece's arm in his, "our affection was always a strong one, for we have had but few near ties. We have still fewer now. We have associations to bring us together, that are not of this world, Margaret."

"Dear uncle!" murmured the young lady, and turned her face aside to hide her tears.

"My niece and I have such remembrances and regrets in common, Mr. Sampson," he feelingly pursued, "that it would be strange indeed if the relations between us were cold or indifferent. If I remember a conversation we once had together, you will understand the reference I make. Cheer up, dear Margaret. Don't droop, don't droop. My Margaret! I cannot bear to see you droop!"

The poor young lady was very much affected, but controlled herself. His feelings, too, were very acute. In a word, he found himself under such great need of a restorative, that he presently went away, to take a bath of sea-water, leaving the young lady and me sitting by a point of rock, and probably presuming — but that you will say was a pardonable indulgence in a luxury — that she would praise him with all her heart.

She did, poor thing! With all her confiding heart, she praised him to me, for his care of her dead sister, and for his untiring devotion in her last illness. The sister had wasted away very slowly, and wild and terrible fantasies had come over her toward the end, but he had never been impatient with her, or at a loss; had always been gentle, watchful, and self-possessed. The sister had known him, as she had known him, to be the best of men, the kindest of men, and yet a man of such admirable strength of character, as to be a very tower for the support of their weak natures while their poor lives endured.

"I shall leave him, Mr. Sampson, very soon," said the young lady; "I know my life is drawing to an end; and when I am gone, I hope he will marry and be happy. I am sure he has lived single so long, only for my sake, and for my poor, poor sister's."

The little hand-carriage had made another great loop on the damp sand, and was coming back again, gradually spinning out a slim figure of eight, half a mile long.

"Young lady," said I, looking around, laying my hand upon her arm, and speaking in a low voice, "time presses. You hear the gentle murmur of that sea?"

She looked at me with the utmost wonder and alarm, saying, "Yes!"

"And you know what a voice is in it when the storm comes?"

"Yes!"

"You see how quiet and peaceful it lies before us, and you know what an awful sight of power without pity it might be, this very night!"

"Yes!"

"But if you had never heard or seen it, or heard of it in its cruelty, could you believe that it beats every inanimate thing in its way to pieces, without mercy, and destroys life without remorse?"

"You terrify me, Sir, by these questions!"

"To save you, young lady, to save you! For God's sake, collect your strength and collect your firmness! If you were here alone, and hemmed in by the rising tide on the flow to fifty feet above your head, you could not be in greater danger than the danger you are now to be saved from."

The figure on the sand was spun out, and straggled off into a crooked little jerk that ended at the cliff very near us.

"As I am, before Heaven and the Judge of all mankind, your friend, and your dead sister's friend, I solemnly entreat you, Miss Niner, without one moment's loss of time, to come to this gentleman with me!"

If the little carriage had been less near to us, I doubt if I could have got her away; but it was so near that we were there before she had recovered the hurry of being urged from the rock. I did not remain there with her two minutes. Certainly within five, I had the inexpressible satisfaction of seeing her — from the point we had sat on, and to which I had returned — half supported and half carried up some rude steps notched in the cliff, by the figure of an active man. With that figure beside her, I knew she was safe anywhere.

I sat alone on the rock, awaiting Mr. Slinkton's return. The twilight was deepening and the shadows were heavy, when he came round the point, with his hat hanging at his buttonhole, smoothing his wet hair with one of his hands, and picking out the old path with the other and a pocket-comb.

"My niece not here, Mr. Sampson?" he said, looking about.

"Miss Niner seemed to feel a chill in the air after the sun was down, and has gone home."

He looked surprised, as though she were not accustomed to do anything without him; even to originate so slight a proceeding.

"I persuaded Miss Niner," I explained.

"Ah!" said he. "She is easily persuaded — for her good. Thank you, Mr. Sampson; she is better within doors. The bathing-place was farther than I thought, to say the truth."

"Miss Niner is very delicate," I observed.

He shook his head and drew a deep sigh. "Very, very, very. You may recollect my saying so. The time that has since intervened has not strengthened her. The gloomy shadow that fell upon her sister so early in life seems, in my anxious eyes, to gather over her, ever darker, ever darker. Dear Margaret, dear Margaret! But we must hope."

The hand-carriage was spinning away before us at a most indecorous pace for an invalid vehicle, and was making most irregular curves upon the sand. Mr. Slinkton, noticing it after he had put his handkerchief to his eyes, said:

"If I may judge from appearances, your friend will be upset, Mr. Sampson."

"It looks probable, certainly," said I.

"The servant must be drunk."

"The servants of old gentlemen will get drunk sometimes," said I.

"The major draws very light, Mr. Sampson."

"The major does draw light," said I.

By this time the carriage, much to my relief, was lost in the darkness. We walked on for a little, side by side over the sand, in silence. After a short while he said, in a voice still affected by the emotion that his niece's state of health had awakened in him:

"Do you stay here long, Mr. Sampson?"

"Why, no. I am going away to-night."

"So soon? But business always holds you in request. Men like Mr. Sampson are too important to others, to be spared to their own need of relaxation and enjoyment."

"I don't know about that," said I. "However, I am going back."

"To London?"

"To London."

"I shall be there too, soon after you."

I knew that as well as he did. But I did not tell him so. Any more than I told him what defensive weapon my right hand rested on in my pocket, as I walked by his side. Any more than I told him why I did not walk on the sea side of him with the night closing in.

We left the beach, and our ways diverged. We exchanged good night, and had parted indeed, when he said, returning,

"Mr. Sampson, *may* I ask? Poor Meltham, whom we spoke of — dead yet?"

"Not when I last heard of him; but too broken a man to live long, and hopelessly lost to his old calling."

"Dear, dear, dear!" said he, with great feeling. "Sad, sad, sad! The world is a grave!" And so went his way.

It was not his fault if the world were not a grave; but I did not call that observation after him, any more than I had mentioned those other things just now enumerated. He went his way, and I went mine with all expedition. This happened, as I have said, either at the end of September or beginning of October. The next time I saw him, and the last time, was late in November.

CHAPTER V

I had a very particular engagement to breakfast in the Temple. It was a bitter north-easterly morning, and the sleet and slush lay inches deep in the streets. I could get no conveyance, and was soon wet to the knees; but I should have been true to that appointment, though I had to wade to it up to my neck in the same impediments.

The appointment took me to some chambers in the Temple. They were at the top of a lonely corner house overlooking the river. The name, MR. ALFRED BECKWITH, was painted on the outer door. On the door opposite, on the same landing, the name MR. JULIUS SLINK-TON. The doors of both sets of chambers stood open, so that anything said aloud in one set could be heard in the other.

I had never been in those chambers before. They were dismal, close, unwholesome, and oppressive; the furniture, originally good, and not yet old, was faded and dirty — the rooms were in great disorder; there was a strong prevailing smell of opium, brandy, and tobacco; the grate and fire-irons were splashed all over with unsightly blotches of rust; and on a sofa by the fire, in the room where breakfast had been prepared, lay the host, Mr. Beckwith, a man with all the appearances of the worst kind of drunkard, very far advanced upon his shameful way to death.

"Slinkton is not come yet," said this creature, staggering up when

I went in; "I'll call him. — Halloa! Julius Cæsar! Come and drink!" As he hoarsely roared this out, he beat the poker and tongs together in a mad way, as if that were his usual manner of summoning his associate.

The voice of Mr. Slinkton was heard through the clatter from the opposite side of the staircase, and he came in. He had not expected the pleasure of meeting me. I have seen several artful men brought to a stand, but I never saw a man so aghast as he was when his eyes rested on mine.

"Julius Cæsar," cried Beckwith, staggering between us, "Mist' Sampson! Mist' Sampson, Julius Cæsar! Julius, Mist' Sampson, is the friend of my soul. Julius keeps me plied with liquor, morning, noon, and night. Julius is a real benefactor. Julius threw the tea and coffee out of window when I used to have any. Julius empties all the water-jugs of their contents, and fills 'em with spirits. Julius winds me up and keeps me going. — Boil the brandy, Julius!"

There was a rusty and furred saucepan in the ashes — the ashes looked like the accumulation of weeks — and Beckwith, rolling and staggering between us as if he were going to plunge headlong into the fire, got the saucepan out, and tried to force it into Slinkton's hand.

"Boil the brandy, Julius Cæsar! Come! Do your usual office. Boil the brandy!"

He became so fierce in his gesticulations with the saucepan, that I expected to see him lay open Slinkton's head with it. I therefore put out my hand to check him. He reeled back to the sofa, and sat there panting, shaking, and red-eyed, in his rags of dressing-gown, looking at us both. I noticed then that there was nothing to drink on the table but brandy, and nothing to eat but salted herrings, and a hot, sickly, highly peppered stew.

"At all events, Mr. Sampson," said Slinkton, offering me the smooth gravel path for the last time, "I thank you for interfering between me and this unfortunate man's violence. However you came here, Mr. Sampson, or with whatever motive you came here, at least I thank you for that."

"Boil the brandy," muttered Beckwith.

Without gratifying his desire to know how I came there, I said, quietly, "How is your niece, Mr. Slinkton?"

He looked hard at me, and I looked hard at him.

"I am sorry to say, Mr. Sampson, that my niece has proved treacherous and ungrateful to her best friend. She left me without a word of notice or explanation. She was misled, no doubt, by some designing rascal. Perhaps you may have heard of it."

"I did hear that she was misled by a designing rascal. In fact, I have proof of it."

"Are you sure of that?" said he.

"Quite."

"Boil the brandy," muttered Beckwith. "Company to breakfast, Julius Cæsar. Do your usual office — provide the usual breakfast, dinner, tea, and supper. Boil the brandy!"

The eyes of Slinkton looked from him to me, and he said, after a moment's consideration,

"Mr. Sampson, you are a man of the world, and so am I. I will be plain with you."

"O no, you won't," said I, shaking my head.

"I tell you, Sir, I will be plain with you."

"And I tell you you will not," said I. "I know all about you. *You* plain with any one? Nonsense, nonsense!"

"I plainly tell you, Mr. Sampson," he went on, with a manner almost composed, "that I understand your object. You want to save your funds, and escape from your liabilities; these are old tricks of trade with you Office-gentlemen. But you will not do it, Sir; you will not succeed. You have not an easy adversary to play against, when you play against me. We shall have to inquire, in due time, when and how Mr. Beckwith fell into his present habits. With that remark, Sir, I put this poor creature, and his incoherent wanderings of speech, aside, and wish you a good morning and a better case next time."

While he was saying this, Beckwith had filled a half-pint glass with brandy. At this moment, he threw the brandy at his face, and threw the glass after it. Slinkton put his hands up, half blinded with the spirit, and cut with the glass across the forehead. At the sound of the breakage, a fourth person came into the room, closed the door, and stood at it; he was a very quiet but very keen-looking man, with iron-grey hair, and slightly lame.

Slinkton pulled out his handkerchief, assuaged the pain in his smarting eyes, and dabbled the blood on his forehead. He was a long time about it, and I saw that in the doing of it, a tremendous change came over him, occasioned by the change in Beckwith — who ceased to pant and tremble, sat upright, and never took his eyes off him. I never in my life saw a face in which abhorrence and determination were so forcibly painted as in Beckwith's then.

"Look at me, you villain," said Beckwith, "and see me as I really am. I took these rooms, to make them a trap for you. I came into them as a drunkard, to bait the trap for you. You fell into the trap, and you will never leave it alive. On the morning when you last went to Mr. Sampson's office, I had seen him first. Your plot has been known to both of us, all along, and you have been counter-plotted all along. What? Having been cajoled into putting that prize of two thousand pounds in your power, I was to be done to death with brandy, and, brandy not proving quick enough, with something quicker? Have I never seen you, when you thought my senses gone, pouring from your little bottle into my glass? Why, you Murderer and Forger, alone here with you in the dead of night, as I have so often been, I have had my hand upon the trigger of a pistol, twenty times, to blow your brains out!"

This sudden starting up of the thing that he had supposed to be his imbecile victim into a determined man, with a settled resolution to hunt him down and be the death of him, mercilessly expressed from head to foot, was, in the first shock, too much for him. Without any figure of speech, he staggered under it. But there is no greater mistake than to suppose that a man who is a calculating criminal, is, in any phase of his guilt, otherwise than true to himself, and perfectly consistent with his whole character. Such a man commits murder, and murder is the natural culmination of his course; such a man has to outface murder, and will do it with hardihood and effrontery. It is a sort of fashion to express surprise that any notorious criminal, having such crime upon his conscience, can so brave it out. Do you think that if he had it on his conscience at all, or had a conscience to have it upon, he would ever have committed the crime?

Perfectly consistent with himself, as I believe all such monsters to be, this Slinkton recovered himself, and showed a defiance that was sufficiently cold and quiet. He was white, he was haggard, he was changed; but only as a sharper who had played for a great stake and had been outwitted and had lost the game.

"Listen to me, you villain," said Beckwith, "and let every word you hear me say be a stab in your wicked heart. When I took these rooms, to throw myself in your way and lead you on to the scheme

ALFRED BECKWITH REVEALS HIMSELF

that I knew my appearance and supposed character and habits would suggest to such a devil, how did I know that? Because you were no stranger to me. I knew you well. And I knew you to be the cruel wretch who, for so much money, had killed one innocent girl while she trusted him implicitly, and who was by inches killing another."

Slinkton took out a snuff-box, took a pinch of snuff, and laughed.

"But see here," said Beckwith, never looking away, never raising his voice, never relaxing his face, never unclenching his hand. "See what a dull wolf you have been, after all! The infatuated drunkard who never drank a fiftieth part of the liquor you plied him with, but poured it away, here, there, everywhere — almost before your eyes; who bought over the fellow you set to watch him and to ply him, by outbidding you in his bribe, before he had been at his work three days — with whom you have observed no caution, yet who was so bent on ridding the earth of you as a wild beast, that he would have defeated you if you had been ever so prudent — that drunkard whom you have, many a time, left on the floor of this room, and who has even let you go out of it, alive and undeceived, when you have turned him over with your foot — has, almost as often, on the same night, within an hour, within a few minutes, watched you awake, had his hand at your pillow when you were asleep, turned over your papers, taken samples from your bottles and packets of powder, changed their contents, rifled every secret of your life!"

He had had another pinch of snuff in his hand, but had gradually let it drop from between his fingers to the floor; where he now smoothed it out with his foot, looking down at it the while.

"That drunkard," said Beckwith, "who had free access to your rooms at all times, that he might drink the strong drinks that you left in his way and be the sooner ended, holding no more terms with you than he would hold with a tiger, has had his master-key for all your locks, his test for all your poisons, his clue to your cipher-writing. He can tell you, as well as you can tell him, how long it took to complete that deed, what doses there were, what intervals, what signs of gradual decay upon mind and body; what distempered fancies were produced, what observable changes, what physical pain. He can tell you, as well as you can tell him, that all this was recorded day by day, as a lesson of experience for future service. He can tell you, better than you can tell him, where that journal is at this moment."

Slinkton stopped the action of his foot, and looked at Beckwith.

"No," said the latter, as if answering a question from him. "Not in the drawer of the writing-desk that opens with a spring; it is not there, and it never will be there again."

"Then you are a thief!" said Slinkton.

Without any change whatever in the inflexible purpose, which it was quite terrific even to me to contemplate, and from the power of which I had always felt convinced it was impossible for this wretch to escape, Beckwith returned,

"And I am your niece's shadow, too."

With an imprecation Slinkton put his hand to his head, tore out some hair, and flung it to the ground. It was the end of the smooth walk; he destroyed it in the action and it will soon be seen that his use for it was past.

Beckwith went on: "Whenever you left here, I left here. Although I understood that you found it necessary to pause in the completion of that purpose, to avert suspicion, still I watched you close, with the poor confiding girl. When I had the diary, and could read it word by word — it was only about the night before your last visit to Scarborough — you remember the night? you slept with a small flat vial tied to your wrist — I sent to Mr. Sampson, who was kept out of view. This is Mr. Sampson's trusty servant standing by the door. We three saved your niece among us."

Slinkton looked at us all, took an uncertain step or two from the place where he had stood, returned to it, and glanced about him in a very curious way — as one of the meaner reptiles might, looking for a hole to hide in. I noticed at the same time, that a singular change took place in the figure of the man — as if it collapsed within his clothes, and they consequently became ill-shapen and ill-fitting.

"You shall know," said Beckwith, "for I hope the knowledge will be bitter and terrible to you, why you have been pursued by one man, and why, when the whole interest that Mr. Sampson represents would have expended any money in hunting you down, you have been tracked to death at a single individual's charge. I hear you have had the name of Meltham on your lips sometimes?"

I saw, in addition to those other changes, a sudden stoppage come upon his breathing.

"When you sent the sweet girl whom you murdered (you know with what artfully made-out surroundings and probabilities you sent her) to Meltham's office, before taking her abroad to originate the transaction that doomed her to the grave, it fell to Meltham's lot to see her and to speak with her. It did not fall to his lot to save her, though I know he would freely give his own life to have done it. He admired her; I would say he loved her deeply, if I thought it possible that you could understand the word. When she was sacrificed, he was thoroughly assured of your guilt. Having lost her, he had but one object left in life, and that was to avenge her and destroy you."

I saw the villain's nostrils rise and fall convulsively; but I saw no moving at his mouth.

"That man Meltham," Beckwith steadily pursued, "was as absolutely certain that you could never elude him in this world, if he devoted himself to your destruction with his utmost fidelity and earnestness, and if he divided the sacred duty with no other duty in life, as he was certain that in achieving it he would be a poor instrument in the hands of Providence, and would do well before Heaven in striking you out from among living men. I am that man, and I thank God that I have done my work!"

If Slinkton had been running for his life from swift-footed savages, a dozen miles, he could not have shown more emphatic signs of being oppressed at heart and laboring for breath, than he showed now, when he looked at the pursuer who had so relentlessly hunted him down.

"You never saw me under my right name before; you see me under my right name now. You shall see me once again in the body, when you are tried for your life. You shall see me once again in the spirit, when the cord is round your neck, and the crowd are crying against you!"

When Meltham had spoken these last words, the miscreant suddenly turned away his face, and seemed to strike his mouth with his open hand. At the same instant, the room was filled with a new and powerful odor, and, almost at the same instant, he broke into a crooked run, leap, start — I have no name for the spasm — and fell, with a dull weight that shook the heavy old doors and windows in their frames.

That was the fitting end of him.

When we saw that he was dead, we drew away from the room, and Meltham, giving me his hand, said, with a weary air,

"I have no more work on earth, my friend. But I shall see her again elsewhere."

It was in vain that I tried to rally him. He might have saved her, he said; he had not saved her, and he reproached himself; he had lost her, and he was broken-hearted.

"The purpose that sustained me is over, Sampson, and there is nothing now to hold me to life. I am not fit for life; I am weak and spiritless; I have no hope and no object; my day is done."

In truth, I could hardly have believed that the broken man who then spoke to me was the man who had so strongly and so differently impressed me when his purpose was before him. I used such entreaties with him, as I could; but he still said, and always said, in a patient, undemonstrative way — nothing could avail him — he was broken-hearted.

He died early in the next spring. He was buried by the side of the poor young lady for whom he had cherished those tender and unhappy regrets; and he left all he had to her sister. She lived to be a happy wife and mother; she married my sister's son, who succeeded poor Meltham; she is living now, and her children ride about the garden on my walking-stick when I go to see her.

GEORGE

SILVERMAN'S

EXPLANATION

*

IN NINE CHAPTERS

George Silverman's Explanation

FIRST CHAPTER

IT HAPPENED in this wise —
But, sitting with my pen in my
hand looking at those words again,
without descrying any hint in them of the words that should follow,
it comes into my mind that they have an abrupt appearance. They
may serve, however, if I let them remain, to suggest how very difficult I find it to begin to explain my explanation. An uncouth phrase:
and yet I do not see my way to a better.

SECOND CHAPTER

It happened in *this* wise —
But, looking at those words, and comparing them with my former
opening, I find they are the self-same words repeated. This is the
more surprising to me, because I employ them in quite a new connection. For indeed I declare that my intention was to discard the
commencement I first had in my thoughts, and to give the preference
to another of an entirely different nature, dating my explanation
from an anterior period of my life. I will make a third trial, without
erasing this second failure, protesting that it is not my design to conceal any of my infirmities, whether they be of head or heart.

THIRD CHAPTER

Not as yet directly aiming at how it came to pass, I will come upon
it by degrees. The natural manner, after all, for God knows that is
how it came upon me.

My parents were in a miserable condition of life, and my infant home was a cellar in Preston. I recollect the sound of father's Lancashire clogs on the street pavement above, as being different in my young hearing from the sound of all other clogs; and I recollect, that, when mother came down the cellar-steps, I used tremblingly to speculate on her feet having a good or an ill-tempered look — on her knees — on her waist — until finally her face came into view, and settled the question. From this it will be seen that I was timid, and that the cellar-steps were steep, and that the doorway was very low.

Mother had the gripe and clutch of poverty upon her face, upon her figure, and not least of all upon her voice. Her sharp and high-pitched words were squeezed out of her, as by the compression of bony fingers on a leathern bag; and she had a way of rolling her eyes about and about the cellar, as she scolded, that was gaunt and hungry. Father, with his shoulders rounded, would sit quiet on a three-legged stool, looking at the empty grate, until she would pluck the stool from under him, and bid him go bring some money home. Then he would dismally ascend the steps; and I, holding my ragged shirt and trousers together with a hand (my only braces), would feint and dodge from mother's pursuing grasp at my hair.

A worldly little devil was mother's usual name for me. Whether I cried for that I was in the dark, or for that it was cold, or for that I was hungry, or whether I squeezed myself into a warm corner when there was a fire, or ate voraciously when there was food, she would still say, "O you worldly little devil!" And the sting of it was, that I quite well knew myself to be a worldly little devil. Worldly as to wanting to be housed and warmed, worldly as to wanting to be fed, worldly as to the greed with which I inwardly compared how much I got of those good things with how much father and mother got, when, rarely, those good things were going.

Sometimes they both went away seeking work; and then I would be locked up in the cellar for a day or two at a time. I was at my worldliest then. Left alone, I yielded myself up to a worldly yearning for enough of anything (except misery), and for the death of mother's father, who was a machine-maker at Birmingham, and on whose decease, I had heard mother say, she would come into a whole courtful of houses "if she had her rights." Worldly little devil, I would stand about, musingly fitting my cold bare feet into cracked bricks and crevices of the damp cellar-floor — walking over my grandfather's body, so to speak, into the courtful of houses, and selling them for meat and drink, and clothes to wear.

At last a change came down into our cellar. The universal change came down even as low as that — so will it mount to any height on which a human creature can perch — and brought other changes with it.

We had a heap of I don't know what foul litter in the darkest corner, which we called "the bed." For three days mother lay upon it without getting up, and then began at times to laugh. If I had ever heard her laugh before, it had been so seldom that the strange sound frightened me. It frightened father too; and we took it by turns to give her water. Then she began to move her head from side to side, and sing. After that, she getting no better, father fell a-laughing and a-singing; and then there was only I to give them both water, and they both died.

FOURTH CHAPTER

When I was lifted out of the cellar by two men, of whom one came peeping down alone first, and ran away and brought the other, I could hardly bear the light of the street. I was sitting in the road-way, blinking at it, and at a ring of people collected around me, but not close to me, when, true to my character of worldly little devil, I broke silence by saying, "I am hungry and thirsty!"

"Does he know they are dead?" asked one of another.

"Do you know your father and mother are both dead of fever?" asked a third of me severely.

"I don't know what it is to be dead. I supposed it meant that, when the cup rattled against their teeth, and the water spilt over them. I am hungry and thirsty." That was all I had to say about it.

The ring of people widened outward from the inner side as I looked around me; and I smelt vinegar, and what I know to be camphor, thrown in towards where I sat. Presently some one put a great vessel of smoking vinegar on the ground near me; and then they all looked at me in silent horror as I ate and drank of what was brought for me. I knew at the time they had a horror of me, but I couldn't help it.

I was still eating and drinking, and a murmur of discussion had be-

gun to arise respecting what was to be done with me next, when
I heard a cracked voice somewhere in the ring say, "My name is
Hawkyard, Mr. Verity Hawkyard, of West Bromwich." Then the
ring split in one place; and a yellow-faced, peak-nosed gentleman,
clad all in iron-grey to his gaiters, pressed forward with a policeman
and another official of some sort. He came forward close to the vessel
of smoking vinegar; from which he sprinkled himself carefully, and
me copiously.

"He had a grandfather at Birmingham, this young boy, who is just
dead too," said Mr. Hawkyard.

I turned my eyes upon the speaker, and said in a ravening manner, "Where's his houses?"

"Hah! Horrible wordliness on the edge of the grave," said Mr.
Hawkyard, casting more of the vinegar over me, as if to get my devil
out of me. "I have undertaken a slight — a ve-ry slight — trust in
behalf of this boy; quite a voluntary trust: a matter of mere honor, if
not of mere sentiment: still I have taken it upon myself, and it shall
be (O, yes it shall be!) discharged."

The bystanders seemed to form an opinion of this gentleman
much more favorable than their opinion of me.

"He shall be taught," said Mr. Hawkyard, "(O, yes, he shall be
taught!) but what is to be done with him for the present? He may be
infected. He may disseminate infection." The ring widened considerably. "What is to be done with him?"

He held some talk with the two officials. I could distinguish no
word save "Farm-house." There was another sound several times
repeated, which was wholly meaningless in my ears then, but which
I knew afterwards to be "Hoghton Towers."

"Yes," said Mr. Hawkyard. "I think that sounds promising; I think
that sounds hopeful. And he can be put by himself in a ward, for a
night or two, you say?"

It seemed to be the police-officer who had said so; for it was he who
replied, Yes! It was he, too, who finally took me by the arm, and
walked me before him through the streets, into a whitewashed room
in a bare building, where I had a chair to sit in, a table to sit at, an
iron bedstead and good mattress to lie upon, and a rug and blanket
to cover me. Where I had enough to eat too, and was shown how to
clean the tin porringer in which it was conveyed to me, until it was
as good as a looking-glass. Here, likewise, I was put in a bath, and

had new clothes brought to me; and my old rags were burnt, and I was camphored and vinegared and disinfected in a variety of ways.

When all this was done — I don't know in how many days or how few, but it matters not — Mr. Hawkyard stepped in at the door, remaining close to it, and said, "Go and stand against the opposite wall, George Silverman. As far off as you can. That'll do. How do you feel?"

I told him that I didn't feel cold, and didn't feel hungry, and didn't feel thirsty. That was the whole round of human feelings, as far as I knew, except the pain of being beaten.

"Well," said he, "you are going, George, to a healthy farm-house to be purified. Keep in the air there as much as you can. Live an out-of-door life there, until you are fetched away. You had better not say much — in fact, you had better be very careful not to say anything — about what your parents died of, or they might not like to take you in. Behave well, and I'll put you to school; O, yes! I'll put you to school, though I'm not obligated to do it. I am a servant of the Lord, George; and I have been a good servant to him, I have, these five-and-thirty years. The Lord has had a good servant in me, and he knows it."

What I then supposed him to mean by this, I cannot imagine. As little do I know when I began to comprehend that he was a prominent member of some obscure denomination or congregation, every member of which held forth to the rest when so inclined, and among whom he was called Brother Hawkyard. It was enough for me to know, on that day in the ward, that the farmer's cart was waiting for me at the street corner. I was not slow to get into it; for it was the first ride I ever had in my life.

It made me sleepy, and I slept. First, I stared at Preston streets as long as they lasted; and, meanwhile, I may have had some small dumb wondering within me whereabouts our cellar was; but I doubt it. Such a worldly little devil was I, that I took no thought who would bury father and mother, or where they would be buried, or when. The question whether the eating and drinking by day, and the covering by night, would be as good at the farm-house as at the ward superseded those questions.

The jolting of the cart on a loose stony road awoke me; and I found that we were mounting a steep hill, where the road was a rutty by-road through a field. And so, by fragments of an ancient

terrace, and by some rugged outbuildings that had once been fortified, and passing under a ruined gateway we came to the old farm-
house in the thick stone wall outside the old quadrangle of Hoghton
Towers: which I looked at like a stupid savage, seeing no specialty
in, seeing no antiquity in; assuming all farm-houses to resemble it;
assigning the decay I noticed to the one potent cause of all ruin that
I knew — poverty; eyeing the pigeons in their flights, the cattle in
their stalls, the ducks in the pond, and the fowls pecking about the
yard, with a hungry hope that plenty of them might be killed for
dinner while I stayed there; wondering whether the scrubbed dairy
vessels, drying in the sunlight, could be goodly porringers out of
which the master ate his belly-filling food, and which he polished
when he had done, according to my ward experience; shrinkingly
doubtful whether the shadows, passing over that airy height on the
bright spring day, were not something in the nature of frowns —
sordid, afraid, unadmiring — a small brute to shudder at.

To that time I had never had the faintest impression of duty. I
had had no knowledge whatever that there was anything lovely in this
life. When I had occasionally slunk up the cellar-steps into the street,
and glared in at shop-windows, I had done so with no higher feelings
than we may suppose to animate a mangy young dog or wolf-cub. It
is equally the fact that I had never been alone, in the sense of holding
unselfish converse with myself. I had been solitary often enough, but
nothing better.

Such was my condition when I sat down to my dinner that day, in
the kitchen of the old farm-house. Such was my condition when I lay
on my bed in the old farm-house that night, stretched out opposite
the narrow mullioned window, in the cold light of the moon, like a
young vampire.

FIFTH CHAPTER

What do I know now of Hoghton Towers? Very little; for I have
been gratefully unwilling to disturb my first impressions. A house,
centuries old, on high ground a mile or so removed from the road
between Preston and Blackburn, where the first James of England,
in his hurry to make money by making baronets, perhaps made some
of those remunerative dignitaries. A house, centuries old, deserted
and falling to pieces, its woods and gardens long since grass-land or

ploughed up, the Rivers Ribble and Darwen glancing below it, and a vague haze of smoke, against which not even the supernatural prescience of the first Stuart could foresee a counterblast, hinting at steam-power, powerful in two distances.

What did I know then of Hoghton Towers? When I first peeped in at the gate of the lifeless quadrangle, and started from the moldering statue becoming visible to me like its guardian ghost; when I stole round by the back of the farmhouse, and got in among the ancient rooms, many of them with their floors and ceilings falling, the beams and rafters hanging dangerously down, the plaster dropping as I trod, the oaken panels stripped away, the windows half walled up, half broken; when I discovered a gallery commanding the old kitchen, and looked down between balustrades upon a massive old table and benches, fearing to see I know not what dead-alive creatures come in and seat themselves, and look up with I know not what dreadful eyes, or lack of eyes, at me; when all over the house I was awed by gaps and chinks where the sky stared sorrowfully at me, where the birds passed, and the ivy rustled, and the stains of winter weather blotched the rotten floors; when down at the bottom of dark pits of staircase, into which the stairs had sunk, green leaves trembled, butterflies fluttered, and bees hummed in and out through the broken doorways; when encircling the whole ruin were sweet scents, and sights of fresh green growth, and ever-renewing life, that I had never dreamed of — I say, when I passed into such clouded perception of these things as my dark soul could compass, what did I know then of Hoghton Towers?

I have written that the sky stared sorrowfully at me. Therein have I anticipated the answer. I knew that all these things looked sorrowfully at me; that they seemed to sigh or whisper, not without pity for me, "Alas! poor worldly little devil!"

There were two or three rats at the bottom of one of the smaller pits of broken staircase when I craned over and looked in. They were scuffling for some prey that was there; and, when they started and hid themselves close together in the dark, I thought of the old life (it had grown old already) in the cellar.

How not to be this worldly little devil? how not to have a repugnance towards myself as I had towards the rats? I hid in a corner of one of the smaller chambers, frightened at myself, and crying (it was the first time I had ever cried for any cause not purely physical), and I tried to think about it. One of the farm-ploughs came into my range of view just then; and it seemed to help me as it went on with its two horses up and down the field so peacefully and quietly.

There was a girl of about my own age in the farm-house family, and she sat opposite to me at the narrow table at meal-times. It had come into my mind, at our first dinner, that she might take the fever from me. The thought had not disquieted me then. I had only speculated how she would look under the altered circumstances, and whether she would die. But it came into my mind now, that I might try to prevent her taking the fever by keeping away from her. I knew I should have but scrambling board if I did; so much the less worldly and less devilish the deed would be, I thought.

From that hour, I withdrew myself at early morning into secret corners of the ruined house, and remained hidden there until she went to bed. At first, when meals were ready, I used to hear them calling me; and then my resolution weakened. But I strengthened it again by going farther off into the ruin, and getting out of hearing. I often watched for her at the dim windows; and, when I saw that she was fresh and rosy, felt much happier.

Out of this holding her in my thoughts, to the humanizing of myself, I suppose some childish love arose within me. I felt, in some sort, dignified by the pride of protecting her — by the pride of making the sacrifice for her. As my heart swelled with that new feeling, it insensibly softened about mother and father. It seemed to have been frozen before, and now to be thawed. The old ruin and all the lovely things that haunted it were not sorrowful for me only, but sorrowful for mother and father as well. Therefore did I cry again, and often too.

The farm-house family conceived me to be of a morose temper, and were very short with me; though they never stinted me in such broken fare as was to be got out of regular hours. One night when I lifted the kitchen latch at my usual time, Sylvia (that was her pretty name) had but just gone out of the room. Seeing her ascending the opposite stairs, I stood still at the door. She had heard the clink of the latch, and looked round.

"George," she called to me in a pleased voice, "to-morrow is my birthday; and we are to have a fiddler, and there's a party of boys and girls coming in a cart, and we shall dance. I invite you. Be sociable for once, George."

"I am very sorry, miss," I answered; "but I — but, no; I can't come."

"You are a disagreeable, ill-humored lad," she returned disdainfully; "and I ought not to have asked you. I shall never speak to you again."

As I stood with my eyes fixed on the fire, after she was gone, I felt that the farmer bent his brows upon me.

"Eh, lad!" said he; "Sylvy's right. You're as moody and broody a lad as never I set eyes on yet."

I tried to assure him that I meant no harm; but he only said coldly, "Maybe not, maybe not! There, get thy supper, get thy supper; and then thou canst sulk to thy heart's content again."

Ah! if they could have seen me next day, in the ruin, watching for the arrival of the cart full of merry young guests; if they could have seen me at night, gliding out from behind the ghostly statue, listening to the music and the fall of dancing feet, and watching the lighted farm-house windows from the quadrangle when all the ruin was dark; if they could have read my heart, as I crept up to bed by the back way, comforting myself with the reflection, "They will take no hurt from me" — they would not have thought mine a morose or an unsocial nature.

It was in these ways that I began to form a shy disposition; to be of a timidly silent character under misconstruction; to have an inexpressible, perhaps a morbid, dread of ever being sordid or worldly. It was in these ways that my nature came to shape itself to such a mold, even before it was affected by the influences of the studious and retired life of a poor scholar.

SIXTH CHAPTER

Brother Hawkyard (as he insisted on my calling him) put me to school, and told me to work my way. "You are all right, George," he said. "I have been the best servant the Lord has had in his service for this five-and-thirty year (O, I have!); and he knows the value of such a servant as I have been to him (O, yes, he does!); and he'll prosper your schooling as a part of my reward. That's what *he*'ll do, George. He'll do it for me."

From the first I could not like this familiar knowledge of the ways of the sublime, inscrutable Almighty, on Brother Hawkyard's part.

As I grew a little wiser, and still a little wiser, I liked it less and less. His manner, too, of confirming himself in a parenthesis — as if, knowing himself, he doubted his own word — I found distasteful. I cannot tell how much these dislikes cost me; for I had a dread that they were worldly.

As time went on, I became a Foundation-boy on a good foundation, and I cost Brother Hawkyard nothing. When I had worked my way so far, I worked yet harder, in the hope of ultimately getting a presentation to college and a fellowship. My health has never been strong (some vapor from the Preston cellar cleaves to me, I think); and what with much work and some weakness, I came again to be regarded — that is, by my fellow-students — as unsocial.

All through my time as a Foundation-boy, I was within a few miles of Brother Hawkyard's congregation; and whenever I was what we called a leave-boy on a Sunday, I went over there at his desire. Before the knowledge became forced upon me that outside their place of meeting these brothers and sisters were no better than the rest of the human family, but on the whole were, to put the case mildly, as bad as most, in respect of giving short weight in their shops, and not speaking the truth — I say, before this knowledge became forced upon me, their prolix addresses, their inordinate conceit, their daring ignorance, their investment of the Supreme Ruler of heaven and earth with their own miserable meannesses and littlenesses, greatly shocked me. Still, as their term for the frame of mind that could not perceive them to be in an exalted state of grace was the "worldly" state, I did for a time suffer tortures under my inquiries of myself whether that young worldly-devilish spirit of mine could secretly be lingering at the bottom of my non-appreciation.

Brother Hawkyard was the popular expounder in this assembly, and generally occupied the platform (there was a little platform with a table on it, in lieu of a pulpit) first, on a Sunday afternoon. He was by trade a drysalter. Brother Gimblet, an elderly man with a crabbed face, a large dog's-eared shirt-collar, and a spotted blue neckerchief reaching up behind to the crown of his head, was also a drysalter and an expounder. Brother Gimblet professed the greatest admiration for Brother Hawkyard but (I had thought more than once) bore him a jealous grudge.

Let whosoever may peruse these lines kindly take the pains here to read twice my solemn pledge, that what I write of the language and customs of the congregation in question I write scrupulously, literally, exactly, from the life and the truth.

On the first Sunday after I had won what I had so long tried for, and when it was certain that I was going up to college, Brother Hawkyard concluded a long exhortation thus:

"Well, my friends and fellow-sinners, now I told you when I began, that I didn't know a word of what I was going to say to you (and no, I did not!), but that it was all one to me, because I knew the Lord would put into my mouth the words I wanted."

("That's it!" from Brother Gimblet.)

"And he did put into my mouth the words I wanted."

("So he did!" from Brother Gimblet.)

"And why?"

("Ah, let's have that!" from Brother Gimblet.)

"Because I have been his faithful servant for five-and-thirty years, and because he knows it. For five-and-thirty years! And he knows it, mind you! I got those words that I wanted on account of my wages. I got 'em from the Lord, my fellow-sinners. Down! I said, 'Here's a heap of wages due; let us have something down, on account.' And I got it down, and I paid it over to you; and you won't wrap it up in a napkin, nor yet in a towel, nor yet pocketankercher, but you'll put it out at good interest. Very well. Now, my brothers and sisters and fellow-sinners, I am going to conclude with a question, and I'll make it so plain (with the help of the Lord, after five-and-thirty years, I should rather hope!) as that the Devil shall not be able to confuse it in your heads — which he would be overjoyed to do."

("Just his way. Crafty old blackguard!" from Brother Gimblet.)

"And the question is this, Are the angels learned?"

("Not they. Not a bit on it!" from Brother Gimblet, with the greatest confidence.)

"Not they. And where's the proof? sent ready-made by the hand of the Lord. Why, there's one among us here now, that has got all the learning that can be crammed into him. I got him all the learning that could be crammed into him. His grandfather" (this I had never heard before) "was a brother of ours. He was Brother Parksop. That's what he was. Parksop; Brother Parksop. His worldly name was Parksop, and he was a brother of this brotherhood. Then wasn't he Brother Parksop?"

("Must be. Couldn't help hisself!" from Brother Gimblet.)

"Well, he left that one now here present among us to the care of a brother-sinner of his (and that brother-sinner, mind you, was a sinner of a bigger size in his time than any of you; praise the Lord!), Brother Hawkyard. Me. *I* got him without fee or reward — without a morsel of myrrh, or frankincense, nor yet amber, letting alone the honey-comb — all the learning that could be crammed into him. Has it brought him into our temple, in the spirit? No. Have we had any ignorant brothers and sisters that didn't know round O from crooked S, come in among us meanwhile? Many. Then the angels are *not* learned; then they don't so much as know their alphabet. And now, my friends and fellow-sinners, having brought it to that, perhaps some brother present — perhaps you, Brother Gimblet — will pray a bit for us?"

Brother Gimblet undertook the sacred function, after having drawn his sleeve across his mouth, and muttered, "Well! I don't know as I see my way to hitting any of you quite in the right place neither." He said this with a dark smile, and then began to bellow. What we were specially to be preserved from, according to his solici-tations, was, despoilment of the orphan, suppression of testamentary intentions on the part of a father or (say) grandfather, appropriation of the orphan's house-property, feigning to give in charity to the wronged one from whom we withheld his due; and that class of sins. He ended with the petition, "Give us peace!" which, speaking for myself, was very much needed after twenty minutes of his bellowing.

Even though I had not seen him when he rose from his knees, steaming with perspiration, glance at Brother Hawkyard, and even though I had not heard Brother Hawkyard's tone of congratulating him on the vigor with which he had roared, I should have detected a malicious application in this prayer. Unformed suspicions to a similar effect had sometimes passed through my mind in my earlier school-days, and had always caused me great distress; for they were worldly in their nature, and wide, very wide, of the spirit that had drawn me from Sylvia. They were sordid suspicions, without a shadow of proof. They were worthy to have originated in the un-wholesome cellar. They were not only without proof, but against proof; for was I not myself a living proof of what Brother Hawkyard had done? and without him, how should I ever have seen the sky look sorrowfully down upon that wretched boy at Hoghton Towers?

Although the dread of a relapse into a stage of savage selfishness was less strong upon me as I approached manhood, and could act in an increased degree for myself, yet I was always on my guard against any tendency to such relapse. After getting these suspicions under my feet, I had been troubled by not being able to like Brother Hawkyard's manner, or his professed religion. So it came about, that, as I walked back that Sunday evening, I thought it would be an act of reparation for any such injury my struggling thoughts had unwillingly done him, if I wrote, and placed in his hands, before going to college, a full acknowledgment of his goodness to me, and an ample tribute of thanks. It might serve as an implied vindication of him against any dark scandal from a rival brother and expounder, or from any other quarter.

Accordingly, I wrote the document with much care. I may add with much feeling too; for it affected me as I went on. Having no set studies to pursue, in the brief interval between leaving the Foundation and going to Cambridge, I determined to walk out to his place of business, and give it into his own hands.

It was a winter afternoon, when I tapped at the door of his little counting-house, which was at the farther end of his long, low shop. As I did so (having entered by the back yard, where casks and boxes were taken in, and where there was the inscription, "Private way to the counting-house"), a shopman called to me from the counter that he was engaged.

"Brother Gimblet" (said the shopman, who was one of the brotherhood) "is with him."

I thought this all the better for my purpose, and made bold to tap again. They were talking in a low tone, and money was passing; for I heard it being counted out.

"Who is it?" asked Brother Hawkyard, sharply.

"George Silverman," I answered, holding the door open. "May I come in?"

Both brothers seemed so astounded to see me that I felt shyer than usual. But they looked quite cadaverous in the early gaslight, and perhaps that accidental circumstance exaggerated the expression of their faces.

"What is the matter?" asked Brother Hawkyard.

"Ay! what is the matter?" asked Brother Gimblet.

"Nothing at all," I said, diffidently producing my document: "I am only the bearer of a letter from myself."

"From yourself, George?" cried Brother Hawkyard.

"And to you," said I.

"And to me, George?"

He turned paler, and opened it hurriedly; but looking over it, and seeing generally what it was, became less hurried, recovered his color, and said, "Praise the Lord!"

"That's it!" cried Brother Gimblet. "Well put! Amen."

Brother Hawkyard then said, in a livelier strain, "You must know, George, that Brother Gimblet and I are going to make our two businesses one. We are going into partnership. We are settling it now. Brother Gimblet is to take one clear half of the profits (O, yes! he shall have it; he shall have it to the last farthing)."

"D.V.!" said Brother Gimblet, with his right fist firmly clinched on his right leg.

"There is no objection," pursued Brother Hawkyard, "to my reading this aloud, George?"

As it was what I expressly desired should be done, after yesterday's prayer, I more than readily begged him to read it aloud. He did so; and Brother Gimblet listened with a crabbed smile.

"It was in a good hour that I came here," he said, wrinkling up his eyes. "It was in a good hour, likewise, that I was moved yesterday to depict for the terror of evildoers a character the direct opposite of Brother Hawkyard's. But it was the Lord that done it: I felt him at it while I was perspiring."

After that it was proposed by both of them that I should attend the congregation once more before my final departure. What my shy reserve would undergo, from being expressly preached at and prayed at, I knew beforehand. But I reflected that it would be for the last time, and that it might add to the weight of my letter. It was well known to the brothers and sisters that there was no place taken for me in *their* paradise; and if I showed this last token of deference to Brother Hawkyard, notoriously in despite of my own sinful inclinations, it might go some little way in aid of my statement that he had been good to me, and that I was grateful to him. Merely stipulating, therefore, that no express endeavor should be made for my conversion — which would involve the rolling of several brothers and sisters on the floor, declaring that they felt all their sins in a heap on their left side, weighing so many pounds avoirdupois, as I knew from what I had seen of those repulsive mysteries — I promised.

Since the reading of my letter, Brother Gimblet had been at intervals wiping one eye with an end of his spotted blue neckerchief, and grinning to himself. It was, however, a habit that brother had, to grin in an ugly manner even when expounding. I call to mind a delighted snarl with which he used to detail from the platform the torments reserved for the wicked (meaning all human creation except the brotherhood), as being remarkably hideous.

I left the two to settle their articles of partnership, and count money; and I never saw them again but on the following Sunday. Brother Hawkyard died within two or three years, leaving all he possessed to Brother Gimblet, in virtue of a will dated (as I have been told) that very day.

Now I was so far at rest with myself, when Sunday came, knowing that I had conquered my own mistrust, and righted Brother Hawkyard in the jaundiced vision of a rival, that I went, even to that coarse chapel, in a less sensitive state than usual. How could I foresee that the delicate, perhaps the diseased, corner of my mind, where I winced and shrunk when it was touched, or was even approached, would be handled as the theme of the whole proceedings?

On this occasion it was assigned to Brother Hawkyard to pray, and to Brother Gimblet to preach. The prayer was to open the ceremonies; the discourse was to come next. Brothers Hawkyard and Gimblet were both on the platform; Brother Hawkyard on his knees at the table, unmusically ready to pray; Brother Gimblet sitting against the wall, grinningly ready to preach.

"Let us offer up the sacrifice of prayer, my brothers and sisters and fellow-sinners." Yes; but it was I who was the sacrifice. It was our poor, sinful, worldly-minded brother here present who was wrestled for. The now-opening career of this our unawakened brother might lead to his becoming a minister of what was called "the church." That was what *he* looked to. The church. Not the chapel, Lord. The church. No rectors, no vicars, no archdeacons, no bishops, no archbishops, in the chapel, but, O Lord! many such in the church. Protect our sinful brother from his love of lucre. Cleanse from our unawakened brother's breast his sin of worldly-mindedness. The prayer said infinitely more in words, but nothing more to any intelligible effect.

Then Brother Gimblet came forward, and took (as I knew he would) the text, "My kingdom is not of this world." Ah! but whose was, my fellow-sinners? Whose? Why, our brother's here present was. The only kingdom he had an idea of was of this world. ("That's it!" from several of the congregation.) What did the woman do when she lost the piece of money? Went and looked for it. What should our brother do when he lost his way? ("Go and look for it," from a sister.) Go and look for it, true. But must he look for it in the right direction, or in the wrong? ("In the right," from a brother.) There spake the prophets! He must look for it in the right direction, or he couldn't find it. But he had turned his back upon the right direction, and he wouldn't find it. Now, my fellow-sinners, to show you the difference betwixt worldly-mindedness and unworldly-mindedness, betwixt kingdoms not of this world and kingdoms *of* this world, here was a letter wrote by even our worldly-minded brother unto Brother Hawkyard. Judge, from hearing of it read, whether Brother Hawkyard was the faithful steward that the Lord had in his mind only t'other day, when, in this very place, he drew you the picter of the unfaithful one; for it was him that done it, not me. Don't doubt that!

Brother Gimblet then groaned and bellowed his way through my composition, and subsequently through an hour. The service closed with a hymn, in which the brothers unanimously roared, and the sisters unanimously shrieked at me, That I by wiles of worldly gain was mocked, and they on waters of sweet love were rocked; that I with mammon struggled in the dark, while they were floating in a second ark.

I went out from all this with an aching heart and a weary spirit: not because I was quite so weak as to consider these narrow creatures interpreters of the Divine Majesty and Wisdom, but because I was weak enough to feel as though it were my hard fortune to be misrepresented and misunderstood, when I most tried to subdue any risings of mere worldliness within me, and when I most hoped that, by dint of trying earnestly, I had succeeded.

SEVENTH CHAPTER

My timidity and my obscurity occasioned me to live a secluded life at college, and to be little known. No relative ever came to visit me, for I had no relative. No intimate friends broke in upon my studies,

BROTHER GIMBLET PREACHES A SERMON

for I made no intimate friends. I supported myself on my scholarship, and read much. My college time was otherwise not so very different from my time at Hoghton Towers.

Knowing myself to be unfit for the noisier stir of social existence, but believing myself qualified to do my duty in a moderate, though earnest way, if I could obtain some small preferment in the Church, I applied my mind to the clerical profession. In due sequence I took orders, was ordained, and began to look about me for employment. I must observe that I had taken a good degree, that I had succeeded in winning a good fellowship, and that my means were ample for my retired way of life. By this time I had read with several young men; and the occupation increased my income, while it was highly interesting to me. I once accidentally overheard our greatest don say, to my boundless joy, "That he heard it reported of Silverman that his gift of quiet explanation, his patience, his amiable temper, and his conscientiousness made him the best of coaches." May my "gift of quiet explanation" come more seasonably and powerfully to my aid in this present explanation than I think it will!

It may be in a certain degree owing to the situation of my college-rooms (in a corner where the daylight was sobered), but it is in a much larger degree referable to the state of my own mind, that I seem to myself, on looking back to this time of my life, to have been always in the peaceful shade. I can see others in the sunlight; I can see our boats' crews and our athletic young men on the glistening water, or speckled with the moving lights of sunlit leaves; but I myself am always in the shadow looking on. Not unsympathetically — God forbid! — but looking on alone, much as I looked at Sylvia from the shadows of the ruined house, or looked at the red gleam shining through the farmer's windows, and listened to the fall of dancing feet, when all the ruin was dark that night in the quadrangle.

I now come to the reason of my quoting that laudation of myself above given. Without such reason, to repeat it would have been mere boastfulness.

Among those who had read with me was Mr. Fareway, second son of Lady Fareway, widow of Sir Gaston Fareway, baronet. This young gentleman's abilities were much above the average; but he came of a rich family, and was idle and luxurious. He presented himself to me too late, and afterwards came to me too irregularly, to admit of my being of much service to him. In the end, I considered it my duty to dissuade him from going up for an examination which he could never pass; and he left college without a degree. After his departure, Lady Fareway wrote to me, representing the justice of my returning half my fee, as I had been of so little use to her son. Within my knowledge a similar demand had not been made in any other case; and I most freely admit that the justice of it had not occurred to me until it was pointed out. But I at once perceived it, yielded to it, and returned the money.

Mr. Fareway had been gone two years or more, and I had forgotten him, when he one day walked into my rooms as I was sitting at my books.

Said he, after the usual salutations had passed, "Mr. Silverman, my mother is in town here, at the hotel, and wishes me to present you to her."

I was not comfortable with strangers, and I dare say I betrayed that I was a little nervous or unwilling. "For," said he, without my having spoken, "I think the interview may tend to the advancement of your prospects."

It put me to the blush to think that I should be tempted by a worldly reason, and I rose immediately.

Said Mr. Fareway, as we went along, "Are you a good hand at business?"

"I think not," said I.

Said Mr. Fareway then, "My mother is."

"Truly?" said I.

"Yes: my mother is what is usually called a managing woman. Doesn't make a bad thing, for instance, even out of the spendthrift habits of my eldest brother abroad. In short, a managing woman. This is in confidence."

He had never spoken to me in confidence, and I was surprised by his doing so. I said I should respect his confidence, of course, and said no more on the delicate subject. We had but a little way to walk, and I was soon in his mother's company. He presented me, shook hands with me, and left us two (as he said) to business.

I saw in my Lady Fareway a handsome, well-preserved lady of somewhat large stature, with a steady glare in her great round dark eyes that embarrassed me.

Said my lady, "I have heard from my son, Mr. Silverman, that you would be glad of some preferment in the church."

I gave my lady to understand that was so.

"I don't know whether you are aware," my lady proceeded, "that we have a presentation to a living? I say *we* have; but, in point of fact, *I* have."

I gave my lady to understand that I had not been aware of this.

Said my lady, "So it is: indeed I have two presentations — one to two hundred a year, one to six. Both livings are in our county — North Devonshire — as you probably know. The first is vacant. Would you like it?"

What with my lady's eyes, and what with the suddenness of this proposed gift, I was much confused.

"I am sorry it is not the larger presentation," said my lady, rather coldly; "though I will not, Mr. Silverman, pay you the bad compliment of supposing that *you* are, because that would be mercenary — and mercenary I am persuaded you are not."

Said I, with my utmost earnestness, "Thank you, Lady Fareway, thank you, thank you! I should be deeply hurt if I thought I bore the character."

"Naturally," said my lady. "Always detestable, but particularly in a clergyman. You have not said whether you will like the living?"

With apologies for my remissness or indistinctness, I assured my lady that I accepted it most readily and gratefully. I added that I hoped she would not estimate my appreciation of the generosity of her choice by any flow of words; for I was not a ready man in that respect when taken by surprise or touched at heart.

"The affair is concluded," said my lady; "concluded. You will find the duties very light, Mr. Silverman. Charming house; charming little garden, orchard, and all that. You will be able to take pupils. By-the-bye! No: I will return to the word afterwards. What was I going to mention, when it put me out?"

My lady stared at me, as if I knew. And I didn't know. And that perplexed me afresh.

Said my lady, after some consideration, "O, of course, how very dull of me! The last incumbent — least mercenary man I ever saw — in consideration of the duties being so light and the house so delicious, couldn't rest, he said, unless I permitted him to help me with my correspondence, accounts, and various little things of that kind; nothing in themselves, but which it worries a lady to cope with. Would Mr. Silverman also like to — ? Or shall I — ?"

I hastened to say that my poor help would be always at her lady-ship's service.

"I am absolutely blessed," said my lady, casting up her eyes (and so taking them off me for one moment), "in having to do with gentlemen who cannot endure an approach to the idea of being mercenary!" She shivered at the word. "And now as to the pupil."

"The —— ?" I was quite at a loss.

"Mr. Silverman, you have no idea what she is. She is," said my lady, laying her touch upon my coat-sleeve, "I do verily believe, the most extraordinary girl in this world. Already knows more Greek and Latin than Lady Jane Grey. And taught herself! Has not yet, remember, derived a moment's advantage from Mr. Silverman's classical acquirements. To say nothing of mathematics, which she is bent upon becoming versed in, and in which (as I hear from my son and others) Mr. Silverman's reputation is so deservedly high!"

Under my lady's eyes I must have lost the clue, I felt persuaded; and yet I did not know where I could have dropped it.

"Adelina," said my lady, "is my only daughter. If I did not feel quite convinced that I am not blinded by a mother's partiality; unless I was absolutely sure that when you know her, Mr. Silverman, you will esteem it a high and unusual privilege to direct her studies — I should introduce a mercenary element into this conversation, and ask you on what terms —— "

I entreated my lady to go no further. My lady saw that I was troubled, and did me the honor to comply with my request.

EIGHTH CHAPTER

Everything in mental acquisition that her brother might have been, if he would, and everything in all gracious charms and admirable qualities that no one but herself could be — this was Adelina.

I will not expatiate upon her beauty; I will not expatiate upon her intelligence, her quickness of perception, her powers of memory, her sweet consideration, from the first moment, for the slow-paced tutor who ministered to her wonderful gifts. I was thirty then; I am over sixty now: she is ever present to me in these hours as she was in those, bright and beautiful and young, wise and fanciful and good.

When I discovered that I loved her, how can I say? In the first day? in the first week? in the first month? Impossible to trace. If I be (as I am) unable to represent to myself any previous period of my life as quite separable from her attracting power, how can I answer for this one detail?

Whensoever I made the discovery, it laid a heavy burden on me. And yet, comparing it with the far heavier burden that I afterwards took up, it does not seem to me now to have been very hard to bear. In the knowledge that I did love her, and that I should love her while my life lasted, and that I was ever to hide my secret deep in my own breast, and she was never to find it, there was a kind of sustaining joy or pride, or comfort, mingled with my pain.

But later on — say, a year later on — when I made another discovery, then indeed my suffering and my struggle were strong. That other discovery was —

These words will never see the light, if ever, until my heart is dust; until her bright spirit has returned to the regions of which, when imprisoned here, it surely retained some unusual glimpse of remembrance; until all the pulses that ever beat around us shall have long been quiet; until all the fruits of all the tiny victories and defeats achieved in our little breasts shall have withered away. That discovery was that she loved me.

She may have enhanced my knowledge, and loved me for that; she may have over-valued my discharge of duty to her, and loved me for that; she may have refined upon a playful compassion which she would sometimes show for what she called my want of wisdom, according to the light of the world's dark lanterns, and loved me for that; she may — she must — have confused the borrowed light of what I had only learned, with its brightness in its pure, original rays; but she loved me at that time, and she made me know it.

Pride of family and pride of wealth put me as far off from her in my lady's eyes as if I had been some domesticated creature of another kind. But they could not put me farther from her than I put myself when I set my merits against hers. More than that. They could not put me, by millions of fathoms, half so low beneath her as I put myself when in imagination I took advantage of her noble trustfulness, took the fortune that I knew she must possess in her own right, and left her to find herself, in the zenith of her beauty and genius, bound to poor rusty, plodding me.

No! Worldliness should not enter here at any cost. If I had tried to keep it out of other ground, how much harder was I bound to try to keep it out from this sacred place!

But there was something daring in her broad, generous character, that demanded at so delicate a crisis to be delicately and patiently addressed. After many and many a bitter night (O, I found I could cry for reasons not purely physical, at this pass of my life!) I took my course.

My lady had, in our first interview, unconsciously overstated the accommodation of my pretty house. There was room in it for only one pupil. He was a young gentleman near coming of age, very well connected, but what is called a poor relation. His parents were dead. The charges of his living and reading with me were defrayed by an uncle; and he and I were to do our utmost together for three years towards qualifying him to make his way. At this time he had entered into his second year with me. He was well-looking, clever, energetic, enthusiastic, bold; in the best sense of the term, a thorough young Anglo-Saxon.

I resolved to bring these two together.

NINTH CHAPTER

Said I, one night, when I had conquered myself, "Mr. Granville," — Mr. Granville Wharton his name was — "I doubt if you have ever yet so much as seen Miss Fareway."

"Well, Sir," returned he, laughing, "you see her so much yourself, that you hardly leave another fellow a chance of seeing her."

"I am her tutor, you know," said I.

And there the subject dropped for that time. But I so contrived as that they should come together shortly afterwards. I had previously so contrived as to keep them asunder; for while I loved her — I mean before I had determined on my sacrifice — a lurking jealousy of Mr. Granville lay within my unworthy breast.

It was quite an ordinary interview in the Fareway Park, but they talked easily together for some time: like takes to like, and they had many points of resemblance. Said Mr. Granville to me, when he and I sat at our supper that night, "Miss Fareway is remarkably beautiful, Sir, remarkably engaging. Don't you think so?" "I think so," said I. And I stole a glance at him, and saw that he had reddened and was thoughtful. I remember it most vividly, because the mixed feeling of grave pleasure and acute pain that the slight circumstance caused me was the first of a long, long series of such mixed impressions under which my hair turned slowly grey.

I had not much need to feign to be subdued; but I counterfeited to be older than I was in all respects (Heaven knows! my heart being all too young the while), and feigned to be more of a recluse and bookworm than I had really become, and gradually set up more and more of a fatherly manner towards Adelina. Likewise I made my tuition less imaginative than before; separated myself from my poets and philosophers; was careful to present them in their own light, and me, their lowly servant, in my own shade. Moreover, in the matter of apparel I was equally mindful; not that I had ever been dapper that way; but that I was slovenly now.

As I depressed myself with one hand, so did I labor to raise Mr. Granville with the other; directing his attention to such subjects as I too well knew most interested her, and fashioning him (do not deride or misconstrue the expression, unknown reader of this writing; for I have suffered!) into a greater resemblance to myself in my solitary one strong aspect. And gradually, gradually, as I saw him take more and more to these thrown-out lures of mine, then did I come to know better and better that love was drawing him on, and was drawing her from me.

So passed more than another year; every day a year in its number of my mixed impressions of grave pleasure and acute pain; and then these two, being of age and free to act legally for themselves, came before me hand in hand (my hair being now quite white), and entreated me that I would unite them together. "And indeed, dear tutor," said Adelina, "it is but consistent in you that you should do this thing for us, seeing that we should never have spoken together that first time but for you, and that but for you we could never have met so often afterwards." The whole of which was literally true; for I had availed myself of my many business attendances on, and conferences with, my lady, to take Mr. Granville to the house, and leave him in the outer room with Adelina.

I knew that my lady would object to such a marriage for her daughter, or to any marriage that was other than an exchange of her for stipulated lands, goods, and moneys. But looking on the two, and seeing with full eyes that they were both young and beautiful; and knowing that they were alike in the tastes and acquirements that will outlive youth and beauty; and considering that Adelina had a fortune now, in her own keeping; and considering further that Mr. Granville, though for the present poor, was of a good family that had never lived in a cellar in Preston; and believing that their love would endure, neither having any great discrepancy to find out in the other — I told them of my readiness to do this thing which Adelina asked of her dear tutor, and to send them forth, husband and wife, into the shining world with golden gates that awaited them.

It was on a summer morning that I rose before the sun to compose myself for the crowning of my work with this end; and my dwelling being near to the sea, I walked down to the rocks on the shore, in order that I might behold the sun in his majesty.

The tranquillity upon the deep, and on the firmament, the orderly withdrawal of the stars, the calm promise of coming day, the rosy suffusion of the sky and waters, the ineffable splendor that then burst forth, attuned my mind afresh after the discords of the night. Methought that all I looked on said to me, and that all I heard in the sea and in the air said to me, "Be comforted, mortal, that thy life is so short. Our preparation for what is to follow has endured, and shall endure, for unimaginable ages."

I married them. I knew that my hand was cold when I placed it on their hands clasped together; but the words with which I had to accompany the action I could say without faltering, and I was at peace.

They being well away from my house and from the place after our simple breakfast, the time was come when I must do what I had pledged myself to them that I would do — break the intelligence to my lady.

I went up to the house, and found my lady in her ordinary business-room. She happened to have an unusual amount of commissions to intrust to me that day; and she had filled my hands with papers before I could originate a word.

"My lady," I then began, as I stood beside her table.

"Why, what's the matter?" she said quickly, looking up.

"Not much, I would fain hope, after you shall have prepared yourself, and considered a little."

"Prepared myself; and considered a little! You appear to have prepared *your*self but indifferently, anyhow, Mr. Silverman." This mighty scornfully, as I experienced my usual embarrassment under her stare.

Said I, in self-extenuation once for all, "Lady Fareway, I have but to say for myself that I have tried to do my duty."

"For yourself?" repeated my lady. "Then there are others concerned, I see. Who are they?"

I was about to answer, when she made towards the bell with a dart that stopped me, and said, "Why, where is Adelina?"

"Forbear! be calm, my lady. I married her this morning to Mr. Granville Wharton."

She set her lips, looked more intently at me than ever, raised her right hand, and smote me hard upon the cheek.

"Give me back those papers! give me back those papers." She tore them out of my hands, and tossed them on her table. Then seating herself defiantly in her great chair, and folding her arms, she stabbed me to the heart with the unlooked-for reproach, "You worldly wretch!"

"Worldly?" I cried. "Worldly?"

"This, if you please" — she went on with supreme scorn, pointing me out as if there were someone there to see — "this, if you please, is the disinterested scholar, with not a design beyond his books! This, if you please, is the simple creature whom any one could overreach in a bargain! This, if you please, is Mr. Silverman! Not of this world; not he! He has too much simplicity for this world's cunning. He has too much singleness of purpose to be a match for this world's double-dealing. What did he give you for it?"

"For what? And who?"

"How much," she asked, bending forward in her great chair, and insultingly tapping the fingers of her right hand on the palm of her left — "how much does Mr. Granville Wharton pay you for getting him Adelina's money? What is the amount of your percentage upon Adelina's fortune? What were the terms of the agreement that you proposed to this boy when you, the Rev. George Silverman, licensed to marry, engaged to put him in possession of this girl? You made good terms for yourself, whatever they were. He would stand a poor chance against your keenness."

Bewildered, horrified, stunned by this cruel perversion, I could not speak. But I trust that I looked innocent, being so.

"Listen to me, shrewd hypocrite," said my lady, whose anger increased as she gave it utterance; "attend to my words, you cunning schemer, who have carried this plot through with such a practiced double face that I have never suspected you. I had my projects for my daughter; projects for family connection; projects for fortune. You have thwarted them, and overreached me; but I am not one to be thwarted and overreached without retaliation. Do you mean to hold this living another month?"

"Do you deem it possible, Lady Fareway, that I can hold it another hour, under your injurious words?"

"Is it resigned, then?"

"It was mentally resigned, my lady, some minutes ago."

"Don't equivocate, Sir. *Is* it resigned?"

"Unconditionally and entirely; and I would that I had never, never come near it!"

"A cordial response from me to *that* wish, Mr. Silverman! But take this with you, Sir. If you had not resigned it, I would have had you deprived of it. And though you have resigned it, you will not get quit of me as easily as you think for. I will pursue you with this story. I will make this nefarious conspiracy of yours, for money, known. You have made money by it, but you have at the same time made an enemy by it. *You* will take good care that the money sticks to you; I will take good care that the enemy sticks to you."

Then said I finally, "Lady Fareway, I think my heart is broken. Until I came into this room just now, the possibility of such mean wickedness as you have imputed to me never dawned upon my thoughts. Your suspicions — "

"Suspicions! Pah!" said she indignantly. "Certainties."

"Your certainties, my lady, as you call them, your suspicions as I call them, are cruel, unjust, wholly devoid of foundation in fact. I can declare no more; except that I have not acted for my own profit or my own pleasure. I have not in this proceeding considered myself. Once again, I think my heart is broken. If I have unwittingly done any wrong with a righteous motive, that is some penalty to pay."

She received this with another and more indignant "Pah!" and I made my way out of her room (I think I felt my way out with my hands, although my eyes were open), almost suspecting that my voice had a repulsive sound, and that I was a repulsive object.

There was a great stir made, the bishop was appealed to, I received a severe reprimand, and narrowly escaped suspension. For years a cloud hung over me, and my name was tarnished. But my heart did not break, if a broken heart involves death; for I lived through it.

They stood by me, Adelina and her husband, through it all. Those who had known me at college, and even most of those who had only known me there by reputation, stood by me too. Little by little, the belief widened that I was not capable of what was laid to my charge. At length I was presented to a college-living in a sequestered place, and there I now pen my explanation. I pen it at my open window in the summer-time, before me, lying in the churchyard, equal resting-place for sound hearts, wounded hearts, and broken hearts. I pen it for the relief of my own mind, not foreseeing whether or no it will ever have a reader.